RECKLESS VOW

Gemma Morr has worked in book marketing for twenty years, connecting imaginations with the worlds in which they belong. She currently lives in Hampshire with her husband and two children. *Reckless Vow* is the second book in her Diamond Back Ranch series following *Untamed Heart*.

Also by Gemma Morr

Untamed Heart

RECKLESS VOW

GEMMA MORR

PAN BOOKS

First published 2026 by Pan Books
an imprint of Pan Macmillan
The Smithson, 6 Briset Street, London EC1M 5NR
EU representative: Macmillan Publishers Ireland Ltd, 1st Floor,
The Liffey Trust Centre, 117–126 Sheriff Street Upper,
Dublin 1 D01 YC43
Associated companies throughout the world

ISBN 978-1-0350-7902-5

Copyright © Gemma Morr 2026

The right of Gemma Morr to be identified as the
author of this work has been asserted in accordance with
the Copyright, Designs and Patents Act 1988.

All rights reserved. No part of this publication may be reproduced, stored in
a retrieval system, or transmitted, in any form, or by any means (including,
without limitation, electronic, mechanical, photocopying, recording or
otherwise) without the prior written permission of the publisher.

Pan Macmillan does not have any control over, or any responsibility for,
any author or third-party websites (including, without limitation, URLs,
emails and QR codes) referred to in or on this book.

1 3 5 7 9 8 6 4 2

A CIP catalogue record for this book is available from the British Library.

Typeset in Granjon by Six Red Marbles UK, Thetford, Norfolk
Printed and bound in the UK using 100% Renewable Electricity by CPI Group (UK) Ltd

This book is sold subject to the condition that it shall not, by way of
trade or otherwise, be lent, hired out, or otherwise circulated without
the publisher's prior consent in any form of binding or cover other than
that in which it is published and without a similar condition including this
condition being imposed on the subsequent purchaser. The publisher does not
authorize the use or reproduction of any part of this book in any manner
for the purpose of training artificial intelligence technologies or systems.
The publisher expressly reserves this book from the Text and Data Mining
exception in accordance with Article 4(3) of the European Union
Digital Single Market Directive 2019/790.

Visit **www.panmacmillan.com** to read more about
all our books and to buy them.

For anyone that ever felt they weren't enough – or were too much. Bullshit. You're just right. Don't let anyone tell you different.

The *Reckless Vow* Playlist

'Sugar' – Sleep Token
'vitamin' – Cloudy June
'weren't for the wind' – Ella Langley
'Heart-Shaped Box' – Nirvana
'Fast Car' – Luke Combs
'Closer' – Nine Inch Nails
'Can You Feel My Heart' – Bring Me The Horizon
'Pink Skies' – Zach Bryan
'Killing In The Name' – Rage Against The Machine
'Let's Get Lost' – Beck, Bat For Lashes
'WILDFLOWER' – Billie Eilish
'Blood Sport' – Sleep Token
'Smother' – Daughter
'Something in the Orange' – Zach Bryan
'Atlantic' – Sleep Token
'Half of forever' – Henrik
'Shake It Out' – Florence + The Machine

Chapter 1
Hestia

'So tell me, cowboy, what's your favourite thing to ride?'

I pinned Jesse with my eyes as I said it, but it was Cole who almost sprayed beer over his cards, the poor fucker still adjusting to my delivery.

Lottie smirked, shaking her head.

'Hestia, girl, you're a damn riot. How can someone who sounds just as ladylike as Lottie here come out with shit like that?' Bailey said, slapping the table as she issued a dirty cackle.

I shrugged, still focused on breaking Jesse's stare. There wasn't even an inkling of a smile, nothing. Damn. Fucking hot *and* a good poker face.

'Oh, don't be fooled by the accent. Lottie's just the other side of my coin, as Cole's been finding out.' I glanced up at him, raising an eyebrow. He was grinning now, glancing back at Lottie with the same besotted expression he'd worn ever since I got here. 'It's just that where she chooses dignity, I always choose violence.'

There was a pause, everyone waiting for Jesse's response. Lottie gave me a knowing smile, which I returned.

'I know what you're trying to do here,' Jesse drawled, taking his time as he looked back at his cards, utterly unruffled. 'And there's no way you're getting one up on me through distraction.'

It'd only been a few days since I'd arrived at the Diamond Back ranch for a few weeks away from all the shit back in London, but I was getting impatient. The flirting had been hardcore, even by my own standards. Trouble was, this guy was a little too much like me. He was willing to push it further than others would, utterly sure of himself and very aware of just how fucking tasty he was – from biceps that strained against his shirtsleeves to the all-American, Old Hollywood chiselled face.

He was also all too aware that he was making me wait, despite having already fucked me with his eyes about a dozen times.

So, I decided something on the spot. When we got to it for real, which I guessed would be any time in the next hour or so, I'd make him beg for it.

'Answer the question, then,' I replied, leaning in against the tall-backed chair, elbow on the armrest. 'Or I'll give you a real distraction.'

That did it. His dark, smoky grey eyes flicked onto mine then dipped down to my chest, where I knew the top buttons of my shirt were pulled taut. Shifting in his chair, he refocused on his cards.

I had him. A surge of triumph coursed through me, and I tingled with the urge to tear his shirt open with one hand and rip his belt off with the other.

'Well, let's see then,' he said, just as slowly as before; but this time he wasn't quite able to stop himself from giving me a quick glance, the corner of his mouth curving up. 'We've got bulls, mean sons-of-bitches but over pretty quick – kinda similar to the broncs.' Cole snorted as he studied his own cards. 'And then there's the regular old horses here on the ranch, but that's nothing. I've been riding 'bout as long as I've been walking, so . . . that leaves buckle bunnies, I guess.'

'Okay, I'm out,' Bailey announced, shaking her head with a

smile in Jesse's direction as she stood up, glancing between us. 'I'm training with Darcy tomorrow, so I'm gonna leave y'all to it.'

Lottie started giggling, waving to Bailey as she rounded the table and headed across the vast living room.

I paused, focusing on my best friend for a moment. The lightness in her laugh was unlike anything I'd heard from her in years, maybe even since university. Her whole demeanour had changed in the couple of months she'd been here, as though she'd finally shaken off the weight of London, a job she hated, and Kyle, ex-boyfriend and professional prick.

It made me so insanely happy to see it.

I'd never known that kind of love, not even with Cal, my ex of five years. Passion, yes, friendship and a shared love of tattoos and music, definitely, but somehow, nothing deeper. We were both messed up, I knew that. Products of dysfunctional parents and traumatic childhoods. Somehow, I'd hoped – tried – for a while to connect through that. As it turned out, neither one of us had been brave enough to talk about any of it, so the soft, vulnerable and breakable bits had remained locked down tighter than ever.

Cole pulled Lottie up onto his lap, his own expression matching her joy as he brushed a thumb over her cheek, watching her laugh. I almost had to look away – the love in their touch was so intense that it felt wrong to intrude.

This time, when I caught Jesse's eye again, I saw the last of his own contemplative glance, as though his thoughts mirrored mine. He quickly smiled in a way that reset my thoughts firmly back on him, on what that mouth would feel like on mine.

'Anyone want some snacks?' he asked, placing his cards face down. 'Another beer?'

Cole and Lottie put in their orders before Cole resumed his poker tutorial. I could tell Lottie wasn't really listening by the way she was watching his lips, playing with one of her curls absent-mindedly.

'Hestia?' Jesse asked as he rounded the table towards me, circling his shoulder as he did so as though it was bothering him. 'Drink? Snacks?'

I pushed my chair back and stood, moving just far enough into his personal space to make myself clear as I flicked my hair over my shoulder.

'I'll give you a hand,' I offered, keeping my voice low. He raised an eyebrow, fighting another smile. 'With the snacks, you perv.'

He laughed then, unable to hold it back. Lottie and Cole looked up together.

'C'mon then,' he replied, sauntering over to the door and glancing back to me, eyes darting from my shirt to my black denim mini and down to my Doc Martens – which I had so far stubbornly refused to swap out for cowboy boots. 'I think I've come up with a way to describe your look, you know,' he added, turning into the hallway as I followed.

'Tread carefully, cowboy,' I warned, allowing myself an extra-long, fully gratuitous stare at his ass. His indigo blue jeans were fitted to perfection and, combined with his casual, confident walk, moved in a way that sent heat flaring right through me. 'These boots have kicked many asses in the past ten years.'

Entering the kitchen, with the light over the table on low and the sound of Lottie and Cole's laughter fading as the door shut, the atmosphere changed.

'Kick any as fine as mine?' he asked, opening the fridge door, pulling out a couple of beers.

I leant against the table, folding my arms.

He turned as if to question my silence, eyes immediately resting on my breasts, barely contained by the buttons.

'Jessica Rabbit . . .' he began, undeterred, putting the beers down on the countertop, reaching up into a cupboard and bringing out several bags of chips, '. . . meets Wednesday Addams. That's your look.'

I narrowed my eyes. Secretly, I fucking loved that. But this was my way in, so I wasn't about to tell him that.

'A cartoonish, psychotic teenager, then?' I said, voice low, as though he was walking a fine line.

His face changed in an instant, awareness flaring. I almost felt bad, even though this was all part of the game. It confirmed what Lottie had said, though, that under the cocky exterior was a genuine guy with a big heart.

'Whoa there.' He put everything down, rounding the counter with his hands raised. 'I meant it as a compliment. Damn, I mean, you've got the whole cherry-red hair, sexy thing going on with all the black clothes . . .' He stopped, clocking my eyes.

'No, no, do go on,' I purred, stepping closer, watching as he realized we were in touching distance, his eyes drifting down once again. 'Up here, handsome,' I added, waiting for him to look me in the eye again.

'I . . . I just meant . . . Wait, are you . . . You're fucking with me, aren't you?'

Dipping my head to hide my smile, I kicked myself, realizing how much harder I found it to do this with him. There was something about his energy, something insistent and relentlessly positive, that made it almost impossible to fuck with.

'Well, if I'm a sexy red-headed psycho –' I replied, snapping my head back up and noting his relief, followed by a flash of challenge in his eyes – 'that makes you . . .' I considered it for a minute, studying his features openly. To his credit he didn't flinch, just stared right back, only reacting as I bit my lip, painted the same intense red as my hair. His grey eyes widened at that, and his jaw flexed. 'I've got it: Austin Butler meets the hot, ex-military one from *Yellowstone*, what's his name? Kayce?'

This time he stepped forward, pushing his dark sandy hair back from his face. It was tanned from the intense summer sun, and his eyes were brightened by the contrast. The shadows of the dim room highlighted his sharp cheekbones, sloping to darker stubble on his cheeks and jaw.

'The hot one?' he asked, reaching out and gently unfolding my arms, taking my hands instead. The brazen look in his eyes and the pure jolt of electricity that shot straight up my arms at his touch almost gave me pause. I knew I could handle myself, handle him in this scenario, but something felt . . . different. He paused too, turning my smaller hands in his, studying the white tattoo on my left wrist. 'What does this one mean?'

I hesitated, suddenly checking myself. It wasn't like it was a personal question as such, but all of my tats had stories, some deeper than others. I'd explained this one many times before, to many people, but I couldn't put my finger on why explaining it to Jesse suddenly felt . . . exposing.

'It's an old Norse compass,' I began, staring at my wrist, feeling his eyes on my face. 'Helps prevent you from losing your way. I did it myself when I was first starting out, just before I opened the studio with my ex.'

'And is he still in the picture?'

I looked up, the gap between us disappearing. But, remembering my earlier promise to myself, I deflected. Not this easily.

'Why don't you give me your own tat tour and I'll tell you,' I countered, slowly retracting my hands from his and stepping back to lean on the table again.

He gave another small smile, and then his fingers began undoing his shirt buttons, working slowly as he watched me.

'I've only got two so far. But . . . maybe I've got room for more,' he said, eventually reaching the last button and opening it up to reveal the tanned skin beneath. *Holy fuck*. Turning around, he slid the shirt off to reveal a broad, toned back, leading right down to that ass. 'So, what do you think?'

Momentarily stunned, I didn't get it together until he peered at me over his shoulder. There was a bucking bull, small but nicely done, on one shoulder, and a larger water dragon at the top of his spine.

'Nice,' was all I could manage, covering my shock by getting up from the table and approaching him, as if to inspect them. But, in truth, I felt like if I didn't touch him again in the next ten seconds I might just fucking implode.

So I did, reaching right out and stroking my finger down the dragon, letting my long, sharpened, gloss-black nail drag slightly on his skin.

'Plenty of space for more,' I breathed, feeling him shudder under my touch. 'Shame I didn't bring my kit with me.'

He turned then, fast enough that we were touching as I looked up into his eyes.

'I've shown you mine,' he growled, his finger grazing my chin, following the line of my neck and down, across my collarbone. 'Only polite to show me yours.'

I almost smiled, feeling as though he'd plucked a line from my own head. Except I couldn't, because my entire body was consumed with the thought of fucking this man until neither of us could stand any more.

'I think you're mistaking this accent again,' I murmured, beginning on my own buttons, teasing him by moving as slowly as I could, the first one popping apart to reveal an obscene amount of cleavage. He swallowed as he watched. 'There's not a single polite thing about me.'

As though unable to stand it any more, his eyes darting to the door as if weighing up the chances of us getting caught, he moved his hands over mine, popping the next two.

I shook my head gently, stepping back to bend over and untie my laces, kicking off my Docs and giving him an entire eyeful of my black lace bra.

'Fuck,' he breathed, shifting position as he leant back against the counter, the front of his jeans straining against the biggest fucking boner I'd ever seen.

'That's more like it,' I smiled, continuing to torture him with achingly slow pops of my buttons, now revealing my whole rack, the tats that stretched from the flames on my neck and down to the *Sleepy Hollow* scene on my chest. 'Explaining every one of these may take a while,' I began, letting the shirt fall to the floor, stepping up to him again.

'I've got time,' he answered, the gravelled edge to his voice growing as his fingers reached out to trail my flames. 'Although I'm having a hard time concentrating right now.'

'Ever fucked a woman with tats like mine?' I asked, failing to maintain my own game of making him wait and reaching out for his belt buckle, freeing it in seconds and running my hand over his zipper as I pulled it down. In the same moment I realized he wasn't wearing anything underneath, his cock straining to be released.

'Oh I've fucked plenty of women with tats,' he murmured, circling his hand around my back and pulling me closer still, hearing the snap of the catch as he undid my bra. 'But no one like you, honey. You are one of a fucking kind.'

As my bra dropped and before I could move first, he made a sound between a groan and a growl, taking my face in his hands and running his tongue over my lips for a moment.

'Why do I get the feeling you might just undo me, Jessica?'

That was it.

I pushed my lips onto his and felt his instant response, his tongue against mine. One hand was on my breast, stroking my nipple, gently pulling it between his fingers. Moaning into his mouth, I found his jeans again and ripped them down, my hand closing around his cock.

'Fuck me right now,' I ordered, taking my lips off his just long enough to look down at the size of him in my hand, my voice too strained to be truly authoritative.

'You're in an awful rush for someone that was keeping me waiting back there,' he murmured as I reluctantly let go of him in order to undo the button on my skirt. 'Oh, no, no, Jessica, you leave that itty bitty skirt right there,' he whispered in that drawling accent of his, finding my mouth again, pressing me to him for a moment before his arms circled me, lifting me up onto his hips.

'What're you doing?' I gasped, his lips now against my jaw, working up to my ear as he took a step forward and turned us against the wall, his hands moving round to grab my ass. My skirt had ridden right up in the process, baring my flimsy lace underwear beneath.

'Do you remember when you arrived?' he murmured, his tongue now moving down to my breasts, teasing me as his cock brushed my thigh. I could barely answer, tilting my head back and only aware of where I was when I felt his hand on my head, gently cushioning it against the wall. He pushed me up against it, his own breathing as heavy as mine. 'You took my hat clean off my head and wore it for yourself?' I nodded, almost whimpering as he lifted my skirt, his fingers tracing the thin lace, slipping inside them briefly. 'Well now, maybe you don't know the rules here, honey, but you wear the hat . . .'

'. . . you ride the cowboy,' I gasped as his fingers moved, pulling my underwear to the side. He kissed me roughly again, pulling a condom from his pocket and ripping it open, swearing under his breath as I helped him roll it down, applying pressure as I did so.

He paused for a moment, his eyes wild, as though he wanted to say something else, but wasn't sure how I'd respond.

'Well, fuck me,' I demanded, saving him from any overthinking, desperate to feel him in me. '*Now.*'

He smiled, edging closer, somehow able to support my weight against the wall with barely any effort.

'I want that mouth around my cock next time,' he demanded right back, eyes burning, fixed on mine and waiting until I smiled, running my tongue over my bottom lip in answer. 'And then I'm gonna kneel right down between your legs and have you ride me that way too.'

Before I could even think to answer, he pushed into me, gently at first, and matched my own moan. It was louder than I'd intended, and I was suddenly aware that anyone could walk in and find us. But as he slid back out and pushed in again, harder, I knew I didn't fucking care.

'Harder,' I whispered, wrapping my hands around his broad, muscled shoulders, giving myself more leverage to move with him.

'Holy shit,' he groaned as I ground myself against him, knowing that there was limited time before we'd make each other explode.

I arched back, eyes closing. His mouth was on my nipple again, circling and sucking it with his tongue as he fucked me, harder and harder until I was biting my lip to stop myself from screaming out. It was pure feeling, my skin tingling wherever it touched his, the world narrowed to the space between us.

Slowly, very deliberately, he moved up to my mouth, slowing as though he was about to come, the kiss deepening. It began to change somehow, gradually at first, then all at once. His hand wove into my hair and his cock thrust deeper, pushing me against the wall with a whole new intensity.

Opening my eyes, I found myself looking straight into his. His expression mirrored how I felt, the realization of a shared feeling.

He paused, eyes now studying my whole face.

'How did I only just meet you?' he asked, his voice suddenly rough, as though emotion had ripped the edges.

For once, I had no idea what to say, too surprised by the way my own feelings seemed to wrap around his, wanting to comfort him somehow, or tell him how I'd never had an experience quite like this before, not even with Cal.

Instead, I was saved by the other feelings that suddenly rose up as he pushed into me again, making me come so hard that I almost saw stars. His mouth covered mine, wrapping me in a gentle kiss as I moaned, hardening as it was followed by his own.

I held onto him as he finished, my arms still circling his shoulders as I rested my head against his chest, eyes closed as I tried to catch my breath. We stayed there, just breathing against each other, one of his hands still in my hair, the other on my ass. He smelled incredible: a deep, warm, smoky scent.

'That was . . .' he began, breaking off as though realizing the next words might just take us into new territory, to somewhere I guessed neither of us was familiar with. I lifted my head as he tucked a loose strand of hair behind my ear.

His eyes blazed into mine, clearly deep in thought, as an unfamiliar but very definite jolt hit me square in the gut.

'Yeah, it was,' I whispered, wanting nothing more than to stay right here with him, and therefore knowing I had to leave immediately.

Shit.

Chapter 2
Hestia

'So . . . when are you going to tell me what happened with you and Jesse last weekend?' Lottie's lips twitched as she came out onto the wraparound deck at the back of the ranch house, handing me a steaming coffee. She curled herself into the wide rocking chair opposite mine. 'And don't you dare bullshit me. Jesse's been as smug as fuck but suspiciously quiet ever since, so I know for a fact you were making way more than snacks in there. And frankly, it's even weirder that you won't tell me all about it.'

I hid behind my Ray-Bans, taking a sip to hide the expression that agreed with her. So instead, I took the tried and tested route – and deflected.

'It was just a quick fumble,' I replied, shaking my head as her mouth popped open. 'Seriously, chill. Not everyone comes on holiday to Wyoming and meets the love of their life, okay? He's hot, we were both horny, so we just . . . hooked up. That's it. No drama. End of.'

I knew I sounded defensive, and I kicked myself internally as Lottie let her mass of curls fall forward to cover her deepening smile. It was impossible not to soften at that, at knowing how well this woman knew me, unlike anyone else.

'That sounds . . . great,' she said, clearing her throat, clearly trying not to laugh. 'Just what you needed, then.'

'Exactly.' I stared out across the incredible view, the soaring mountains ahead casting a long shadow over the green valley floor. This place was crushingly beautiful, and about as far from East London as I could've got. 'I'm here for a break from the hellscape of home, from all of the bullshit with Cal. Any other activity, including screwing cowboys, is entirely recreational. Fuck yoga – getting hammered up against a wall is my kind of stress relief.'

Lottie choked on her coffee, eventually recovering enough to laugh. I loved the sound of it, the way her whole face came to life.

'I've missed you,' she gasped, holding out her free hand to me. I took it, my inked skin and dark nails against the natural, unmarked beauty of hers. She smiled, likely noting the same thing. 'You know it's okay to like someone, though, right? I know it's been a shitshow with Cal, but Jesse isn't him.'

I shrugged, hating just how aware I was of that, how the last moments of our kitchen encounter had replayed over and over in my mind.

'Right. I just want to do my own thing right now, though, you know? Just me. Although I'll always want you around.' I winked at her, watching as her perceptive, all-too-wise gaze read my real thoughts, just as she always had.

'Just as long as you know you don't have to do it alone,' she said, stroking a finger over the sharp tips of my nails. 'I know that big old wall of yours has been up for a long fucking time, but you can share yourself with someone and still be independent. I swear it. Wouldn't have believed it myself before coming here.'

'You're a walking Hallmark movie, Lottie Wright,' I replied, lowering my glasses and smiling at her now sheepish expression. 'And I am so fucking happy for you. That man is a sweetheart and *almost* as hot as you.'

She raised her eyebrow, still smiling, knowing exactly what I was doing in ignoring the truth in her words. I knew they were true, but about as unreachable as me becoming a cowgirl and learning how to line dance. I groaned, remembering the event was tonight.

'What?' she said, letting me go in order to reach for her coffee again.

'The line dance; I just remembered. I really can't go in my normal clothes, can I?' I glanced down at my black jeans and T-shirt, the fierce, masked face of the lead singer of my favourite metal band at odds with the sunny, raw wilderness spread out before us.

Lottie considered it, then shook her head.

'I'd lend you some of my stuff, but . . .' She gestured to my ample chest. 'Pretty sure it'd give a very different look.' I groaned, now contemplating the idea of clothes shopping, not something I was into or good at. 'Ask Bailey,' Lottie suggested. 'She might have something?'

I thought of the perky, no-bull natural redhead. In the few conversations we'd had she'd projected an air of quiet confidence, someone driven in their ambition and not afraid to work for it. But there'd also been a tiny hint of something else. I smiled. Two birds with one stone – something to wear tonight and a new distraction, maybe even some . . . recreation.

It was mid-afternoon before I got my shit together enough to wander down to the barn. What felt like a lifetime of working into the evenings at the studio and getting up late was deeply ingrained, and anything before 11 a.m. felt like a punch in the mouth. In reality it was only three years since Cal and I had quit uni a year early, both bored to hell with degrees we'd realized would never pay us back.

I was still grateful to him, despite the dumpster fire our relationship had become, for believing in our ability to become the artists we'd slowly turned into, growing our client list into a waiting list. The money he'd inherited from his grandad had allowed us to rent the studio space and kick it all off, and somehow, three years had gone by in a fucking blur.

And for what?

The nasty, critical voice in my head that sounded a hell of a lot like my stepdad – the one I drank a little bit harder than I should've to blank out – was always there for moments like these. As I approached the vast, rust-red barn, watching dust flying from the corral opposite, I shoved it down and flicked my hair over one shoulder. The studio was doing fine without me for now; Cal and another talented artist we knew, Blake, were holding it down. No need to worry.

Reaching the fence, I resisted leaning against it, knowing everything out here was covered in a fine film of dirt. It'd been an eye-opener to see Lottie in her element, totally unbothered by smudges on her cheeks, shovelling up horse shit and getting stuck into every aspect of ranch life. I couldn't imagine how constricted and fake she must have felt back home, having to become someone so entirely different to her real self. Kyle may have been an utter bellend, but at least the situation had forced a change for her.

'Oh hey, cowpoke!'

Bailey's voice rang out across the corral as she urged her horse, Dunkin, into a gallop right towards the fence, pulling up at the very last moment and sending a small shower of dirt towards me.

'Jesus wept,' I yelled, jumping back, not able to prevent my boots from being covered in it. 'You pull that kind of shit with all your visitors?'

Bailey cackled, looking back at the other woman in the ring on her horse, still practising turning around big, rusting barrels placed at intervals. She was clearly learning, taking wider loops than I'd seen Bailey do.

'Only the ones I really like,' she said, winking. 'You want to try, honey? I reckon you'd be quite something on a horse.'

I eyed her, speculating.

'Fuck no, you've got the wrong Brit. Never ridden a horse in my life, *genuine* city girl and very happy to stay that way.'

She tilted her head, eyes narrowed under the brim of her hat.

'I call bullshit,' she replied. 'We'll have you in the saddle before you leave, I know it.'

'I'm gonna need an incentive,' I added, giving her a sly smile, imitating her own accent, watching as she tried to hide a grin.

'Hot damn, girl,' she shook her head. 'Lottie was right about you. Pure firecracker.'

I knew it. There was a flicker of interest, just as I'd felt in her truck when she'd picked me up at the airport.

'Well, this firecracker needs an outfit for the line dance this evening. Apparently "goth Barbie", as Lottie loves to call me, isn't going to cut it. Have you got anything that might work?'

She considered me for a moment.

'Maybe. I mean, you're welcome to have a look in my closet, but honestly, I think we're a different shape, honey. You're all tits and hips, in the best way. If you want to get into town, I think Cole's around somewhere, or Jesse? They're both working on the cabin right now, but they'll spare an hour or so, I'm sure. Pretty sure Lottie's tied up with the guests today.' She paused, seemingly weighing something up. 'I'd give you a ride myself, but I need the rest of the afternoon with Darcy. The rodeo's only another week away.'

I nodded, conflicted about seeing Jesse again at close quarters, having only seen him at à distance since . . . the kitchen.

'Maybe a ride another time?' I said, hoping the suggestive undertone translated.

Bailey smiled again.

'Sure thing, cowpoke. Just so long as you know I'm focused on competing and all this.' She gestured behind her to the corral, where Darcy was slowing, leaning down to pat her horse on the neck. 'I'm not in the right place for anyone . . . no matter how tempted I am.'

'Oh, I get it . . . more than you know,' I added after a pause, not missing the flash of concern in her eyes as I took my sunglasses off my head and put them on, the bright sunlight threatening to give me a headache. 'Okay – I'll go find Cole. Does he know which shops to try?'

Bailey just laughed, manoeuvring Dunkin backwards before turning towards Darcy, reeling off the names of a few shops to try in Jackson. I waved, steeling myself as I began the walk towards the cabin.

———

'I hope Bailey warned you that all I'm good for is holding bags and driving?' Cole offered as we arrived in Jackson, a half-smile on his lips. I totally saw it, why Lottie had fallen so hard; hard enough that it had scared her at first, something a long conversation one night after I arrived had revealed.

'Just point out the shops and I promise I'll be quick. I fucking hate shopping. Don't suppose there are any that are a bit less . . . you know, mainstream?'

He grinned as we pulled into a space just off the main square, somehow parking the giant truck with ease.

'Well, most things here cater for the tourists,' he admitted as we got out and started strolling down the street, weaving through them. They all had their phones out, taking photos of everything from the random archway made of what looked like giant deer antlers to the knife-edge peaks soaring behind the low-rise buildings and fir trees. 'But there is a place some local ladies go. It's not cheap, but it's run by Deanna, and I reckon you and her might just get along.'

I side-eyed him.

'Dare I ask why?'

He couldn't hide a smile.

'You'll see,' he said, eyes crinkling with mischief.

A few minutes later, on the other side of the square, we entered the shop. The clothes were fairly standard western fare by the look of it. As I turned to Cole to say so, he was tipping his hat to a woman walking towards us from the back of the shop.

'Oh hey, Cole, haven't seen you for weeks. That new lady of yours keeping you busy up at the Diamond Back, huh?'

The first thing I saw was her lip piercing, followed by a smoky-eye look, a cute, super-short fringe and shoulder-length black hair.

'Something like that,' he admitted, suddenly a little shy. 'Dee, this is Hestia Hampton, Lottie's best friend from England.'

Her eyes widened, focusing immediately on my neck tattoo.

'Oh hey,' she breathed, holding out her hand to me, both of us smiling as we realized we were wearing very similar rings. 'I love your look – omigod, is that a Sleep Token tee? I fucking *love* them!'

Within moments we were deep in conversation, barely registering Cole's laughter and a promise to wait outside until we were done.

'I don't know how anyone gets anything done up at Diamond Back with Cole and Jesse around,' Dee admitted, taking a long, professional look at me before striding around the store and picking out various tops and jeans to try. 'They're not my usual type but . . .' She held up a dark plaid shirt, nodding. 'I'd make an exception.'

'Tell me about it,' I murmured, once again having to shake off the memory of Jesse holding me up against the wall, the way his fingers had smoothed over my skin and dipped into my underwear. *Ugh*. I had to stop torturing myself. 'Oh – actually, I really like that.'

I pointed to a tee that was somehow western but had some edge: a faded black colour, a human skull, pink flowers blooming from the eye sockets.

'Really? That's one of my designs,' Dee said, blushing instantly at the praise.

'Oh wow, I love it! You're an artist?' I asked, slightly disbelieving to have found someone like me here, deep in cowboy country.

'Well, I guess . . . sort of.' She shook her head. 'I mean, running this place is my main income right now, but my real love is painting, drawing and –' she gestured to my tattoos – 'I definitely want more of those.'

We talked as I tried things on, even managing to find some cowboy boots in my size that I could just about tolerate – black, obviously, with silver detailing on the stitching.

'I can't make it to the line dance tonight, but come hang out again? Maybe come meet some of my friends over at the Jackson Collective – there's a whole bunch of creative people over there,' Dee said as I paid up. 'You're not heading home too soon, I hope?'

I shook my head, suddenly aware of how fast my time here was going – already over a week in. We said goodbye, and as I went outside, Cole grinned.

'Told you,' he said, taking my bags from me despite my protests. 'So, we finally gonna see country Hestia?'

The dancing had already kicked off by the time Lottie, Cole and I arrived. Third-wheeling wasn't exactly the vibe I was going for, but given the alternative was to squash into Jesse's truck with Bailey, I chickened out.

'Oh man, Lil would've loved this,' Lottie said as we went in, Cole's arm wrapped territorially around her shoulder. 'She's an amazing dancer, right, Cole?'

He nodded, giving her a look nothing short of pure adoration as he leant down and kissed her forehead. I'd yet to meet Lottie's cousin, the owner of the Diamond Back, currently on a well-earned holiday in the UK. But from what I heard, she sounded fun.

'What can I get for you ladies?' he asked, looking over to me, his smile switching to an irritatingly satisfied expression at my new clothes.

I couldn't bring myself to get into blue jeans, but the new boot-cut black Wranglers did things to the shape of my ass that even I couldn't dispute. I was wearing Dee's skull tee tucked in, and my new black boots. Lottie had lent me one of her new summer straw cowboy hats, decorated with a black leather band and various multicoloured beads and silver charms.

'A beer, but only if you stop looking so damn smug,' I replied, suddenly wondering why he'd glanced over my head.

'Well hell, Cole, I think that's the first time anyone's accused you of that.'

The sound of his voice alone made my stomach drop, but as I turned, I realized just how close he was behind me. Cole laughed, turning back to the bar to place his order.

'Hey Jessica, how's –' He cut off, leaning back to look me up and down. 'Fuuuck . . . Well now, don't you look the country part.'

The use of the nickname he'd given me in the kitchen . . . the temptation to launch straight into full flirt mode was overwhelming, but as Bailey joined the group and her friend Darcy too, I tried to restrain myself.

'Not sure I qualify as Wednesday any more,' I said, fighting to keep my face neutral as I turned back towards the bar, feeling the heat of his body as he leant into me from behind, his incredible smell and the feel of his hand on my lower back forcing my eyes shut for a moment.

'Definitely a little more Lainey Wilson now,' he murmured next to my ear as the others shared out drinks. 'But you'll always be more Jessica Rabbit to me.' He paused, choosing a moment when no one was looking our way, his lips brushing against my neck, travelling along my jaw. 'So are we going to stay here, pretend to dance and then eye-fuck all evening, or are you gonna come with me out back and see if I can't make you come just as hard as last time? We might even get a dance in afterwards, if you can still stand up straight.'

For once, I wasn't capable of answering. There was something about this man that levelled me – and part of me wanted it, wanted him desperately, but the other part was a warning bell so loud I could hardly think.

As though on autopilot, I reached behind me, grazing my nails down his thigh, my palm stroking what I knew was waiting for me.

'Give it five minutes,' he whispered. 'I'll be by my truck.'

With the briefest touch to my waist, he left, leaving me to pull myself together just in time to receive my drink from Lottie.

'You okay?' she asked, frowning as she clocked my face.

'No,' I admitted, gesturing to her neat whiskey. 'Can I?'

'Um . . . sure?' she said, eyebrows disappearing under the brim of her hat as I knocked it back in one and handed her my beer.

'I owe you one,' I gasped, gritting my teeth at the fire that raged down my throat.

'Hestia, what –' she began, reaching for my arm, but I was already backing away.

'Yoga,' I replied, not waiting for her to fully register before I turned and went outside, walking to the back of the car park where Jesse's black truck was parked, not making eye contact with any of the new arrivals still pulling up.

'I make that no more than three minutes. You *must* be keen.'

Jesse waited on the far side of his truck, hidden from view thanks to the wall behind and the sheer size of his truck in front. His trademark cocky smile turned to something quite different as I rounded the bonnet and without slowing, pressed myself into him and reached up, pulling his mouth onto mine.

He groaned as our lips parted, every memory from the other night flooding in. In a gesture that felt inevitable, his hands circled my ass and waist, lifting me up again as he had before.

As my back pressed against the truck, the full weight of his glorious body on mine, I switched off everything else.

Especially my head.

Chapter 3
Jesse

Her body was . . . something else.

I gripped her ass harder, slowing our movements, determined to make it last even a little longer and cursing my damn impatience. I should've waited until later, back at the ranch where we could do this in private, make it last more than the ten minutes I dared to give it out here, where anyone could find us. There was too much to feel, to take in. From soft, full lips to the rounded, mouth-watering curves of her hips and thighs, to those piercing blue-green eyes that reached right into my fucking chest and squeezed my damn lungs every time she looked my way.

But it wasn't just that. I'd known it from the instant she arrived, arching her brow and lifting my hat straight onto her head, tucking her arm into mine like we'd been friends for years. Hestia might just be the most beautiful woman I'd ever seen, bar none, but that beauty carried right on inside. Honest, funny, smart . . . and the filthiest fucking mouth I'd ever heard on anyone. Her smile alone was enough to make me rock hard in seconds.

Cole was right.

I was fucked.

'What's the matter, cowboy? Can't keep up?' she whispered, lips brushing against my jaw, forcing me to grit my teeth as her voice and the breathy moan that followed almost pushed me over the edge.

'Look at me,' I growled, waiting for her eyelids to flutter open, her head tilting back as she arched against the truck.

The effect was too much, the image forever branded in my mind as the single hottest moment of all my twenty-eight years to date. The way her lips parted, moaning my name as her orgasm began, eyes still holding mine, lips curving as I had no choice but to follow her.

'Hestia, *fuck*,' I groaned, burying myself inside her as hard and deep as I could, claiming her, never wanting it to end.

She gasped as I came, eyes closed again, a smile of pure joy lighting up her face. My heart pounded, waves of intensity smashing into me from every side, but even then I couldn't look anywhere else.

My eyes were fixed on her, as though if I stopped, my heart would too. The world was tilting, finding a new angle – a whole new fucking axis.

I'd felt it before, just for a second, in the kitchen – and I thought she had too, but this . . .

Fuck.

'Jesse,' she started as we finally slowed, my cock twitching at the sound of my name in her mouth, the way her accent shaped it, made it something else. 'Are all line dances this good?'

I held her eyes for a moment, unable to suppress a chuckle.

'Best one yet,' I replied, now distracted by the rosy flush that followed her cheekbones, the way the floodlights turned her hair to glistening fire. I reached up, running my thumb over the colour in her cheeks, watching as her lips parted.

'We should probably . . .' she began after a moment, glancing over to our left as the sound of voices echoed across the car park.

'Right, shit, sorry,' I replied, startled by the realization that I'd completely zoned out to everything else, to the fact that we were outside, in a public place with only my truck between us and everyone else.

I had one hand on her hip as we gently disconnected, eyes meeting for a moment. That same expression as in the kitchen hovered in hers, an unanswered question. Forcing myself to focus, I lowered her down, reluctantly releasing her once I knew she had her balance.

'Listen,' she murmured as we adjusted ourselves and I wrapped and dumped the condom in a nearby trash can, trying and failing not to think of what it'd be like to fuck her without one. 'This is just a physical thing, right? I mean, I'm not here for that long, and . . .'

Her voice was softer, the ball-breaking certainty fading for a moment to reveal something else. My chest squeezed tight and I resisted the urge to touch her again, wanting to bring her into me and hold her for a moment, maybe even kiss her, knowing what would start up all over again . . .

'Whatever you want, Jessica,' I replied, offering out my hand for her to shake instead, figuring this was the only way to touch her without pushing it too far. Her lips curled at the corners, eyes lighting up as she clearly imagined what she wanted.

'Deal,' she breathed, giving her slow smile as her fingers slid into mine and shook my hand firmly. I felt her hesitate as she looked into my face, my attention drawn to the goosebumps gathering down her arms, the now visible nipples hardened beneath her shirt.

'Let me get you my jacket,' I began, reaching into my back pocket for the truck keys, but before I could, she'd reached up to me, shaking her head with a small smile.

'I'm not cold,' she whispered, letting her lips graze my ear. 'Now come dance with me.'

Even some four days later, the memory alone was making me shift in my jeans again. And given I was on my way to see my mom and sisters for Sunday dinner, I needed a distraction, like now.

I spent the rest of the drive with the music turned right up, windows down and my elbow resting on the door, humming along and running through a few issues I needed to iron out in roping practice this week ahead of the rodeo next weekend.

'Howdy.' My brother-in-law, Dean, opened the door to Mom's apartment as I arrived, a troublemaking grin on his face. He took the pack of beers I offered up. 'C'mon in! Although, with the line of questioning Clara's got for you, I'd turn right around and—'

'So who is she?'

Clara, my eldest sister, all but pushed her husband out of the way to get to me. Our other, more reasonable sister, Belle, was trying to call her away in the background, telling her to give me a minute.

'Good to see you too,' I smiled, giving her a patronizing pat on the arm and barging past her, chuckling as she called me an asshole under her breath.

In the tiny kitchen, Mom turned at the commotion, her face lighting up as I stepped inside.

'Jesse, honey!' she exclaimed, taking off her glasses for a second and turning to pull me into a hug. I returned it as hard as I dared, that shitty voice in the back of my head telling me I'd never know when it would be the last time. 'Now, let me look at you. Is Lil working you too hard?'

'Nah,' I replied, picking up what looked to be her drink from the counter and handing it to her, swapping it out for the oven mitt in her hand. Face flushed from the cooking, she gave a grateful nod and took a sip, watching as I dipped down to check on the chicken in the oven. 'She's over in London, anyhow. Lottie's in charge right now, doing a fine job.'

'Uh-huh,' Mom hummed as Clara stood in the doorway, her

tall frame filling most of it as she narrowed her eyes at me. 'You gonna answer Clara's question?'

I turned back to catch them grinning at each other.

The relief at seeing Mom have one of her good days, of their tag-teaming me again, was almost enough to persuade me to say something. But frustrating my busybody sister was too tempting.

'Who do you mean?' I asked, reaching over to the fridge and taking out a beer, angling the cap under my canines to pull it off, then flicking it at Clara with my thumb and forefinger as if tossing a coin.

Dean laughed from behind her in the corridor as she caught it in her right hand.

'The redhead, smartass. I heard from three different people about my brother dancing the whole night with one girl, a redhead with tattoos and an accent, ignoring just about everyone else.'

I shrugged, smiling to myself as I caught Mom's eye. She studied my face thoughtfully.

'Chrissy was kinda pissed, from what I heard,' Dean added, ducking under Clara's arm to stand inside the kitchen. 'Aren't you guys—'

'We're done,' I clarified, refusing to feel guilty. 'I've told her, and we've talked about it. I can dance with whoever I like and so can she.' I shrugged again. 'And I'm not sure why it's any of your business.'

Clara dead-eyed me, and I returned it. She sighed.

'Why won't you just tell me, before I have to hear about it from everyone else?' she complained. 'It's—'

'Clara, would you set the table?' Mom asked, an edge to her tone that we knew all too well from our childhood – not so much a question as a command.

Clara nodded, rolling her eyes and tossing the beer cap into the trash, her parting glance a promise that she wasn't about to let up any time soon.

'I received a *huge* box full of meds this morning,' Mom said after a few moments, the silence having settled between us. She waited for me to turn to her, her head tilted to the side, arms folded. 'Now, I didn't have time to add it all up, but I'm pretty sure there's at least two or three thousand dollars' worth in there. And given Belle can't save for shit, and Clara and Dean have just paid the down payment for their new place . . .'

Smiling, I shrugged again.

'I don't want you worrying about it,' I said, trying to ease the frown gathering on her brow. 'It's my money to spend how I like, okay? Lil pays me well, and I don't much care for shopping. You know that.'

She shook her head slowly, letting out a deep breath.

'I don't know what I did to get a son like you,' she said, reaching out to squeeze my arm. 'But I don't want to be the reason you can't live your life because you're paying for my bills.'

'Mom, stop,' I replied, pulling her into another hug. It was hard to give back to her, to express my thanks for her years of sacrifice for us, without it becoming emotional for both of us. I still couldn't imagine what it must have been like to care for three kids as a single mom, with no help from anyone. 'I want to do it, okay? I've got you. And those two assholes out there, if they need it.'

I dodged her half-hearted attempt to slap my wrist as she tried not to laugh, defending my sisters, who had never, and would never need defending.

'Okay, well, there's one other thing I need you to do,' she said, turning back to check on the progress of the pans on the stove.

I nodded, ignoring the undercurrent of worry, wondering if there was another complication, another diagnosis from her latest doctor's appointment.

'. . . Tell me why your face changed like that when Clara mentioned the redhead.'

She was studying me the way she'd always been able to do.

About to brush her off, I hesitated as I caught her eye, that same worry reminding me that she might not be around to have this conversation in a few years' time. That my honesty now might bring her a little happiness – even a little hope.

'She's . . . just visiting, from the UK. Lottie's best friend, Hestia. I don't know her that well, we're just, you know, hanging out, having fun.'

She raised an eyebrow, gaze still trained on my expression.

'Then, honey, if I didn't know better,' she began, glancing over to the door to check we were still alone, 'I'd say you're in trouble. Because I'm not sure I ever saw you look that way with Chrissy, and she's about the most serious you've ever been about someone.'

I swallowed, about to shrug it off, but the image of Hestia's mischievous smile, the way her words could cut me down and make me laugh in the same breath . . .

'She's pretty special,' I admitted, keeping my voice low and smiling at Mom's satisfied expression. 'And just about the most beautiful woman I've ever met,' I added, offloading the thoughts I'd had to keep to myself for the past couple of weeks. Cole had guessed quick enough and given me shit about it briefly before backing off, either because Lottie told him to or because he saw something in it. Maybe the same thing Mom had seen.

'Well, then,' she said, straightening up and putting her glasses back on, 'I want to meet her.'

Surprised, I opened my mouth to object, not knowing how I'd even broach that with Hestia, especially after agreeing to just keep things physical. But I could also picture them talking. I knew Hestia's big heart and quick wit would win Mom and my sisters over in minutes.

'I . . . well, we're not exactly . . .' I began, stopping as she chuckled under her breath.

'Jesse, darlin' – are you blushing?'

I ran my hand through my hair, looking up at the ceiling for a moment and trying to laugh it off.

'Whatever,' I answered after a beat. My turn to shake my head at her. 'I'll ask her, as a friend.'

She dipped her chin in a nod, turning to the oven.

'You do that,' she agreed, stifling a smile as Clara and Belle appeared again in the hall, tentatively edging closer. 'Just be warned, honey, I've got a feeling those two are gonna be working overtime to get you blushing all over again right in front of your beautiful friend.'

I sighed, resigned, as all three of them started cackling, Clara already whispering something in Belle's ear.

Fucking kill me now.

Chapter 4
Hestia

In the week that followed, one thing was crystal fucking clear.

Abstinence was not an option.

There was no point sugar-coating it to anyone, least of all myself – Jesse and I had quickly become fuck buddies. Friends with benefits. A situationship, if you will.

No other thoughts, barely any eye contact, certainly no talking that implied any kind of further involvement. Purely physical. I'd suggested it right as we'd finished up against the truck at the line dance and he'd agreed, his slow smile on our formal handshake almost prompting a repeat performance on the spot.

Christ, that man was delicious.

Not that we'd had a chance to repeat anything since, given how busy everyone was in the lead up to the rodeo this weekend. I'd dived into helping Lottie with the guests, learning the basics of how to take care of the horses with Bailey and using any free time to sketch out new tattoo designs. My favourite spot was at the lake by Lottie's new cabin, the sheltered position often turning the still water to glass, reflecting the burning sky in the late afternoon. Increasingly my designs were drawing more on the natural world. My morbid delight at finding an animal skull among the trees made me think of Dee's store, knowing she'd likely understand my excitement.

But now, on the way to the rodeo with Lottie in Cole's truck, a very unfamiliar feeling was dawning.

'Stop it. You look fucking gorgeous, Hes. Trust me.'

I pulled down the sunshade, using the inset mirror to check myself again. Lighter make-up, except for the ruby-red lips – those I refused to give up. Lottie had curled my matching hair into soft, voluminous barrel waves under the straw cowboy hat, but it was the pale blue denim minidress that really made me pause. My black cowboy boots added an element of comfort, but it was so . . . country.

'I don't think I've had bare legs in public since secondary school,' I murmured. 'Remind me why I agreed to this?'

Lottie giggled, squeezing my arm.

'Because you love me and are humouring my over-the-top excitement at having you here? And because it's too hot to wear black today, and frankly, I was just really fucking curious to see you in any other colour.'

'Blasphemy,' I grumbled. 'It's never too hot for black.' But as I glanced over and saw her bright blue eyes dancing with amusement, I rolled my own and offered her a small smile. 'Only for you, cowgirl.'

We approached the rodeo, following the queuing traffic for the car park, the muffled sound of the loudspeaker blaring outside and a sea of cowboy hats as people walked in.

'What about certain cowboys?' Lottie said, her voice light. 'I hear Jesse had a lot of, um . . . *feelings* about your outfit at the line dance, and that was only, what? Fifty per cent country?'

I bit my lip to hide my smile as we parked up, just one of hundreds of pick-up trucks, seemingly part of the Wyoming uniform.

'Look. It's just a bit of fun, like I said before. There's nothing else to read into. For a guy, he's . . . not bad. I'll admit it – nice ass, arms to die for, face like a movie star . . .' I stopped as her smile turned into a grin.

'Great sense of humour, kind, thoughtful . . .' she continued as we got out, waiting for me as I rounded the front of the truck.

'Whatever,' I replied. 'It doesn't mean anything else, okay? What happened between you and Cole is pretty rare, Lots. It just doesn't happen like that for most people, certainly not me.'

She hooked her arm through mine as we got to the entrance, showed the tickets on her phone to the attendant, and we were through. A vast dirt-floor arena stretched out in front of us, surrounded by stands with banked seating, some covered and others open to the fierce sun. The full impact of the noise – the sounds of the gathering crowd, the occasional sounds of horses and – *shit*, was that a bull over there?

Lottie laughed at my expression.

'I forget that you haven't seen any of this before,' she added, walking us over to the covered stand where our seats were located. 'It's so . . . *American*, isn't it?'

I just nodded, my eyes drawn to the event already starting. A calf was released out of a gate at one end of the arena, followed by a couple of cowboys moving at warp speed, circling ropes above their heads as they chased it.

'Listen,' Lottie added as we reached our seats finally, attracting a fair amount of looks from the surrounding spectators. It was likely because they didn't know us – Lottie had said her arrival had caused a wild amount of interest in town. 'I guess I'm just letting myself feel delusional about having you here and enjoying the cowboys as much as I have.' She smiled as I did, unable to do anything else in the face of her genuine joy. 'I'm just aware that very soon you're going to head home and . . . honestly, it's going to feel like I'm missing a fucking limb.'

I gripped her hand, feeling a sudden prickle of emotion behind my eyes.

'Me too,' I whispered.

'Ugh, don't,' she said suddenly, looking up and blinking. 'None of that. You're here and we're making the most of it. Now – Jesse's up in a sec, then Bailey. This is a big day for them both, there's a fair amount of prize money up for grabs, I think.'

As we watched and waited, a shadow fell across us. We both looked up into the smiling face of a cowboy, tipping his hat.

'Howdy,' he said, eyes flicking over my outfit before going back to Lottie. 'Lottie, right? I'm Carter, I was on the cattle drive at the Diamond Back a couple months ago.'

'Oh, right, yes – I remember!' She smiled. 'How are you? You competing today?'

He shook his head, glancing to me again.

I raised an eyebrow. I had a feeling I knew where this might go.

'No ma'am, just watching with a few buddies.' We both glanced behind us, clocking the handful of other cowboys now nodding and smiling in our direction. 'I don't suppose you and your, err . . . friend here will be going out to Shelby's later? It'd sure be nice to catch up over a drink?'

Lottie's face changed, suddenly catching on. Honestly, it was adorable – being so into Cole that it didn't even seem to cross her mind to think of any other men in that way.

I stood up, taking charge.

'Hestia.' I introduced myself, leaning over Lottie to shake his hand. 'I think we will be, yes, although Lottie will be with Cole. You know him, right? Big fucker, arms like the Hulk?'

Lottie covered her mouth and dipped her head, shoulders shaking slightly.

'Yeah, yeah, I know Cole.' He acknowledged my tone with an

amused nod and a curious smile, but otherwise unperturbed. He was cute, admittedly. 'Maybe see you later, then?'

'Maybe.' I smiled sweetly. 'Mine's a bourbon. No ice.'

'Yes, ma'am,' he replied, tipping his hat again and shaking his head as his friends laughed.

'Oh, Hes – look,' Lottie said, still laughing but pointing to the arena.

And there he was. Clad head to toe in rodeo gear, from the tan leather chaps to the Diamond Back branded shirt, his smile breaking out as he roped the calf in record time. As the crowd roared and he pulled up his horse, Jesse seemed to search out the crowd, looking from under the brim of his hat to shield his eyes from the sun.

Lottie jumped up, cheering and clapping, and in the same moment he saw us.

I held myself still, expression neutral, but my heart picked up as he fully took off his hat and tipped it towards us. Running a hand through his hair, he placed it back and despite the distance, winked before turning away.

'Well, *I've* never received that before,' Lottie noted as she sat back down. 'Greatest sign of respect from a cowboy to fully take their hat off—'

'Tell me he doesn't ride bulls?' I asked, noticing a sudden commotion to the right, where one of them seemed to be kicking the shit out of the gate.

'Not any more,' Lottie clarified, smiling at my blatant deflection. 'He stepped away before he received more than a broken back . . . besides, Cole told me that his mum got sick around the same time. His dad left years ago, so he wanted to step up for her and his sisters.'

The myriad of sarcastic responses dried up and evaporated. Combined with what I knew of Jesse already, the picture building around him was . . . *fuck*.

As Lottie turned to me, suspicious of my silence, with considerable relief I saw the barrels being set up and heard Bailey and Dunkin's names over the tannoy.

Attention turned, we watched as the first few racers belted out of the gate, their speed and precision breathtaking as they thundered across the arena, a blur of colour and dirt. There were milliseconds in the time differentials.

'These are some of the best racers in the state,' Lottie explained as the crowd cheered again, just as Bailey's name was announced. 'Qualifying here takes you on to the championships in Cheyenne. It's a big deal . . . big money, too, Bailey says. More than she'd get in a year at the ranch.'

We held our breath as the countdown started, a roar as Dunkin rocket-launched up the centre of the arena, Bailey no more than a flash of auburn hair against the horse's golden coat. The first turn was the tightest we'd seen yet, cutting so close to the barrel that I couldn't believe it wouldn't be knocked down. On to the next, and again, as Dunkin dipped down, Bailey leaning with her, it looked like the perfect turn until –

'Shit, *oh God*, no,' Lottie yelled, both of us springing up as Dunkin lost her balance, her leg striking the heavy barrel hard. She half went down, struggling bravely to stay upright as Bailey vaulted off in the next moment, her hat flying into the dirt. Officials began running in as Dunkin limped away in distress, eventually slowing as Bailey ran after her, calling her name. 'Oh fuck,' Lottie whispered, her hand over her mouth, tears welling in her eyes. 'She's going to be devastated. Right before qualifying, too . . . and poor Dunkin . . .'

'It's okay, they'll be okay,' I offered, putting my arm round her shoulders, a huge jolt of relief at seeing both Jesse and Cole among the cowboys striding into the arena to help. But, as we watched Jesse supporting Bailey while she led Dunkin out, we both knew my words were hollow. There was no way Dunkin was going to be barrel racing again any time soon.

My solution was tried and tested.

'Shots, right now,' I ordered, Bailey tucked under my arm, grim stoicism setting her features. 'There's fuck all you can do about it tonight, I heard the vet say that. Dunkin's patched up and comfortable, right? She's had more ketamine than half of East London on an average Saturday night, so I'd say she's having the best time out of all of us. Let's get wasted and forget about it for now, okay?'

'Can't argue with logic like that,' Jesse interjected as he joined our group at a table near the stage. Shelby's was exactly what I'd imagined a bar in Wyoming might look like – a ton of dark wood, from the floors to the chairs, wall-mounted wagon wheels and old painted signs. The walls behind the bar were jam-packed with framed pictures of bands and artists who had played over what looked like a history spanning decades. 'To Dunkin's recovery,' he toasted.

All five of us tipped back the small glasses, Lottie groaning as she tasted the contents.

'I fucking hate tequila,' she grimaced.

'Since when?' I asked, reaching out for Bailey's beer and passing it to her, rubbing her shoulder.

Jesse watched us, open curiosity in his stare.

'Since Kyle,' Lottie murmured, prompting what was almost a growl from Cole, his arm moving from the back of her chair to her shoulders.

'Prick,' he hissed.

'Bang on,' I nodded, noticing the guy from the rodeo near the bar, seemingly telling one hell of a joke as the others fell around laughing. 'Kyle is a grade-A wanker. Still, at least you got an upgrade out of it.'

I winked at Lottie and returned Cole's smile.

'And somehow you've managed not to say I told you so,' Lottie noted, looking up at me from under her eyelashes, even making Bailey chuckle. 'Hes knew that Kyle wasn't good for me from day one . . . but I wasn't really up for listening.'

'There's still time,' I countered, giving her a wink, pausing as Jesse smiled at me before sipping his drink. 'Shame I don't have the same radar for myself.'

Lottie shrugged.

'Cal's not so bad, though, just . . . a mess.'

It was my turn to shrug as I glanced at Bailey. She was all but folded in on herself, clearly resting the blame for what had happened squarely on her shoulders.

'Bailey, honey!' a voice called from nearby. A group of women, including Darcy, beckoned her over.

'Anyone I need on my radar over there?' I said to her, gratified as a shy smile bloomed. 'You just give the signal if you need me. Or if you need more shots.'

'Thanks, darlin', I will,' she said, getting up and slouching over to them to be enveloped in a many-armed hug.

Jesse studied me as I watched the group. Bailey was nodding self-consciously at their attempts to console her, managing the occasional smile.

'You're a real ol' mama bear, huh?' he said softly, angling his chair towards me as Lottie and Cole leant into each other, deep in conversation.

I shook my head, not quite meeting his eye.

'I hate seeing good people beating themselves up.' I looked back over at the bar area. The guy from the rodeo, Carter, returned the glance, touching the brim of his hat. 'Anyone in pain, actually. Mental or physical.'

'Ever think about the medical profession?' he asked, leaning forward, chin in his hand, his depthless grey eyes flickering over my face.

'Did psychology at university,' I said, suddenly wary at his serious expression, the depth of his interest in my answers. 'Turns out, being fucked up yourself isn't a qualification for helping others in the same boat.'

He kept his expression neutral, but his eyes darkened for a moment. There was a level of understanding there, beneath the banter. Unnerved by him yet again, I picked up the last spare shot and downed it.

Shifting gears, his expression softened and a mischievous smile grew. 'So, seeing as you know exactly what I'm thinking, given your degree and all, I reckon it's only fair I get to know you a little.'

He gestured towards the bar, catching a bartender's attention and nodding, setting up a fresh rack of shots. I paused, knowing exactly what he was up to, but simultaneously not wanting to back down from the challenge.

'You don't have to get me drunk to get in my –' I began, stopping as he chuckled, nodding to Cole and Lottie, now getting up to go dance.

'Highly recommend the corridor behind the bar,' Lottie called, waving with a coy smile as Cole led her away.

'Honey, I am mighty fond of how good you are to go at any moment,' Jesse replied, thanking the bartender as eight shots arrived. 'But I still don't know much about you. And I want to. So – here's the game. I guess something about you, and if I'm right, you drink. If I'm wrong, I drink.'

I knew full well this had all the hallmarks of an extremely stupid decision, and yet . . .

'Do your worst, cowboy.'

Leaning in, I took off my hat and shook out my hair, running my fingers through it. He stilled for a moment, eyes darting across my face, then down to the denim dress and my bare legs below.

He cleared his throat and sat back in the chair, folding his arms as he studied me through narrowed eyes. It was impossible not to stare at the way the rolled-up sleeves of his shirt strained against rock-hard biceps, two buttons open at his throat revealing the beginnings of his tanned torso . . . how it felt to be pressed against it, those arms flexed as they held me up . . .

'When it comes to men, you don't have a specific type,' he began, watching my expression carefully. 'But you do like bigger guys. Maybe ones that don't work out in a gym, but ones that can pick you up just as easy as that glass right there.'

I rolled my eyes, picking up the shot and knocking it back.

It was a fireball, the cinnamon burning a path right down to my core. God. We were going to be *fucked*.

'Congrats, Sherlock,' I drawled, forcing myself not to smile as he did. 'Except you missed a bit. Men . . . or women.'

He raised an eyebrow as comprehension dawned, a tiny shake of his head as he blew out a breath.

'Jesus, Jessica.' He cupped the back of his neck for a moment and shifted in his seat.

'I've got one,' I murmured, leaning into him. 'You're the type to wonder if me and Lottie ever had a moment, right? Maybe a little more than friends?'

He looked up, eyes glued on mine for a moment before reaching out for a glass, not dropping my stare as he knocked it back with a wince in answer.

'I swear to God, Jessica, if that really happened, I'm gonna do whatever you goddamn well tell me to for a live-action replay.'

I cackled, all pretence of trying to play a smart game washed away. *This man*.

'Sorry, gorgeous, she turned me down. I tried.'

He bit his lip for a moment, clearly still picturing it as he shook his head.

'Well now, I like Lottie an awful lot, but . . . she's a goddamn fool. *Look at you*, for crying out loud.'

I paused at that same intensity as before in his voice weaving through despite the banter. Too close to the surface, for both of us.

'Next question,' I said instead.

Time seemed to slow, the rest of the bar melting away as he correctly guessed my favourite music genres and that I'd never owned any pets. Thankfully, he was wrong about what car I drove at home – none – and that I was an only child.

Fireballs and previous drinks accumulating, my head was starting to spin.

'Last question,' I said, unsure if I was slurring my words now or not. The glazed look in his eyes suggested he was unlikely to notice.

His pause was the longest yet, but when he spoke, the words were sure.

'You've told yourself you'll never get married. You're afraid of really committing your whole self to someone.'

My thoughts spun, the truth of his words like the burn of alcohol in my throat. Painful.

'Bullshit,' I lied, shaking my head and instantly regretting it. I gripped the table and waited for his outline to become solid again. 'I'd get married. It's just a piece of fucking paper, right? People do it all the time.'

He grinned, shrugging.

'I don't buy it,' he replied, leaning forward, his face just inches from mine, and reaching out to trace my fingers with his. 'If I asked you – if I said, Hestia, you are more than I could've ever imagined in a woman and I'll be fucking damned if I let you go home to England and never see you again, will you marry me so you can stay – you'd agree?'

I shut the real words out, just listening to the tenor, the undertone of challenge. I never backed down, ever, to anyone. And fireballs or not, I was not about to back down to a cocky, half-cut cowboy.

'Sure, why not. Fuck it, let's go one better – I'll book the registry office, or whatever you call it here. Where's the best place to get married in Jackson?' The surprise on his face was replaced with a belly laugh as I hiccupped, holding my hand to my mouth as I got my phone out. 'You think I won't do it?' I asked, trying to get a grip on my focus, typing the place into my browser as Jesse named it. 'There – that's it, right? Look – "register your interest", fifty dollar deposit.'

He just laughed, shaking his head.

'All front, honey,' he murmured, lighting the fire in my gut all the brighter. I picked the next available date and my phone autofilled the form. I clicked to pay, not giving a fuck about spending the money to prove a point.

'There,' I grinned, flipping the phone round to show him the confirmation page. 'I thought a spring wedding would be nice. Still snow on the mountains, but maybe warm enough to consummate things right outside, seeing as there's no way I'd let you keep a suit on for long.'

I picked up the last shot and handed it to him, watching as he knocked it back without complaint, banging the table with his fist as it went down, laughing.

'Holy fucking hell, woman,' he cried, shaking his head. 'You know something? You're just the kinda crazy I could get to love.'

There was a hesitation between us, a sliver of reality entering a surreal situation.

Time to leave.

I stood up, the room swirling like the rope in Jesse's hands at the rodeo.

'Whoa there, cowgirl . . .' Cole's voice. He appeared at my side, strong hands holding me up as the room began to tilt.

'Don't tell me you two have had that whole fucking rack of shots between you?' Lottie scolded. 'I told you leaving them alone together was a mistake,' she said to Cole, taking my other side, tucking my arm into hers.

'He started it,' I said, my words now blurring together freely, trying to point in Jesse's direction, and frowning when I realized he'd gone.

'And you finished me off,' Jesse said, appearing as if from nowhere behind me. 'Just like you always do.'

'Dear fucking God,' Lottie groaned. 'Right, we're going home before this escalates.'

Jesse and I giggled together as we were escorted out of the bar, a pair of naughty schoolkids next to Cole and Lottie's barely concealed amusement.

'. . . dread to think where these two could end up if left to it,' I heard Lottie say. And as I was about to object, I had a vague sense I'd just done something particularly stupid, even by my own standards.

But, for the life of me, my body and brain wholly engulfed in one giant fireball, I couldn't remember what the fuck that was.

Chapter 5
Hestia

The progress on Lottie's new cabin by the lake was startling. Despite a batch of guests arriving the day after the rodeo, the ranch now at capacity and Lottie in full-on manager mode, Cole and a couple of hired hands had maintained a determined pace. Even in the almost three weeks I'd been here, it'd gone from a bare frame to a full, watertight cabin, roof on and windows in.

Lottie was desperate for them to have a space together, the intensity of their feelings shining through, growing brighter daily. I felt more than a twinge of sadness at the thought of leaving them and the ranch, with my flight now coming up in just four days. The only consolation was knowing Lottie was the happiest I'd ever seen her, and that she was surrounded by great people.

Averting my eyes from Cole's topless form sitting astride the roof in just jeans, boots and his hat, I felt thankful Jesse was nowhere in sight. The temptation of him in the same position would've been enough to make me either scale that house like Spider-Man, or wade into the lake – clothes on.

I had no memory of the other night, only a vague sense of unease. I'd put it down to seeing Bailey doing her damnedest to cope with the guilt she felt about Dunkin's accident, the sense of loss and disappointment almost palpable. I didn't know how else to help her, given my previous suggested distraction had backfired and landed me with a two-day headache. Come to think of it, I didn't have many suggestions that didn't involve alcohol and hangovers, a fact some overpaid, smug therapist had deigned to point out to me once.

I'd left uni not long after. The thought of a career spent pointing out the bleeding fucking obvious for obscene fees somehow grated against my moral code. The irony was, I had since become a de facto therapist for many of my clients, inking their problems, solutions and scars right into their skin.

Returning to my latest sketch, legs tucked up on the outdoor sofa in the cookout area overlooking the lake, I picked up my phone as the screen lit up.

> Your drawing is FIRE!

I smiled, opening it and navigating into Messages. I'd taken the plunge and called Dee yesterday, getting her mobile number and sharing a couple of the cow skull sketches I'd made.

> Is there any way you'd sell it to me? It would look SO good on a tee.

I paused, looking up as I heard footsteps. Bailey.

> Yeah, it's yours if you want it. But no payment. It's a present for not forcing me into blue denim in your store.

'Hey, cowpoke,' Bailey said, trying a small smile as she approached.

'Hey,' I replied, gathering myself up and standing. 'You okay? How's Dunkin doing?'

She nodded, and as her smile broadened, I felt a surge of relief. Bailey cared so much for Dunkin, and it'd hit me harder than I'd thought possible to see them both hurt. I liked her a lot – her honesty, the sincerity in her ambition, the obvious love she had for the animals and people here.

'She's healing up real well, no lasting damage according to the vet, thank the good lord. But it's the championships. They've given me a wildcard entry, as I didn't qualify . . . but it means I need another horse. Like, now.'

'That's amazing about the championships – but is that possible? Like – where do you even buy horses?' I asked as we began walking together.

She laughed, the sound echoing as we skirted the lake shore, a couple of birds startled out of the trees that ran the length of one edge.

'Plenty of places, but there's a horse sale on tomorrow morning, a couple hours out of town. Would you want to come along? I know horses aren't your thing, but—'

'I'm there,' I said, hooking my arm through hers. 'Now, while it's true I know sweet fuck all about horses, I do know people. You concentrate on finding a good horse, and I'll let you know if the owner's a dick and trying to scam you.'

She huffed a laugh again.

'Deal. Oh, and Jesse's coming along too. He's got the best eye outta all of us for horses. And maybe even people, too.'

I returned her knowing look with a serving of side-eye.

'Quit it, or I'll get the shots out again.'

―――

The next morning, so early that my eyes watered under my sunnies, the three of us climbed into Bailey's truck. I opted for the small back seat of the double cab, with Jesse the last one in as he secured and double-checked the horse trailer behind the truck.

As I clutched my flask of coffee like a lifeline, I looked out at the passing scenery – the jagged peaks of the Tetons spearing the sky, the deep greens and earthy browns of the pines. Wildflowers in every shade sprinkled the verges and endless fields in the distance; two birds of prey circled on the currents high up. This place had a way of making you feel like a very small, very insignificant piece of a vast jigsaw in a way a city couldn't. People weren't the main characters here.

'You okay back there?' Jesse said, turning to check. 'What happens if you take those glasses off? You burn up or something?'

Bailey chuckled.

'Fuck around and find out,' she speculated. 'You leave her be. She's a night owl, not used to the hours us country folk keep, huh darlin'?'

I grunted my agreement, clinging to the caffeine.

'How are you so cheerful this early in the morning?' I murmured, wrapping Lottie's oversized fleece-lined jacket around myself more tightly. Despite reaching the high twenties during the day, summer mornings in Jackson were barely in double digits.

'Oh, I don't know,' he said, turning back to face out the front of the truck as Bailey stepped on the gas, the main highway stretching out into the far distance. 'The sun's out, life's good, Dunkin's on the mend and . . . well, I've rarely had more fun getting over three-day hangovers.'

I only just hid my smile as he glanced in the rear-view mirror.

'You got any Lainey Wilson?' I asked, watching as his expression changed with the memory dawning, the words he'd whispered right before our last . . . encounter. 'Wake me up with some country music. I've heard she's good.'

By the time we reached the sale, I was humming along to some of the tracks. There were similarities between the heartfelt lyrics and darker undertones of the kind of music I liked, the guitars much lighter and more playful, but it suited the scenery, the whole vibe. I put on my hat as I slid out of the truck, finally removing the glasses.

'There you are,' Jesse smiled, lifting the brim for a moment.

I flinched away, knowing I looked as tired as I felt, no make-up to hide behind. He frowned as Bailey wandered over to the huge outdoor ring, horses already lined up and ready to show.

'Sorry, I just . . . I look like shit, so . . .' I began, surprised when I felt a gentle touch under my chin, his finger brushing my skin and lifting my head.

'You're a whole other person in the morning, aren't you?' he said, his voice as soft as his eyes. Before I could respond, he added, 'But you don't look like shit, honey. You look like you need another coffee and a hug or something, but you're beautiful. You know that, right?'

Caught out again, my thoughts stalled.

'Y'all coming? Jesse, what'd you make of this pinto?'

Bailey's words rang between us, but Jesse made no attempt to leave. Instead, he stepped closer, putting an arm around my shoulder from the side, squeezing it for a moment. The unexpected gesture and the kindness behind it, despite having done all kinds of other physical things with this man . . . suddenly felt intensely intimate.

'Thanks,' I whispered, resting my head against his side for just a moment.

But then I felt it again. The same feeling as in the kitchen, and again at the line dance. A tiny shift, a small crack appearing at the surface, growing into a fissure in my gut.

As he gently pulled back, I glanced up, disconcerted to find that his expression reflected mine – a frown, now masked by a small smile, as though he'd felt it too.

He looked up and over to Bailey.

'I'm on my way. She moves well,' he answered, staying close to my side as we approached the ring, the outside crammed with buyers. Moving me ahead of him, as we reached Bailey he positioned himself to shield me from the jostling crowd behind.

As they discussed the horses, Bailey pulling up the catalogue on her phone, I tried to unpick what the hell had just happened. Why was it that he could lift me up and fuck me against a wall – twice – but a brief side hug from him sent me into a spiral?

'I might get some more coffee,' I said a few minutes later, my muddled brain none the wiser. 'You want some too?'

'Not for me . . . but you want me to come with you?' Jesse asked, while Bailey also declined the offer, craning to see one of the horses emerging from the back of the ring.

I shook my head.

'Bailey needs your expertise. It's fine.'

'If anyone tries anything, you just come right back and find me. I ain't got no problem cracking skulls first thing in the morning.'

Rolling my eyes at him, I couldn't help smiling as I left. As if anyone would give a shit about me being here. I strolled around, looking for any sign of coffee, until a short queue of people caught my attention.

I joined the end, taking in the animated conversations around me, mostly about horses but often about family and snippets from everyday life, friends catching up. There seemed to be an invisible web connecting everyone here, a genuine sense of community and a shared lifestyle that I'd never experienced at home. Everyone here was likely part of a ranch in some way, worked with the land they lived on and met the same people over and over at sales and rodeos, one generation after another intertwined. The solitary way

I lived, the way most people lived back home in London, seemed so . . . empty in comparison.

Shouts suddenly echoed through the yard; something bashed against metal, and a gate slammed shut. I could see dust rising from a fenced-off corral near the white barn at the far end, and then came a gut-wrenching sound like a horse screeching in pain.

I looked around, wide-eyed, catching the grimace of the older woman in front of me. Seeing my confusion, she shook her head.

'The Taylors are assholes,' she murmured as we watched two men approach the gate, clearly trying to find out what was going on, only to be dismissed by whoever was inside the corral. 'Ain't nothing good that happens to animals in their hands. I've seen that horse before. She's just got spirit, is all. Looks a bit different, funny mix of somethin' – but she'd do someone proud. But she won't be told, not in the way they do it anyway.'

I nodded, the sound of the horse's pain still echoing in my mind.

'What'll happen to her, if no one buys her?' I asked quietly as we moved up the queue and the woman placed her coffee order.

She winced.

'You're not from round here, are ya?' I shook my head. 'Well, I'm sorry to say that she'll likely end up getting taken over the Canadian border. They still take horses for slaughter up there. It's a damn shame, but ain't nobody got time to work on horses like that any more.'

I ordered my coffee, holding up a hand as she walked away. That's when it hit me: the way she'd described the horse, the painful memory that now surfaced.

Your mother and I don't have the time to indulge you any more. If you won't take good advice from us, you'll bloody well take it from a professional. We don't need your nonsense. Darken someone else's door with it.

Gritting my teeth, I gripped the cup and stared at the gate.

My feet made the decision for me as I began to stride across the yard. I knew I would likely draw attention, and despite the cowboy hat, the rest of me was all city.

Even as I reached the corral, my head and heart were warring. I knew fuck all about horses. This wasn't my world. I was leaving to go home in a couple of days with no way of knowing when I'd come back. There was nothing I could do, was there?

Except, when I approached, what I saw stopped me dead.

In the far corner of the corral, hidden behind high fencing, one man was holding the horse – a shimmering dark copper colour all over – while another brought what looked like a long, thin pole down across its back. Rearing up, the horse jerked sideways and body-slammed into the fence, crying out again in pain, eyes flashing, tremors rolling through its body. A lump gathered in my throat, tears immediately springing up behind my eyes.

'Hey!' I yelled, banging my fist against the gate. 'What the fuck are you doing? Stop it right now, or I'll call the police.'

Both faces whipped towards me, and after a moment, one of them started laughing.

'Ain't your business, woman. Fuck off.'

I'd worked long and hard to box my anger away, lid on firmly. But in that moment, it didn't just come off – the whole fucking box exploded.

Throwing my coffee against the side of the barn, I tried to wrench open the gate, but there was some kind of lock on the side. Instead, I climbed up the bars, placing both hands on the top to vault over and landing with a thud in the dirt on the other side.

'You okay, ma'am?' said a voice from behind me. I turned briefly, meeting the eyes of a concerned but kindly looking older cowboy.

'I need Jesse and Bailey, from the Diamond Back, big red trailer over by the main ring – can you find them, quickly? Please?'

He nodded as our gazes met before turning away and striding out over the yard.

'What the hell are you doin'?' yelled the guy with the stick, his expression darkening as I strode towards him. 'Like I said, this ain't your—'

'It *is* my fucking business, because I want to buy that horse, right now. But only if you back the fuck away from it with that pole. Touch that horse again, and it won't be money I'll be giving you. Believe me.'

The bemused smirk on the other man's face turned dark as he fought against the horse, now throwing her head up in fear as I approached.

'You? Want this piece of shit?' he said, eyebrow raised.

I'd heard some of the prices thrown around in the sale ring, but even so, I had no idea what would swing it here or the implications of what I was doing.

'I'll give you five hundred dollars and you'll hand her over right now,' I demanded, coming to a stop in striking distance of the pole.

He grunted, shaking his head in disgust.

'Who the fuck even are you—'

'Five hundred,' I repeated, cutting him off. 'And your worst fucking nightmare, if you want me to be.'

Eyes narrowed, he glanced down at me, his gaze lingering on my face.

'A thousand,' he countered. Even though I knew he was full of shit, the relief that he was engaging with my offer was so overwhelming that tears almost welled again.

'Seven fifty. Final offer.'

The other guy looked over at him, acknowledgement passing between them.

'Fine. I want it in cash,' he said, finally throwing the damn pole to the ground, the horse flinching as he did so. 'We ain't letting her go until we got it.'

My stomach dropped. I only had cards on me, no easy way of getting hold of cash.

'Hestia?'

I turned to see Jesse and Bailey at the gate, Jesse registering my expression. Without hesitation, he hooked his leg up on the gate and vaulted over, striding right towards me. The urge to meet him in the middle was unbearable.

'What the fuck?' he said as he reached me, taking one look at my face, his hands on my shoulders for a moment. 'What did they do?'

He turned to face them, his jaw hardening as he took in their stance, the horse pressed against the fence and the pole in the dirt.

'Fucking assholes,' he growled, starting towards them. I caught his hand, pulling him to a stop.

'I need cash – seven hundred and fifty. I bought her, the horse. I have the money, I just need to get it from an ATM, or a bank.' He looked back at me, stunned. 'Please, Jesse. I need your help.'

Staring, his forehead creasing as his eyes flicked between mine, he took a breath and reached out with his spare hand, gently wiping my cheek. Then, without a word, he let go of my other hand and reached into his jeans pocket, pulling out a thick roll of notes.

Before I could say anything, he turned and walked over to the guy holding the horse's head.

'It's five hundred,' he said, holding up the cash. 'Or, it's five hundred and my fist in your face, followed by a call to the livestock board to report this shit. Your choice.'

The man shook his head, but handed over the horse's reins as he snatched the money.

'Congratulations,' he spat. 'You just bought the biggest pain-in-the-ass mule in the state. Looks like they're made for each other.'

He gestured towards me with a flick of his head and I saw Jesse's stance change, his fist curling and back tensing.

'Jesse, you bring that poor girl here. I'll help ya load up.'

I turned at the steel in Bailey's voice. She was jogging across the dirt towards us, her forehead drawn into a grim line.

'You okay?' she mouthed, frowning as I looked over, nodding briefly.

The two men stared at them before turning away as Jesse soothed the horse, now skittering sideways, the bleeding open wounds on her back visible as she drew closer. As they stalked off, Bailey approached the horse, working with Jesse to walk her slowly to the gate.

I realized my hands were shaking as I held one to my mouth, not able to take my eyes off the horse. Her eyes were white-rimmed and terrified, the pain and fear obvious; her distress radiated, hitting me square on. My own chest ached in response.

Jesse glanced back at me, murmuring something to Bailey before coming over. This time, just as before, my feet took over and I moved towards him, our bodies meeting in a rush as I pressed against him, my hat falling into the dirt.

Wordlessly, he wrapped his arms around me as my tears fell for real now, my hands gripping his shirt until my knuckles turned white. Rage, sadness and rejection took turns churning through me, a storm dredging the sand beneath the waves and turning the water dark.

Only Jesse's steady breathing, the feeling of his hand holding the back of my head, stopped me from drowning.

Chapter 6
Hestia

We were half an hour into the drive back to the ranch when it hit me. It wasn't that I'd just bought a horse despite my utter ignorance about them, or even the fact that I had about forty-eight hours to figure out what the fuck to do about it before I flew home. Bailey had tried to reassure me that there were charities, horse shelters that would likely take her in. Take her off my hands.

But it was exactly that — her being palmed off, discarded as though she was worth nothing — that I couldn't bear. Those men had beaten and brutalized her, and from what the woman in the coffee queue had said, it was because she wouldn't fit the mould they wanted to force her into.

It was too close to home. Combined with the overwhelming tiredness and the impending prospect of facing my broken relationship back home, having to keep running the business in spite of it every day . . .

'Can you pull over? I need some air — just for a few minutes,' I asked, avoiding Jesse and Bailey's worried expressions in the rear-view mirror.

'Sure thing, honey,' Bailey replied softly. 'There's a gas station just up about a mile or two ahead, okay?'

I nodded, gripping the door handle as I stared out towards the mountains, seeing nothing. I felt Jesse's eyes on me the whole way, as heavy on my shoulders as if his hands held me upright, forcing me to keep it together.

Finally we pulled in, the gas station no more than a large hut with a few pumps outside, backing onto the shaded fields of the valley floor. The sun was still climbing behind the jagged mountains to our right. I jumped out as we came to a stop, half walking, half stumbling to the grass at the side of the building, suddenly aware of the nausea roiling in my gut. I leant against the wood as I reached it, eventually sinking down into a crouch as my legs gave way.

'Hey, whoa there, what's going on?'

Jesse approached, his boots crunching on the gravelled dirt as I closed my eyes to the beginnings of a tightness in my chest, my heart starting to pound. A feeling I hadn't experienced for years, another thing I'd worked to keep under the surface.

'Don't – just leave me be,' I mumbled, trying to move away as I heard him behind me, my eyes still clamped shut. Wasn't it enough that he'd already seen me cry? I didn't want to have an anxiety attack right in front of him too.

'Nope, not gonna happen,' he replied, his tone firm. I felt his hand on my arm, cool plastic against my hand. 'You're gonna drink a little water, then tell me what's going on.'

I grasped the bottle, opening my eyes to realize he'd already undone the cap for me and so I took a sip at first, then a longer drink. Heart still pounding, I leant my head against the hut and tried to focus my breathing.

'Jesse, you don't have to do this, just go – leave me to it. It's just an anxiety attack, I've had them before . . . I'll be okay in a few minutes,' I began, stopping as he leant over me to screw the cap back on the water, his face right next to mine.

'I don't think you get it, Jessica,' he murmured, leaning into a crouch himself, his body now bracing mine. 'I'm not leaving you anywhere, least of all like this. Now, I know you're used to being the boss and that's all good with me,' he paused, brushing stray hairs out of my face. 'But right now, you're on my orders. And we're gonna go back to the truck, 'cause those horses need to get home, and your new girl needs to see a vet. I'm sitting up back with you and you're gonna tell me all about those tattoos of yours, take me on a whole tour. Starting with this one, right here.'

His fingers brushed below my collarbone, circling the moon above the scene of Sleepy Hollow.

I knew he was trying to distract me, to take the lead in a moment where I couldn't. I thought of the horse – whose name I didn't even know – standing in the trailer, likely in pain and scared, needing to get back to the ranch.

'Okay, but I feel a bit shaky,' I said, knowing how pathetic I sounded, hating that I knew I needed help, but glad that he was stepping in and taking charge.

'I've got you,' Jesse replied, one arm circling my back and pulling me up slowly, the other reaching over, his hand grasping mine. 'You good?' My head spun as I tried to nod, the edges of my vision darkening. 'Okay, okay – I'm gonna lift you, sweetheart. No troublemaking now. Just pretend you've been on the fireballs again, all right?'

As I mumbled a protest I felt my feet leave the ground, my head rolling against him. Bailey called out in concern, Jesse cheerfully reassuring her that I was just being dramatic and he was humouring me.

'Asshole,' I mumbled, listening to his responding chuckle, the way it reverberated in his broad chest.

'And she's back,' he whispered as we approached the truck. He lifted me gently onto the back seat as Bailey held the door open.

'Sorry,' I said to her, holding my forehead as I tried to get a grip on my breathing.

'For what?' she frowned, shaking her head. 'It's nothing. We'll be home in no time, okay? Get you and that poor girl of yours right.'

Jesse climbed into the back seat from the other side as Bailey closed my door and jumped into the front, the truck starting with a roar and pulling back onto the highway in a few smooth turns.

Space in the back was suddenly very limited, Jesse's broad shoulders and long legs dominating.

'Come here,' he ordered, gesturing for me to move towards him and gently pulling me over when I frowned, confused. Raising his arm and the seatbelt, he tucked me against his chest so my head rested on his shoulder, taking my weight. 'Right, now ... you owe me a story about why you've got a headless horseman right over your heart.'

As ever, there was a natural ease and smoothness to his tone, the same confidence that'd shone through from the first moment I'd locked eyes with him. But as I lay back against him, wrapped in his smoky scent, I felt the depth behind it. The way his hand rested on my waist, holding me there, as if guiding me to fall into step with the steady beat inside his chest.

'I just liked the story,' I lied, my voice as unsteady as his was sure, forcing myself to focus on his breathing instead of my own; the way it tickled my neck as he leant closer.

'Bullshit,' he whispered in my ear.

I shivered, unable to help myself, thoughts of his lips on my neck intruding over everything else, remembering the way he'd worked his way down to my breasts, right over the ink.

'It's a reminder,' I blurted, my voice dropping to a whisper, eyelids closing as I felt his fingers tracing mine. I realized I wanted him to know the real reason, even if I had no idea how to tell him, or why he'd care. 'To never give in to fear.' I hesitated, the words sticking in my throat. 'The headless horseman isn't the danger, it's the feeling he inspires. The only thing to fear is my reaction to it.'

He stilled, his abs tensing, his grip tightening on my waist.

'Who made you feel like that?' he murmured, an unmistakable edge to his voice, hardening to a point.

I just shook my head, what few words I'd had turning to the dust that rose from the wheels of the truck as we flew down the highway. Signs were now appearing for Jackson.

He didn't press it, saying nothing else. Eventually, his body relaxed again and his hand closed over mine.

'I've got you,' he whispered, and for the second time that day, tears rose behind my eyes. Unable to trust myself to reply, I moved the hand he held instead, weaving my fingers between his.

I knew that if I turned my head even slightly, made any kind of eye contact, there would be no way to stop what would follow. And it wasn't just Bailey right there in the front, but the prospect of knowing that his kiss, our touch, would be entirely different to those that'd already been.

So we remained still, his chin eventually coming to rest on my head, his thumb tracing soft circles on the back of my hand.

By the time we reached the Diamond Back, most of the anxiety had ebbed away. I leant against the fence and watched as Bailey and Jesse worked to get the horses out, now strangely aware of his physical absence.

'Hes?' Lottie ran down the road towards me, her phone in one hand, clutching her hat to her head with the other. 'Jesse messaged me . . . is that –'

She slowed to a walk as Jesse backed my horse – MY horse – out of the trailer, expertly manoeuvring as she swung round, ears flat against her head and teeth bared, about an inch from taking a chunk out of Jesse's arm.

'Fuck, is he . . . does he need some help? I don't know how to –' I straightened up abruptly, wary of getting in the way but unwilling to watch the horse literally tear a strip off him.

'Don't worry, he's got it,' Lottie soothed, frowning both at my distress and the very clear abuse the horse had suffered. 'I can't believe someone could do that,' she hissed as she reached my side.

'I couldn't let them do it,' I said, turning to her, watching her anger dissolve as she took in my expression. 'I didn't mean to buy her . . . I just didn't know what else to do, it seemed like the only way to stop them—'

'Hes, stop,' Lottie cut in, eyes darting between mine. 'Don't fucking apologize for a second, okay? You did the right thing.' I nodded, gritting my teeth as I looked back to Jesse, shielding my eyes from the blazing sun. He was leading her round to the barn, talking to her as they approached the other stalls, some of the ranch's horses calling out. 'What else happened? What's going on?'

I shrugged, shaking my head.

'It's nothing. Can we go down there now?'

Lottie's eyes narrowed, studying me for a moment, but ultimately giving me the grace she knew I needed. Instead, she tucked my arm around hers, pulling us together as we walked towards the barn.

Bailey was now leading her new horse, muscular-looking with a dark, rich chestnut coat that shone in the sunlight.

'He's a looker,' Lottie called out. 'Bet he moves some with those legs – what's his name?'

'Buckeye.' Bailey appraised him as they walked, scratching his neck. 'Y'know – as in the horse chestnuts – think you guys call them conkers? Anyways, he moves like wildfire, similar feel to Dunk. I'm gonna let him have some space in the field just there, I'll see you later.' Then, looking directly at me, she added, 'Chin up, cowgirl. You did a damn good thing today. I'll give my friend Rosie a call tonight if you like, at the sanctuary.'

I nodded, but as we turned into the barn, walking over to the stall where Jesse was gently reassuring the horse, I knew I couldn't do it.

'If there was a way I could stay for longer,' I began, watching as Lottie's eyes widened, 'would it be a pain in the ass for you? I'd have to sort stuff out with Cal and see if he can cover my clients, but . . . I just don't know if I can leave. Not just yet.'

Lottie launched herself at me, her elation forcing a smile despite everything as I hugged her back as tightly as I could, closing my eyes as I was deluged by dark curls.

'Are you fucking kidding me? I've been dreading you leaving . . . ohmygod! Yes! Please stay, as long as you can.'

She rattled through some of the practicalities, talking more to herself than me, allowing me to look away, straight into Jesse's waiting gaze.

The same feelings as in the truck came rushing back, of a kind of safety and peace that I'd rarely known before. There was little trace of the flirtation so readily at the surface, a serious undertone in his eyes, maybe even . . . worry?

'Thank you,' I said to him, suddenly keen to break the intensity as Lottie suddenly caught our stare, her monologue coming to an abrupt halt. 'For everything. I'll transfer over the money – just give me your details.'

'Um . . . I've got to prep some guest stuff,' Lottie said, squeezing my arm before stepping back. 'See you at dinner?'

I nodded, smiling as she turned and walked out of the barn.

'You really do love that girl, huh?' he said, stepping out of the stall and checking the catch was on firmly.

I nodded fervently.

'She's family.'

He came closer, forcing me to look up, and I could almost hear the questions swirling behind his eyes.

'I'm glad you're staying,' he said, scuffing his boot against the floorboards. 'And I don't care about the money, I'd pay it a hundred times over to stop you crying.' My breathing hitched as he reached out, brushing my cheek. 'Although . . . there is one thing you could do in return, if you like.'

He broke into an achingly beautiful smile, the tiniest hint of mischief in his tone switching the situation onto more familiar ground. One I knew, one I could navigate.

I raised my eyebrow.

'If it involves fireballs, I'm going to need three to five business days to prepare,' I replied, glancing into the stall as the horse snorted, steadily working her way through some hay in a net.

His smile became a grin.

'I'm going over to see my mom and sisters later this week, over in Driggs. It's about an hour away, across the border in Idaho. Come with me, I could do with the back-up.'

I almost took a step back, confused.

'You want *me* to meet your family?' I clarified, waiting to see if this was some kind of joke.

'I want you to come help me even up the odds of surviving the visit,' he replied, his voice still light, but the look on my face clearly bothering him. 'My mom's sick, she doesn't get much of a chance to meet new people, but she loves to talk and chew things over. I know she'll lo—' He paused, correcting himself. 'She'll really enjoy talking to you, if you wanted a break from the ranch, all this.'

His vulnerability was laid out in front of me, the weight of his feelings in my hands.

'Sure, course I will,' I replied quickly, an unfamiliar swooping sensation in my chest as his face lit with surprise, then pleasure.

'Well, all right then,' he smiled, putting a hand to the back of his neck and holding it there for a moment along with my gaze before turning towards the other end of the barn. 'I've got to go help Cole with something. Why don't you stay for a while, let her get used to you? The vet's coming first thing in the morning. Bailey's patched up the worst of her cuts until then.'

'But I don't know what to do with her . . . I don't even know her name,' I called as he walked away.

'Ah, yeah. If she had one originally, those assholes didn't know it or wouldn't share it. Sure you can come up with something better, anyway.'

He shared one last smile before disappearing through the open gap, leaving just me and the sounds of the horses, the smell of warm hay.

Before I could turn to look at her, I felt something soft brushing my shoulder. Making sure to move slowly, I glanced up to find her inquisitive eyes on me, her nose searching my coat, huffing a breath as she found no food. Tentatively, I reached out and stroked her nose, only realizing how close the colour was to my own hair when it tumbled forward over my shoulders. Her coat was soft, the skin around her muzzle turning to fine velvet.

'Which is more dangerous?' I murmured to her, watching as her small ears both pricked forward towards me, listening. 'A natural redhead like you, or one that chooses it like me?'

As if offended, she threw back her head from my touch, ears flattening in a way that gave her an utterly ominous expression, and turned a full 180 in her stall, presenting me with her ass instead.

I laughed, not able to help it – holding a hand to my mouth as she startled, looking around at me in a way that suggested she was less than impressed – and in a way that, for all the differences between us, seemed just like something I would do.

CHAPTER 7
JESSE

I knew Hestia likely needed some space, just to process everything that had happened at the sale. So that was my excuse for avoiding her, not wanting to add to her mental burden or make her feel like she owed me in any way. But the truth was . . . I couldn't do it.

Couldn't speak to her without wanting to touch her, kiss her, hold her again. It had been days since the sale, but even now, as I knelt by the side of the part-completed deck of Lottie's cabin, I could still feel the impression of her body against me in the back of Bailey's truck. The smell of her hair, soft and sweet, like the late summer wildflowers that blanketed the meadow beyond the lake ahead. The way she'd gripped my hands, as though I was the only thing tethering her to this earth.

For about the tenth time in half an hour, I looked around the side of the cabin and towards the barn where she was sitting on a low stool, her back against the open barn door. Legs out and ankles crossed, she was sketching intently, barely aware of anything else. Occasionally her hand trailed across her chest, glossy black nails tracing invisible lines around the Sleepy Hollow figure.

I knew it was irrational, but rage began to build yet again at the memory of her pain, the tremor in her voice when she told me the meaning of that particular tattoo. Her silence when I asked who had made her feel that way.

Was that same person the reason why she felt compelled to rescue that horse? That meant she was disbelieving when I asked her to meet my family? That'd caused her to have anxiety attacks and deal with them alone?

The urge to find whoever had hurt her, even so much as *looked* at her the wrong way, and beat the living ever-loving shit out of them was overpowering.

I swore under my breath, almost accidentally firing the nail gun into my damn boot.

'I'm taking a break,' I grunted at Cole, putting it down before I actually did some damage. 'Want a drink? I'm going up to the house.' A sudden idea hit as he nodded, his brow furrowed as he registered my expression. 'Is Lottie up there?' I added, waiting for his nod before turning.

'You okay? Finish up if you want, it's been a long day,' Cole called out, but I shook my head and carried on up the path, taking the shortcut over the grass ridge to reach the main drive, avoiding the temptation of looking down towards the barn. Work was the only thing keeping me sane right now. If I had nothing to do, then . . . I screwed my eyes shut for a moment against the memory of how her hands felt in mine, the look of open affection and trust in her eyes when we'd last spoken.

'Hey! Just the guy,' Lottie said as I reached the kitchen, taking off my hat with a sigh. 'What do you think . . .' She trailed off as I strode over to the fridge, pulling out a can of soda.

I turned to her, concern in her eyes as she stared.

'What is it?' she asked. 'Are you okay? Is Cole . . .?'

I nodded, opening the can and taking a gulp of the cold, sugary sweetness, hoping it'd take the edge off the oppressive feeling.

'We're fine, it's just –' I bit my lip, suddenly wondering if this was a good idea, before my anger reminded me it was. 'I have a question about Hestia. One that I don't want to upset her by asking.'

Lottie's eyes widened for a moment as she perched on the edge of the kitchen table, hands on the edge.

'Okaaay,' she replied, clearly curious but also wary.

The real question lay thick on my tongue, the one about why Hestia felt so alone, why she so clearly pushed people away. With one exception, seemingly. The one staring at me like a startled deer.

'When we came back from the sale,' I began instead, trying to keep my voice level, trying to guard myself from the swell of emotion in the pit of my stomach, 'she told me the story behind her Sleepy Hollow tattoo. Right after we had to pull over when she had some kinda anxiety attack.' Lottie's face crumpled, turning to look at the floor as her hands gripped the table. 'I asked her who had made her feel afraid . . . but she wouldn't answer me. Couldn't, I don't think. But I – I want to know, even though . . .' I paused, hating how the next part of my thought process made me feel. 'Even though maybe I can't do anything about it. I just want to understand, make sure I never do anything that might trigger her in that way again.'

Lottie nodded slowly, meeting my eyes.

'You really like her, don't you?' she asked, voice as gentle as her eyes as she studied me.

I held them, nodded just once as my jaw clenched.

'I'm not sure what she'd want me to share, but I know you, and I know . . . she trusts you.' She sighed, moving her hair from her face, letting it fall over her left shoulder as she frowned. 'It was her stepfather that made her feel like that,' she added, almost wincing as she stared into the space between us. 'You might've heard what an almighty asshole my dad can be from Cole, but Hestia's stepfather . . . he's a whole other level of nasty prick.'

My grip tightened on the can, and I knocked the rest of it back before I could crush it, placing it down on the counter.

'Did he hurt her?' I growled, dreading the answer, unsure how I'd be able to contain myself if . . .

'No, not physically,' she confirmed, watching me carefully. 'It was all emotional, headfucks and manipulation. Probably not a surprise that she ended up with a hot mess like Cal.'

I clenched my fists.

'And has he . . .' I started, relief coursing through me as she quickly shook her head.

'All emotional, again. But it means . . . well, you've seen what it means,' she shrugged. 'She's been alone, in her own head, for a long time. She let me in, thank fuck, but with men . . . I don't know.'

I nodded again, raking back my hair and reaching for my hat, checking the time on my phone and realizing I was going to be late.

'Shit,' I muttered. 'Sorry, I've got to meet someone, lost track of time . . . Listen, don't tell her I asked. I don't want to make her uncomfortable. It's just . . .' I sighed, knowing how it would sound.

'It's okay, I get it,' Lottie ventured with a small smile full of the natural kindness we'd all come to know and love about her – one of the *many* reasons Cole was willing to work to the bone every day on her behalf. 'You don't have to explain.'

I gave her a grateful smile, putting on my hat as I stepped back out and walked over to my truck.

———

Half an hour later, I pulled up outside a small two-storey house on the other side of Jackson, looking out at the surrounding land.

'Jesse, right?' The realtor emerged from inside the house as I mounted the steps to the porch, shaking my hand before gesturing to the land. 'Prime grazing – you thinking of keeping animals?'

I nodded, not wanting to give him any ammo to reinforce his sales pitch.

'Does this back onto Elk Creek?' I asked, suddenly realizing I recognized the far ridge, the tree line that eventually rounded the mountainside over towards the Diamond Back.

'It's part of it, actually,' the realtor confirmed. 'The last person to live here had worked on the main ranch for years. Left it to his daughter, but she's over in California, so no need for it.'

I nodded, taking a last look at the house as I held out my hand again.

'Well, I'm sorry to waste your time, in that case,' I replied. 'I don't do business with Elk Creek.' He hesitated before taking it again, mouth half open. 'I'd love to say it wasn't personal, but it is. I'd rather set fire to my money than hand it over to a Sinclair.'

I tipped my hat, taking no small pleasure in his stunned disbelief as I started up the truck and rolled straight back out.

It cushioned the deflated feeling, the one that'd wondered if this was finally the opportunity to start out for myself, finally use all the carefully amassed savings from my bull riding winnings and buy my own place. The hazy, half-assed vision of bringing Mom over to show her, seeing the pride in her face and relief at knowing I was settled, no matter how things turned out with her health . . . It faded away with the daylight that was gradually retreating behind the peaks beyond.

But fuck it – nothing was worth buying from the asshole who'd tried his level best to fuck Lil over, and her mom, Carrie, before her.

I shrugged it off, gunning it back down the highway, somehow not quite ready to go to the ranch. The fact was that property around Jackson was expensive, the holiday rentals and second homeowners long having pushed up prices. There were still

Jackson residents willing to only sell to other full-time residents – like the house I'd just visited – but the places were few and far between.

As I approached the Diamond Back turning, I didn't slow. Instead, with a vague plan to head down and drop in on Jace, my ex-rodeo buddy, I carried on. I pictured telling him the problem, knowing exactly how he'd respond: *So quit fucking belly-aching and get back on a bull. Win your way to a bigger choice of places round here.*

I slowed the truck, pulling off into the opening of a long drive on the right, turning the thought over and over. Could I do it again? Mom was stable now, a system in place, albeit with expensive medication to keep her going. Finally glancing up, I realized the drive was the one that led down to Harebell, the hunting and fishing lodge built by Lottie's grandfather, still owned by the Diamond Back.

Seconds later, like a starting gun going off in my head, I got out my phone and made the first of two calls, smiling as the first picked up, the sound of a voice I hadn't heard in over a year.

Chapter 8
Hestia

I was still mulling my horse's name over when Jesse pulled his truck up outside the ranch house. We hadn't seen much of each other since the sale, but I couldn't tell whether it was intentional or not, at least on his part. Other than a couple of brief conversations, checking on both me and the horse, he'd spent every spare minute on Lottie's cabin with Cole, or out with ranch guests.

I began to feel his absence physically, like the low, dull throb of an impending headache. I realized then it was an effort not to notice or wonder why he hadn't sought me out, to watch out for him wherever I went around the ranch.

So, by myself, I'd made a promise to myself. In the quiet of the barn where I'd now all but taken up residence next to the horses' stalls, I'd set aside all the shit of my past and forge ahead alone – without fucking it up. Again. This trip was a chance to actually make the most of the break from home that I'd come for.

'Hey, stranger,' I said, jumping into the passenger seat, watching as he appraised my outfit. A quiet smile raised one side of his mouth and he tilted his head, blowing out a breath.

'There are no half-measures with you, huh?' he chuckled, moving off as I buckled up and put on my sunglasses, the only non-Western coded item on my body.

I'd gone all out. Indigo flared jeans – borrowed from Lottie – a fitted, scoop-neck cream tank top with a faded charcoal grey horseshoe pattern; black cowboy boots; and a stack of silver and turquoise bracelets with matching silver hoop earrings. I'd even got up early – for me – and blow-dried my hair, soft waves now falling across my chest.

I smiled, ignoring the unexpected feeling of nerves in the pit of my stomach.

'Too much?' I replied, tucking my red bra strap under the top, noting how his eyes followed my fingers, the way his tightened on the wheel.

'Always, Jessica,' he murmured, glancing over again, smile broadening. 'But that's why . . .' He trailed off, looking back out of the windscreen as we approached the end of the drive. Then, his voice low, 'Don't ever change, y'hear?'

I frowned as we pulled onto the highway, contemplating his change in direction, the tone of his voice. Fishing in the side pocket of his door, he pulled out his own sunglasses and put them on. The Old Hollywood vibe complete, I gave in to gawping at his sharp jaw and deepening tan against the worn cowboy hat . . . the way his shirtsleeves dug into his biceps.

'Think I've got a name for her – my horse,' I blurted, staring straight ahead and mentally eye-rolling at myself, the desperation I felt to move to safer ground – anywhere to avoid the big, complicated feelings that threatened when he was around. Jesse would make an awesome friend – the best, even – so it was time to grow the fuck up and chill the fuck out. 'And, given I owe you for . . . everything that day at the sale, you get the deciding vote.'

I chanced a look back at him, relieved to see his face relaxing a little but remaining focused on the road.

'All right,' he replied after a pause. 'But honey, you don't owe me. Not a thing.'

I swallowed, determined to keep it light, pushing aside the fact that technically, he was right. I'd paid back the five hundred dollars after getting Jesse's bank details from Lottie, via the ranch payroll. Neither of us had spoken about it, but then I doubted he'd had any spare time to check his account since. 'So, I thought that given I was named after a Greek goddess, maybe that could be a theme.'

He huffed a laugh under his breath, shaking his head slightly again.

'Well, hell. Should've known,' he began, but before I could ask what he meant, he added, 'So what kind of goddess are you then, Hestia?'

The sound of my name in his mouth was almost too much.

'She, um . . . represents the hearth and home,' I murmured, more disconcerted than ever as his jaw flickered. 'The sacred flame.'

There was a silence for a moment, filled only by the low rumble of the radio.

'The goddess of . . . home,' he repeated, more to himself than me, the knuckles of his hand on the wheel turning white for a moment.

My gut lurched. No doubting it now. Something big had shifted since the sale, leaving us in new, shaky territory that neither of us seemed to know how to navigate. I took a breath.

'Right. So, I've been going over the options . . . and given how my horse is, well, a bit of a handful, and in what I've seen so far, has more than a hint of the underworld about her . . .' His cheek twitched at that, and he gave a small nod of agreement. 'So, what about Persephone? I mean, it's a bit of a mouthful, but maybe Sephy for short?'

'Hmm,' he considered, slowing as we came to a stoplight. 'I see where you're going, and I like the underworld bit, that definitely works . . . but maybe it's too regal or something, I dunno. She's more sassy than that, y'know?'

I nodded, totally getting his train of thought. There was nothing ethereal about her. She was way too blunt and direct, if a horse could be that.

'Shame she's not a he,' I said, thinking aloud, turning over the underworld vibe. 'Something like Damien would work.'

Jesse chuckled, and I glanced over as he did the same.

'Yeah, now you've got it,' he said, his smile growing as mine did, my brain turning it over, still thinking, when –

'I've got it,' I cried suddenly, inspiration striking as the lights turned green. 'Luci! Short for Lucifer!'

This time his laugh was full, the strange atmosphere between us suddenly dispelled by the sound. I joined in, the relief palpable.

'Genius,' he said, banging his free hand against the wheel. 'Bailey's gonna be pissed – she's been chucking ideas around all week, but Luci . . . yeah, that's the one.'

'Okay, done,' I breathed, shifting to pull my knee up under my chin, finally starting to relax. 'I was starting to feel bad for not having chosen one, like some kind of fucked-up mum guilt.'

He laughed again.

'You're taking this whole thing pretty serious, huh? Lottie said you've been at the barn all week. Is your . . . is the business back home okay without you, then, for a while longer?'

I nodded, thinking back to my last call with Cal, strained and barely civilized. I'd had to swallow my anger at his reticence to step up and shoulder responsibility for the business as a whole for once. I knew he wouldn't want to disappoint our clients, though, many of them having become friends, so that's what my hope was clinging onto.

'For a while, I think. My ex – he's also my business partner. He's taking care of it. It's just, I've had a ton of responsibility over the past few years, you know? But not directly for one living thing.' He nodded, his expression turning serious again. 'I mean, not including Lottie at university. She had a bit of a wild ride in the first couple of years with me, away from the prying eyes of her asshole dad.'

Jesse grunted in agreement, and I guessed he knew all about it from Cole.

'Wild ride, huh?' he asked quietly, risking a quick glance, eyebrows raised.

I shrugged, avoiding the innuendo.

'For her. She just did things my way for a while until she found her own style. You know, just giving less of a fuck, making her own choices ... ditching lectures, smoking, drinking, wild sex ... standard shit.' He bit his lip, rubbing the back of his neck in the same gesture as the other day, as though he was dying to say more but stopping himself. 'It's why her dad hates me,' I added cheerfully. 'But he's in good company. My stepdad is level pegging for prick of the century.'

'Yeah,' he agreed after a moment. 'I know the feeling.'

I paused, sensing that he was opening a door to me, just enough to let me glimpse the room beyond.

'So, is it just your mum and sisters we're seeing today?' I asked gently.

'Yep,' he replied, seemingly gathering himself together. 'There's Mom – Jean – and my big sisters, Clara and Belle. It's just been us since ... well, ever since I can remember, anyway.'

His meaning was clear, the silence between the words thick with it. He hadn't even had a chance to find out if his dad was an asshole; his absence made it the default.

'Anything I need to worry about?' I asked, shrugging at his half-smile response. 'What? You're their baby brother.'

'You? Nah,' he shook his head. 'I've got a feeling it'll be me in the firing line.'

Less than an hour into the visit, I realized he was right.

His mom lived on the top floor of a low-rise condo block on the edge of town, a big, airy apartment with a view of the Tetons in the distance, beyond the town. After the initial greetings, we got settled on the generous balcony at the back, and I was struck by the similarities in the four of them. The same dark, sandy-coloured hair, a shared sense of relaxed confidence – even the same smiles. Jean was tiny in comparison to Jesse's 6′ 2″, tucking into his side as he pulled her into a hug, her neck craning right back as she beamed at him.

'Well now,' she finally exclaimed, reaching out to pat my arm from her chair. 'My boy wasn't wrong. You make quite the cowgirl – and yep, I think I agree with him – you're just about the prettiest girl I've ever seen too, notwithstanding my own girls, of course.'

'I am?' I asked, glancing over at him, positioned furthest away in the corner, two seats left empty for his sisters, both prepping lunch in the kitchen. He sat with his ankle resting on his knee, leaning on the arm of his chair, a careful smile almost hidden in the shade under his hat.

Jean laughed.

'Oh, he's being all coy now,' she replied.

'Not like you at all,' Clara interjected, stepping outside and shielding her eyes from the sun. She was the taller of the sisters, and the initial vibe I'd got from her – maybe a little more reserved than Belle? – was now counteracted by the devilish smile she flashed in my direction. 'In fact, I can't remember the last time Jesse ever brought a girl to meet us. Can you, Bells?'

Before I could interject, as Belle followed her sister, she turned to me and gave a small, knowing wink.

'Nope,' she agreed. 'Although we did spot the last buckle bunny from a distance . . .'

I clamped my mouth shut, struggling not to join in as the three women dissolved into giggles. Jesse rolled his eyes.

'All right, all right, I knew that was coming,' he drawled,

leaning back against his chair and taking off his hat, running a hand through his hair. His smile was soft, as though watching their amusement at his expense was all worth it.

'We're only messin',' Jean said to me. 'We know y'all are just friends. Besides, I need to hear more about what you do. Jesse said you're a tattoo artist and did some of your own, that right? I've got a few, but none as good as yours.'

They listened as I explained my business, how it all started. They were curious and without judgement, genuinely interested in the process and leaning in for a closer look when I showed them my first ink, the compass on my wrist.

Jesse just watched in silence, taking it all in, but his eyes were fixed on me. Even when I looked back at him for a moment, he didn't flinch away. There was an intensity to it that made my heart lurch, as though he was committing the scene to memory.

Before I could look away, Clara caught us, taking a pause as I hurriedly shifted back to Jean, listening to her own tattoo stories.

'Jesse got his first tattoo right after his first bull ride,' Clara said quietly as we got up, Jean declaring it was time for us all to have some lunch inside. 'You seen that one yet, Hestia?'

'Oh – yeah, the one on his back . . .' I began, coming to an awkward stop as I realized what she'd made me reveal, given there was no way I could've seen it without him being topless.

Jesse laughed as he got up, rolling his eyes at both sisters and their barely suppressed smiles.

'Sorry, honey, I couldn't resist it,' Clara apologized, touching my shoulder, a sheepish edge to her grin.

I tried to smile back, but mortification was slowly curdling my insides. Everything about today was off, the usual defences and deflections just out of my reach.

'All right, enough – get inside before I start airing out all of *your* stories,' Jesse threatened, towering over us and coming to a stop directly behind me. 'And Clara, you best be afraid. Don't think I don't remember your dating chaos.'

As she protested, Belle and Jean chiming in with stories, I tried to follow, stopping abruptly as his arm wound around my waist.

'Don't you feel embarrassed about anything we've done,' he whispered in my ear, not missing the way my eyes closed for a moment, opening straight into his as I turned my head back slightly. 'They love calling me out for my past, that's all. I wouldn't undo you seeing my tattoos for all the money in this world.'

His gaze became fierce, burning my insides. In no more than a couple of moments he released me, gently moving me inside as the women turned back to us. My heart was pounding as I sat at the table, accepting Belle's offer to add things to my plate.

'I think the better story is Jesse's first bull ride itself,' Jean began.

'Jesus . . . Mom,' Jesse chuckled, piling up his plate, stealing the bread right from under Clara's nose with a smirk. 'You three are determined to get it all out today.'

'Seems like you beat us to it, brother,' Clara countered, and even I couldn't help myself – joining them as they all cackled.

'Like I said – firing line,' Jesse said to me with a pointed expression, tearing off a chunk of bread and aiming it at Clara's head.

'I'm sorry, Hestia,' she said between laughs, deflecting his missile. 'I'll stop.'

I shook my head as Jesse protested at me receiving the apology. 'You're fine. I was wondering how Jesse was ever kept in check as a kid, but I get it now.'

'Yeah, some might even say it drove me to bull riding,' he grumbled, not quite able to hide his own smile. 'Less of a pain in my ass being trampled by a three-thousand-pound death trap than listening to these two.'

'Sounds like a chicken and egg situation,' I mused, catching Clara's eye, open curiosity in her stare. 'Does the crazy come before or after you get trampled by the three-thousand-pound death trap?'

'I like her,' Jean announced to Jesse as both sisters laughed, Clara nodding at me in approval.

'I used to,' Jesse agreed, matching my grin as I attempted to focus on eating some of the bread Clara had passed to me, failing miserably as I took him in instead.

'So what happened on the first bull ride, then?' I asked eventually, suddenly aware that all three women had seen our shared look and were now glancing at each other.

'I swear,' Belle began, clearly relishing being able to retell it again. 'If only I'd recorded it . . . funniest damn thing I've ever seen. The ride itself was good, whatever,' she said, waving it away as Jesse held up his hands at her dismissal of his triumph. 'He made it past the bell, but when he jumped off, it was like he forgot there was still a bull in there with him – and that bastard was nasty. Jesse just stood there, waving at the crowd, listening to the bunnies whistling and hollerin' his name,' she giggled as Jesse scoffed. 'But when the bull turned and came right back for him, head down, one of the wranglers had to haul him up and over her horse – his ass in the air, legs jiggling as she rode him out of the ring.'

She dissolved into giggles as the rest of us joined in.

Jesse shrugged.

'Won the tournament, though.'

Another couple of hours later, the chat settling down and heat removed from Jesse, I was gently grilled by Jean about all aspects of my life.

I didn't mind – she was easy to talk to. I'd liked her instantly, but seeing her inside their dynamic, it hit differently. The way Jesse doted on her, the small gestures of affection between them, hinted at the kind of parental relationship I'd only dreamed of.

'He's been my rock, this whole time,' Jean admitted when she mentioned her illness, early-onset Parkinson's. 'You all have,' she said to the three of them. 'It's a pain in the ass having to slow down and rely on people, you know? But today has been great. I'm sure glad he met you, honey. Good friends are important.' She looked me over, noting my hesitation, the inference in her words. 'How long you staying? Come see me again, won't you, before you head home?'

From her, said in that way, the consequence of even my extended trip coming to an end suddenly hit me. Of possibly not seeing her ever again after that . . . of not seeing Jesse.

'Definitely,' I said, matching the tightness of the hug she now gave me as the three siblings stood by. 'But only if we can take it up a notch next time and get the *really* embarrassing childhood photos out.'

We left amid their laughter, walking back out into the blinding sun of the car park.

'Thank you,' he said, as we reached his truck and climbed in, waiting as the engine sprang into life, the A/C working overtime to cool the stifling air.

'What for?' I asked, genuinely puzzled.

He opened his mouth for a moment, then paused, as if rethinking.

'What?' I asked, unable to hold back from asking. 'Tell me. We've . . . we're dancing around each other,' I admitted, barely able to hold on as he looked at me straight. He knew it too. 'Why are you thanking me? I loved meeting them.'

He sighed, eventually looking down. Then, as if he couldn't help it either, he reached out for my left hand, holding it in his own.

'For doing something for me. That you didn't have to do, that could've been really difficult. I guess I'm not used to that . . . the boot's usually on the other foot, y'know?' He looked up as his fingers brushed mine, goosebumps forming as I read his expression.

It was that fierce intensity again, his eyes molten. 'Not that I mind. I'll be there for my mom, sisters, Lil, Cole . . . anyone that needs me,' he added softly. 'But it's a fucking weird feeling when someone else does it just for you.'

His words were a gut punch. There was sadness right behind them, a loneliness that spoke so directly to me, at my core. To my absolute horror, I felt emotion gathering, rising up and threatening to form tears.

'I get it,' I murmured, bottling out of his gaze and staring at our hands instead. 'I've felt the same way.'

'No more dancing, Jessica,' he whispered, waiting for me to look up again, knowing he noticed the difference in my eyes. 'It's fucking rough being alone sometimes. You don't have to hide it, not from me.'

There were seconds before my first tear fell, my fingers tightening around his. Desperately, grasping at anything, I voiced the first thought that came to mind.

'I'm sorry I revealed too much to them, about your tattoo—'

'Honey, know that I say this with love for my sister, but so fucking help me I will kick her ass back over the state line when I see her next for pulling that stunt,' he growled, rolling his eyes. 'Listen to me,' he urged, leaning forward, his other hand reaching out to softly pull one of my waves through his fingers. 'The only issue I have with them knowing we've been more than friends is that they might think it's *only* that. Because that's all it's ever been before, and . . .'

He stopped himself again, searching my face as deeply as the words he sought.

'No dancing, cowboy,' I whispered, watching as his eyes drifted to my lips.

'. . . And you . . . you're more than that. I don't know what yet, but both of those times we had together . . . it wasn't just a quick fuck.'

I stopped breathing, my body registering the panic in one part of my mind while the other part desperately wanted to lean forward, to meet his mouth with mine. I knew he felt the same, his hand now reaching up to brush my jaw –

A sudden noise jolted us out of it, my phone vibrating against the dash, threatening to fall off as it moved across the plastic.

I grabbed it, using the distraction to pull on my seatbelt as Jesse shifted back into his seat and settled at the wheel, moving us out of the car park.

My thoughts still racing, hands trembling slightly, I opened the screen to an email notification from . . . 'The Old Jackson Courthouse, Wyoming's Premier Wedding Venue'.

The uneasy feeling from last week, the result of the fireballs . . . everything came crashing back in like a direct hit to my temple. I read the message confirming my deposit and inviting me and my fiancé to come and view the venue, make all of the arrangements.

'You okay?' Jesse asked in the same quiet voice as before, frowning slightly at my expression.

I nodded quickly as I set down the phone and put my shades on – I was on the verge of telling him, but I lacked the guts. Did he even remember? Would it even bother him as it clearly did me? I was such a fucking idiot.

And as Lainey Wilson played, prompting him to throw the hint of a smile my way, I gathered up every last thread of feeling and shoved it all back down, aware of just how close I'd come to completely unravelling in front of him – to him.

Chapter 9
Hestia

I spent the next few days doing anything I could to not spiral.

The sensation, deep down, was ever present, as though that moment with Jesse in the truck had opened something that now refused to close. The contents were beginning to leak bit by bit, and it was only constant activity, wearing myself out to exhaustion every day, that allowed any kind of relief from it.

I'd thrown myself into learning how to care for Luci, asking Lottie with as much nonchalance as I could muster whether I could help around the ranch. She'd heard my desperation; I knew she had. But she also knew to leave me to it, for now. There was a big cookout coming up this weekend for the ranch guests: a full house of ten, plus all of the newer staff who'd come on board since Lottie had taken over.

'Hestia, get in here – I want you to meet someone,' she called as I emerged from my room – her room, technically. Since I'd arrived, she and Cole had bunked up, an arrangement that seemed to have pressed fast-forward on what was already a breakneck romance.

As I stuck my head around the door she smiled and waved me in. She was sitting in an armchair by the far window, laptop resting on her knees. The room had the unmistakable feel of a bachelor pad with 'Lottifications' everywhere. I suppressed a chuckle, remembering how she'd done the same to our shared flat at uni – carefully placed soft furnishings and dried and silk flowers intertwining with my stuffed rats in various jaunty poses, the results of my brief taxidermy hobby.

'I'm catching up with Lil,' she said, grinning and moving over in the chair so I could squeeze in next to her. I did so, looking up to see her blonde twin on the screen. 'Lil, this is Hes!'

I looked back at Lottie, then at her cousin again, leaning forward slightly. I'd seen a few photos, noticed the family resemblance, but never seen them together.

'Am I high or something?' I asked to their shared bemusement. 'Sorry – hey Lil, fucking awesome ranch by the way – but seriously, you guys look . . . Are you definitely not sisters?'

They both laughed, Lil raising her eyebrows. She was in an unmistakably English room with high ceilings and a vast period fireplace in the corner of the screen. There were even Union Jack cushions on the sofa next to her.

'Well, I wouldn't put it past either of our daddies, now, would you, Lottie?' Lil asked, still laughing.

'It'd have to be yours, then,' Lottie replied, trying to straighten her face. 'Your mum's got better taste.'

I joined in at that; the thought of Lottie's charmless dad worming his way into the life of two hot women was beyond reasonable odds.

'So, I hear you've already bought a horse and made friends with one of my cowboys, huh?' Lil asked, reaching for a mug beside her, tendrils of steam rising from it. 'You another fake city girl like Lottie here? That's good going.'

I side-eyed Lottie and received an innocent shrug in return.

'That's about the gist of it,' I replied, smiling at Lil's amusement.

'But I'm a real city girl, haven't got a fucking clue about any of it. Never ridden a horse, not planning to.'

She chuckled.

'Aww, come on, Lottie – get her out on Penny, she's about as bombproof as they come. Hestia, girl, you can't know what ranching is really like unless y'all get up on four legs.'

Lottie nudged me, eyebrows raised in question as I rolled my eyes.

'I'll think about it,' I shrugged, not admitting that I already felt oddly envious of Lottie's easy grace on horseback, the effortless connection between her and Jasper. But the prospect of making a total ass of myself, or bizarrely, having the horse reject me somehow – possibly violently – had been enough to stop me asking for a lesson. 'What about you, then? How're you liking my hometown?'

Lil grinned again, taking a sip of her drink.

'I feel like a goddamn traitor for saying it, but I fucking love London – there's so much to do, and the history of this place is crazy. Folks are *totally* different here, but I've met some awesome guys. Actually –' she paused, almost flustered by her own excitement – 'I've had an idea for the ranch, Lottie. Some of these guys I met – over in East London, that's your neighbourhood, right, Hestia?'

I had to think for a moment before nodding; Lottie's brow creased as she noticed.

'Well, they were talking about coming over to the US or Canada, wanting to stay for the summer and experience ranch life. I showed them our socials and they wanted to know if we offered a volunteer programme. As in, they work and help us run things for paying guests – all the jobs that keep Cole and Jesse out twelve hours a day – and we give them a place to stay in return.'

'I love it,' Lottie breathed, biting her lip as she turned the idea over in her head. 'We'd need more accommodation, though . . .

maybe a bunkhouse, but nicer? We're almost there with the cabin ... the builders could move on to a new project in a couple of weeks. Want me to run the numbers?'

Lil nodded eagerly, a slow smile spreading across her face.

'Cabin's almost done, huh? Bet Cole's mighty pleased with that?'

Lottie ducked her head for a moment, wearing the same intense smile she always did around all things Cole.

'Yeah, I mean, it's been backbreaking work, but it looks great.'

'Well, I'm sure you'll make it worth his while, honey,' Lil chuckled and I joined in, sharing a knowing glance with her. 'Any other news on that front?'

I glanced at Lottie, not entirely sure what Lil was getting at, surprise deepening as Lottie began to blush.

'What . . .' I began, looking between them.

'Oh, nothing,' Lottie said, dismissing her cousin with a mock glare. 'Lil keeps teasing me about Cole proposing.' At my shock, she shook her head. 'He hasn't – there's just a lot of wedding stuff going on at the moment, with his brother's wedding coming up at the end of August. It's just, I keep telling Lil that where I'm from, people tend to wait a few years before getting married, if at all.'

'And I keep saying that when you know you've met your person, waiting some arbitrary amount of time ain't gonna make no difference.' Lil shrugged. 'We get married younger, quicker than city folk, maybe. Well, some of us.'

Lottie launched into trying to find out about Lil's love life, but I barely heard it. Somehow, for some reason, I'd just never pictured either of us getting married. Lottie was too driven by her career, and me . . . well, people like me just didn't get married.

But now, here on the ranch, Lottie was a different version of herself. A happier, healthier version, living by her rules, not her dad's – or Kyle's. And Cole . . . genuine, wholly trustworthy and hot-as-hell though he was, for some reason, I just hadn't factored in marriage there.

Some hours later, headphones in and volume way up as I groomed Luci, I kept replaying the conversation. Moving around her in the way Bailey had shown me, I used the stiff-bristle brush to clear the dirt and hairs from her coat, slowing for the more sensitive areas around her shoulder and back and carefully avoiding her healing wounds.

Just as the track I was listening to became extra heavy, the drums and guitar dropping to a ribcage-shaking depth, someone tapped me on the shoulder.

'Fuck,' I said, jumping in tandem with Luci, who promptly bared her teeth for a moment towards Bailey, standing at the stall door, grinning. Next to her was . . . 'Dee! Hey!'

I pulled my headphones around my neck and came out of the stall.

'Thought I'd bring Dee up to see why you've been too busy to come into town,' Bailey began, as Dee gave me a brief hug. 'We've been friends since high school, don't get to see each other too much these days, so two birds with one stone and all that.'

'Ah, okay – yeah, it's been a bit intense,' I admitted, dusting the dirt and hairs off my hands as Jesse entered the back of the barn, leading Domino back in. He tipped his hat to us, his face shaded by the brim.

'Don't apologize,' Dee replied, her eyes following him for a moment before turning back to me, raising her eyebrows suggestively. 'I always forget how good the, um, views are up here.' I bit my lip as she fought back a giggle, Bailey shaking her head. 'Besides, I have a gift for you!'

She grinned at me, the liberal highlighter across her freckled cheekbones shimmering in the shafts of sunlight. I realized how similar our look was – one part country, regulation cowboy boots and black denim, one part alt girl. The beginnings of a sleeve tattoo up her right arm caught my eye as she pulled out a small tissue-paper-wrapped parcel from her bag and handed it to me.

'But what –' I began, stopping when she rolled her eyes.

'Just open it,' she replied, eyes lifting as I heard Luci shuffle to the door behind us, the velvety touch of her muzzle on my arm as she tried to smell the parcel.

'Well, look at that,' Bailey mused, shaking her head at Luci as I ripped the tissue open to reveal a T-shirt, a faded charcoal grey. 'Gentle as a goddamn lamb with you now. She likes you, Hes.'

'She likes the hand that feeds her,' I murmured, but reached back to give Luci a gentle scratch on the neck as I unfurled the T-shirt. On the other side, printed in shades of white, pink and green, was the skull design I'd created by the lake a couple of weeks ago. 'Oh my God, I love it,' I breathed, barely noticing as Jesse's shadow fell across us.

'New line?' he asked, glancing at me as Dee answered, his eyes quickly assessing my face. We'd fallen back into what seemed to be our pattern since the visit to his mum's place – withdrawing from each other after moments of intensity, both retreating into our own shadows.

'Actually, Hestia,' Dee continued, turning to me, 'I also wanted to ask you something, now Bailey tells me you're staying awhile.' She gestured towards her sleeve tattoo. 'I've been getting this done by a few different artists, people I really admire, each of them adding a different element.' Her glance up at me was a little sheepish. 'And I kinda looked your work up after we met, found your studio in London . . . I love your stuff, kinda obsessed with the indigo blossom designs.'

'You want me to add to the sleeve?' I guessed as she nodded, biting her lip. I felt Bailey and Jesse's eyes on me as I reached out for her arm to take a closer look. The existing work was incredible, definitely a mix of styles and techniques, but all together, it worked. I felt the sudden urge to do it, a creative itch in my fingers that I realized hadn't been there for a while. 'I'd be honoured,' I said, smiling as she gave a small squeal of excitement. 'Did you have something in—'

'Yes! You really will? I mean, name your price, of course . . . Oh man, this is so cool . . . yeah – your skull, the one on the T-shirt, maybe combined with the blossom?' Jesse shifted to my right, as though preparing to leave. I caught his soft smile as he turned. 'We've got an open day at the Jackson Collective, it's a whole bunch of artists and creatives here, in a couple of weeks – maybe we could do it then? We've got some spare kit, if you didn't bring your own.'

We made arrangements while Jesse and Bailey prepped some of the horses. My mind was already buzzing with ideas, ways of integrating my design with her sleeve. As I voiced a couple and was met with wild enthusiasm, I felt a strange sense of cohesion; a tangible snap as this element of my home life slotted right in next to the ranch and to Luci, who was now resting her head against my back.

'You're gonna be one busy woman,' Bailey winked, returning from the tack room with a saddle over her arm. 'I'm gonna ride out on Buckeye with Dee – do you wanna come? We can take it slow? Penny could do with some exercise. She's getting mighty lazy since Lil's been gone. She's as gentle as they come, though, perfect for a greenhorn like you.'

I considered it for a moment, Dee clocking my hesitation.

'It's not as hard as it looks,' she offered. 'I know it's easy for us to say when we've done it our whole lives, but you just need to hold on really. Penny's a sweetheart like Bailey said, she'll take care of you.'

I turned back to Luci, who was now beginning to nudge me. Smiling, I took a small apple from my pocket and offered it up to her, realizing how much of my initial wariness around horses, around her, had begun to evaporate. If a creature like Luci, previously beaten and broken by people, could learn to trust again, couldn't I try it?

But as Bailey led Buckeye out of the stall and past us, prancing sideways a little as he checked out Luci and received shit-eye with a side of flattened ears in return, I chickened out.

'Another time,' I said, not missing the calculating stare from Jesse, now across the stalls with Penny. 'If I fall off and fuck up my hand,' I gestured to her sleeve, 'I promise you don't want to try my first left-handed tattoo.'

Dee grimaced.

'Yeah, okay – deal. But maybe afterwards? Surely one of these guys might give you a lesson or two, start off in the corral, get the hang of it before riding out?'

I shrugged.

'Sure, maybe.'

I waved them off from the entrance of the barn, laughing as Domino and Buckeye seemed determined to race each other despite Dee and Bailey's efforts. Eventually, beyond the main gate, as the vast meadow field opened up, the women let them fly. In seconds, they were no more than blurs of colour shrouded in a fine dust.

'It's freedom,' Jesse said, making me jump as I wandered back to Luci's stall. He came out of the stall, hanging up Penny's head collar on a hook. She was fully tacked up for riding.

'What is?' I asked, forcing myself to keep my distance.

He gestured out towards the meadow.

'That's why we love to ride,' he clarified. 'The feeling of freedom. Just you and your horse, nothing else to complicate shit.' I didn't try to speak into the pause between us, just took him in, steadying myself as my heart threatened to ratchet up a notch. 'You can be alone but not lonely, if that makes sense.'

He knew it did, after our last conversation in the truck. I had a sense this was his way of reaching out, of making a bridge back between us.

I nodded, not wanting to shut him down.

'It looks easy, but I'm sure that's just years of practice,' I started, stopping as he shook his head, turning back to Penny's stall and opening the door.

'You don't need years,' he added, disappearing for a moment and then leading her out, approaching me slowly and ignoring the downright satanic expression Luci pulled to my right. 'How's about one more favour?'

I raised my eyebrows, unsure where this was going.

'I know Lottie's asked you to help with the cookout this weekend, and thing is, the easiest way to get down to the spot we use is to ride. I'm taking some guests out in half an hour, but we could do just five, ten minutes now, in the corral. I'll show you how to get on, hold on, just walk around a little. What do you think? I swear I won't let anything happen to your hands.' He smirked a little, sneaking the quickest glance over the rest of me. 'Or anything else. Penny is our very best beginner's horse, not a mean bone in her body.'

My gut reaction was to refuse. It wasn't just the thought of sitting on top of a massive animal with a tiny brain, sweet and unassuming though Penny looked. It was knowing that Jesse would touch me again, that the fires he would light across my skin would threaten to merge into one and burn me from the inside out.

But . . . as I looked between his open expression, the clarity in his stormy eyes, and Penny's calm, stoic vibe . . . I couldn't refuse him.

'Five minutes,' I murmured, unable to help matching his smile.

I followed him out into the corral, half blinded by the sunlight after the peaceful gloom of the barn. My heart was pounding as we walked across the soft dirt.

'All right,' he said, giving Penny a pat on the neck as I stood next to her, suddenly conscious of the enormous gap between the ground and the stirrup Jesse had just pulled down. 'If you put your left boot in the stirrup and your left hand on the pommel –' He waited for me to do so, stretching as high as I could reach while she stayed mercifully still. 'Then on three, you push up, and I'll lift you the rest of the way.'

Swallowing, I nodded, waiting for his countdown – and on three, as I pushed off the ground, his strong hands gripped either side of my waist, lifting me as easily as . . .

Flashes of our hook-ups thundered into my mind, but almost before I realized it, I'd swung my leg over Penny's back and was sitting astride her. The imprint of his hands remained as he stood back, grinning. Penny all but dozed next to his arm, utterly unperturbed.

'Holy shit,' I murmured, registering just how far away the ground was.

He chuckled.

'Right foot into the other stirrup,' he said, adjusting the reins and hooking them over the pommel. I nudged the toe of my boot in and tried to adjust myself in the saddle, surprised at how comfortable it actually was, the way the raised back and tall pommel held me in place. 'Now, sit back a little, keep your back straight – that's it, that's perfect,' he instructed, clicking his tongue and holding the reins at Penny's head to ask her to walk forward. The motion was strange, a gentle rolling from side to side, but as I sat back, trying to move with it as I'd seen Lottie do before, it wasn't as terrifying as I'd imagined.

'This is . . . okay,' I said, smiling as he beamed at me, walking backwards to check my position as Penny walked slowly on. 'Do I need to hold the reins?'

'Sure,' he replied, before explaining how they worked, his

fingers brushing against mine as he lifted the soft leather into my right hand. 'Try a stop with her, just a gentle pull towards you.'

He let go of her head, her small ears pricking towards him. I did as he'd instructed, pulling back for a moment and staring at him in astonishment as she came to an easy stop.

'I did it!' I said stupidly, before leaning down as much as I dared to pat her neck.

'You look good up there,' he said, taking me in as he adjusted his hat. 'Natural cowgirl.'

As I opened my mouth to protest, he moved closer, gently taking my boot in his hand and sliding it out from the stirrup, keeping his hand on my leg.

'Were you nervous?' he asked, looking straight up into my face.

For a second we were back in his truck, hands clasped, moments from a kiss that felt as though it might change it all.

In a whisper, he added, 'No dancing, Jessica.'

Everything around us blurred into nothing; even the fact that I was sitting astride a horse faded away.

'Not of riding,' I murmured, my pulse beginning to pound as his eyes flared.

'Unhook your other boot,' he ordered, a new, raw quality entering his voice. 'Then swing your right leg over the front and slide down. I'll catch you.'

I hesitated, feeling the ground being pulled from beneath me, slowly. But I did it anyway, his hands clasping my waist in the same place as I dismounted. This time, they didn't let go.

'Why do I make you nervous?' he asked, waiting for me to look up, not knowing what to do with my hands, our bodies just inches apart. I met his eyes again, every feeling and emotion rushing in together and meeting with a crash.

'I don't trust myself around you,' I whispered. 'Every time you touch me . . .'

He clenched his jaw, leaning down.

'I don't know how much longer I can go without having *you* touch *me*, Jessica,' he said, running one finger up from my chest, slowing at the nape of my neck. 'No matter how much I imagine it, or how many times I fuck my own hand in the shower. I want it to be you. *I want you.*'

I held my breath, vaguely aware that Penny had wandered off in the corral, of the sounds of distant voices, that we weren't alone.

Reaching between us, I ran my fingers over his belt buckle, increasing the pressure as I moved down. His grip on my waist hardened, his finger trailing up to my jaw, hooking it under my chin to bring me closer.

'You coming out on the ride today, Hestia?'

Cole's voice was distant enough that Jesse and I didn't spring apart, still held in each other's stare.

'Not today,' I called back, keeping my focus on Jesse, knowing he'd read between the lines. 'Soon, though.'

'Promise?' he whispered, his thumb tracing my lower lip for a moment.

I almost lost it there and then, only just withstanding the violence of the urge to consume him, to let him consume me right there.

I nodded, not sure there was a choice any more. Knowing, with more certainty than I'd known anything before, that I wanted him right back.

Chapter 10
Jesse

'So, you going to tell me why we're going into town right now, in the middle of the working day?' I asked Cole, trying to work out why his eyes were darting all over – up to the house, the cabins, the drive. 'Or do I get some kinda prize if I guess? Maybe you'll finally open that dusty-ass wallet and buy me that drink you owe me?'

Cole just side-eyed me as we shrugged our shirts back on, skin still warm and damp from working in the sun all morning. Truth was, I was just glad to have a break from my own thoughts, especially the ones that pulled up emotion so deep, they scared the shit out of me – like the memory of Hestia meshing so quickly and easily with my family. Not to mention the other thoughts that wove alongside them and hardly let me look at her, even from a distance, without wanting her.

'I'll buy you a drink if it means you shut the hell up,' he offered, fastening buttons as the sleeves strained over his arms. He had the kind of definition gym bros trained for their whole lives and never achieved.

'We going shirt shopping or something?' I replied, ignoring him, ignoring my own head and enjoying the way he was fighting not to smile at me. There was something satisfying about cracking Cole, whose hardened, gruff exterior made most folks assume he had an attitude to match his physical dominance. But really, just below that grumpy mule layer was a guy to trust your life with – and one hell of a drinking buddy. 'You sure that's not one of Lottie's shirts? It looks like—'

'Jesse Bennington!'

We both spun round to see Bailey marching over, her face set as firmly as her words.

Now Cole smiled, shaking his head as he did up the last button. 'What did I do –' I began as he chuckled, taking a step to the side as if to let Bailey have a clear shot at me.

'How long have we been friends?' she asked, resting her hands on her hips as she reached us.

'I ... err ... I don't know? About ten years, maybe?'

My brain scrambled, flipping back through memories, landing on the rodeo season after graduating high school. She'd been in Clara's year, the one above mine. Always a familiar face, but not one I knew well until we started meeting regularly on the circuit.

'Ten goddamn years,' she hissed, taking another step towards me. 'And I have to find out second-hand from Clara that you finally took someone home to meet your mom? That Hestia, your *oh so goddamn casual* friend, was the one you introduced to them as the most beautiful woman you've ever met?'

I was gonna fucking *scalp* Clara.

'I – well, look, it was actually Mom that suggested it,' I retorted, knowing how lame it sounded. Cole's raised eyebrows and Bailey's glare confirmed it. 'Ugh, okay, fine. Yeah, I wanted her to meet Hestia, and my nosy, big-mouth sisters. I just thought, well ...'

Bailey shook her head, rolling her eyes.

'I'm fucking with you, you dumbass,' she crowed, her expression breaking out into a huge grin. She punched me on the arm.

'I'm just happy about it, that's all. I know what you're like in keeping your family outta your love life. So, y'know, it's good to see somethin' change.' I shrugged, smiling as Cole snorted. 'Hestia's a goddamn riot and I want her to stay around, so I'm glad she might just be finding a reason to.'

I looked up at her, holding tight to the thought that Hestia might just stay; the thought of what was slowly unfolding between us.

'Anything else you need to know ahead of time?' I asked, only just dodging another punch on the arm. I turned towards Cole's truck as he beckoned me over, the trip into town clearly still at the forefront of his mind.

'Enough of your sass, Bennington. But yeah, when you guys make it official, if I hear that through anyone other than you or her, you'll be wishing you were facing down a bull and not me.'

I laughed, climbing into the cab and flipping her off with a grin as she did the same.

'I fucking knew it,' Cole murmured as we wound down the drive, his smile smug. 'So, are you guys . . . together, or . . .?'

'Oh, no, no. This isn't about me and Hestia. You're not off the hook, dude. Are you gonna tell me why we're about to get half-trampled by tourists in town when it's over eighty degrees?' He glanced at me, a mix of amusement and exasperation in his eyes, keeping his mouth firmly shut. 'This better be good,' I grumbled, turning over the possibilities, the reason why the smile at the corner of his mouth never faded out, not for the whole way in.

We parked up in Jackson, using one of the free spaces behind Dee's store. It was on permanent loan to any of us from the Diamond Back, an arrangement Lottie had brokered recently to allow us to drop off and pick up guests easily among the hordes of tourists.

'She's smart, huh?' I murmured to Cole, clarifying as he gave me a questioning glance. 'Lottie. Everything she's done for the ranch since she arrived. Small things like this, right up to getting us booked out for the whole season.'

Cole's whole expression softened, just like it always did when he thought of Lottie.

'You have no idea,' he replied as we stepped onto the sidewalk, heading for the far side of the square, where some of the fancier shops were. 'That's why –' he continued, weaving in and out of people blocking the way, most with their phones out, taking pictures or videos of the scene around them – 'I've kept this quiet. Because my girlfriend has a knack for finding out about everything, and this is the one thing I want to surprise her with.'

I matched his stride as we reached the corner, where he slowed.

'And that is . . .?' I asked, trying to get a read on his face.

Finally, he stopped, gesturing towards the store. The jewellery store.

'That I want her to be my wife,' he said, smiling as my mouth dropped open.

'Holy fuck,' I whispered as I thought about how awesome that would be – the visible happiness they'd both been unable to hide since getting together, cemented for ever. '. . . Holy fuck!' I shouted it this time, grabbing Cole's shoulder with one hand and clapping him on the back with the other. 'That's awesome!'

He received it with a laugh, glancing back at the store window.

'She hasn't said yes yet. And wash your mouth out or you'll get us thrown out of the fancy store, okay?' he said, watching as I pinched the brim of my hat and nodded.

'Wait – are you picking *up* a ring or picking *out* a ring?' I asked, suddenly realizing the implications of him bringing me along.

'The last one,' he murmured, opening the door into beautifully cool air conditioning, which only just counteracted the clammy sensation of knowing he was going to rely on my opinion for something as important as this.

'Cole, I don't know shit about rings,' I whispered, glancing around the glass display cases, the bright white walls and polished wood floors. 'Why didn't you ask Hestia or something?'

He didn't reply, already talking to the saleswoman, someone I vaguely recognized. But then, as most Jackson-born residents had grown up together, it wasn't so surprising.

'Jesse, you remember Mrs Cornell? Amber's mom, from high school? She was in your class, right?'

I drew a blank, smiling as I faked a, 'Right, yeah, of course,' response, only to remember just as I shook her hand, her eyes assessing me. She was pretty, with distinctive hazel eyes that I was sure I recognized . . .

A memory hit me: making out under the bleachers, being discovered by the football coach with her hand wrapped round my dick and mine unhooking her bra.

That Amber Cornell. Eyes just like her mom's, apparently.

Cole's shoulders were shaking slightly again as he leant over a glass case nearby, and I vowed to pay him back for this.

'Are you settling down any time soon, like Cole?' Mrs Cornell asked, the polite, cool tone of her question undone by the lift of one eyebrow that told me she remembered *exactly* who I was.

'Um, maybe, yeah . . .' I began, strolling over to join Cole. 'Not quite at the jewellery stage, though.'

She made a humming sound that somehow implied she doubted I'd ever make it there.

'Well, Cole, just let me know if I can help. Like I said on the phone, I'd stick to something similar to the metals she already wears, and any stones you know she likes. Otherwise, it's usually just going with your gut, okay?'

He nodded, smiling up at her briefly as she moved over to the front of the store to welcome in another couple.

'You're an asshole, you know that?' I hissed at him under my breath, ignoring the low rumble of his chuckle in response. 'You knew exactly what you were doing bringing me here, didn't you?'

He scanned the dozens of rings in the case, resting his hands on the side.

'I figured you could do with a break from everything recently,' he said, moving over to the next case on our right. 'And a reminder of how far you've come since high school.'

I rocked back a little, pushing my hat up and staring at the back of his, about to protest. But the progress was undeniable – from Amber and countless encounters in high school, through to buckle bunnies, ending up with a couple of longer, true relationships. Like Chrissy. Sweet, unassuming and . . . just not quite right.

And now Hestia. There was no mould to shape whatever I had with her, no reference point for it. She somehow felt like everything and yet, officially, in terms of labels, nothing – or no *one* thing, at least.

'I guess,' I murmured, suddenly fast-forwarding to what this scenario would look like for me and her, whether I could picture myself buying her a ring . . . whether she would ever accept it. Glancing around, I knew this store was as far from Hestia's vibe as it was from mine. I smiled as I imagined asking to see some rings with colourful stones, preferably a skull or two.

'You know how much of dork you look every time you think of her,' Cole said, still not raising his eyes from the rings.

'Sure I do,' I shot back. 'Picked it up from you, big guy.'

He snorted and we both chuckled, attracting looks from the other couple and forcing ourselves to behave. We fell silent for a moment, just the low hum of the air con in the background.

'Why is this so fucking difficult?' he sighed, keeping his voice low. 'No one tells you that *this* is the impossible task, not the whole finding "the one" thing.'

'How did you know?' I asked before I could stop myself, knowing how keen I sounded and exactly what Cole would guess.

This time he looked up at me, straightening up until our eyes were level again.

'Same way you know when the bull is gonna spin right or left, dip his shoulder or throw his head around. It's in your gut,' he said, gesturing to his own. 'The whole is better than the sum of the parts, you know?'

I swallowed as he turned back to the rings again, now throwing myself into concentrating on them instead of the damn fluttering sensation in the place he'd described. The one that recognized his words and scrambled my fucking brain.

'Even so soon after meeting her?' I added, watching as he froze, hovering over a platinum band studded with tiny diamonds, a larger round diamond set above it.

He stood, calling Mrs Cornell over, asking to see it, utterly unflinching despite the hefty price tag.

'The way I see it,' he said to me, turning the delicate band over in his palm, both of us watching the diamonds reflect tiny rainbows across the wall as the sun caught them, 'time doesn't mean a damn thing. All I know is that I love that woman more than my own life, and I know she feels the same way. We've been together for, what, a few months? But it might as well be years. It makes no difference.'

I smiled, gripping his shoulder.

'You know I'm gonna give a best man speech no one will ever forget,' I replied, already cataloguing the details I could use to maximize his embarrassment.

'I'd expect nothing less,' he sighed, but it turned to a grin as he took one last look at the ring – Lottie's ring – and handed over his card to Mrs Cornell.

Chapter 11
Hestia

The rest of the week had passed in a blur of prep for the cookout, taking over on managing the catering set-up for Lottie, who'd moved over to general logistics. She'd hired a traditional covered wagon for us to take the food and supplies on, opting to sit up with Cole as he drove the two horses on the front.

That left Bailey and a couple of the casual ranch hands leading the ten guests, and at the back, Jesse, in charge of escorting me. Penny had been nothing short of an angel, patiently allowing me to go along for the ride and barely needing any direction.

Chastened at the thought that Jesse and I had been so close to behaving like animals in the corral, I was determined to keep this evening chill. To have fun as friends first, despite the pressure we could both feel below the surface. It completely baffled me that despite years of fuck buddies and dysfunctional relationships, keeping a simple, emotionless friends-with-benefits situation with him seemed . . . difficult.

Emotionally distant? You're the fucking OG Ice Queen, Cal had accused me once; an off-the-cuff comment in a moment of banter, but one that'd nagged at me for years. I'd cut him down in response, saying it took one to know one – something both of us knew to be absolutely true.

Sex, the physicality of feeling, in one cage of my mind. Emotion, the real deep and dark stuff – that was buried deep. Hidden. Open only to a tiny handful of people.

'You gonna come along to the rodeo next week?' Jesse asked, bringing Jasper closer. 'Think Bailey's kinda nervous, being without Dunkin and all.'

'Yeah, for sure.' I nodded fervently. 'I was wondering if I could stay backstage maybe? Help out a little?' He gave me a questioning glance. '. . . I'm not saying anything bad's going to happen this time, but it was fucking horrible watching from the stands last time, not being able to do anything.'

He nodded, then looked ahead to the guests for a moment.

'You might need to dress down a touch compared to last time, though, sugar,' he smiled. 'Distracting every last bull and bronc rider in there is the quickest way to fill up the local hospital.'

I side-eyed him with my sweetest, most innocent smile.

'I'd say that's a them problem,' I countered. 'Not my fault if they can't keep their eyes on the prize.'

Smiling back at me, seemingly fighting a laugh, he shook his head.

'For me, then, if no one else. May as well wave a red flag and lie down in the dirt if you're gonna come along looking like you did last time.'

I frowned, not computing.

'But you . . . Do you rope bulls?' I asked, suddenly confused. I was wondering if I'd missed something from the first rodeo, but I knew I'd only seen calves being roped.

He shook his head, a sheepish smile spreading.

'I'm gonna get back on a bull,' he said, searching out my reaction. 'It's been a year or so, but . . . I don't know. Been thinking about it for a little while and kinda confirmed it when we saw my mom last weekend. I miss it. Not sure I'm ready for it to be nothing but a memory just yet.'

As though from nowhere, horror engulfed me, shock and fear morphing into anger before I could stop it.

'Because you don't want the story of your first rodeo to be the one they tell? You want the story of how you were fucking trampled to death after you finally snapped your neck for good?'

His mouth opened in surprise, and he leant back slightly to assess my expression.

'Hestia, it's not—'

'Don't fucking patronize me,' I snapped. I knew I was straying into overreaction territory, but the fear . . . the image of him lying in the dirt . . . 'I'm no expert, but I know that shit is dangerous. Beyond dangerous. Fucking suicidal.'

My hands closed into fists on the reins, Penny reading it as a signal to slow down. Realizing, I released them, gently nudging her with my heels as Jesse had shown me earlier. She obliged without complaint.

'Shit, I didn't realize . . .' he began, seemingly baffled by my anger. 'Honestly – and hear me out, okay? I know it's risky, I do. But I've learnt a lot since my last season. I know what mistakes I made and how I'd do it different now.'

I gritted my teeth, trying to listen to him but also rationalizing why I felt the way I did.

'Why?' I asked, still struggling to get a grip on the part of me that wanted to fucking slap him, force him to see sense. 'Are you bored at the ranch? Not enough life-threatening action going on?'

He raised his eyebrows.

'Other than missing the circuit, the people and some of my friends still in it . . .' he began – and for one awful moment the thought of all the women, the buckle bunnies, entered my mind. 'The money can be really good. I don't want to get rich; I just want to be able to buy my own place, help my mom pay for her medication. The stuff she's taking is really helping, her doctor says it buys her another couple years maybe, but it's hundreds of dollars a month. She can't really afford it, and me and my sisters help . . . but it'd let me sleep easier at night if I knew I could pay for it for as long as she needed.'

His words doused my flames.

'Oh . . . right,' I replied, closing my eyes for a moment and shaking my head.

Frowning, he pulled Jasper closer still, our legs almost touching.

'Why does it bother you so much?' he murmured, trying to search my face, hidden below the brim of my hat.

I swallowed hard, knowing I owed him an explanation but needing to hold back from the raw truth.

'Because I care,' I said, fixing him with a direct look that I knew would be hard to hold. 'Because the thought of your head smashed open . . . having to tell your mum . . .'

'Hey, hey,' he said, reaching out and taking my hand in his. 'Plenty of riders get injured, but that's why there are wranglers in there. It's rare to get more than a broken bone, okay? And it sucks, but they mend.'

I took a deep breath.

'Can't I just bribe Lottie to give you a pay rise?' I offered, the pressure in my head easing as he gave a soft laugh. He gave my hand a last squeeze before centring himself in his saddle again.

'Bribe her with what?' he asked, rewarding my sideways glance with a mischievous half-smile.

'I don't know . . . releasing sex tapes, something on those lines,' I replied, matching his chuckle with a shaky laugh as the anger gently ebbed away.

'You're pure fire, aren't you, honey?' he said, his look so familiar, so *affectionate*, that I turned away.

'The eternal fucking flame,' I said wryly. Then, pointing to the flames on my neck, 'You were warned.'

We wound on and up through the pastures, Jesse expertly

steering our conversation to safer ground. Voluminous clouds drifted across the sun from time to time, giving temporary shade, but despite the ever-fresh mountain air, it was relentlessly hot.

By the time we reached the cookout spot a half hour later, everyone except Lottie and Cole – shaded and effort-free on the wagon – was melting. There was a stone-built firepit area surrounded by log benches, several long, rustic wooden tables fixed down into the earth, and a small wooden hut – a *very* rustic bathroom – near the treeline. The creek wound behind that, glinting like molten glass when the sun re-emerged, its slow flow creating a stress-melting rush of white noise.

As Bailey led some of the guests over to the creek, offering up a swim, I helped Lottie offload the supplies from the wagon, including the food prep tables.

I looked up as Cole approached, a primal expression on his face. Jesse was smiling in the background, clearly in on something.

'One thing we need to do before all that,' Cole growled to Lottie as he approached. 'This is one part of the creek we haven't tried.'

She held her hands up to him, squealing as he scooped her up.

'Cole! Fuck – no, I've got to prep dinner . . . I can't—'

He stopped her mid-sentence, gently placing his lips over hers, waiting until she all but melted into him. As he turned, pressing her lithe body into his, the sound of her laughter echoed all the way down to the water.

I smiled, my heart aching with happiness for her – for them.

'Want a dip before dinner?' Jesse offered, sauntering over, removing his sunglasses as he approached and hooking them into his shirt pocket. 'It's kinda tradition here. The creek's too shallow for swimming, but it's good to dip into when it's hot.'

I brushed aside the warnings in my head, knowing we were surrounded by chaperones.

'It's gonna be fucking Baltic, isn't it?' I said, setting down the utensils I was holding and falling into step beside him.

'Baltic?' he asked, confused.

'Freezing,' I clarified. Then, smiling as we approached the water, watching as Bailey even led Buckeye in, 'It's all very well you teaching me rodeo shit, but you clearly need some help with proper English.'

'Yeah?' he challenged as we both chucked off our boots and rolled up our jeans. The bootcut style allowed for a full roll-up to the knees. Grinning, he jumped in from the bank, sending a small cascade of water over me.

'Bastard,' I giggled, doing the same right back. The water was definitely cold, but it felt amazing after our long, sticky ride. Jesse turned; the guests were descending into shrieks and hysterical laughter as a water fight broke out. Struck by a sudden idea, I moved into the centre of the creek, just out of sight of everyone but him, and took off my tank top.

'Fucking carnage,' he laughed, glancing back to me for a moment, doing a full double take as I leant forward. My red lace bra was valiantly working overtime to keep everything inside as I dipped my tank top into the water, lifting it up before twisting the water out.

I returned his stare as it unashamedly rested on my breasts before lifting back up to my face.

'You all right there, cowboy?' I asked, shaking out the top before lifting it over my head and putting it back on, icy-cool against my overheated skin. I realized it was now pretty transparent, giving a neat little window to substantial cleavage.

His mouth opened a little, but nothing emerged.

'Now, the word we'd use in proper English for this would be "gawping" – maybe even "gobsmacked".'

Chuckling, I dipped my hands in the current and used the

water to push my hair back from my face, pulling it into a high ponytail.

'Jesus Christ, Jessica,' he breathed, turning to adjust his jeans.

'Nope, Greek goddess, remember?' I added, climbing out and pulling myself up the bank. 'Now, I'm pretty sure Lottie will be busy for a while, so you're on fire-building duty, okay?'

He touched the brim of his hat.

'Yes, ma'am.'

Dinner was a success.

As the dying sun bled out behind the mountains, the coral sky now smudged with indigo, almost every plate was clean.

Lottie's tried and tested Dean family recipes did most of the heavy lifting, but after spotting a couple of guests wearing band T-shirts I recognized, a sneaky change to the playlist on Cole's Bluetooth speakers had a group of us rocking out as I took the drinks orders. The rest of the group looked on with a mix of amusement and fascination as we sang along to 'Killing In The Name' by Rage Against The Machine, Jesse's smile turning to a laugh as I belted that famous repeated line with everything I had.

Cackling with the guests as the track finished, I finally let Bailey change it back over to the country playlist.

'Something tells me that's your anthem, right?' Jesse appeared at my side, gathering a long rope in his right hand.

'One of them,' I answered with a grin, now mid-clear-up, stacking pots and pans back into the crates we'd used to bring them over.

'You'll have to share the others sometime,' he said, glancing over at the group for a moment. 'Maybe in my truck. I was thinking of upgrading the sound system anyway . . . maybe one that can cope with the drums and bass guitar you like.'

I imagined sharing my favourites, one in particular that I'd started associating with him. I wasn't sure either of us was ready for it.

'Not sure you can handle it,' I remarked, reaching out to pick up the heavy crate, only for him to gently move me aside and lift it himself, walking it over to Bailey at the wagon.

'Try me,' he challenged, ignoring Bailey as she laughed at us.

'You two,' she said, vaulting up into the wagon to pull the crate in. 'She's the match and you're the kindling.'

'Well, this here matchstick is gonna be my assistant for a minute,' he winked, shrugging at my confusion as he announced to the guests that alongside having our campfire-brewed coffee, we were going to be running a roping competition.

'Now, y'all are gonna be aiming for our wooden cow over there.' He gestured to a crudely carved log cow, complete with long curved horns. 'But Cole and I thought it might be more entertaining to demonstrate on two moving targets.'

Lottie suddenly looked up from her clearing, shaking her head as Cole approached, already circling the rope over his head.

'Not a fucking chance,' she said, glancing at me for a moment, catching the momentary tilt of my head to the left.

'Now, what you want here is a nice smooth motion, just a gentle flick of the wrist,' Jesse instructed, only half watching us as he also lifted his rope in the air.

'Go,' I shouted to Lottie, both of us bolting away from the serving tables towards the creek.

'Fuuuck,' she yelled, laughing as the rope landed around her, Cole letting go of his end to prevent her from tripping over.

As I turned to glance back at Jesse, his rope landed over me to raucous applause from the guests behind, the metalheads hollering their approval the loudest. He dropped it too, allowing me to step out before he came over, as Cole took charge of organizing the guests into teams.

'Prettiest damn thing I ever had in my rope,' he said, gathering it up again. 'I didn't hurt you, did I?'

I shook my head.

'You likening me to a cow?' I teased, holding his gaze for a moment. Then, before I could stop myself, I added, 'But you don't need a rope, you know.'

His whole expression changed, fingers tightening around the loops for a moment.

'You can tell me to fuck off,' he started slowly, watching me carefully. 'But if you're free August twenty-fourth, will you come with me to Cole's brother's wedding?'

It was leftfield enough to give me pause. I felt the weight of his stare, that same depth of sincerity as clear and urgent as the mountain current.

'Your plus-one?' I clarified, giving him a soft smile, a strange churn of nerves as he returned it.

'My plus-one and then some,' he whispered, tracing a finger along the neckline of my tank top. 'But please, for both our sakes, no see-through tops. I'm not gonna fit a giant fucking boner in my good suit.'

I shrugged as he turned back to help Cole.

'No guarantees, cowboy.'

He shook his head, still smiling as he approached the group.

It was almost enough to distract me from the undercurrent of anxiety ahead of the rodeo. On the ride back, with the very first stars puncturing the eastern sky, I ended up riding next to Cole.

'You have a good time?' he asked, striking me yet again with how such a giant bear of a man could have such a calm, kind vibe. His voice was gravelled and deep, blending effortlessly with the scenery around us as it faded into twilight.

'Until I was openly compared to livestock, yes,' I joked, receiving a throaty chuckle in response. 'I have got a question, though, on the whole rodeo thing.'

He nodded, pushing Domino forward a little to keep in step with Penny.

'Shoot,' he said, tilting his head as I figured out how best to word it in my mind.

'Is there any way . . .' I began, then stopped, knowing how my question would come across. 'Can Jesse be talked out of the whole bull riding thing? I know it's his choice, I just . . . Can't you earn decent money from roping? Or something else?'

Cole narrowed his eyes, looking out towards the mountains on our left.

'I'm not sure he can,' he said, sighing. Then, to my surprise, 'Between us, I'm not a fan of it either – but that man is two things, sugar, and it'd help you to know what they are right now. One is stubborn. Once he's landed on something and he wants it, ain't nothing shaking him off, bulls included.'

I bit my lip, glancing over to where Jesse and Bailey rode together with the guests, deep in conversation.

'Yeah, I got that,' I said. 'And the second?'

Cole paused, straightening up as he rolled his broad shoulders back.

'That man has a heart so damn big that there ain't a challenge or a setback in this world that will stop him doing something for the people he loves.' His stare was intense, a frown appearing on his brow. 'So as I see it, it's our job to go with it and see if we can't help him out. Make sure he's got a soft landing if he falls.'

I felt his message loud and clear, knowing that we weren't talking about rodeo any more.

'I don't want him to fall in the first place,' I murmured, dipping my head, running my hand over Penny's soft neck. 'He deserves better.'

Cole was silent for a few seconds, leaving enough space that I wondered if he'd heard me.

'We get what we need,' he said softly, eyes fixed on Lottie up ahead.

I nodded, dwelling on the implication as we crossed into the familiar meadow below the ranch. Through the fir trees, the main house glowed on the ridge above. The rest of the ride was quiet as night gathered around us, the impending darkness mirrored in my mind.

Chapter 12
Hestia

The day of the rodeo was another scorcher, and everyone else was up and out before the sun had a chance to slow things down. My daily routine now started and ended with Luci, although Jesse had offered to take over her morning feed, predicting – correctly – that having to get up at 6 a.m. *and* be coherent *and* outdoors would be intensely painful for me.

Not wanting to give princess vibes, I'd taken over cleaning and prepping the tack he needed for guest rides. He hadn't asked, but a quick dig for information from Lottie had revealed the process and I'd just got stuck in, with a few pointers from Bailey.

His response had been fucking adorable. Genuine surprise flickering through his eyes, telling me I didn't have to, that he understood I wasn't a morning person.

'I wanted to,' I'd replied; then, as his expression became unbearably soft, 'Besides, I've seen the state of the tack. And I'm willing to bet I've had more experience with leather than you.'

He'd roared at my suggestive eyebrows, a sound imprinted on me, repeating now in my mind as I smiled into a bowl of granola. It was barely 9 a.m. but I was alone in the kitchen, trying not to replay the whole thing over and over.

My phone rang.

It was Cal. His name was like a slap, jolting me from the safe haven of my thoughts. Bracing myself for combat, the edge of his words still sharp from last time – hell, from the last six months – I finished my mouthful and picked up.

'This is going to cost a fortune,' I said, suddenly aware that my tone was already hard, defences raised. 'I thought we agreed to stick to email from now on?'

'I'm fine, thanks for asking,' Cal spat, moving in and out of range of the microphone. 'I'm just between clients and I had five minutes so I thought it'd be quicker this way.'

'Okay, okay,' I sighed, putting him on speaker and carrying on with my breakfast. 'What's up?'

Apparently placated at a chance to offload, he delved into his issues, general ramblings about the studio and even a mention of a new relationship; someone called Becca. The same frustrated, claustrophobic feelings that had threatened to bury me back home before I arrived here rose all over again. Resting my elbow on the table, chin in my hand, I was dragged back into his erratic current, stupefied into barely moving as footsteps approached and entered behind me.

I turned to see Jesse, frowning as he met my gaze. He gestured towards the door as though asking if he should leave.

Shaking my head, I mouthed, 'Five minutes.' He nodded slowly, poorly disguised concern across his face as he took a mug from the cupboard and poured himself a coffee from the pot. Then, with a glance at me noting the absence of a coffee on the table, he poured a second.

'. . . So what do you think I should do?' Cal was asking, and I realized I'd totally zoned out.

'Whatever you want,' I replied, my tone flat as Jesse brought the coffee over. 'Thanks,' I murmured, attempting a half-smile but knowing it was more of a grimace.

It was Cal's turn to sigh.

'Sorry, am I getting in the way of your holiday plans while I try and keep *our* business running?'

On the point of turning away, Jesse stopped, coming back to face me as he leant against the counter. I could feel my anger rising, drowning the sensible voice that told me not to go there, not to fall back into our usual cycle.

It was like riding a fucking bike.

'You know what, Cal?' I spat, suddenly wishing he was here in person to tear apart properly. 'You gave up the right to ask me what to do and solve all of your problems a few months ago. Longer, actually, when you checked out of *us*. You want to talk about holidays? What about the two weeks when you just fucking disappeared earlier this year?'

Jesse's expression had darkened, setting down his coffee on the counter as though ready to intervene.

'Are you seriously having a go at me for having a fucking breakdown?' he yelled, his dial instantly turning from one to ten, just as it always did in response to me.

I pushed back from the table and took a breath, closing my eyes for a moment, letting the darkness calm me just enough to take it down a notch.

'No, and I didn't at the time either, remember? I just got on with it, covered your clients and admin without fucking complaint and did what needed to be done. But this is a break for me, okay? I need a break, and I deserve one. Look –' I paused, desperate to not sink to his depths. 'Why don't I just postpone my clients for now so you can concentrate on yours, and I'll go through the business inbox later, make sure we're up to date with all the admin. Okay?'

There was silence at the other end before he drew a breath.

'Look, if I annoyed you by bringing up Becca . . .'

'You didn't, Cal. What you do with your personal life is not my business, and vice versa. I'm moving on.' I kept my eyes low, feeling Jesse's on my face, assessing me. 'I've got to go. If you have any business-specific issues, just email me. I think it's better for both of us that way.'

We hung up and I leant back against the chair, pinching the bridge of my nose. My nails dug deep into my skin, but somehow the pain took the edge off the echo of the words.

'Honey, if I smoked, I'd offer you a cigarette right now,' Jesse said. His voice was soft, but when I looked up, his eyes were hard.

I shook my head.

'Quit years ago,' I mumbled, knocking back as much of the coffee as I could handle, hoping it might somehow burn out the feeling Cal left me with. As I stood up, tucking my phone away, Jesse rounded the table towards me.

'Come here, for fuck's sake,' he gestured, holding an arm open towards me.

I hesitated, just for a second, then stepped into him. His warmth, that same intoxicating smell enveloping me as his arm did. My eyes closed instinctively as I leant against his chest, wrestling internally with how comfortable this felt and therefore how much I did and didn't want to return home.

'You still coming to the rodeo?' he asked, his voice muffled as he rested his head against mine for a moment, his lips against my hair.

'With fucking bells on,' I murmured. I could feel a sudden surge of resolve firing up in the brief safe haven of his hold.

Jesse chuckled as I gradually released him, all too aware of how much longer I could've stayed. My anxiety around his first bull ride for months was resurfacing in the wake of Cal's distraction.

'You want to come over with me, Cole and Bailey? Lottie's staying here with the guests this time, I think. We're going pretty soon, so . . .' He glanced at my pyjamas: black shorts and one of Lottie's oversize vintage Disney tees, featuring a very faded Thumper.

'You told me to tone it down for the rodeo,' I shrugged, finally managing a real smile when I saw his. 'But listen . . . I don't want to tell you what to do – I have no right, I know. But . . .'

'Spit it out, Jessica,' he said, glancing down at the T-shirt, pulling on the hem.

'Just be careful, please,' I begged, not intending for it to come out with the intensity it did. 'I just can't imagine—'

He closed the gap between us, leaning down. In one heart-stopping moment he pressed his lips against my forehead, his hands on my shoulders.

'I swear to you, I'll be fine. And as soon as I'm done, I'm coming to find you and the others, collect my winnings and then spend it all on fireballs. See if we can't get ourselves barred from Shelby's this time? Maybe dodge the chaperones and see what other trouble we can cause?'

The implication was crystal clear. Once again, I wondered if he'd remembered the dare I'd taken on, the booking I'd made to prove a point. I assumed he hadn't, figuring he would've suggested cancelling it. Just as I kept intending to do.

'Don't tempt me,' I replied, watching as his gaze slid over mine, then down to my mouth, my body.

He bit his lip, taking a step back.

'Too late for that, honey,' he murmured as he turned for the door. 'See you there.'

———

As Lottie dropped me off – with a wistful look at the buzzing crowds before she headed home – I knew I'd been right to brazen it out and arrive alone. Partly because the anxiety before the event would have driven me over the edge here, among the energy of the crowd. And also because I'd dressed as . . . battle-ready me.

It steadied my nerves to climb into clothes that felt like a second skin, to slowly and carefully prep my make-up as I would at home. The result was tiny black denim shorts, a blood-red corset, black platform Doc Martens and my hair curled but half pinned up. Soft waves fell around my flame tattoo, and silver dagger earrings next to a row of mixed studs followed the curve of my ear. My make-up was dark, especially around my eyes; my lips were the colour of my corset.

Finding my way around to the chutes as Lottie had instructed, I showed my pass to the steward, who looked mildly shell-shocked by my outfit. The staring continued as I went in, suddenly adding to my nerves. What if Jesse actually hadn't been joking, and I would now utterly distract him and cause . . .

Mentally slapping myself, I resolved to pull it the fuck together just as I saw Bailey and her friend, Darcy, practising in a smaller corral out of sight of the crowds.

As Buckeye thundered down the centre of the corral, I marvelled at how Bailey had managed to build a rapport with him so quickly. It was remarkable how well they worked together, the horse clearly hanging on every signal she gave him.

'Hey, Hestia!' Darcy waved, trotting over as I approached the fence. 'Whoa – you look awesome! You here by yourself?'

I nodded.

'Lottie had guest stuff to do at the ranch, so she dropped me off. It's all good though.'

'Well, damn, cowgirl,' Bailey said, recovering her breath as she came over, patting Buckeye's neck. 'That's quite a statement. Sure you're at the right place? The Jackson Collective's over in town.' She winked, pushing her hat back a little. I shrugged, suddenly wishing Dee were here, that we could buddy up on the alt vibes.

'That's next week,' I said, feeling a jolt of excitement at the thought of creating Dee's tattoo. 'Call this a trial run.'

'Well, honey, I sure appreciate it,' Bailey smiled. 'But I know you're here for Jesse – he's up real soon, just over there.'

She pointed to the bucking chute, where a gaggle of cowboys were gathered in a mass of denim and hats, a number of cute, mainly blonde, women among them.

'How do you stand it?' I asked them, gritting my teeth against the wave of anxiety taking over my gut. 'The pressure, I mean?'

Darcy explained her own feelings, grounded in her trust of her horse, as Bailey considered me.

'You're nervous as all hell for him, aren't ya?'

I met her gaze, seeing the unflinching realness in her green eyes, and nodded. 'I'm ready to fucking throw up,' I admitted.

Darcy and Bailey shared a look.

'I'm not gonna lie to you, bull riding is . . . Well, it takes skill and experience to pull it off and walk away without too much bruising. But, honey, Jesse is pretty good. He's grown up an awful lot since last year, too. All the shit with his mom has put things in perspective.'

I nodded, staring out at the chute.

'It's eight seconds, that's all,' Bailey added. 'The whole thing'll be over in thirty, from start to finish. He'll be fine. Don't fret.'

I wished them luck for their event and headed over to the chute, careful to avoid the main throng of cowboys – I was genuinely worried about distracting Jesse. Taking a few steps up into the seating next to the chute, I spotted two things in quick succession. The first was the bull, incomparably vast, with short, pointed horns currently attempting to fuck up the small steel pen surrounding it. Shouts and whoops from the cowboys surrounding it did nothing to calm my nerves, especially as at that moment, I saw Jesse.

He seemed relaxed, perched on top of a nearby gate, talking to two other guys. In full rodeo gear, from the Diamond Back jacket to the black leather chaps, he looked so at ease, so at home that some small trickle of relief dampened my fear. I stood for a moment, leaning on the back of the seat to get a better look, and the movement caught his eye.

He stopped talking mid-sentence, eyes flaring as he took me in. I gave him a small smile just as the other two men turned in my direction, one of them wolf-whistling before I had a chance to sit down. Resisting the urge to give him shit-eye, I turned away instead, moving down to a seat nearer the arena, out of their sight.

As the event began, my hands clasped together, I had to turn to deep breathing to get me through the first twenty minutes. The bulls were ferocious, comprised of pure, rippling muscle. As they tore out of the gates and threw themselves around, the cowboys on top resembled nothing more than rag dolls.

The first three riders did well, all staying on until the bell rang before jumping off to safety, the wranglers in the arena keeping the bulls at bay. With no one injured so far, my nerves dissipated slightly – until the bell rang for the fourth rider. Leaping off the bull and away from its head, he somehow caught the edge of its hoof mid-buck, clipping his head as he went down. He landed face first in the dirt and it took two wranglers to drag him out, dazed but awake. Even at this distance, I could see his helmet was badly cracked.

'*Fuck, fuck, fuck,*' I whispered, thankful that no one was sitting near enough to hear.

I gripped the edge of the seat either side of my legs, and as Jesse's name was announced, my fingers turned white, nails digging into the hard plastic.

'. . . He's back from an extended break. Give it up for a Jackson favourite, Jesse Bennington!'

The scene before me wound right down to slow motion, only the curses and yelling from the chute filtering through as horns and hooves connected with metal. I couldn't bring myself to look;

I just stared straight ahead at the grooves in the dirt where the last cowboy had been dragged through.

Then, with a sound like a gunshot, the gate opened and the bull emerged, writhing in the air as Jesse sat astride. He was gripping a rope with his left hand, his right raised in the air. Hand to my throat, I forced myself to watch the green digits of the huge timer on the wall instead, begging them to reach eight seconds – begging anything, anyone listening to my thoughts to keep him safe.

The noise of the crowd built, cheers and roars growing in intensity as my heart thundered, the seven turning to eight. I gasped as the bell sounded and a moment later, Jesse let go and leapt – landing on his feet, well away from the bull.

The whole arena exploded. Everyone around me was on their feet as he punched the air, jumping onto the nearest gate to avoid the still whirling bull, now being herded back into its pen. Seconds later, as cowboy after cowboy patted him on the back, the announcer gave the score. The crowd roared again and Jesse whooped, shaking his head as he found himself in first place.

There were several other riders still to go, but I knew I couldn't handle it. Shaking, I got up, walking as quickly as I could to the end of the row and back down the steps towards the back of the chute.

A whole throng of women had appeared, whistling and whooping as Jesse emerged not twenty feet away. He was grinning, surrounded by friends and fellow riders. A few of the women approached from both sides. I hesitated as he looked around, his head turning in my direction, but as a wave of nausea hit, I knew I would just kill his buzz. Instead, I walked away, suddenly grateful for the corset, the way it physically held me together as I strode past the practice corral. I knew the three of them had come in Bailey's truck, having spotted it near the entrance on the way in. The car park would be quiet, everyone now inside.

As I approached the exit, the adrenaline slowing, tears quickly rose. With no one else around and one arm wrapped around myself, I let out a sudden sob. Knowing more were coming, I all but ran for the truck as it came into view, stumbling against it as the first tears fell.

Trying to breathe through it, I let myself sink down, leaning against the huge wheel. *Jesse was fine. He was fine. No injuries. He might even have won it.*

'Hestia?'

My head jerked up as with horror, I realized Jesse was running towards me, confusion and pain etched so clearly in his features that for a moment I thought he *had* been hurt.

'Are you okay?' I croaked, forcing myself up to standing again, unable to see anything except him, the rodeo flags and stands and noise behind us nothing more than a blur.

'Yeah, I'm fine,' he replied, breathing heavily as he reached me, instantly drawing me into him, half crushing me against his chest. 'Why are you upset? Where did you go? I saw you leave . . .'

The relief – the shattering realization that he was okay, that he'd run to find me despite this being his big moment, was suddenly more than I could ignore.

'I was so fucking worried,' I whispered. 'I still feel sick. Watching you get thrown around in there . . .'

His expression changed in an instant, one hand moving to my cheek as he gently moved us back against the truck, wedging me firmly between the solid metal and his body.

'I'm fine, sweetheart. Stop now, you're killing me,' he murmured as another tear slid down my cheek. Then, almost to himself, he whispered, 'I didn't realize you cared so much?'

I couldn't answer, could only gaze back into his eyes, reading me as closely as I was him. He knew the answer, I realized. Just as I'd started to.

'I can't help it,' I replied as he leant down, tilting his hat up and out of the way. 'It's just how I feel about you.'

All of the moments to date between us, from that first hook-up in the kitchen to what had almost happened in his truck after visiting his mum, flashed before my eyes. The restraint we'd both maintained since then, a string pulled taut with the constant tension, finally snapped.

My hand wound round the back of his head, and I tilted my face up as he met me in the middle. His lips were soft at first, a sensation of relief waking up every nerve in my body. The kiss intensified, building, until we were almost crushing each other with the desperation to feel more, to take in more of one another.

I knew I'd never felt this before, this deep sense of something settling into place. Any sense of fear evaporated, replaced by a need for more. For all of it – all of him.

'I can't describe how I feel about you,' he breathed as we parted for a moment, removing his hat with his free hand, the other woven into my hair. 'But I do know that if I can't have you right now, I'm gonna fucking explode.'

He reached into his pocket, and I heard the truck locks click open.

I smiled between breaths.

Before I could reply he moved us over, opening the door to the back of the cab. Picking me up by the waist, he lifted me onto the edge of the seat, waited for me to shift back, then climbed in, closing the door behind him.

Behind the darkness of the window tint, as he pressed the key again to lock the doors, I reached behind me to undo my corset.

He shook his head, moving towards me, settling between my legs.

'Leave it on,' he said, leaning down to kiss the tops of my breasts. 'You look so fucking beautiful like this.'

He made his way slowly up my neck, his tongue following the curves of my flames. Following instinct alone, I reached out for his jeans, flicking the button open and pulling down the zipper.

'I swear to you,' he whispered as he reached my mouth, kissing me gently, reverently. 'Next time will be slower, somewhere with space that I can take my time on you, just you. But right now, I need to fuck you. Can I do that?'

I grabbed his jaw with my hand, deepening our kiss in response, not wanting words to get in the way. Not when I knew he understood me physically, maybe better than I understood myself. He took over on his jeans, pulling himself free before working on my shorts, his expert hands working them down, followed by my underwear, in seconds.

Despite the space restrictions, I lay back and watched as he braced himself over me, lightly brushing his fingers between my legs, holding my gaze and smiling as I squirmed. In seconds his cock followed. He used a hand to guide himself into me, not trying to be gentle this time but hearing my moans for what they were – a plea for more, to thrust harder, go faster.

'Hestia,' he groaned as I ground into him over and over, only slowing slightly when I realized this would be over in seconds if we kept the same pace. He watched me, his eyes bright, as unlike before I sought out his mouth, putting every ounce of feeling into a kiss instead.

He slowed to a stop, still inside me, and kissed me right back. It began to change, our lips gradually slowing, a softness developing that I couldn't prevent from taking over. I wanted to cry all over again, traitorous tears threatening at the corners of my eyes.

As I gazed at him, watching as he gently brushed a thumb under my eye, I realized his expression mirrored my own. Those beautiful storm-cloud eyes were glimmering with the same emotion.

I reached up, brushing under his eye as he'd done for me,

melting into his mouth once again as he responded. I was holding his face as seconds later we began to move again, his cock somehow pushing deeper than before, making me gasp aloud. Covering my mouth as if wanting to absorb every sound, he groaned, the sound reverberating as my body responded, tightening around him as I started to come.

'I never want this to end,' he breathed against my ear as I cried out, grabbing fistfuls of his shirt as the feeling cascaded over me. His own breathing became ragged, pushing harder and harder until he followed.

We lay there, just breathing. He was braced on his arms to stop himself crushing me with his body weight.

'Jesse,' I whispered, waiting for him to look up, then bringing his mouth back to mine. We kissed again, even slower than before, a hundred words compressed into a handful. 'Does this make me your buckle bunny?'

He laughed, shaking his head as he stroked my hair.

'Only if I've won, honey.'

We stared at each other for a moment, knowing the spell was breaking, the threads of life outside winding back around us.

'Want to go and see if you have?' I asked as he kissed my forehead before drawing back. Never more thankful for condoms, I pulled my underwear and shorts back up as he leant into the front of the cab and grabbed tissues from the glovebox.

'Sure you want to go out there again?' he asked, checking my expression as he cleaned and zipped up.

'If I can stay with you,' I admitted, using the rear-view mirror to check the state of my make-up. Thankfully, waterproof everything was my go-to, covered with violent amounts of setting spray. Almost nothing had moved.

He just smiled, reaching over one more time, no hesitation on either side as our lips met again. Fire flared in my core. I knew that in a different setting, we'd be straight back to it.

'Nuh-uh,' he half moaned as I gently bit his lip. 'Next time I want you for hours.'

When we both jumped out of the truck, exchanging sheepish grins as we checked for anyone around us, it felt only right that he took my hand.

I locked my fingers through his, staying as close to his side as possible as we walked back into the rodeo together.

Chapter 13
Hestia

My gloves on and stencil applied, Dee was almost vibrating with excitement as she looked down at the guide now on her arm. Nestled within part of her existing sleeve, the horns of the cow skull wove through the end of a snake's tail above, the blossom cascading down her arm to her elbow.

'Honey, it's going to look like I tattooed this drunk if you don't simmer down,' I mock-scolded, picking up the tattoo machine, thankful it was the same brand as mine back home.

'Sorry, sorry,' Dee laughed as she all but skipped into the chair, startling as the band in the corner started up. We both watched the beginning of their set for a minute, amid the bustle of the Jackson Collective space. It was an open day – throwing the doors of Jackson's artistic community open to everyone, locals and tourists alike. Artists and creators of every description, from photographers to sculptors, musicians to hatmakers, had set up stands in a huge community hall. The idea was to showcase Jackson's home-grown talent and invite others, like me, in to demonstrate our passion.

I smiled to myself, realizing that I'd used a very 'Jesse' word just then, adjusting my grip and the needle depth slightly as I herded my attention back to the task at hand. A vision of accidentally tattooing Jesse's face on Dee's arm crossed my mind and as she turned back to me, I chuckled under my breath.

'What?' she asked, smiling as I shook my head.

'Nothing, just trying to get myself in the zone a little. It's been . . . almost two months since I last did any work. And this week I've been distracted with, well, the rodeo last weekend, and Luci . . .'

'The *rodeo*, huh?' Dee asked after I got started. Within seconds I could feel the muscle memory returning to my fingers, my creative brain locking into the detail. I knew this design would look incredible, especially with the rest of her look. 'Yeah, I heard a few things about that.'

'Oh?' I murmured, feigning innocence.

She paused, as though assessing my expression.

'It's a small-town thing, the gossip,' she explained, careful to keep her voice in line with the volume of the band. I could feel eyes on us now I'd started – people are always curious about the tattooing process. 'So don't take it personal that people were yapping about you, but yeah . . . there was some talk. Something about the return of Jackson's star bull rider, getting an incredible score and then high-tailing it out of the rodeo after a woman.'

'Huh,' I replied, raising my eyebrow as I completed the curve of the horns, really starting to get into my groove. 'He did, did he?'

A quick glance at her face confirmed that she was holding back a laugh.

'Yeah. Funny thing is, by all accounts a little while later he came striding back in again, holding hands with – and I quote – "some hot goth chick".'

I snorted.

'He was just being . . . nice,' I admitted, smiling as she chuckled. 'I got a bit freaked out by the bull riding, that's all. If you think about it, it's a pretty fucking weird thing to do, not to mention fairly suicidal.'

I realized how much I didn't want to lie to her, or anyone else, about me and Jesse. But we'd agreed on returning to the Diamond Back after the rodeo that we would keep things as quiet and low-key as possible while we figured it out.

My stomach squirmed as I thought of him, of the snatched moments we'd had together since. The week had been manic with guests, Jesse out from dawn to late, not to mention silently suffering the physical after-effects of being jolted and thrown around on a bull. I knew his shoulder was hurting; I had noticed him rotating it, wincing, too many times over the past few days.

'So, are you guys . . .? Or is it complicated with stuff at home?' Dee asked, her voice tentative.

I sighed a little, turning my head to begin part of the blossom, switching inks. My signature style was using an indigo ink, something Dee had specifically requested.

'Yeah, it's kind of complicated,' I confessed, trying to explain without going too deep. 'I still run my studio at home with my ex, and he's only a recent ex. But . . . Jesse is . . . I like him. A lot.'

We were skirting the real truth, as though walking along the edge of an abyss, teetering above the blackness below. In that darkness, way down, was every failed relationship I'd had, and the knowledge that – aside from Lottie and one, maybe two others – I didn't know how to let people in for the long term. I didn't know what it was to make a relationship work, not really. Therefore, the odds of something working out with Jesse were . . . low. At best.

'Oh, I get that,' Dee agreed, nodding and saying hi to someone passing, being careful not to move. 'I mean, he's fucking gorgeous, obviously. Must make it even more difficult with only being here for a little while, I guess.'

I hummed an agreement as I concentrated, registering yet another lurch in my gut at the inevitable, not yet able to picture just how we would say goodbye. I'd always known that leaving

Lottie would be hard, but now, with Jesse – not to mention Luci, Bailey, Cole, Dee – the list was growing unbearably long.

'What about you?' I said, keen to switch the topic away from myself and clear Jesse from my mind, if only for the next couple of hours while I worked. But even as Dee talked about a recent date and her own ex, he was still there on the periphery of my perception.

Just over two hours later, Dee's arm wrapped and admired as I met a whole host of fellow artists, she wrapped me in a careful hug.

'I fucking love it,' she breathed, helping me to clean up. 'Do you want to borrow the machine and the rest of the kit while you're here? It's a spare anyway. Just in case you feel . . . inspired up there at the Diamond Back.'

I laughed, thanking her, and agreed to take care of it.

'Want to come look at all the other stuff? There's something I want to show you in particular as well,' she enthused, glancing down at the new part of her sleeve and grinning again.

Her natural enthusiasm was catching; I'd almost forgotten the satisfaction of seeing a client as in love with my creation as I was with the process of doing it.

'Show me everything,' I agreed, linking arms with her and carrying the kit in a bag on my shoulder. 'Are those belt buckles over there?'

We reviewed a whole selection of buckles – not something I'd ever imagined being interested in. But learning from Dee what they meant and assessing the metals, from silver to brass and steel, and designs from bucking broncs to one particularly beautiful cow's skull, I found myself choosing two: the skull, not dissimilar to my tattoo design for Dee, and a turquoise-studded silver one that I could picture with my black Wranglers.

'Okay, now – this is what I really wanted to show you,' Dee said, barely suppressing a squeal as we reached one of the largest stands, already crowded with other customers. There were endless cowboy hats of almost every colour and shape on racks, with four people at benches in front, customizing them. 'These guys are going to be supplying my shop soon – I'm branching into offering hat customization for bachelorette parties and girls' weekends. We get so many weddings now in Jackson.' She stopped, catching the eye of one of the women serving, waving and pointing at me. 'I, um . . . well, as a little thank-you for this and the other T-shirt design, I kind of had one made up for you.'

Taken aback, I watched as the woman brought over a large box, greeting Dee and offering it up to me.

'Are you sure?' I asked, my eyes flickering over the slightly intimidating price tags on the hats nearest to us. 'This is really generous . . .'

As Dee lifted the lid, allowing me to pull it out, my mouth fell open. It was jet black with a braided black leather band around the crown, and a silver skull and a turquoise 'H' charm woven into the ends of the braid.

'Oh my God, Dee,' I blurted eventually, putting my bag down, desperate to try it on. 'Oh wow, it fits perfectly.'

I turned to her and the woman, both nodding.

'I knew it,' Dee said, grinning. 'Got a knack for guessing sizes. And obviously the black looks awesome against your hair.'

'I fucking love it,' I said, grinning right back and pulling Dee into a hug, mindful of her arm. 'It's so thoughtful of you.'

'I really don't want you to go,' she murmured into my shoulder before we pulled apart. 'I was hoping I could bribe you to stay.'

It wasn't until much later in the day, back at the ranch and freshly showered, that I began to dwell on her words. What the ranch had come to mean, the growing depth of my attachment to it – let alone the people. The thought of wearing my new hat at home, in London, felt entirely alien. But the strangest part about it wasn't the hat – that felt comfortable in every sense. It was the thought of the city, my life there, that felt . . . off.

My stay was open-ended right now, but I knew that hovering in the distance was a moment when I'd have to make the call to go home. Luci was recovering beautifully, even being borderline pleasant to Bailey as well as to me; she might well become a useful asset to the ranch. My tourist visa was ultimately the deciding factor, given I didn't have Lottie's flexibility with dual citizenship.

In my bathrobe, I slipped into the kitchen, suspecting tonight would be a quiet one – likely a movie in bed and an early night. Lottie was exhausted. The cabins were booked solid for another few weeks through to mid-September, and even with a full staff it was all hands on deck.

As I grabbed a bottle of beer from the fridge, the side door opened, and Jesse came in from the dimming twilight outside.

'Oh, hey,' I said, giving him a smile and resisting a sudden self-conscious urge to hide my make-up-free face, my wet hair slicked back from it.

With a quick check down the hall to the rest of the house beyond, he strode across the kitchen and without a word, gently took my face in his hand, kissing me.

Only just remembering to hold onto the bottle, the fridge door hanging open, I felt myself dissolve into him. His mouth was soft against mine, his movements gentle, but the urgency behind his kiss . . . the force I always felt around him, pulled tighter than ever.

'Hey,' he replied as we parted, his voice rough as he held my gaze. 'I've been waiting for that all day.'

I closed my eyes, resting my forehead against his for a moment, feeling the now familiar sensation of wanting more – to stay next to him, safe against his body – warring with my recent thoughts of what it would mean to say goodbye.

I swallowed, hard.

'I've got something for you,' I murmured instead, forcing myself back. 'You want a drink?'

I gestured to the bottle, not missing the slight puckering of his brow as he made his way to the sink and began washing his hands, the foam from the soap turning black as he scrubbed.

'Sure,' he replied. 'You all good?'

I nodded, beckoning him to follow me as he finished up, taking another bottle and leading him back down the hall to my room. Bailey was out tonight, Lottie and Cole already crashed out in his room.

He followed, crossing the threshold slowly, eyes not leaving me as I closed the door behind us. Grabbing the two items I'd bought for him off the bed, as our eyes met again, I was suddenly aware this was the first time we'd been alone in a bedroom together.

'I got you something,' I said, careful to keep an arm's length between us, just for now. 'Well, two things.'

'Okaaay,' he replied, smiling as I handed over a small paper bag and a gift bag. Then, with a glance to my bathrobe, he added, 'I've got something for you, too.'

He delved into the paper bag, drawing out a small brown bottle and squinting at the label.

'Arnica oil,' I said softly, daring to step closer, running a hand over his left shoulder. His eyes shot to my face at the touch, flaring. 'I've seen you wincing a little, am I right? Guessing you hurt it last weekend?'

He said nothing for a moment, studying me.

'You got this for me?'

I rolled my eyes.

'I don't know anyone else stupid enough to get thrown around on a wild, three-thousand-pound animal and do fuck knows what to their body,' I retorted, unable to hold back from returning his smile in response. 'You put a few drops in the bath. It'll help your bruising heal, tone down the aching.'

'Your bath?' he asked, stepping into the remaining space between us, forcing me to tilt my head right back to maintain eye contact.

'If you like,' I breathed, feeling my body respond, suddenly desperate for him to remove my robe, his clothes.

He made a rumbling sound in his throat as he reached into the gift bag, pulling out a small, tissue-wrapped object.

'And what's this?'

I shrugged as he unwrapped it.

'I'm new to this whole buckle bunny business,' I murmured as the metal inside glinted in the low lights of the bedroom. 'But I thought of you when I saw it . . . and me. Well, *us*.'

The tissue fell to the floor as he freed the skull belt buckle. He turned it over for a moment, running his thumb over the skull as he looked back at me. His eyes had become molten, just as they had been in the truck.

'You thought of us?' he asked slowly, softly, as though afraid saying the words again might render them to dust.

I nodded, too afraid to say more, knowing with every cell that he was feeling the same as I was in that moment. He leant down slightly, his lips coming to brush mine.

'I fucking love it,' he whispered, his tongue tracing my lower lip as my mouth opened to him. 'I don't know what I did to deserve it, but it's beautiful. Thank you, Jessica.'

We fell into another kiss, fuelled by my insistence this time, pulling him to me and letting the feelings wash over the thoughts and doubts that whirled in my head. As I scraped my nails over his existing belt buckle, threatening to take it off, he smiled.

'Hold up there,' he breathed, circling my waist and moving us back onto the bed, letting me fall back, holding himself over me. 'I said I had something for you before the belt comes off.'

On the verge of grabbing him and forcing him back into our kiss, instead I inhaled as he gently undid the tie on my robe and opened it out, running his fingers over my breasts and down, not stopping until they slipped between my thighs and I gasped again.

'Oh fuck, honey,' he moaned, feeling just how wet I'd become.

'What something do you have for me?' I asked breathlessly, barely able to breathe as he began to circle his fingers there.

'The promise I made in the truck,' he whispered, leaning down to kiss my jaw. I arched my neck to his touch as his fingers slid into me.

'Oh, holy shit . . .' I moaned, unable to help myself as he made his way down my body, pausing at my breasts. 'Get your clothes off, now.'

He chuckled, making slow, painfully wonderful small circles with his fingers inside me.

'Not yet, sweetheart.'

And slowly, using one arm to hold me down, his mouth reached my hips, nipping and kissing the skin as he worked across, joining his fingers with his tongue.

In less than a minute I was barely in control, coming hard as he fucked me with his hand, giving me only another minute to pause, stroking the inside of my thigh as I tried to breathe before he began again. Ignoring my half-hearted protest and insistence on being fucked properly, this time he just used his mouth. So gentle at first, growing more insistent as I felt myself building up again.

'I want you,' I murmured, running my fingers through his hair.

But he ignored me, instead using his tongue inside me until I came again, only partly stifling a cry with my arm over my face.

'Now,' he murmured, the sound of his belt buckle finally opening, the zip following. I watched, eyes half-closed, as he took off his shirt, his jeans and boxers dropping together as he shrugged everything off. 'I'm willing to wait to use this,' he said, gripping his cock. 'So if you've had enough, or it's too much . . .'

'Don't you dare go anywhere,' I breathed, my core muscles

having long melted into the bed, preventing me from sitting up to reach it myself. 'Now fuck me properly.'

His eyes wild, he leant back over me, using his hands to turn me gently until I was on my front, pulling my hips back up towards him.

'Don't be gentle,' I hissed as he teased the end of his cock against me, wanting him, needing him to . . .

I gasped as he entered me, no hint of gentle touch. He slammed against me and I cried out with him, impatiently waiting for him to do it again, and again, and again.

'I don't know if I'll ever have the patience to fuck you slowly,' he moaned as I stifled a cry again, his movements becoming rougher, his fingers inching forward to stroke me around his cock.

'Jesse,' I moaned, only half aware of what I was saying. 'Don't ever stop – I only want you.'

He came in the same moment, the sensation of his cock pumping into me as he finished. We collapsed together, just breathing into the cotton sheets as I tried to piece my thoughts back together.

'Did you mean that?' he murmured a minute later, turning his head towards me, the skin above his cheekbones flushed.

I knew what he meant; I could still feel the truth of it etched into every pore of my skin. But now, in the quiet calm, it took on new meaning.

I nodded, just holding his gaze as he moved closer to my face, his lips now brushing mine with such care, such a worshipful touch, that I was suddenly terrified of what he might say.

'Want me to run us a bath?' I said, jumping in before he could say anything else. At his raised eyebrow, I added, 'I could fuck you all day, cowboy, but even I need a break in between.'

He chuckled, nodding.

I half expected the bath to turn into an action replay, but instead it felt . . . relaxing. He told me about his day and I reciprocated, lying back against him, my head resting on his shoulder.

'What's your real hair colour?' he asked suddenly, continuing to twirl strands of it.

I laughed at the realization.

'Actually, it's not dissimilar to your hair colour,' I said, turning back to see his face. 'A kind of dark, dirty blonde.'

'The best kind,' he murmured, running a finger over my chest, around the outline of the headless horseman. 'And I still haven't had a full tat tour,' he noted. 'The first time I see you fully naked, and I don't know what half of it means.'

I laughed, gripping the sides of the bath and slowly standing in front of him, watching as his expression became hungry again.

'There's too many . . .' I said, slowly turning, shivering as his hands reached up to hold my hips, running down my legs, eyes everywhere – from my ass to the viper that wound around the back of my left thigh, circling down to my calf.

Looking back to him, I stilled. He said nothing, hands still on my lower legs, but his expression screamed everything I knew I felt too.

'Would you do one for me?' he asked suddenly, his eyes on my wrist, the white Norse compass on the inside. 'I've got an idea.'

Barely half an hour later, the small desk in the corner of the room pulled out, my borrowed kit cleaned and prepped, we sat opposite each other.

'So you don't mind me free-handing this? I can stencil it?' I offered, eyebrows raised as he shook his head, offering his upturned arm on the desk.

'I trust you, Jessica. Besides, I've stalked you online. I know how good you are.'

I couldn't help laughing, his sheepish expression giving way to a beautiful smile.

'Okay . . . well, I'll do my best. But you're going to need to hold completely still for this, and I'll warn you, the inner wrist gets fucking sore. I'll go as quick as I can.'

He nodded briefly, watching as I reached for my gloves.

'It's so painful that I actually think you might need some help,' I added, unable to deny myself the amusement, justifying that it might actually work . . . kind of.

So as I shrugged my robe off my shoulders, letting it fall to my waist, he barely noticed as I gently took his wrist and, prepping the ink, got to work.

He simply stared for a moment, his eyes, his whole attention entirely focused on my breasts.

'What are you trying to do to me?' he asked hoarsely as I followed the faint outline of the pen I'd used to give a rough idea of the design just minutes ago.

'Distract you,' I replied softly, concentrating just as resolutely. 'Never done it half-naked before, might check with Lottie, see if it could be a new marketing tactic.'

He barely laughed, still too fixed on me to respond properly.

'So why this design, why here?' I asked, shifting my grip slightly, taking the next bit a little more slowly, all too aware of the increased margin for error. The design he'd requested – the same cow's skull as the design on my T-shirt, wreathed in flames – was small, but not without a fair bit of detail.

He shifted his gaze to my face, then to the emerging design on his skin.

'I wanted something of you,' he said simply, holding my eyes in his as I stopped, looking up. 'Your skull design and . . . your flames. And right here, on my wrist . . . I want to see it. Every day. I want the reminder of you . . . if you're not here.'

A lump gathered in my throat as I forced myself back to work, not daring to say another word as I continued.

Eventually the quiet between us settled, just as it had in the bath. I'd finished within the hour, allowing myself to smile as I triple checked it, setting aside the machine so I could wrap it gently.

'Do you like it?' I asked, strangely nervous as he held it out.

We were both standing, me still naked. He didn't answer until he reached me, his right arm circling my waist.

'I love it,' he murmured, kissing my nose first, finding my mouth moments later.

'Don't go,' I whispered as he drew back, aware that it was late, with another full day ahead in not many hours. 'Stay here, with me.'

He did. And with creeping exhaustion, curled around each other, I watched as he finally fell asleep. I waited a few moments, eyes heavy in the darkness, as his breathing softened, his hands still on my skin. When I kissed him softly on the forehead, he didn't stir.

'Jesse,' I whispered, tears instantly springing forward, falling onto the pillow as I closed my eyes, 'I think . . . I'm in love with you.'

Chapter 14
Hestia

As life sped up over the next couple of weeks, I was both grateful and . . . lost.

Cole was busy off the ranch, his brother's wedding rapidly approaching. Jesse picked up his slack, taking over more work than ever. In turn, I offered to step in, taking his morning round feeding and prepping the horses as well as sorting and cleaning tack for the day.

I could see how touched he was by my offer. Initially he tried to resist, knowing how I loathed mornings, but ultimately he was too tired to refuse.

So, my head won over my heart. I made myself as busy as everyone else, giving myself the extra distance from him – from all of them – that I needed.

Because I couldn't begin to process how I now knew I felt – the words that'd scared me so fucking shitless when I'd said them aloud that I'd struggled to sleep since. Only the fact that he hadn't heard me, crashed out and blissfully unaware, was keeping everything together. It was contained, and all I needed to do was stamp it the fuck back down and bury it.

Jesse deserved the fucking world.

Not an emotional wasteland like me.

Avoiding Lottie was harder. She knew things were off, but she gave me space. After her experience with Cole, trying to get to know him and fall in love in the midst of a busy working ranch, she was trying to give me the time I knew she hadn't had.

I missed her.

I even missed the old Cal; those moments when we had worked as friends . . . That had evaporated like the mists that hung over the pitch lake water. He'd messaged a couple of times, apologetic for our last angry phone call, trying to work his way back in.

My new routine became a silent meditation after the first week: measuring out feed for the horses, taking the buckets around, starting to brush down one after another. My soundtrack was the soft sound of crunching as they ate, their warm breath on my hand as I greeted them.

'Hey, baby demon,' I cooed, entering Luci's stall and delivering her breakfast. I took small satisfaction at the way she now approached me, her head low as I scratched her favourite spot. 'I'm going to have to rename you at this point,' I added as she instantly rested her head on my arm. 'You better be a bitch to someone today, okay? You've a rep to keep.'

Checking her wounds, relieved as the healing continued, I kissed her on the nose as I backed out. She followed me to the door, ignoring her food and putting her head over as I locked it behind me.

'See you later on,' I murmured, reminding myself that for her, too, I wouldn't always be able to keep that promise.

In danger of choking up, I glanced down towards Lottie's cabin, where Jesse and Cole were now setting up for the morning. There were only a few last touches to the deck needed before the kitchen got delivered, which would be soon. Taking a breath, I headed back up to the ranch house, determined to keep my hands and brain busy.

Breakfast. I'd make them breakfast and take it down there.

That way I could still see Jesse, but only briefly, with Cole's presence to keep things neutral. I didn't trust myself with him alone any more.

The challenge of cooking food was exactly what I needed – and two espressos and half an hour later, I was walking up the freshly laid dirt track to the cabin. Pushing loose strands of hair out of my face, my hair pulled up into a high pony, I looked out over the lake as the sun set the morning sky ablaze. Half squinting as I approached, I almost missed Jesse watching me from the deck. He set his tools aside and stood up.

'Hey,' he said softly, jumping off and stepping over to close the distance between us.

His kiss was immediate, gentle at first, then more insistent. My body leapt into its core response to him, leaving me breathless as we parted.

'I've missed you these last few nights,' he whispered, reaching down to take the bag I held between us. 'I'm sorry it's been so crazy. It'll settle down once the wedding's done and some of the guests head home next week.'

I nodded, still startled by breakneck speed with which my feelings had torn through my flimsy defences. Stepping back, I scrambled to keep it normal.

'I thought you guys might be hungry,' I replied, looking up as Cole walked round the side of the cabin.

'We get takeout now?' he smiled, nodding with gratitude as I handed over the wrapped bacon sandwich.

'Don't get used to it,' I replied, handing one to Jesse. I hadn't missed his questioning glance, recognizing I'd pulled away too quickly. 'I just know you're all on overtime, so I figured I'd get domestic for once.'

Cole smiled as they perched on the deck, wolfing down the food in seconds.

'You not eating?' Jesse asked quietly, his brow still furrowed.

'I had mine at the house,' I lied, unwilling to explain that my stomach had barely stopped churning for days now; how it made eating difficult. 'Couldn't wait. Chef's privilege.'

Cole grunted a laugh as he finished, getting up.

'Hold up a minute there, would you?' he asked, turning to go into the cabin. 'Got something I want your opinion on.'

As he disappeared inside, Jesse reached out a hand to me, gently pulling me down to sit beside him on the deck.

'Talk to me,' he said, real concern now spreading across his features. 'What's wrong?'

I just shook my head, resolutely staring at my lap when I couldn't meet his eyes.

'I'm just tired, that's all. We all are,' I replied, chancing a look up.

'Bullshit,' he whispered, eyes narrowing. 'You've been off all week, longer. Is it because I haven't been around as much? Honey, I'm sorry – you've got to know it's not because I don't want to be. I've missed being with you so much—'

Snapping back up to standing, I shook my head so vehemently that he stopped dead. This right here, this was why it couldn't work between us.

He was too good for me. I'd known it the moment we'd visited his mum – before that, even. At the sale, after it. In his every gesture, his every thought towards me, there was nothing but light and kindness.

And I . . . I was the vacuum that would pull him into darkness. I would ruin him with my issues, my fucked-up past and emotional destruction.

It only confirmed my feelings. This *was* it; this *was* love. That I would rather walk away and protect him from my chaos than make him suffer.

Cole's footsteps back onto the deck broke the tension. Holding what looked like a small box in his hand, he gave me a sheepish smile, turning to a more knowing one as he looked at Jesse.

'So . . . uh, I wanted your opinion on something,' he began, stepping down to the grass next to me. 'Now, I realize it looks a little like I jumped the gun, and I know you're maybe not as, um . . . traditional as Lottie, maybe, but I know what you think will be important. To her and me.'

I raised my eyebrow, unsure why my heart rate was speeding up.

'Okay,' I replied slowly, tilting my head to try to see what was in his hand. 'Sharing is caring, cowboy – spit it out.'

With a quick glance at Jesse – whose eyes were still trained on me, a tightness to the corners of his mouth – Cole revealed a deep-blue velvet box.

As I suddenly realized what it was, he opened it, revealing . . .

'Oh shit,' I murmured, my hand drifting to cover my now open mouth.

The ring that nestled in the box was . . . stunning. A silver band with a raised diamond set in the top, surrounded by a halo of tiny diamonds.

'I know it's all so fast,' he began, anxiety winding into his voice. 'And I'm not planning to ask her straight away, especially when things are still difficult with her dad.' He glanced at me, almost pleading. 'But I know she's *it* for me, and . . . I want her – *need* her to be my wife.'

Swallowing hard, I felt my eyes fill immediately. Jesse moved to get up, but I shook my head quickly, asking him to wait.

'It's beautiful, Cole,' I replied eventually, keeping my voice steady as I looked up at him, his relief registering instantly. 'And I know it's been quick, but you have nothing to worry about, or wait for. Lottie will say yes. She'd marry you tomorrow if you wanted.'

It was his turn to look down, his emotion barely concealed.

'And you . . . you wouldn't be against that?' he asked quietly, glancing back up for a moment, his deep brown eyes fearful.

'What? Against it?' I questioned, reaching out to put a hand on his arm. 'What makes you think that? I – You guys are made for each other. I've never seen Lottie so happy.'

He nodded.

'I just . . . well, Lottie said you're not really a big fan of marriage, that it's not something you'd want. So, I don't know . . . you guys are so close. I just wanted your blessing, I guess.'

Looking skyward for a moment, forcing the tears back, I stepped in towards him and gave him a hug.

He responded after a surprised pause. My thoughts swirled, processing the idea that a huge bear of a man like this, the backbone of the ranch, could be so vulnerable for the sake of my best friend as to want *my* approval.

I pulled back, still holding his arm.

'You have my blessing, in fucking spades,' I urged him, tightening my grip. 'Don't let her prick dad or my fucked-up thoughts on marriage derail this. Lottie loves you more than you can know – and if you feel the same way, why wait? Isn't that the way things are done here?' I gave him a small smile, relieved that he returned it; Lil's words were ringing in my ears from before. 'Listen. Lottie's always been the better side of our coin,' I continued, catching Jesse's pained expression in the corner of my eye. 'I have some really fucked-up stuff in my past, Cole.'

I hesitated, but realized this was my chance to warn Jesse as much as it was to explain to Cole.

'My stepfather was . . . abusive, emotionally,' I began, forcing myself to continue as they looked at each other briefly, open anger registering on Jesse's face. 'When he married my mum . . . well, he took the chance to use their wedding to tell me just how he was going to fuck me over, to control my life and hers. It was the beginning of the worst time of my life.'

'It's okay, you don't have to tell me,' Cole reassured, his voice softer than I'd ever heard before.

I shook my head.

'I need you to know where it comes from,' I murmured, roughly wiping my face as tears escaped. 'It's not about you or whether I like you enough for Lottie, okay? That's not even a question. I just . . . I guess I just associate getting married with . . . hell.'

They were both silent for a moment as I fought to get it together.

'Are you sure you want to come to Jay's wedding?' Jesse asked, his voice barely above a whisper. 'I don't want it to bring anything up, or—'

Cole moved in and gave me a brief hug in return.

'I'll give you guys a minute.'

Hands on my hips, I stared down at my boots and wiped my eyes again as the quiet returned.

'I'm so fucking sorry,' Jesse said, his hand flinching as though he wanted to reach out, but stopping himself. 'That must be . . .'

'. . . A head-fuck?' I finished with a bitter smile. 'Yeah. It is. Even ten years later.'

'Listen, we don't have to go,' he said, studying my face carefully. 'Jay and Cole would understand. We could just hang out, just the two of us.'

My heart lurched at the way he was so ready to support me at his own expense. The thought of time alone with him, a whole day of *us*. I wanted it so badly, wanted him so much that the feeling became painful. My gut twisted with it.

'No, it's okay,' I said, backing up. 'It'll be good for me or something. Don't worry.'

His eyes burned into mine as I turned, making myself walk away. One step after another until my body was on autopilot, knowing full well he was still watching; that one stumble would have him running to me to pick up the pieces.

So I kept going, hoping that I loved him enough to not stop.

'Hes?'

Lottie's head emerged around my door, make-up and hair already done. The wedding wasn't for another few hours, but Cole's best man duties had already begun. He was swinging by to pick us up in less than an hour.

'Want a coffee? Irish coffee?' she offered as I turned to her, finishing my make-up in the mirror. 'Valium?'

I grimaced, waiting as she strode across the room and grabbed me into a hug.

'What's this for?' I asked gruffly, squeezing her back. 'You look fucking gorgeous, by the way.'

'Because I know how hard weddings are for you,' she whispered into my neck, pulling back gently so as not to disturb the pinned curls all over my head.

'Aversion therapy,' I shrugged.

'And – you look . . . stunning,' she said. 'I've never seen this look before?'

I glanced back at the mirror, noting how different I looked without my darker, smudged eyes, the complete coverage I normally favoured with my foundation. This time I'd kept it light, letting my tan and freckles through, opting for light, clean make-up – baby pink blush, soft highlighter. Long half-lashes and eyeliner only, a raspberry pink lip stain.

The truth was, I'd started applying my usual look, feeling more and more fake as I went. It felt so obviously like a mask, an attempt to be funny, ballsy, sweary Hestia, that I'd washed it all off. This version of me . . . I didn't know her. But somehow, that matched my insides.

'Thanks . . . I'm trying it out,' I replied, struggling to keep my voice normal. Behave normally. 'Besides, my dress is doing *a lot* of the talking.'

She chuckled.

'Did you forewarn Jesse?'

I tried to smile back, but my stomach turned over at the thought of it. I'd ordered the dress a while ago, just after the cookout, when my head, heart . . . everything felt different.

Lottie's eyes narrowed, finally reaching out a hand and pulling me over to the edge of the bed to sit.

'Okay, okay. Enough. Spit it out. Leaving you be to figure things out with Jesse is one thing, but you look fucking miserable.'

I gritted my teeth, warring with myself about how much to share. She'd never accept that I wasn't good enough for Jesse, that I would pollute and poison something so good. So I went for the other side of my turmoil, the other factor that complicated it, that would prevent us even exploring what could be – even if miracles were possible and I wasn't a fucking mess.

'I guess . . . I'm just suddenly really aware of how little time I have here, that whatever I feel about Jesse . . .' I stopped, twisting my hands together. 'I can't just stay like you. My visa only has another three, four months, max. Then that's it. I'm out and can't come back for, what, another year?'

'You'd want to stay longer?' Lottie breathed, eyes widening. 'Because of Jesse? Does that mean you really—'

'It doesn't matter, though, does it?' I replied, trying not to shut down the excitement she was trying so hard to hide. 'He has enough going on in his life without my bullshit. His mum, this place, the fact that I can't watch him bull ride without wanting to throw up.'

Lottie pursed her lips, placing her hand over mine.

'Listen. Lil comes home in a couple of weeks – let's talk to her. We might be able to get things organized for a work visa, if we can get you on payroll. There are options, Hes. But as for Jesse . . .' She paused, her expression softening. 'He doesn't see what you guys have like that, from what he said.'

I stared at her, searching her eyes.

'What did he say?'

'It was in confidence,' she began, but as I dead-eyed her, she rolled hers. 'But the gist of it was that he would go to the ends of the fucking earth for you.'

I bit my lip. That was just Jesse, though. He would always give himself to other people, regardless of the impact on his own wellbeing.

'Thanks,' I said softly, taking a deep breath. 'But let's just get through this afternoon first. I don't want to be a downer.'

She stared at me for a moment, her brow furrowing.

'I wish you could see what I see,' she murmured, reaching out to pull out a pin from one of the curls, winding it around her finger as it fell, bouncing onto my collarbone. 'What everyone that really gets to know you sees.'

I shook my head.

'Don't be nice to me,' I begged, pointing to my face. 'If I cry off my eyelashes I'll be pissed, took fucking ages.'

'Fine,' she said brightly, getting up and adjusting her robe. 'You're absolutely not the kindest, most giving person I know, with a fucking huge heart that you don't know what to do with. Absolutely not. Now put the damn dress on and meet me out front.'

Almost smiling, I got up.

'You're extra hot when you're mean, you know,' I replied, catching her smile in return, expanding as she flipped me off.

Less than ten minutes later, my biggest concern shifted to keeping my rack in my dress.

It was a simple, raspberry-red satin shift with thin straps, the neck and back dipping low, and I was in desperate need of tit tape. The chances of finding any in Jackson Hole – fuck it, Wyoming – were likely slim to none.

Steeling myself, I put on the pale, metallic gold heels, the straps winding up above my ankles. The dress still almost brushed the floor, a thigh-high split on one side allowing me to walk, but after two months of boots, heels felt like hell.

My hair was unpinned, brushed into waves, and with a last look at the woman in the mirror, I knew exactly who I looked like.

There were voices outside the front door, the sound of a truck pulling away as I opened the door and stepped out, checking the decking carefully so as not to catch my heels in the gaps.

Head down as I lifted the front of my dress to take the step onto the drive, I realized the voices had stopped.

Looking up, brushing my hair back from my eyes, I saw three sets of eyes staring right back.

'Holy hell,' Lottie said finally, her mouth half open as she looked to Cole, also wide-eyed. 'I've never . . . wow.'

But I wasn't listening. I could only focus on the grey eyes nearest to me, the way they clung to me, as though to look away would be to starve. Jesse's expression was stunned, what had been a relaxed pose in a sharp, dark navy suit turned to stone.

'Thanks,' I said quietly, stepping over as Jesse cleared his throat, looking away, towards Cole's truck.

'We should go,' he said, his tone as rigid as his body language. My heart dropped. I'd walked away from him earlier, pulled back from his attempts to help me.

Cole nodded as Lottie took his arm, her pale blue dress, the twin to mine, shimmering in the afternoon sun that sliced across the drive.

'Jesse,' I called, keeping my voice soft. He hesitated for a moment, then turned back to me, waiting until I drew level with him. 'I'm sorry for earlier. It was a lot – I didn't mean –'

He shook his head gently, meeting my eyes again briefly.

'Nothing to be sorry for,' he whispered, his voice rough. 'Never is, honey.'

'Then what?' I urged, unable to bear the pain in his eyes.

He hesitated again.

'I can't . . .' He looked back at me, burying his hands in his suit pockets. 'I don't know how to do this.'

A feeling of cold dread gripped my insides. Suddenly, the thought that Jesse was about to push me away felt like a gut punch.

'What do you –' I began, stopping as he finally gave in, turning fully and taking his hands from his pockets to hold mine instead.

'I don't know how to pretend, Jessica,' he murmured, looking all over me, his eyes like fingertips over my skin. 'Like I don't think you're the most beautiful, incredible woman I've ever met. I don't know how to give you space or time or whatever you need right now . . . because I can't not touch you, or not want to be with you.'

I just stared back at him, floored by the force of feeling in his voice, how he so clearly meant it with his whole heart.

'Guys?' Lottie called, forcing us back to reality.

Gradually, he let go of my hands, a space opening up between us as we walked to the truck, together but apart.

And amid the occasional concerned glances from Lottie, the small talk and greetings as we arrived at the wedding venue, that's how we continued. Forcing my thoughts to stay in the moment, right there with everyone, the wedding itself didn't prompt the anxiety it could've. Cole's brother Jay and his new wife, Lianne, were so clearly in love, their families and friends all in tune with those vibes, that I almost relaxed.

But I kept my eyes down, never daring to stray close to Jesse despite our physical proximity. I felt his presence like a guiding hand on my back, his gaze on me throughout.

It wasn't until after the dinner, as evening stole over the party during Cole's short and sweet speech, that I started looking up. As his words became more personal, bringing tears to both Lottie and Lianne's eyes, it hit me. This was going to be Lottie and Cole sometime soon.

And I couldn't do this to her. I had to find a way to show up for both of them, and . . .

'Come with me,' Jesse asked, holding out his hand as he stood. 'Please.'

I wanted to run. My response to emotion was so engrained that refusing it brought flutters of panic up from the depths.

But I couldn't.

I placed my hand in his, and we navigated the packed dance floor towards the open double doors leading onto a vast wooden deck. The venue backed onto the beginning of the wilderness, facing away from Jackson's lights. As Jesse led me outside, the Wyoming night subsumed us, everything behind fading away. The deep velvet sky was studded with infinite stars, the towering mountain peaks the only true blackness against it. The coolness of the air was offset by his warmth as he drew me close to him.

'Are you doing okay?' he asked, one hand gently circling my waist, the other brushing against my arm.

'I think so,' I whispered, my heart racing, not able to help myself leaning into him, overwhelmed by the sensation of peace as we stayed that way. As the moments passed, he rested his chin on my head, and I could feel him working up to something.

'Why won't you let me in?' he whispered, his lips brushing my hair.

I closed my eyes, not wanting the peace to end but drawing back a little.

'I have,' I replied after a moment, looking up, biting my lip as he locked me into his gaze. 'That's the problem,' I added, my throat threatening to close.

He frowned, his fingers brushing my jaw.

'Did I do something that last night we spent together?' he asked, his eyes flashing to his wrist, to the tattoo that lay under the shirt cuff. 'Since then, I . . .'

'You didn't do anything wrong,' I whispered, laying a hand over his heart. 'It's me. It's always me. My fault.'

'Hestia, stop.' His voice was pained, his beautiful face shaped by it. 'Just tell me what's going on.'

I held my breath, the lump in my throat building. There was nothing else to say, every other explanation fading to nothing.

'I care about you,' I whispered, watching as his eyes softened. 'I care . . . too much. I don't know how . . . or what to do—'

But before I could finish, he took my face in his hands, tilting it up, our lips agonizingly close.

'I care about you too,' he murmured, stroking his thumb against my jaw as I struggled to take it in. 'More than you know. And if you'll let me, I want to figure this out.' He paused, studying my reaction. 'But Jessica, honey, you have to let me in.'

Desperate to say the words I really felt in return, feeling them churn over and over in my mind, I did the only thing I knew how.

Slowly, gently, I brought my lips to his.

The response was instant, a lit fuse sparking into a chain reaction between our bodies. A release: days of barely touching each other falling away and taking us back to the moments after our last night together.

'Take me home,' I whispered, shuddering as his hand brushed the bare skin on my back.

'I need you to understand how much I want there to be an *us*,' he insisted, his breathing ragged. 'This isn't just sex for me, not now.'

'You don't know what you're letting yourself in for,' I whispered, searching his eyes, wanting him to understand how difficult it would be. 'I've never . . . I feel more for you than I ever have, but –'

'Let me find out for myself,' he returned, stroking my hair. 'I'm not gonna run away if things get complicated.'

And even though I knew it was wrong, that I was giving in to my own selfish desire, I moved back into him. He wrapped himself around me in response as I gripped him back, unwilling to let go, for now.

Chapter 15
Hestia

'You really do look like her,' Jesse mused, propping his head on his hand as he lay next to me. His hair was mussed from last night, the soft morning light turning it a deep, burnished gold.

I raised an eyebrow, wondering for one horrific moment if he was about to name an ex.

'Jessica Rabbit,' he replied, melting into a smile as I did, my arm bent under my head on the pillow. Glancing down to the end of the bed, I could see the red satin pooled on the floor beyond, right where he'd slipped the straps off my shoulders.

We were here again, in our safe space between reality and the depths inside both of us.

'I didn't get a chance to tell you how good you looked in that suit,' I murmured, reaching out to run my finger over his broad shoulder, following the hard grooves of the muscle down his arm. 'I was trying so hard to hold it together that I didn't say.'

'Honey, I know it's your style to show, not tell,' he said, a sly smile emerging across his lips as he leant down towards me. 'And knowing what I do now, I'm even more in awe of you.'

Confused, I moved my finger to his lips as he brought himself in to kiss me.

'What do you mean?' I asked, barely able to hold off the urge to let the fire take over again, but too curious not to know.

'That you went ahead and came to the wedding, even though it hurt; that you went through hell in your past.' He kissed my finger. 'That's no small thing. I know you think your demons are bigger than you, but I see you in there, fighting. And I'm fucking rooting for you, honey.'

I felt his words seep in, heard them repeat in my mind as he finally closed the gap between us, his mouth finding mine for a moment. Once again, as though my tears were wired to his voice, the familiar prickle behind my eyelids began.

'I don't know what I did to deserve finding you,' I whispered as we drew back, lips still touching.

'Well, you did, Jessica. And I'm right here, always. You don't have to be alone.'

I looked down, not brave enough to share just how much of a nerve that'd hit. I found his hand instead, the touch of his skin an instant relief as he twined his fingers with mine.

'Now I've got a suggestion,' he said, a more playful tone taking over. 'Given we've got the whole day off, and despite having slept with you . . .' I looked back at him as he paused, apparently trying to count. 'Damn, I actually can't remember how many times,' he admitted, his sheepish smile somehow drawing my own smile in return. 'Anyway – what I mean to say is, I've never even made you breakfast. But given my pretty basic kitchen skills, and the fact that I want it to just be you and me right now, why don't we head on out into town?'

Within the hour, we were parked up outside Molly's Diner. Jesse took my hand as I stepped onto the pavement with him. Town was busy already: locals and tourists wandering around, the beginnings of a queue at the diner door.

'This okay?' he asked as my fingers tightened around his.

His eyes were clear under the brim of his hat as I nodded in return.

'As long as I don't get tackled by buckle bunnies for stealing Jackson's star bull rider,' I replied, smiling as he chuckled.

'I'd like to see them try,' he smirked as I side-eyed him. 'With those nails and that mouth, ain't no one round here that'd stand a damn chance.'

'Hey, Chrissy,' he said as we entered, raising his hand to a petite blonde with a Molly's T-shirt tucked into her tiny denim shorts.

She waved back, shooting me a curious glance before gesturing towards the one free booth near the back.

'Friend of yours?' I asked as we headed over to it, looking back to see her talking to two other women behind the counter. Their gazes lifted to meet mine as I shifted focus back to Jesse.

'Kinda,' he said, then after a half-beat added, 'An ex, actually. Reformed bunny.'

I raised my eyebrows as we slid into the burgundy leather seats, sitting opposite each other.

'How far am I from your usual type?' I asked, trying to keep my voice casual, but judging by his deep chuckle, failing spectacularly.

'Are you jealous, Jessica?' he teased, moving my legs between his under the table, squeezing them with his knees.

I shrugged, grabbing the menu and starting to read.

'Damn. You are *cute* when you're jealous,' he mused, grinning as I dead-eyed him back.

'Long time no see, cowboy!'

We glanced up as Chrissy appeared next to the table, her smile as big as her considerable rack. Her voice was bubblegum sweet and her substantial lips were glossed with sparkling pink.

'Oh hey,' Jesse said, smiling. 'Thanks for holding the table, I figured it'd be crazy on rodeo Saturday.'

'Right,' she agreed, her smile fading slightly as her eyes flicked over to me. 'Are you visiting for the rodeo?'

I turned to her fully, sweeping my hair back as I raised my Ray-Bans. Her eyes fell on my tats, the way the twining flowers at the bottom of the Sleepy Hollow scene descended under the neckline of my top.

'No, actually,' I replied, feeling Jesse's eyes on my face. 'I'm here for the bull rider.'

I gave her a slow smile, enjoying the surprise that now lit her expression as she glanced at him, struggling to recover. Jesse glanced down, amusement radiating.

'Well . . . that's . . . can I get you both started? Some coffee?' she started, then with a glance at me, 'Or tea?'

'Black coffee, thanks,' I replied, waiting for Jesse to order before reaching across the table to put my hand on his. 'Choose for me on the food? I'll have whatever you have.'

It was petty, I knew it was, but I couldn't deny the satisfaction as she glanced down at our hands together.

'You're just here for the bull rider, huh?' he teased as she left, shaking his head. 'You enjoyed that, didn't you?'

'Not as much as last night,' I shrugged, leaning forward over the table, watching as his eyes drifted south to the buttons that strained on my tank top. 'Just wanted to make things clear to her.'

'Does that mean you're gonna be okay with the bull rider entering the rodeo tonight?' he asked, his eyes pinched despite his smile.

Immediately I was back in the stands at the last rodeo, watching helplessly as he was tossed around, horns and hooves just inches from his face. I must have known then just what he meant to me, even if I couldn't admit it to myself at the time.

'If I can go to a wedding, I can stand a rodeo,' I said, knowing I wasn't convincing either of us.

'I won't do anything stupid,' he urged, his eyes pleading. 'I swear. But a couple more wins and I'm gonna be in line for some serious prize money, you know? It'll take a huge weight off of Mom's shoulders.'

I nodded as the coffee arrived.

'At least a bull ride is just eight seconds, right?' I said as he nodded.

'If you hang on that long, yeah.'

'Much easier than a wedding, then,' I countered, releasing his hand to circle my mug.

He considered me for a moment, smiling as he added cream and sugar to his.

'Okay, how about this – would you rather go to another wedding, or try barrel racing in front of the rodeo crowd?'

I laughed, the thought of desperately clinging on to Buckeye in the way Bailey did so deeply unlikely.

'You mean, fall on my ass in the dirt in front of hundreds of people, or a wedding?' I corrected, grinning as he shrugged. 'Ugh. Okay – barrel racing. It'd be over quicker.'

He nodded. 'Would you rather . . . go to a wedding or sky-dive? No, wait – what do they call it? Base jumping – right off the top of the tallest mountains back there.'

He pointed out towards the jagged peaks in the distance.

I shuddered.

'No way. I can't do heights,' I admitted, watching as he reacted with surprise.

'So, heights, huh? That your limit?'

'I mean, don't ask me to climb into a confined space with a bunch of spiders, but yeah. I'm sure there's no better view than those mountains . . .' I paused as our food arrived, glancing with alarm at the volume of it – pancakes, eggs, bacon, fried potatoes . . . 'But don't ever ask me to climb one.'

'Okay, last one,' he warned, offering me the maple syrup before taking it for himself.

'When do I get a turn?' I asked, my heart stuttering at his smile in response.

'When you've answered my last one. Truthfully.'

I sipped my coffee, waiting. He stopped for a moment, looking me straight in the eye.

'Would you rather . . . live here in Jackson, or in London?'

The insinuation was like a bell ringing directly in my ears, the complexity of the answer too much to distil into one word.

I opened my mouth, then closed it, knowing what it would mean, what he would take from it. A promise, one I didn't know if I could keep.

'Jackson,' I whispered, feeling his legs grip against mine. 'London made me, it's my home, but . . .'

'No mountains, right?' he added softly, picking up his fork. 'Or Molly's.'

I managed a half-smile, grateful for the steer away from the depths.

'No mountains,' I replied, tilting my head. 'No Molly's, bulls or bunnies.'

After we'd finished, me swearing I wouldn't need to eat again until tomorrow, he gave me a curious glance.

'So what *is* in London? Why live there?'

I leant back against the padded back of the booth, somehow knowing and not knowing the answer.

'It's where I've always been, since I left home anyway,' I began, my head straying back to my old flat, the studio. 'It's where Cal and I started the business, where our friends are . . .' I tailed off, realizing how I'd worded that, knowing he was too perceptive to let it pass.

'Are you two still . . . friends?' he asked, a sudden hardness to his jaw as I considered it.

'We're not in a relationship, Jesse,' I clarified. 'That ended way back. It's the business that's kept us working together.'

I sighed, suddenly plunged back into thoughts of having to return to it, of dealing with Cal again. As Jesse leant over, brow creased, my phone buzzed. Confused, knowing it was only set to vibrate with calls, I turned it over to see 'Diane' on the screen.

Cal's mum.

'What the hell?' I muttered, shooting Jesse an apologetic glance as I picked up, holding it to my ear as our bill arrived.

'Hi Diane,' I answered, passing my wallet to Jesse, which he promptly pushed away. 'Is everything okay?'

'Oh, hello love,' she said, a quiet, underlying tiredness in her tone immediately setting me on edge. We'd always got along, even during the time Cal and I were falling apart. 'It's not great news, I'm afraid. Cal's . . . unwell. He's been admitted to hospital again.' She paused for a second, her voice cracking. 'It all happened last night, when he was alone. His new friend found him.'

I froze, thinking – knowing – why.

'Shit. Is it the same as before?' I asked, Jesse now watching with concern.

'Yes,' she choked as I closed my eyes, leaning on the table. 'Not quite as bad, but . . .' She seemed to gather herself, exhaling deeply. 'Hestia, I don't want to have to ask this of you, but I think he needs help – with the business, at least. I knew he wasn't coping, but . . . I'm not sure he can do it without you. He fell out with Blake last week and he took off – it sounds like things have been too much. I know how hard you've both worked for it. I just thought you'd want a chance to fix things before it goes too far.'

I swallowed, feeling Jesse's hand on my arm.

'Okay,' I whispered, 'I'll see what I can do. Is someone with him?'

'I'm here right now,' she said, sighing. 'Taking turns with his . . . friend.'

'Becca, by any chance?' I asked, remembering the phone call, how hard I'd been on him.

'I'm sorry, love, yeah, it is,' she replied, further sadness in her tone.

'It's okay,' I lied, leaning into Jesse's touch for a moment, the realization sinking in. 'I'll let you know when I've made plans.'

We hung up and I swore under my breath, Jesse waiting until I looked up at him.

'Long story,' I clarified. 'I'll tell you in the truck.'

Back outside and climbing in, my head began to spin in the sudden quiet.

Launching into an explanation, I included the last time Cal had landed in hospital after a huge bender, taking so many pills that the doctors hadn't known if he'd wake up with any kind of brain function.

Jesse's face darkened, one hand gripping the steering wheel as the implication dawned.

'So . . . you've got to go home, for your business? For . . . him?' he questioned, bowing his head for a moment.

'I think so . . . unless there's a way I can convince Blake to come back and run things, but it sounds like Cal's fucked that up too.'

He swore, his whole upper body tensing.

'Will it be temporary? You can come back here, right?' he checked, turning to me. There was no disguising the pain in his eyes.

A sense of hopelessness washed over me at the awful inevitability of what was now playing out.

'Maybe,' I said, barely able to tolerate the desperation that widened his eyes. 'I'm not sure how, without losing the studio. It's everything I've worked towards . . . but I . . .'

'Hestia,' he murmured, leaning over to me, his hand brushing my neck, along my jaw. 'I can't lose you. Not so soon, please.'

I nodded, biting my lip, unable to see a way out.

'I was always going to have to go back,' I replied, lifting my hand to cover his.

'I know, but . . .' His brow furrowed as he struggled with the words I knew were there, waiting to be said. 'Things have changed,' he added, looking into my eyes, a sense of urgency building. 'I hoped – maybe with some more time . . .'

I nodded, a numbness building in my chest, trying to block out the creeping dread.

'Let's go back to the ranch,' I suggested, my voice flat. 'I'll make some calls, okay?'

He stared at me for a moment longer before setting off, a new kind of silence gathering between us as we headed back.

A couple of hours later, with calls made and no solution in sight – Blake point-blank refusing to help, thanks to Cal's behaviour – I wandered back out of the house. Jesse, unable to bear the waiting, had headed down to the cabin to help Cole.

As I walked down the drive, I knew I'd decided. What I had to do, what needed to be done. I stopped, knowing that if I didn't arrange it now, I might back out later. A quick search on my phone confirmed flights out to Denver tomorrow evening, a whole host of connecting flights back to London between that evening and the day after.

My stomach lurched at the thought of leaving – of Jesse.

'Oh hey, cowpoke,' Bailey called, tilting her hat against the bright sunlight as she led Dunkin out. 'You noticed how that wild horse of yours has turned into everyone's favourite?'

I forced a smile, focusing on Luci – the original reason I'd stayed for longer in the first place – and remembering just how far she'd come in that time.

'Yeah, she's a charmer,' I said, shaking my head as I approached the corral. 'Starting to feel guilty about the name now.'

Bailey snorted.

'You know, I'm not sure she's even been broken yet. She's pretty young, and those assholes that had her before you didn't do fucking squat, other than hurt her.'

'Does that mean she can't be ridden yet?' I asked, more aware than ever of how little I really knew about horses, despite all the other stuff I'd done since arriving.

Bailey nodded, running her hand down Dunkin's previously injured leg, clearly checking for something.

'Yeah, makes it hard to justify keeping them on here, you know? Everyone's got to earn their place. Breaking horses is hard work.'

I bit my lip, almost afraid to walk back into the barn, knowing how Luci would greet me; that now, with what I had to do, the trust she'd put in me was worthless.

'Hey, do you remember the friend you mentioned before – the one at the horse shelter?'

Bailey's attention snapped back to me, frowning as she stood up.

'Rosie? Yeah,' she nodded. 'She's Dee's cousin, actually.'

I nodded. Dee was yet another person I would have to say goodbye to.

'I was wondering . . . maybe we could give her a call? I think I'm going to have to head home sooner than I thought. I don't want Luci to be a burden to Lottie and Lil, especially if she can't be ridden.'

'You are? Oh, shit,' she replied, walking Dunkin over to where I leant against the fence. 'I mean . . . yeah, I can give her a call. That sucks, though. Does Jesse—'

I nodded quickly, looking down at my well-worn boots, scuffed and softened into the most comfortable things I owned.

'Can you stay for the rodeo at least?' she asked, her voice lowered. 'Damn, sugar. We'll miss the hell out of you.'

'Yeah,' I said, remembering the flight times, knowing which one I could book. 'Unless . . . is me being there just going to distract him more? Maybe it might be better to stay away?'

She shook her head, holding my gaze.

'He'll be able to focus better with you there,' she said quietly, digging the toe of her boot in the dirt. 'When the only person you can think about is elsewhere, somewhere you can't go . . . that's the most difficult thing in the world.'

Her words sounded as though they came from experience, a sadness creeping in that I suspected wasn't directly related to me and Jesse.

I sighed, adjusting my hat as she gave me a look of understanding.

'I can't bear it, Bailey,' I admitted, my knuckles turning white as I gripped the fencing. Somehow it was easier to admit it to her, as the person I knew the least well, next to Cole. 'I feel like I'm torn right down the fucking middle. But maybe . . . maybe this is better for Jesse. To happen now, I mean, before we go any further.'

I didn't mean the words, I knew I didn't.

'Sugar, I'm not sure there's much further to go?' she questioned, a sad smile growing. 'I mean, I've noticed how much you guys light each other up, but it's deeper than that, isn't it? I don't want to interfere, but you should know that in all the years I've known Jesse, since high school, I know for damn sure he's never looked at anyone the way he does at you.'

Another twist in my gut, the words landing so close to home that I almost flinched.

'I'm going to see Luci,' I murmured. 'Would you call Rosie? See if we can visit her tomorrow, maybe? Or even a phone call if not.'

She nodded slowly.

"Course. You need anything else, just holler.'

I walked slowly into the barn and picked up Luci's brushes from a shelf.

'Hey, baby girl,' I whispered as I let myself into her stall, her liquid black eyes studying me for a moment before she nuzzled my arm. 'I'm so sorry,' I whispered, unable to stop the tears as they came, running unchecked as I started brushing her, hating myself all the more as she leant against me. The person she trusted most in the world.

Getting ready to leave her.

Leave a whole world behind, including someone who'd come to mean everything.

Chapter 16
Hestia

'I can't believe this is it.' Lottie's voice trembled, her head on my shoulder as we hugged. 'Your last day. What the fuck am I going to do without you?'

I'd woken up with one aim today. To get through it without crying. And yet here I was, at fucking 10 a.m., already forcing back emotion.

'Are you kidding me?' I said, pulling back and grasping her shoulders with my hands. 'I've never seen anyone so in their element. This place is all you, Lots. The cabin's almost done, you and Cole will finally have your own place to walk around naked and get as noisy as you like – you won't even notice I'm gone.'

Her eyes were glassy as she looked up for a moment, blinking, then back at me, trying to smile. We both knew the truth, of how much we'd come to rely on daily chats, small moments together that we'd not even had in London. It'd been like our uni days again, having my ride or die on call for good and bad.

'I mean, I am looking forward to that,' she admitted, hiccupping a laugh. 'But . . . it's just been amazing having you here. It feels like everything's complete, you know? Especially seeing you and Jesse . . .' She tailed off as my face changed, the yawning void of pain twisting my gut. 'He didn't say a word this morning,' she added, eyes creased in worry. 'He knows, right?'

I took a step back, taking the nearest seat at the kitchen table and shaking my head.

'He was there when Diane called and I said I'd try and find a solution, but he disappeared to help Cole and . . .' I hesitated, another ripple of pain beginning, almost taking my breath away. 'I didn't see him again after that. I went to bed pretty early . . . I don't know if he saw me asleep or what happened.'

Lottie drew out the chair opposite and sat down, facing me, our knees interlinking.

'I know Jesse a little now,' she said, waiting for me to look up, her eyes pinched as she took in my distress. 'When something is bothering him, he goes inward, into his own head. I know he won't want to be making things any harder for you. He always thinks of himself last, you know? So don't take it to mean he doesn't care about you, I know he does.'

'Maybe it's for the best,' I murmured, avoiding her gaze. 'Jesse needs someone that won't add to his list of responsibilities and problems, you know? Maybe it'll be good for us both.'

She sighed, just the sound of the kitchen clock between us.

'Look at me,' she ordered, her tone moving into business mode. As I did so, she narrowed her eyes. 'Do you love him, Hes?'

I flinched, startled, opening my mouth to respond and then closing it. There was no way of hiding it from her, not at this proximity, with her blue eyes piercing right through every façade I could manufacture.

'I don't know,' I lied, trying anyway. 'I don't know what it feels like—'

'*Bullshit*,' she hissed. 'Lying to yourself is one thing, but you can't fucking hide it from me.'

'So what?' I challenged, throwing up my hands, watching as her expression hardened. 'So what if I do? What difference does it make? Even if I wasn't a fucked-up mess incapable of loving someone like they should be, I can't stay anyway – I don't have an American passport! What are we supposed to do? Fucking get married and hope for the best?'

She sat upright, levelling me with her coolest stare.

'Yeah, maybe – that's one route,' she said, refusing to respond to my incredulous expression. 'Or there are work visas, either here at the ranch or elsewhere. It'd take some organization, but it's possible. But that's not the issue, is it?'

I clenched my jaw, only just refraining from folding my arms.

'Things don't always work out perfectly! Not everyone has everything together.'

She shook her head, slowly getting up from her chair.

'I know you've had more shit than most to live with, but at this point, Hes, you're making a choice. You are one of the smartest people I know, capable of doing anything or fixing anything you choose, but you're just not choosing to do this.' She paused, not flinching from my stare. 'You know I'm saying this with love, but maybe it's better that you do have a break, go home and reassess.'

Though delivered calmly, her words stung.

'Fine,' I replied, mirroring her calm, pretending I couldn't feel the cracks appearing deep down. 'I'm leaving after the rodeo. Are you coming?'

She shook her head, halfway to the door. We stared at each other for a moment until in the same moment we walked towards each other and hugged again.

'I love you, Hes,' she whispered.

'I love you too,' I mumbled, her hair blurring as tears formed.

Taking a breath as we let go, I watched as she walked out without turning back, lifting her hand to her eyes as she went.

I returned to packing, killing time before Dee arrived. My thoughts swirled, dwelling on Lottie's reaction, dismissing it.

This wasn't a choice I could make. Cal was self-destructing and taking our business with it, and regardless of being in love with Jesse . . . I stopped, midway through stuffing T-shirts into the corner of my case. Torturous thoughts of the moments between us, the seconds between when we'd both known exactly what the other felt and thought.

Despite that, neither of us had said it to the other. Surely, if he felt the same . . . wouldn't he have said it?

The sound of a car horn jolted me out of it. Grabbing my hat and sliding on my boots, I ran out of the front door, straight into Jesse.

'Shit, sorry,' I said as he reached out for me, his hands brushing my waist as I stepped back.

He glanced at the car, Dee smiling tentatively behind the wheel.

'You going out?' he asked, his voice rough.

I looked into his face, suddenly noting the darkness under his eyes, the way his face seemed drawn and pale.

'Yeah, to the horse shelter. Need to find a place for Luci,' I said, fighting with myself, resisting the urge to reach out and comfort him. 'I'll be at the rodeo later, okay?'

He hesitated, thoughts clearly churning.

'Can we talk then? I need to tell you –' He stopped himself. 'We just need to talk.'

I nodded, heart beginning to race.

'Okay,' I agreed, not able to help myself reaching out for a moment, brushing the side of his hand with my finger as I walked past, down the steps to the drive.

His eyes blazed as he looked back at me, the depth of feeling so painfully obvious that I almost ran straight back.

But instead, climbing into Dee's car, I shut myself down to it.

Rosie's ranch was entirely different to the Diamond Back. On the other side of Jackson, bordering the Wind River Reservation, it nestled into the valley, surrounded by open fields dotted with barns and more horses than I could count.

'Thirty-two horses and two donkeys,' Rosie admitted with a wry smile after Dee had made introductions. Her accent was a strange blend of the Wyoming twang and something else I couldn't quite catch.

'How do you cope with so many?' I asked as she led me over to the nearest barn. Dee was staying behind at the ranch house to watch Rosie's little girl, Addie. Not much of a kid person, I had to admit to being taken with the way she'd stomped outside in her own tiny cowboy boots, demanding a snack as we'd arrived. 'And with Addie, too?'

She shrugged.

'Just getting stuck in,' she admitted. 'I've always been a sucker for animals. My family moved to Sydney in Australia when I was about Addie's age, so I grew up in the city. Ended up living on a farm in the Australian outback for a couple of years after that, so when I came back here, I knew I wanted that same life again.'

'Do you miss the city?' I asked as we stepped into the barn. It was smaller than the one at the Diamond Back, but perfectly kept.

'Sometimes,' she replied, eyeing me with curiosity. 'You thinking about staying here, maybe? Dee mentioned something about Jackson's hottest bull rider.'

I smiled back at her, hoping it didn't come across as the grimace it felt like.

'Just a bit of fun,' I lied, desperate to not talk about it, think about him, for a few minutes.

She chuckled as we approached the first stall, a small, pale grey pony popping its head over the top.

'Well, I'm sure I'm not the first to warn you, but bull riders and cowboys . . . they've got a rep for a reason, you know? Fun's one thing – and good for you – but there's always a queue of women behind those guys. Especially him, right?'

The pony nudged her hand, rewarded when she pulled a couple of mint sweets from her pocket.

'Right,' I admitted – then, not able to help myself, added, 'But Jesse isn't like that, not really.'

She raised an eyebrow as I stroked the pony's nose.

'Come on now, neither of us are naive country girls who've never left the Midwest,' she countered. 'Men are all the same. They're all magpies, after the next new shiny object.' She held up her hands as I frowned. 'I'm not being a bitch, I'm just saying what I've experienced. And you are one hell of a shiny object.'

I knew what she was saying. There was a complete lack of malice in her tone.

'Yeah, you're probably right,' I sighed.

'I'm just saying, from one city girl to another, if you want to stay here, make it something for you. It's an adjustment, for sure. Took me the best part of a couple of years to settle in. Dee says you're a tattoo artist? There's a great creative community here.'

'Yeah, met a few people at the Jackson Collective,' I replied. 'Everyone's been really welcoming.'

'And now you've got yourself a horse, too?' she asked, sharing more mints with the next horse down. 'Bailey told me about the sale. Fucking assholes. Tell me about Luci, then. She not gonna cut it as a ranch horse?'

I explained that she wasn't broken in, that the thought of taking her to another horse sale to sell her on again was more than I could bear now I was going back home.

She considered it, leaning on the stall door.

'Well, I only usually take them in when there's nowhere else to turn, otherwise I'd end up with twice as many as I have now. But Bailey rates her, tells me she's got a sweet nature despite the rough start. So why don't I take her on for a while? I've been wanting to show Addie how to work with young horses, so maybe we can see if we can get Luci into ranch shape? That way, if you do come back, she may be able to go back to the Diamond Back.

Or we could sell her on to someone we know is decent, and split the profit maybe?'

I exhaled with relief.

'Thanks, Rosie,' I breathed, 'that would be amazing.'

'Well, all right then,' she smiled, eyes on the crossed swords tattoo on my right forearm. 'And maybe I can wheedle a tattoo out of the bargain too? Dee hasn't shut up about hers. Apparently half the Collective are queuing up to ask you.'

'They are?' I questioned, taken aback.

She considered me for a moment.

'It'd be great to have more interesting people like you move in round here,' she said, shooing the grey pony back as it attempted to steal the remaining mints in her hand. 'Think if you opened up for business here, you'd be pretty busy. I know people who fly to other states to get work done, too. Sure they'd come here for you.'

I thought it over, wondering if she might be right.

———

I was still wondering as I attempted to manhandle my heavy case out of the ranch house that afternoon. I was barely able to look at the now empty bedroom behind me, so full of moments of me and Jesse that I almost walked into my second cowboy of the day.

'I've got it,' Cole said, lifting it like it was nothing, a sad smile on his face. 'You sure you don't want me to take you to the airport after the show? It won't take me long to help Bailey pack up.'

I shook my head, wanting – needing – the anonymity of a taxi driver to drop me off. The thought of getting emotional with Cole was not something I was up for.

Especially when the biggest goodbye of them all was going to hurt more than I might be able to bear.

We talked about Luci on the way into town, avoiding anything that might bring us close to Jesse.

'She can just stay at the ranch, you know,' Cole said as we parked up near the chute entrance, my stomach already starting to churn as a group of cowboys walked past in full gear. 'Lottie doesn't mind at all.'

'I don't want her to be a burden,' I explained, catching his glance. 'It was my decision to buy her – I caused the problem, so I need to solve it. She's taking up money and room where she is. Plus, Rosie can help break her in. Project for her little girl, Addie.'

He smiled at that.

'Another firecracker in the making,' he replied, nodding to me. 'But Luci's not a burden, any more than you are,' he continued, with a sideways glance at me as we showed our passes at the gate and left my suitcase in one of the luggage lockers. 'To any of us, least of all Jesse.'

I felt myself tense all over, suddenly glad to hide under my hat. I wished he could be right.

'Thanks,' I said simply, eyes on the gaggle of people ahead. Competitors with numbers on their backs, bull and bronc riders surrounded by rodeo officials, and a sprinkling of women, conspicuous in their tiny skirts in a sea of leather chaps.

Among them, I realized with a start, was Chrissy – Jesse's ex from the diner. In full glam she was radiant, a fitted denim minidress and pale straw cowboy hat, cream-coloured boots and a cascade of pale blonde hair.

Cole caught my gaze as I forced myself to look away, Rosie's words about shiny objects ringing loudly in my ears.

'You met Jesse's sister, Clara, right? She's watching today,' he said, his voice soft, as though he'd guessed my thoughts. 'He wanted to let you know. Up in that stand there, to the right of the chute.'

It was where I'd sat previously, in those fear-laced moments right before . . . the other moments. In the truck afterwards.

'Okay,' I croaked, feeling that same anxiety wind itself around me again.

'He'll be fine,' Cole reassured me. 'And if I don't see you before you go, look after yourself, you hear?'

I nodded as he pulled me in a gentle hug, utterly subsuming me within his vast reach.

'Cole?' I asked, stepping back to look up, almost stalling at the kindness in his warm eyes. 'If . . . if there was going to be a, um . . . special moment coming up, would there be a specific time to come back and visit?'

A laugh rumbled in his throat as he smiled.

'I'm not a hundred per cent sure . . . maybe sometime around Thanksgiving or Christmas,' he said, shrugging. 'I'll message you. But are you sure you won't be back before then? Is there no chance?'

'Honestly . . . I don't know.'

He nodded, his smile fading to concern at my expression.

'I'll miss you, Hestia. We all will.'

I nodded. I was reaching my limit, the internal floodgates only just holding back. Smiling as I turned, especially when he touched the brim of his hat to me, I headed up the stairs just as the bull riding was announced.

'Hestia! Over here!' Clara waved, a spare beer in one hand.

I picked my way over, receiving a hug as I arrived.

'So I hear you're leaving us, huh?' she said after the initial greetings, her curiosity clearly too great not to get straight into it.

I explained about the business, the whole situation with Cal.

She rolled her eyes at that.

'Men are fucking useless sometimes, huh?' she replied, shaking her head. 'I mean, not all of them, but I always think things are best left to women to manage, if you actually want to get it done . . . You're coming back though, right? We're throwing a big party for Mom next month, it's her goddamn sixtieth, can you believe it? She's asked if you'd come.'

'I want to,' I said, pausing as the announcer read out Jesse's name. My stomach churned and I clutched the beer bottle. 'But I don't know if I can.'

Her face changed, as though she'd suddenly understood something, a frown appearing.

'Oh . . . shit. Does Jesse know that?' she asked, my own face giving it away before I had a chance to answer. 'Well. Fuck.'

'I need to speak to him,' I said, trying not to flinch as the gate opened to the first bull rider, the crowd roaring.

She nodded, watching with me as the bull flung him off in under eight seconds, making a dash for the fence and away from the flailing hooves.

'Do you guys have a few more days at least? Maybe make some plans?' she asked, leaning back, looking over towards the chute. I knew she was looking for him – so I stared dead ahead, watching the wranglers get the bull under control and back in the pen.

'My flight is in a few hours,' I murmured, catching her surprise in the corner of my eye.

She said nothing for a moment, just looked into her beer, taking a breath. I glanced over, watching what looked to be turmoil.

'I don't want to leave,' I confided as she looked back at me, intensity in her grey eyes. They were so similar to Jesse's that I almost couldn't hold her gaze.

'Go find him,' she blurted, a real sense of urgency in her voice. 'Get out of here together, spend whatever time you have left together. Fuck the competition.'

I recoiled, surprised.

'What?'

She grimaced to herself, seemingly considering her words carefully.

'He's told me just how much he cares about you,' she said quietly, and I felt myself still. 'And it's my guess that you feel the same. Am I wrong?'

Pinned to the spot, I could only shake my head.

'Then go. There will be plenty more bulls to ride next week. You're only here for another couple of hours.'

Butterflies releasing, I stood as she did, her hand squeezing my shoulder.

'I'll see you again,' she said, nodding. 'I know it. Now go talk to him.'

In a daze, unsure why I couldn't do otherwise, I climbed back down the steps, blindly looking for him, any sign of the now familiar Diamond Back jacket. Wincing at the sound of angry hooves against metal as I approached the chute side on, I suddenly saw him in the back corner, talking to another cowboy.

I stopped, reaching out for the barrier next to me, suddenly overwhelmed with what we were about to do.

The scene I'd envisaged in my mind melted away as even at this distance, the tears welled up, resting right on the edge of rolling over. I hesitated, suddenly contemplating the coward's way out, to turn and just keep walking, walk all the way to the damn airport.

At that moment he looked up, stopping mid-sentence as he saw me, the other man glancing in my direction as in the next moment, he began striding towards me.

I let go of the barrier, teeth clenched as I all but ran to meet him, our bodies colliding in a crush.

We said nothing for a second, his arms wrapped tight around me as I buried my face into his shirt, breathing him in. I felt his hand on my hair, holding me gently in place as he kissed my head.

All the words I'd put together, all the ways of saying goodbye suddenly felt meaningless. There was no way this could somehow be made to feel anything other than devastation.

'I'm sorry,' I choked, forcing myself to pull back, stopping as he held tight to my waist. 'I know you're about to ride—'

But he wasn't listening. Reaching down and pulling my chin up, he kissed me, hard.

That kiss, his mouth . . . it was everything we'd said to each other, everything we'd done and everything we hadn't had the chance to. It was need and yearning and love, all in one. My tears fell freely as every barrier I'd raised fell down, the raging torrent of feeling crashing against them all.

'Hestia,' he breathed, an urgency in his voice I'd never heard before as we parted, his thumb wiping my cheeks. 'I need you to know—'

'I can't do this,' I choked, the guilt of what I was about to do swallowing me whole. 'I'm leaving. I couldn't find another way. My flight's in—'

'No,' he begged, his fingers guiding my face back to look at him, his own tears gathering. 'We've got to find a way to make this work with you here – I can't . . . I don't want to be without you, Hestia. I need you to know. I love you. I'm *in love* with you.'

Part of me, the part that loved him back so fiercely that I could barely breathe, felt the kind of joy I'd never imagined knowing. That he returned my feelings, that a man like this could love someone like me. But the other part, the darkness that swirled below, that told me I could never deserve anything so good, pulled me down, drowning out everything.

I closed my eyes to it for a moment, the sensation of pain building in my chest.

'Oh, Jesse . . . fuck,' I breathed, trying to stop the sobs building. 'You can't. You need someone whole, someone that will give you everything you deserve—'

'I want *you*,' he whispered, his lips on mine again for a moment, lifting me to him. 'I need *you*. I love *you*.'

The tears came for real then, great racking sobs as he pulled me into him, holding me tight while the rodeo swirled around us.

'Let's get out of here,' he urged, 'come on. I don't need to ride. We can go back to the ranch and talk things through.'

'I can't,' I whispered, feeling him tense against me. 'That's what I'm trying to say. My flight's at nine thirty.'

'Tonight?' His voice suddenly broke, the strength he'd held for us both failing.

I nodded, pulling back as I wiped my face again. 'I'm so sorry,' I said. I'd never hated myself more than in this moment, watching his shock register, pain gathering in every corner of his face. 'I never meant for this . . .'

'Please don't walk away,' he begged. 'We'll find a way. Fuck it, I'll come with you to London. I just – I can't be without you.'

I felt it then, the first fracture. I had to go. This could only get worse. Guilt, shame, love . . . all roiling together in a nauseating swirl.

'I think I should go,' I said, stepping back. 'Just promise me you won't ride tonight, not like this.'

From the corner of my eye, I saw Cole watching us. I knew he'd be there for Jesse, would stop him from riding. I glanced at him, gesturing to Jesse.

'Oh, fuck . . . Hestia, no, please.'

Almost doubled over, as though punched in the stomach, he reached for me as I shook my head.

I glanced to Cole, his eyes widening at my silent signal and marching over, his stare fixed on Jesse. So, with what little strength I had left, barely able to see through the tears, I turned and walked away.

Chapter 17
Jesse

I could hear myself gasping, but somehow I couldn't breathe.

She was walking away. The woman I loved was walking away from me.

'Hestia,' I yelled, the sound swallowed by the crowds, the PA system announcing the results of the roping and the upcoming bull riding. My voice was hoarse, breaking as I straightened up, roughly swiping at my face to wipe away the tears.

We had to talk. I had to make her understand, make her see that I wanted her, *needed her*, any fraction of her she was willing to give. I didn't care if she didn't feel whole right now, because I'd help her, support and love and give everything to her, until she realized just how incredible she was.

I half choked, half yelled her name again as I started to walk forward, her red hair still visible in a sea of denim, black and brown. Determined, I'd buy a seat on the plane, fuck the cost, fuck everything else. We'd talk until we could kiss again, until she could feel how right it was that I loved her . . . and maybe, one day, when she was able, maybe she'd feel the same way.

'Jesse, stop. Let her go.'

Cole's voice arrived at the same time as his hand on my arm, bracing himself as I turned to him, shaking it off.

'I can't, just let me—' I began, side-stepping him, cursing my chaps and the way they slowed me down, restricting my movement.

'No,' he reiterated, striding in front of me, blocking my path with his body, blocking my line of sight to her. 'Just let her leave.'

'Get outta the fucking way,' I growled, knowing full well what this would mean if he didn't move. 'I need to talk to her, just let me—'

Some of the people around us had paused, seeing the two of us square up.

'Jesse? Where's –' Clara barrelled into me, eyes wide, frowning at the way we'd positioned ourselves. 'The fuck is going on?'

'Hestia left,' Cole murmured, his eyes still fixed on me, unblinking. 'But Jesse wants to go after her, even though it's not gonna end well.'

With every second I knew my chance of stopping her was fading. A huge surge of grief buried low was rising up and up, threatening to drown me.

'Fuck this,' I snapped, taking off my hat and throwing it down. 'So help me, Cole, get the fuck out of my way before I lose my shit and end up doing something I'll regret.'

I could hear Clara trying to talk me down, other voices in the background behind her, but all I could see were the tears streaming down Hestia's face, feel the way she'd clung to me. My chest was cracking, rending everything inside. The pain was suffocating.

Oh God, Hestia, I need you.

Cole's body was still, unyielding even as I stepped up to him and drew my arm back. Just a flash of sadness in his eyes, as though he was willing to take whatever I was about to give because he knew, he understood. *Fuck him. Fuck this.* Anger surged as I imagined her stepping into a cab even as we stood here, wasting time. I clenched my fingers into a fist, preparing to launch myself into his impassive stance until . . . another arm wrapped around my arm from behind.

'Whoa there, Jesse! You lost your damn mind? The only thing you'll end up with after punching Miller is a broken hand. C'mon now – Jesse!'

Cole's eyes flicked to the voice behind as I closed mine for a moment.

I turned to see my buddy Jace and his brother, Jonah, all decked out for the competition just like me. Jace released my arm as I shook it off.

'You okay?' Jonah asked, glancing between me and Cole. 'You want us to back you up—'

'Oh for fuck's sake,' Clara suddenly declared, throwing herself into the middle. 'Simmer the hell down, all of you. Jesse – running after Hestia right now isn't gonna help, especially if she doesn't want you to. Cole is just trying to stop you getting hurt some more. And you two –' she pointed at the brothers – 'need to mind your business and get the fuck back to the chutes. Now.'

I nodded as they looked back to me to check, tipping their hats with sheepish expressions towards Clara, who kept her eyes on them like a hawk as they left.

Finally clocking the small crowd that'd gathered round, I gritted my teeth and scooped my hat back up off the ground, catching sight of a familiar, long absent face among them.

Tristan Sinclair. As tall and imposing as his older brother and dad, and just as out of place – more at home in suits than jeans, his smart mouth and hard eyes making him a likely target for a post-rodeo brawl.

He caught my stare for a moment, then looked over to Cole, his expression blank.

'What the hell is *he* doing here?' Cole muttered under his breath, staring just as I had been, watching as Tristan turned and walked off, heading back over in the direction of the stands.

'Thank fuck Lil's not here,' I replied, grateful for the distraction.

Cole nodded, his brow deeply furrowed as he glanced back at me.

'Look, I'm sorry, I just . . .'

I shook my head, kicking at a couple of stones in the dirt.

'I get it. I know what you're trying to do,' I murmured, unable to help looking towards the parking lot, as if by some miracle Hestia was going to come wandering back.

'Go on and get outta here,' Clara urged, holding out a hand to take my competitor number. 'Ain't no way you're riding tonight. Hand it over and I'll take it back to the office for you. Go get a drink or something, okay?'

The anger was fading as I clenched my jaw, knowing she was right and hating it all the same. Taking the number off and handing it to her, I could feel the pain seeping through me, as though the anger had kept it at bay and now . . . it really fucking hurt.

'I'm sorry, Jesse,' she said, holding my hand for a moment as she took my number. 'Truly, I am.'

Not trusting myself to speak, I walked towards the car park, Cole walking with me, matching my silence.

Other than putting one foot in front of the other, I had no idea what to do next. It was like someone had erased the path I'd been walking until now. All colour had drained away; there was nothing left to say or do. What I'd begun to see as my whole damn future was on her way to the airport and it seemed like there was absolutely nothing I could do about it.

'I need to try,' I said, stopping abruptly as we neared Cole's truck. 'Just one conversation – and if she doesn't want to know, I'll let her go. I fucking swear it. I just . . . I've got to try, Cole.'

I didn't bother to shield the gut-wrenching ache that I know was showing in my face. His look in return was one of pity – empathy.

'I just don't think she's going to—'

'Imagine it was Lottie doing this,' I cut him off, all but begging, taking off my hat and running my hand through my hair, pulling at it as though it would somehow ease the pain in the rest of my body. 'Would you just let her go? When you know what she is to you?'

He paused, knowing exactly what he'd do – and exactly what he was preventing me from doing. Instead, he reached into his pocket and pulled out his phone, tapping the screen twice until I heard ringing.

'Hey,' he said after a moment, then with a glance at me, 'he's not great. Look, you know her best. Do you think she might listen if Jesse goes after her, tries to persuade her to stay . . .?'

Nodding, he held the phone out between us, tapping the speaker icon.

'Jesse?'

Lottie's voice was strained but firm, Cole's eyes on mine.

'Yeah,' I answered, sensing, deep down, where this was going to go.

'Listen to me, okay? I love that woman – she's a sister to me, more. But believe me when I say that she needs to sort this out herself. You can tell her until the end of time that she's not this awful, undeserving person she seems to think she is, but she needs to see it for herself.' She stopped, her voice growing thin for a moment, Cole frowning in concern. 'I think . . . no, I *know*, she feels more for you than she's saying and that with some time apart she might just realize it.'

Drawing a breath, I braced myself against the truck with one hand.

'I love her, Lottie,' I rasped, bowing my head to the floor, hating the pain in Cole's face on my behalf. 'I can't let her walk away.'

'And we love you, Jesse,' she countered, her voice hardening. 'This is the moment where we need to protect you, okay? If Hestia is going to fucking self-destruct, or see the truth, she needs to do it alone. I know you love her, but that's exactly why you've got to let her get on that plane.' She drew in a sharp breath, as if steadying herself. 'Believe me, it's just as hard for me to say as it is for you to hear.'

Cole finally took the phone back and off speaker phone, turning as he spoke to Lottie in low tones for a moment before hanging up.

Still leaning on the truck, I let her words sink in, hearing the sense in them. Hating it. Hating it as much as I loved Hestia.

'Jesse.'

I turned to see Cole, resignation on his face and truck keys in hand, holding them out to me, waiting.

'Just take the damn truck. I know Lottie's making sense, but if that was her going to the airport, I'd fucking hate the guts of anyone trying to stop me. I don't want that between us. So just call me if you need me, okay?'

Swallowing hard, I nodded, took the keys and jumped in.

Grateful that the whole town – and most of their cars – were inside the rodeo, I quickly wove my way out and onto the highway, pushing Cole's truck hard.

But, in the quiet of the cab, Lottie's words replayed on a loop. The longer I drove, the more they made sense, the feeling deep in my gut confirming that Hestia wasn't going to let me in until she could stop hating on herself.

I could love and protect her as much as I wanted from the outside, but she was the only one who could really let me inside. And right now, she wasn't ready.

As I thought it over and over, the truck slowed. I eased my foot on the gas as the airport came into view, imagining bursting in there and following her through, trying to persuade her to stay in a damn airport lounge . . .

It wouldn't work. Lottie was right.

Barely coasting now, I forced myself to keep it together, rolling slowly into a space at the far end of the lot overlooking the runway.

That's where, not more than an hour later, head in my hands and heart fucking numb, I watched her plane take off.

Chapter 18
Hestia

It wasn't until I reached Denver on the smaller plane that I had officially cried myself out. Every time I thought it was under control, something would echo through my mind – Lottie's cool stare as she told me I just wasn't choosing this, that I was lying to myself. Or the raw, unfiltered pain in Jesse's face as he realized I wasn't choosing him either, that I was about to walk away from us with no knowing when or if I could return.

Even knowing that he loved me, needed me.

Gritting my teeth to it as I settled into my seat for the much longer leg back to London, headphones on, I'd almost made it when one of Jesse's favourite tracks began playing.

After weeks of country music slowly trickling through my playlists, my music app was now suggesting more – and this one, 'Something in the Orange', was one Jesse had played many times in his truck.

It hit me like a brick to the chest as a sudden onslaught of vivid detail washed over me. All of the times leading up to now when I'd felt the love he'd just declared, in his touch, the way he kissed me like it was something he *needed*. I realized I knew it, recognized the feeling so easily, because it was everything I needed too.

And for the sake of Cal, someone I knew now had never even come close to meaning anything like Jesse to me – for a business I'd run away from in the first place, unable to bear the thought of working alongside his chaos – I'd just thrown away the one person that I'd ever really, truly fallen in love with.

Curling myself into the window, I covered myself with the blanket and sobbed in silence, only stopping as exhaustion took over long after we'd taken off. An uneasy, dream-laced sleep followed as I crossed the ocean that now lay between us.

Arriving back in London among the grey skies, the soft patter of rain on the train windows as we sped from west to east, I felt numb. Everything felt small and enclosed, from the heavy clouds overhead to the narrow roads and tiny cars – not a Ford pick-up truck in sight. The sheer volume of people crowded onto the tube was suddenly claustrophobic, their glances at my clothes – my cowboy boots, Wranglers edged with rodeo dust, and cowboy hat on my lap – making me feel as though I'd landed from another planet.

Sighing, I buried myself in opening some of the messages that'd come through since I'd landed. There were four from Lottie. My heart fluttered at the thought of her at home right now, maybe even prepping coffee or having breakfast with Jesse.

> I miss you already.

> I'm sorry if I was harsh before. I just thought, somehow, you might just stay for good. I know it's stupid but I thought my Hallmark movie life might just extend to you too.

> I love you, Hes. Call me when you're home xxx

> Cole asked me to tell you that he got Jesse home after you left. He didn't ride. x

My eyes filled instantly, this time through relief. The darker thoughts that'd edged in, the ones that tortured me in the black silence between sleep and numb reality, had been lined with the possibility of him riding. That somehow he'd forced his way back past Cole and got back on the bull, not caring whether he made it through or not.

I shivered at the thought, the ramifications of any element of carelessness on a killing machine like those bulls.

Taking a breath, I opened a message from Diane telling me that Cal had just been released home and was being looked after by Becca. She was offering me the spare room at her place, a few tube stops up from mine and Cal's, just in case I preferred.

Her offer was kind and meant in good faith, but I couldn't kick the feeling it left me with; the inference that I might somehow get in the way of Cal and his new relationship, in the flat we co-owned. All of my belongings were still there – the old spare bedroom had morphed into my bedroom when we'd ended our relationship months ago.

As the tube hurtled through central London, that feeling grew, overtaking the sadness below it until it turned, curdling to anger. I knew it was partly aimed at myself, but a big fat chunk of it was for Cal. For barely being able to act like a functioning adult and step up when I needed him, as a business partner if nothing else. More than that, even as I tried to temper the feeling with empathy, knowing very well how it felt to have your mental health on the edge, I couldn't quite reconcile this experience with what had happened before.

Last time he'd ended up in hospital, after deliberately overdosing himself on God knows what, he'd been in for two weeks. Now he was out within forty-eight hours?

Finally dragging my case off at my stop, the rain seeping through every fibre of my clothes, I walked through familiar streets as a stranger.

I almost knocked as I reached our navy blue door, then paused with my hand poised above the original Edwardian brass handle and pulled out my key instead.

This was still half my place, Becca or not.

Inside, it was quiet, and as I reasoned he might still be resting or asleep, I left my case at the bottom of the steep stairs ahead, planning to come back for it later. With a sad smile, I realized only someone like Cole or Jesse would be able to lift it without dragging on the noisy wooden steps, even if they could fit up the narrow staircase.

Pausing halfway up, catching what sounded like a brief animal noise, I frowned. Cal couldn't keep a fucking cactus alive, I puzzled, resuming my steps up, bracing myself to be introduced to some kind of pet, one that would inevitably end up being donated to a friend.

The living room door at the top was closed, and I used my body weight to push against it, remembering how much extra effort the heavy fire door hinge needed.

As it swung open, my eyes fell on anarchy. Food wrappers, pizza boxes, cans and glasses strewn across every surface, and in the corner, the TV on but silent, a grainy porno playing out the story of two women clearly having a much better time than me.

Blissfully unaware of my presence, like a horny mirage on the sofa opposite, was Cal, complete with a blonde woman sitting on his face, making the same noise I'd heard on the stairs as she pumped his dick in her hand.

I was temporarily stunned. Clearly, his imagined sickbed was nothing more than a fucking figment of Diane's imagination. It was a few seconds before I gathered myself, the first inklings of rage bubbling up through my tiredness.

I formed a fist, letting the door rest against my boot. I figured it was only polite to knock.

'Sorry to interrupt,' I yelled as I banged on it once, then again. I watched with grim satisfaction as the blonde half screamed, abandoning Cal's cock to cover her chest, leaping back as he scrambled, wide-eyed, to figure out what the hell was going on.

'This what the hospital prescribed, then?' I asked, not bothering to look away as the woman ran into his bedroom, Cal pointlessly covering his lap with a cushion. 'I had no idea eating someone out was medicinal.'

'Jesus fucking Christ, Hestia,' he panted, ruddy exertion across his cheeks as he ran his hands through his dark hair. Any hint of a sickly, pallid hospital complexion had clearly magically disappeared between the woman's legs.

'Feeling better, then?' I asked, folding my arms. When he just gaped at me, I shook my head, not bothering to hide my disgust. 'So did you lie to your mum about being ill? Or is she in on whatever this fucked-up hoarder-sex chaos is?'

'What? Neither,' he finally replied, getting up and promptly forgetting the cushion, sending him scrambling.

'Oh Cal, for fuck's sake, I've seen your dick more times than I ever care to remember,' I sighed, suddenly exhausted. 'Now, which one is it? You better start talking really fucking quickly before I call her and ask.'

I pulled out my phone, tapping the screen with the tips of my nails as his eyes widened in horror.

'I can absolutely explain,' he began, stopping as the woman

emerged from his room. Other than the hair, her look was eerily similar to mine – or what mine had been before I'd left London.

'You never did have much imagination, did you, Cal?' I mused, rolling my eyes as she stared. 'I take it you're Becca,' I added, too exasperated to even attempt niceties.

'Yeah, and who the hell are you?' she snapped, folding her arms as Cal groaned.

'No one. You should go,' he said, at the same moment that I snarled, 'I'm the one who picked out the sofa you were just fucking on. The one paying half the fucking mortgage.'

There was a pause, her eyes sliding to his.

'Just let me put some clothes on,' Cal said, holding up his hands to me as he glanced back at Becca. 'I can't do this naked.'

'That ship sailed a while ago,' I retorted, rolling my eyes.

She glared at me. 'I don't know what you think you're trying to do, but you can't just walk back in here. It took him ages to get over you. We're together now.'

I couldn't help it as a laugh bubbled up at the thought of wanting him – this. I gazed around the miserable turmoil I'd lived in with him for years, blanking it out with more hours in the studio and local bars than I'd realized.

'Honey, he's all yours,' I replied, an uncomfortable jolt as I heard Jesse's voice in the words. 'Cal, I'm going to the studio. If you can keep your dick in your pants long enough, meet me down there. We need to talk.'

'Fuck – Hestia, wait,' he yelled from his room; our room, once.

'No, don't think I will,' I called back, turning in the doorway to face the stairs, Becca's glare still on my face. 'Best of luck,' I added, not waiting for a response as I walked back down the stairs and grabbed my bag. I pulled it outside as Cal's footsteps thundered down the stairs behind me, cut off as I slammed the front door shut.

I pulled out my phone again, preparing to call Diane. Instead I saw another message from Lottie.

> I've told Lil you're back in town – why don't you meet up? She extended her stay there too – coming back in two or three weeks I think. Here's her number x

'Hestia! Wait!' Cal called out, following me down the road.

'You know, Cal, I think it's bad form to not finish the job,' I muttered as I shot a quick message back. The thought of meeting Lil, someone connected to the ranch – to Jesse – was more appealing than I could admit to myself. 'In fairness to you, she looked close.'

'Stop it, for fuck's sake,' he hissed, pulling me to a halt, almost yanking my phone out of my hand.

'*Are you for fucking real?*' I yelled, only just resisting the urge to push him back. 'Your mum calls me, thousands of miles away, to say that you're back in hospital again and the business is in tatters, only for me to come home to find some random woman riding your face? Do you know how FUCKED UP that is?'

He stared back, a toxic familiarity in both of our poses, halfway between aggression and defence.

'I *was* in hospital,' he growled. 'It just wasn't quite as bad as Mum thought, okay? It's been really fucking rough this last month, even with Becca—'

'Oh fuck off, Cal,' I spat, grabbing my case handle and beginning to drag it again. 'Every bloody month is tough for you. You know what I've realized? Being around normal, healthy, *emotionally regulated* people? The life you live – that I lived with you – is the fucking symptom *and* the cause of everything rough in our lives.'

'Oh right, right,' he mocked, following me, his mouth a hard line. 'So is this the part where you tell me you're going to join Lottie's little fairy tale over there and start shacking up with some fucking American beefcake dick?'

I gave a bitter laugh, turning the corner onto the busier main road, looking out for a cab. I couldn't bear the thought of lugging my case for the ten-minute walk to the studio with Cal bitching in my ear.

'Not start, Cal,' I corrected, walking again as no cabs appeared. 'Continue. And believe me, no one's been receiving fucking limp-wristed mediocre hand jobs on my watch.' It was petty, but I couldn't help it. I never could when it came to him – that incessant need to wound and scar each other, then patch it up with sex until the next time, never quite healing in between. That was why, as I heard his footsteps speeding up behind me, I wasn't surprised when he grabbed me roughly by the shoulder and turned my head towards him.

His dark eyes burning even in the grey gloom, he brought his face so close to mine that the stubble on his jaw grazed my chin.

'And how was he? Did he fuck you nice and hard, just like you like? Are you still aching down there? I haven't forgotten how good that tight little—'

At one time, I would've leant into his hateful passion, knowing just how good the sex to follow would be. Instead, in a split second, I leant back, giving myself enough space to swing my hand up, and slapped the side of his face with resounding crack.

As he staggered back slightly, mouth open in shock, I pointed at him.

'Don't you fucking *dare* touch me or speak to me like that again, do you understand?'

Two women walking by behind him stopped. One of them called out to ask if I needed help. I shook my head, giving them a grim smile.

'Now, I'm going to the fucking studio, and if you can't behave yourself, I will call your goddamn mother first and an ambulance second, because that's what you'll need once she's done with you.'

'Christ,' he swore, holding a hand to his face as he followed me.

'Listen, Hestia – look, I'm sorry, okay? Can we just start again? Go and get lunch or drinks or something.'

I shook my head, marching on, knowing he'd have to behave once we got to the studio, with clients and our crew of artists there.

'No. Not interested. We can talk *business* at the studio. Who's in today?'

A tense pause followed, just the sound of the wheels on my case between us.

'Look . . . um, that's why we should go somewhere else instead. I can explain, but—'

I turned to give him a quick head shake.

'Oh, no, no, no. You're not getting away with anything – you're going to grow a pair and straighten shit out right there. No persuading me into drinks and fuck knows what else in some overpriced shithole.'

I glanced around at the places and streets I knew so well, all coated in a film of grime from the pollution. Sirens blazed down towards Liverpool Street, and as I strode on, feet still entirely comfortable in my cowboy boots, I wondered what the hell I was doing here.

'Before we go in, you need to know that it was a fuck-up on my part, okay? I'm owning that, no excuses.'

We turned a corner, the familiar black door of our studio straight ahead. Even as his words landed, they didn't wholly compute. I just wanted to be back in my space, my place of creative calm, the simple meditation of my craft having been the salve to so many situations over the years.

Crossing the road as we approached, I realized it was dark inside.

I slowed to a stop, tapping my phone to check the time, suddenly wondering if jet lag had messed with my time perception. But no – it was 2.30 p.m. Way into our opening hours.

'Where is everyone?' I asked, glancing back to realize Cal had slipped back, allowing a greater distance to open between us. His eyes were wary, holding up a hand.

'Wait – let me just explain first . . .'

Ignoring him, I took out my keys, jamming the right one into the lock before he could stop me, and walking into . . . another living nightmare.

It was trashed.

I let go of my case, leaving it in the doorway, and stepped through. My mouth was fully agape as I took in the utter carnage around me. It made our flat look like a fucking show home.

Graffiti was sprayed everywhere – even, I recognized with a start, Cal's old tag sign from our uni days. It mocked my own hand-drawn cherry blossom on the back wall. Broken glass was scattered across the floor, cans and more rubbish strewn over every surface.

I went further in, heart in my mouth as I turned the corner into the back room, *my* room. My custom-made red chair was covered in what looked like vomit. It stank – of piss and stale beer. As I turned, unable to disguise my horror, Cal appeared in the doorway.

For one awful moment, I tried to rationalize it. A break-in? Squatters, even. But as I looked up at one of Cal's own spray-paint tags right above his head, I knew.

For years we had swum together in a filthy pit of past trauma, each holding the other down until neither of us could see a way out. Until Lottie had left – my one chink of light in the darkness, the one person I knew was always there, holding onto me through everything. That had forced me to move, to let go of Cal's grip and swim out, climb up.

And there, at the top, had been Jesse – and Lottie, Bailey, Cole, Dee, Luci . . . a whole other world I'd never allowed myself to imagine existed.

Now the contrast was gut-wrenchingly sharp.

Cal had always, and would always, be on a mission to self-destruct. The minute I'd decided to pull myself out of his fucking black-hole orbit was the minute he'd decided to literally piss all over the only good thing we'd actually shared.

'You fucking *bastard*,' I snarled, watching as he tried to think his way through the possible excuses.

'It was just one of those things – listen, it was a heavy night, Dion got hold of a whole load of pills and the party got really fucked up . . . I didn't mean it to go this far. We can get it cleaned up, I swear . . .'

I launched myself at him, restraint lost as I pushed him back into the wall, screaming at him in frustration as his hands closed around my wrists, forcing me back.

'I fucking *hate* you,' I yelled, fresh tears welling, stinging as they fell, the skin still raw.

'I fucking hate myself too,' he shouted back, struggling as I put all my weight into getting free of him. 'Just like you hate yourself. Just like we've always been. You can't change any more than I can. Look at you! The same thing every fucking time!'

With a final shove, I brought the hard heel of my boot down on his soft trainer. He let me go with a yelp, swearing as he stumbled.

'No, it's not,' I shouted, moving back from him, closer to the front door. 'It's not the same. I don't think I do hate myself, Cal. I hate what's happened to me in my past, and I hate that I've wallowed in it for so long. But I'm *done*.'

I half stumbled, half ran out, swearing as I realized my damn case would prevent me from storming off in the way I so desperately needed to.

Pulling out my phone and navigating to the Uber app, I blindly booked the first one I could see, my hand shaking as I tapped the screen.

Moments later, Cal emerged, eyeing me warily.

'I'm going to sort it out and clear it—'

'Don't you fucking dare go in there again,' I hissed, internally begging for the cab to arrive, desperate to get away from him, from the fucking horror inside the place I'd loved. 'I will deal with this, and when I'm done, I'm going to buy you out of the business and never see you again. If you try anything, anything at all to stop me, I swear to fucking God that I will make your miserable life even more of a living hell.' I paused, seeing the Uber approach. 'We are done, Cal.'

'What do you want me to do? I can prove it, I can prove I was in hospital,' he said, a new desperation in his eyes, pulling out his phone. 'I'll get someone to send me my notes or something.'

The driver opened the boot of the car, jumping out to help me lift my case in.

'You still don't get it, do you?' I said, opening the back door, gripping it like a shield between us. 'I didn't come back for you. I don't care –' I stopped myself, making a sudden, new pact with myself. I did care about him, deep down, but not in the way he might want. 'I don't want you to hurt yourself, Cal. But I didn't come back for that.'

'So what, then?' he replied, throwing his hands up.

I shook my head as I sat down, quietly giving the driver the name of the first hotel that came to mind as he climbed back into his seat.

'For our business. For everything we put into that,' I replied softly. 'And because I didn't deserve to stay.'

He swore as I closed the door. The driver waited for a gap in the passing traffic to pull out.

'I'm sorry, Hestia,' Cal shouted, his voice muffled through the glass. 'I can't do it without you.'

I looked back at him – at five years of my life.

As the cab pulled away, I faced forward, determined to keep it that way.

Chapter 19
Hestia

Almost a week back in London, and I was still a stranger in my home city.

Staying at a small budget hotel on the other side of Shoreditch, working from a nearby café run by a friend, I was more aware than ever that my situation was precarious at best. Thanks to my aggressive saving habits, built in early on in a bid to build any sense of security in my life post-uni, I had a sizeable lump sum put aside to work with.

But – if I was going to buy Cal out of our business, find myself a place and get some kind of new life together . . . shit was about to get expensive.

I'd resisted calling Diane, not quite able to bear the thought of upsetting her in the way I knew it would. Away from the shock and anger of my first day back, the whole thing had actually felt incredibly . . . sad. Seeing Cal locked in a toxic spiral; realizing I'd passively allowed myself to spiral with him for years, figuring that's all there was for me.

Until . . . Wyoming. *Jesse*.

I slid my headphones on and nestled into the dim back corner of the café, blocking out the aggressively emo tunes. Sienna, the manager and a longtime client of mine, winced apologetically from behind the bar. I smiled, shrugging, knowing it was what her regulars wanted, knowing what I would do to counteract it.

So, against a backdrop of country music, I continued to unpick Cal's trail of destruction. Industrial cleaners were now booked to deep clean the studio in a couple of days. I spent the next couple of hours reaching out to our crew of artists and existing clients – chatting briefly to some, emailing others, spinning the studio closure as a refurb.

As I paused after ordering some lunch, Jesse's song started to play. I hesitated over the playlist, about to skip, but . . . couldn't.

Every emotion from those last moments at the rodeo flooded back over me, replaying his tortured expression, the way he'd told me he loved me. It haunted me every night as I tried to get to sleep, sometimes lying there for hours, wondering if he regretted it, regretted me.

Holding my arm around myself, I opened my messages, reading the last few between us. Our proximity at the ranch had meant there weren't many, but the few that were there . . . I could picture his easy, confident smile, the way it changed when he drew close to me. How he felt on me, in me . . .

I closed my eyes, digging my nails into my side.

I wanted to message him so badly. I wanted to speak to him, tell him everything, beg for forgiveness. But without any solution, without seeing any way of going back to Wyoming . . . wouldn't we just be in the same place as before? Wouldn't it be selfish to message him now, rather than let him just forget and move on?

As my lunch arrived, my phone lit up, startling me out of my reverie.

Dee.

Staring at it in disbelief, I picked up.

'Dee?'

'Oh hey! Goddamn, it's nice to hear your accent again,' she giggled. 'How's home?'

I swallowed the real answer, not willing to risk a breakdown in public. In truth, hearing her Wyoming drawl was enough to trigger a lump in my throat as it was.

'It's so nice to hear your voice,' I admitted, feeling her pause down the line, cursing myself for not disguising my tone better. 'It's been . . . fine, I guess.' I shifted in my seat, grimacing at myself, knowing I couldn't lie. 'Actually, no. It's been hard. I hadn't realized how much I'd checked out of my own life.'

'Oh, honey, I'm sorry,' she soothed. 'We all miss you. Jesse most of all, I think. Still, you know how guys can just tuck it all away and get straight back on the horse, right?'

I hummed in agreement, another twist of pain at the mention of his name.

'Listen, I had something I wanted to ask. The Collective open day was a huge success, a whole bunch of us have been talking about doing another one maybe. I know you're back over there now, but if you were gonna come over again, there's a big fucking queue of people here wanting your magic on their skin.'

I blinked, not expecting it.

'I was just thinking it over, you know, trying to join up some dots. I want to expand my own clothes line, swap out some of the branded stuff for my own. Better margins and all that. Your design did so well, I just wondered, with demand for your tattoo skills too . . . and Bailey told me about the whole volunteer idea Lil's had for the Diamond Back. I don't know, I just think there's so much space for you here, honey.'

I felt a surge of gratitude for Dee, for thinking of me. For all of them.

'Oh . . . I . . . yeah, I mean, that all sounds amazing,' I began, trying to compute it against the backdrop of all I'd started organizing for the studio in the past week. 'I just – I'm trying to sort things out here a little. My ex – my business partner, he's kind of fucked things up with the studio.' I sighed, suddenly deflated. 'Then there's visas and all of that stuff, even if I could come back.'

'Well, look, I don't want to add any complication, but maybe just think on it. I just wanted you to know you had options, from someone . . . not quite so tied up in all the emotional stuff, you know?'

'Thanks, Dee. It means a lot,' I replied, feeling myself strain against the need to hold it all together.

We said our goodbyes, hanging up shortly after, a silence ringing in my headphones. I stared at the screen, seeing her shop in my mind instead, the buzz of the Collective open day. In a second, the Messages app was open, my last message to Jesse there on the screen. Before I could stop myself, I tapped out a message.

> I'm so sorry for how we said goodbye. What you said meant everything.

I paused, warring with myself, desperate not to hurt him further but needing him to know. I tapped send before I could delete it, adding:

> Please take care of yourself x

The messages appeared in boxes on the screen, and then the tiny ticks below to show they'd been sent. As I half swiped to close the app, in the next second, a second tick appeared next to each message.

He'd read them. He was reading them right now.

I closed my phone, putting it screen facing down on the table, my heart racing as though he could somehow see me.

Wolfing down my lunch, I eyed my phone like an unexploded bomb, driving myself insane with wondering if he'd messaged back.

Glancing at the clock on the back wall behind me, I realized I had limited time left before meeting up with Lil as arranged earlier in the week. The thought of meeting Lottie's blonde twin felt like exactly what I wanted and needed.

An hour later, walking into the pub I'd suggested, I spotted her immediately.

Head thrown back in laughter, she sat on one of the sofa seats, cowboy boot up on the edge of the coffee table in front, hand linked with a guy to her left. She looked every inch the cowgirl, and he looked every inch like he couldn't believe his luck.

'Howdy,' I said, smiling as I approached, watching as she jumped up, her smile and mannerisms so incredibly Lottie that I felt a pang of sadness.

'Hestia! Holy shit, girl,' she said, stepping over the guy, who watched with amused curiosity as we hugged. He was cute, with cropped brown hair and inquisitive eyes, an earring and an impressive full sleeve of tats on his left arm. His fitted T-shirt left nothing to the imagination as Lil pulled me back, gripping my arms to look at me.

'You are so damn pretty in person,' she chuckled. 'Jesse wasn't exaggerating. I know we met on screen, but there's only so much you can tell like that, you know?'

I smiled, shrugging.

'Hey, I'm Jamie,' the guy said after an affectionate glance at Lil. 'I've heard a lot about you.'

'I deny everything,' I joked, giving him a brief hug too before sitting down, resisting the urge to check my phone again. The initial surge of adrenaline at knowing Jesse had read my messages had mutated into anxiety as nothing came back through in return.

As the three of us talked – them about their sightseeing, adventures in and around London and trips out to other parts of the country Lil had wanted to see – I found myself holding onto her voice. It was so unmistakably of her hometown; even the way she said 'Jackson' made me smile.

'You know, I've got to admit that hearing you . . .' I shook my head as I took a sip of my drink, suspecting I should've steered away from alcohol, the way it opened things up. 'I really fucking miss the ranch. Everyone.'

'Everyone, huh?' she said, raising her eyebrows for a moment, watching my reaction. 'Yeah, my hometown has that effect on people.' She glanced at Jamie, smiling. 'I was only telling him that before you came in. And look –' She pointed to my cowboy boots with satisfaction. 'I told you. Once you're in, that place doesn't let you go.'

I smiled back, not needing to admit that I hadn't been able to swap the boots out for my DMs or any of my other shoes.

'So if you do get volunteers over there, on the ranch,' Jamie started, tracing his finger on the back of her hand. 'How are you going to get them to leave?'

Lil laughed again, her eyes lighting up as they met his.

I had to look away. The emotion was so obvious, so visceral that it felt like a slap.

'Well, I'll be needing security of some kind,' she answered, her voice dipping as he smiled with her. 'Hey, did I mention Jamie had an idea alongside the volunteering, Hestia? It falls in your wheelhouse, kinda.'

I shook my head, knocking back the rest of my drink, hoping it might numb the growing tension in my gut.

Jamie explained his idea, of offering a creative retreat at the ranch, of writers and artists coming to take some time out in the peace and sanctuary of the space there. It made complete sense. Yet more memories of sitting by the lake sketching came to mind.

'I love it,' I said simply as Lil clapped her hands together. 'I've done a couple myself, a few years ago. People pay good money for that kind of thing,' I added, thinking how well it would complement the ranch – how much more space there was to use alongside the horses and all the existing activities Lottie managed.

'We'd need someone to help manage it,' Lil said softly, catching my eye as I looked up. 'You've got the kind of skill set we could justify a visa for, you know,' she added, her eyes fixed on my reaction. 'I've looked it up. Might take a little while to organize, but it's all possible.'

I drew a breath, suddenly connecting dots. I hadn't spoken to Lottie since coming back, but we'd messaged back and forth. The tenor of hers had been apologetic, full of love and promises to make things better, whatever that meant.

'You've been speaking to Lottie, haven't you?' I surmised, studying Lil just as hard as she kept her face entirely neutral. Jamie's expression told a different story, a sly smile hurriedly tucked away as he got up to get us more drinks.

'I talk to my cousin, yes,' she admitted, shrugging. 'What of it?'

I sighed.

'It's not just about visas, Lil,' I admitted, scuffing my boot against the worn floorboard. 'I'm not sure . . . well, it's complicated with Jesse—'

'No, it's not,' she cut in, shaking her head, meeting my surprise with the same kindness in her eyes I'd seen a thousand times before in Lottie's. 'It's simple. You don't feel like you deserve Jesse, and you think he's better off without you, right?'

I opened my mouth for a moment, but the simplicity of condensing all of those feelings into such a short statement somehow stopped me.

'Look, I'm not saying there's a hell of a lot more detail to it than that,' she admitted, suddenly reaching out to me, taking my hand in hers. 'But you're wrong. I know I don't know you that well, but can you please take it from someone that lost their soulmate – a real love, whatever you want to call it – because they believed the very same thing as you do?'

I stilled at the sudden urgency in her voice. She gave a quick glance back towards the busy bar; Jamie was talking to the barman.

'If that's what you have with Jesse – and goddamn, Hestia, if you have something with that man, know it from the depth of my fucking heart, he is the best of all of us. Don't throw it away. Not for anything. Because that kind of connection doesn't come around often. Believe me.'

She leant back as Jamie returned, smiling as he placed the glasses down, giving me one last look of understanding.

I felt stunned, unable to brush off the depth of genuine feeling in her voice. I believed her, wholly; I wanted to know her story, and I was surprised Lottie had never mentioned anything about it. But then, Lil clearly kept it incredibly private, given how she'd just clammed right up.

We talked about everything and nothing for another hour or so, steering towards more neutral topics before eventually making arrangements to meet up for dinner in a few days' time, on her last night in London.

I was feeling conflicted as we hugged goodbye. Lil shot me one last look as she headed off in the opposite direction with Jamie, her smile fading to something else, a reminder of her words.

I stewed on them as I walked, using them to distract from the visit I'd now have to make to the flat to collect more of my stuff. My heart lurched as I saw message notifications on my phone, then hardened when I realized they were from Cal, not Jesse. He was reassuring me he was alone and that we could talk, discuss the flat.

There was no way I could go back to living there, or keep paying the mortgage on top of rent for myself elsewhere. He was going to be difficult about it, I knew that too – and it would be an additional expense if I had to get lawyers involved.

Eventually, after letting myself into the front door and closing it very firmly behind me, I launched myself unwillingly up the stairs.

'Hey,' Cal said, appearing at the top, kettle in hand. 'Want a coffee?'

I eyed him cautiously, determined to keep this interaction civil for the sake of getting my stuff out, and nodded.

'Do you have any clothes left, Cal?' I asked dryly as I reached the top of the stairs. He was back in the kitchen now, wearing only his boxer shorts. 'I mean, it's an improvement on last time but, you know.'

I didn't wait for his response as I walked past him and on to my room at the very back, opening the door to . . . everything I had left behind weeks and weeks ago. It felt like a time capsule, dust motes spiralling in what little September sun filtered through the window. I sat on my comfy seat next to it, wondering how I'd ever thought I could just come back to this life as though nothing had happened.

Footsteps sounded behind me and I turned to see Cal coming in, holding out a cup of black coffee. I nodded a thanks as I took it, waiting for him to leave, then stifling a groan as he perched on the edge of the bed instead.

'I am sorry, Hes,' he urged, turning one of the many silver rings on his fingers, something he always did when nervous. 'Can we just start again? Like this is the first time you've come back in? I've tidied up in the other room, why don't we—'

'No,' I blurted, softening at his expression. 'Thanks. I just want to get some things together and go, okay?' I chickened out of talking about putting the place up for sale, knowing it would give him the ammo to extend the conversation. 'I'm busy – this was only a quick stop.'

He looked away for a moment, shoulders sagging. For a brief moment, I saw the man I'd met under all of the ink: the wide-eyed good-time guy who'd charmed his way into my life and become the centre of my world.

'The studio's being cleaned up in a couple of days,' I added, meeting his gaze as he turned back. 'Why don't we meet after that and sort things out? I don't want things to get . . . nasty or difficult. I just . . . I think it's better if we divide things up and move on properly.'

He frowned, covering it with a nod.

'Sounds like it's all figured out,' he said, standing. 'I'll leave you to it, then.'

Walking out, he closed the door softly behind him.

Sighing, refusing to take his bait and start a new, likely more explosive conversation, I put on my headphones instead. Climbing onto the chair, I reached up to take a small roll-on bag from the top of the wardrobe.

As my mind fell back on the task at hand, running through a mental checklist of items I knew I wanted, the music paused as my phone pinged.

I pulled it from my pocket as I opened the drawer in front of me, glancing down just as I scooped up a T-shirt I wanted.

> Are you there?

I dropped the T-shirt in shock, my heart somersaulting.
Jesse.
Fuck.
Forcing myself to breathe, fingers beginning to tremble, I typed back.

> Yes?

I tapped send, hand over my mouth as it sent, and moved back to the chair, sinking into it as his name appeared on the screen. He wanted to FaceTime.

Shit, shit, shit.

With a brief thought to how I looked, knowing I'd made enough of an effort to meet with Lil to be passable, I picked up, barely breathing.

In another second, he was there, sitting up against the headboard in his room. The shock of seeing his face, his kind, beautiful eyes wary, the torturous echo of his last words to me playing out, almost choked me.

'Hey,' he said gently, his brow furrowing as I immediately teared up, holding up a finger as I desperately tried to gather myself, mortified. I took my headphones off and switched over to my phone speaker, shaking my hair out.

'Hi,' I finally replied, trying a small smile as he glanced down, so clearly struggling himself that the urge to reach out and touch him was overwhelming. 'Oh fuck, Jesse,' I whispered, a sob rising already. 'I miss you so much.'

He shook his head, pleading.

'I miss you too,' he breathed. 'Are you all right?'

I tried to nod, wanting to reassure him, but it turned into a shake instead.

'Hestia,' he started, his eyes burning already. 'I can't do this. I can't be without you, honey. I'm trying, I'm really fucking trying, but . . . I—'

'I know,' I agreed, all efforts at pretence dissolving. 'I don't think I can either.'

'Wait . . . you don't?' he said, shifting himself, the phone wobbling for a second. 'Does that mean . . .'

'Oh fuck, I don't know,' I whispered, rubbing my forehead as I closed my eyes, the weight of the past week weighing them down. 'I don't know anything any more. But I know . . . I feel like I'm fucking dying without you.'

He looked away at that, returning his gaze a few seconds later, his eyes glassy.

'Honey, I meant every word I said to you before you left,' he said, his voice unbearably raw. 'It wasn't just something to make you stay.'

'I know,' I murmured, drinking him in, willing myself to remember every detail of his face.

That's when he shifted again, a different kind of pain flitting through his features. A flash of white on his right arm appeared.

'What's that?' I asked, curiosity turning to concern as he bit his lip.

'Um . . . I, uh . . .' He exhaled, as if steeling himself. 'I just had a bit of fall last weekend, it's nothing.'

'Jesse,' I said, strength returning as my anxiety rose. 'Fall from what?'

He held my gaze, not flinching, eyes pinched as he finally held up his right arm, a cast on his wrist visible, his sleeve rolled back.

'I rode at Sunday's rodeo. It got a bit rough.' He cleared his throat as I put my hand to my mouth. 'But I still won – just. Decent money, too,' he added. 'The next round is even bigger and I've qualified now.'

'This is my fault, isn't it?' I said, remembering the way he'd folded in on himself as I left. 'I distracted you and fucked it up by leaving like that, and now—'

'No, honey – Hestia, sweetheart, stop,' he clarified, shaking his head. 'I was fine, I managed to concentrate. I just messed up the landing, that's all. He was a big, crazy fucker, twisting every which way. It's why my score was so good.'

'You're the crazy fucker,' I swore, holding my finger under my eye to dab at the gathering wetness there.

He exhaled, his mouth parting into a smile.

'God, I want to touch you,' he admitted. 'I can't stop thinking about you. It's driving the rest of them fucking insane.'

I smiled back, watching how he focused on my lips for a moment.

'So, how are we going to solve this, Jessica?' he breathed, his use of my nickname sending fire through every part of my body.

I shook my head, a hundred different thoughts colliding at once.

But before I had the chance to voice any of them, the door swung open behind me and Cal walked in, in full sight of Jesse.

'Thought you might want these,' he said, his tone suddenly icy as he dropped scraps of black lace onto my bed, vaguely recognizable as my underwear.

Only I couldn't focus on the underwear, because this time, he was entirely naked – what little coverage the boxers had provided, gone.

In horror, stunned into silence, I didn't even flinch as he stepped over, kissing me square on the mouth before strolling out again.

'Oh – say hi to your friend for me,' he called.

There was a deep, sickening silence as Jesse's expression hardened.

'I've got to go,' he said, moving himself to the side of the bed.

'Jesse, that was not what it—'

'Hestia, I . . .' He stopped himself, swearing under his breath.

'Please, Jesse, listen t—'

'Bye, Hestia,' he choked, the screen returning to black as he disconnected the call.

I remained still, squeezing my eyes shut. The usual thought spiral began, the self-hatred shouting me down, pulling me into the rage that overtook everything, that told me to find Cal and kick off what would become either the end of him, or me, or both of us. Because this time, I wasn't sure I'd be able to stop.

Getting up slowly – abandoning my bag, my clothes, anything that once belonged to that Hestia – I walked out of the room, clutching my phone in one hand and my headphones in the other.

Cal was waiting in the doorway to the living room, an anticipation in his features that I knew better than my own face. All of it had been planned. He would take whatever opportunity he could to force me to where he wanted me.

But now, in the decimated remains of whatever we had been on the verge of rediscovering, I remembered the version of myself that Jesse knew.

That he loved.

That he'd protected and supported, held and cared for.

That Hestia wouldn't reach for the kitchen knife on the side just there. She wouldn't threaten Cal with it, maybe even throw it at him.

Holding onto that with everything I had, I approached him. He tensed, waiting.

The plastic of my headphones creaked under the force of the fist I'd created as I bared my teeth to him.

'My lawyer will be in touch,' I hissed, taking the first step down the stairs, gripping the handrail.

'What?' he scoffed as I started to walk down, forcing one step after another. 'What the fuck for?'

'For this place. For the business,' I added, willing myself to the door, feeling the pull back to him, the rage begging to be unleashed.

He laughed.

'What? No fight left in you? Did your big cowboy fuck it all out of you? Or should that be ex-cowboy? He hung up pretty fucking quick.'

I need you. I love you. I choked on the lump in my throat as Jesse's words replayed.

'Bye, Cal,' I replied, registering the stunned silence behind me as I pulled open the front door. 'I hope you get the help you need one day.'

I stepped outside and pulled the door shut behind me, forcing myself to breathe again as I sank down into a crouch against the brick wall.

Only Jesse's words held me upright as I repeated them, over and over.

Chapter 20
Jesse

I dropped the phone onto the bed, the weight of it suddenly more than I could hold.

So this was it – this was what it felt like.

Before now, before Hestia, I'd always been the one to walk away, to break up and cut my losses in relationships before anything real happened. Guarding myself was natural, I figured. Watching Mom for all that time alone; catching those moments when she thought we were asleep, her head in her hands in the kitchen, tears pooling on the chipped plastic tabletop. Me, fucking helpless, as my whole chest caved in with the hurt on her behalf, hating the asshole who'd called himself my father for barely six years, before leaving . . . for good.

Mom was the victim of having loved someone who didn't deserve it, a man who'd walked away from all four of us. My sisters were old enough to remember when it happened. The tears she had shed during our childhood had hardened into frown lines and pursed lips as we grew older, the silence of forced restraint rather than peace.

But now, for the first time in my damn life, I understood it. What it felt like to have your heart ripped out, to see the love you'd offered up be tossed aside like trash.

I folded over at the waist, the pain from my wrist streaking white-hot fire up my arm. But for the first time in a week, I couldn't feel it. Not over the pain in my fucking chest.

But this . . . this wasn't the Hestia I'd come to know, was it? The person I'd felt, held, kissed . . . the one who'd looked at me like she was finally able to trust a man, to see *me* – the real me, right in the fucking core of my bones.

What if this was the real her? The one in London who'd fallen back into bed, into life with her ex? Back in love with him?

The hope that'd welled up from her messages, the hours spent contemplating whether to risk it – all of that collapsed in on itself. Even looking up London flights, ready to back out of the rodeo . . . for nothing. For something that had clearly just been in my head.

Fucking tears, more fucking tears formed and fell in silence. I was a wreck, a goddamn burnt-out shell.

And even now, even like this . . . I still loved her. It was the clearest part of my vision in the chaos.

The ranch house was quiet, but it was only a matter of time before someone would come back in and I'd have to snap out of it, act like I was coping. Gulping air, bracing myself against the bed with my good arm, I made a list of the shit I needed to do before leaving for the rodeo. I'd get up, get some cold water on my face and then pick something to –

My phone rang and I whipped round to grab it . . . then realized it wasn't her. I stared at the screen, crushed under an ache so fucking heavy that I had to take a few seconds before I could trust my voice.

'Yeah?' I said, tapping the button, listening as my brother-in-law launched into a sales pitch. He was making way too much effort to get me to agree to go to the rodeo a couple of days early with him and his buddies.

'Dean,' I sighed, trying so damn hard to sound as though I wasn't something to worry about, to confirm his thoughts that

Clara was overreacting about my mental state. 'I'll go to the rodeo early, quit it already. Want me to go to the grocery store and pick up some stuff to take with us?'

He laughed, undeniable relief winding through the sound.

'I knew it, man. I told your sister it'd take more than some random British chick to take you down and out. Don't forget the beers, okay? It's time we put shit right over a few cold ones.'

The call ended soon after, silence returning.

Some random British chick. I ran my fingers through my hair, wincing. How could something, someone as precious as Hestia just be . . . *dismissed* in that way? Like she didn't have the power to fucking shred me inside.

But I knew it wasn't Dean's fault, or any of them. I'd built the wall they saw and worked hard to maintain it. The fact that there was a fucking huge hole in the middle of it was for me alone to know.

There would be plenty of time to pack in the next couple of days, but the moment I heard Lottie and Bailey downstairs, it felt like the perfect time to get to the grocery store. I knew I was hiding, knew that they'd know that too; but right now, it was all I had.

'Jesse?'

Fuck.

'Yeah?' I replied, turning to see the familiar concern in every angle of Lottie's face, mirrored in Bailey's behind her.

'We're going down to Shelby's later. There's a band that Cole was saying . . . Jesse?'

I turned away, unable to hold my gaze on her, hear the accent, without thinking of Hestia and seeing her in my mind. The last thing I wanted to do was make Lottie feel bad, but I had to leave.

'Nah, you go on ahead, I'm gonna sit it out,' I murmured, giving them both a small nod as I opened the front door, a rush of warm, grass-sweetened air washing over us.

'How long you gonna keep sitting out?' Bailey asked, stepping forward, one hand on her hip, a calculated expression forming. 'It's not gonna help or bring her back.'

Mouth half open to respond, I started walking as the words landed.

'I'll sit it out until I give a fuck about music, or nights in a bar, or anything else again,' I replied, taking the porch steps two at a time.

'Jesse, she didn't mean to—' Lottie began as Bailey cut her off.

'The hell I didn't! Jesse Bennington, get your mopey ass over to that bar later. You might not give a fuck, but we do. Don't make me drag you in there!'

I almost smiled, keeping my head down as I half turned back, flipping her off. She chuckled.

'That's settled, then. Eight p.m., cowboy.'

Bailey was many things, but easy-going and forgiving were not two of them.

That was why, just after eight, I forced myself to keep my word and ended up in among a whole bunch of them. With Bailey on one side and Jace on the other, swept up in the rodeo talk and holding a beer in my hand, it almost felt normal, until . . . Lottie and Cole. The way they moved around each other, like he was her gravity and she his, eyes constantly meeting, hands touching or wandering across each other's bodies.

It was painful to watch, to feel.

Knocking back the rest of my beer, I gestured with my empty bottle to the rest of them and the bar in the background beyond, taking a couple of orders from those running low. Finding a space between the seated regulars and the groups of out-of-towners, I placed my order, glad for the relief of stepping away from everyone I knew.

'Wait, let me guess,' a voice to my right sounded.

I stifled my frustration, desperate to be left alone.

'Guess what?' I asked, turning my head to my right, recognition dawning as Chrissy sidled up with one of her friends. I gave them both a small smile. She looked as she always had, a little ray of sunshine in a pair of boots, all fluffy blonde curls and glossed lips – an undeniably pretty smile. One that widened the longer my eyes lingered on her.

'You've ordered a bourbon, neat, of course.' She paused, holding a finger to her chin for a moment. 'With a little ice, not too much though.'

I tilted my head, my smile becoming sheepish as my drink and the couple of others arrived. She giggled, glancing back at her friend, who, with one more look at me, wandered off into the crowd.

'Some things never change, right?' she said softly, only just audible over the music as she stepped up to me.

I shrugged, paying for my drink and then taking a sip. She gestured to me, wanting to try it, something she'd done when we'd been together. It was something I'd always found cute about her . . . and 100 per cent a tactic to get me to look at her lips. I handed her the drink without a word, not quite knowing why, watching as she grasped it with long nails shaped . . . like Hestia's always were. Sharpened to points, painted darker than I'd ever seen Chrissy wear, in fact.

'Wyoming whiskey, right?' she asked, smiling up at me from under her lashes as I nodded.

'Yeah, last one to take the edge off before we head up to Livingston Peak. You coming up for the rodeo?'

She pouted for a moment, handing back the glass, fingers lingering on mine. We locked eyes, hers almost pleading, just as they had when I'd called it off months ago.

'I wanted to, but Danny didn't have room in the truck with the rest of the team, and Jeanie's car's in the shop. Some engine thing got busted up.'

She shrugged and rolled her eyes at my incredulous look, trying not to laugh at her lack of car knowledge. It'd always tickled me that her family were all car mechanics or racers – both, for some of them – but she'd somehow avoided all the shop talk, resolutely staying clear of cars as a life path for herself.

It made me realize, in that moment, that there'd been nothing wrong with me and Chrissy – it was all in my head. She was cute, kind and funny, eager to please.

'Well, you can come on up with me if you like? I was gonna go up with Dean on Friday, but his truck was looking kinda full, so I was thinking of driving anyway, bit more room to spread out. You barely fill up a whole seat, so I reckon I can tuck you into my cab.'

She giggled, swatting my arm, but instead of the small rush of fun that I'd always felt from flirting, there was . . . nothing. I could see it, the whole situation. Her in that cute shirt and skirt, hand on my arm as she moved closer, my wariness making her double down on her efforts, just like she used to do.

'Just you and me?' she asked, moving her hand down onto the top of my jeans, finger skirting over my belt.

'Why not,' I agreed, her smile in response curdling my insides with guilt. The fuck was I doing? Giving her hope now, after all this time, when I had no intention of—

All thoughts gave way to nothing as she reached up, hand on my face, and . . . kissed me. Her lips pressed into me, forming a question, the answer slow as I scrambled to make sense of what was happening. That it wasn't Hestia.

Hestia.

As if she heard it, Chrissy pulled back.

'I'll look forward to it,' she murmured, putting a finger to her lips.

'Chrissy,' I began, needing her to know, not wanting her to think—

'It's fine. I know what's happened,' she replied, searching my face for a moment, her smile fading to nothing. 'I know she left and you're not yourself. Bailey told me as much. But I don't care. I'm still here, Jesse.'

There was a silence between us, despite the music and the noise of the crowd around us. I could feel how easy this would be, to just fall straight back into whatever we'd had; maybe just let it unfold, even though the balance would never be right between us.

'I better get these drinks to everyone,' I said instead, reaching back to the bar, downing the rest of my drink in one. The memory of fireballs flashed right behind my eyes. 'But I'll pick you up on Friday. Say, ten?'

She nodded, her nails gently grazing my arm as I stepped away from the bar. I felt the weight of her stare all the way back to the group.

Chapter 21
Hestia

Much as I'd somehow managed to walk away from Cal without landing myself in jail as a result, I hadn't managed to avoid one of the many bars on the way home.

I drank steadily through the afternoon and into the early hours, eventually letting one of the hot women working behind the last bar walk me back after her shift.

'So . . . can I come up?' she asked as we stopped outside the hotel doors, tucking a strand of hair behind my ear in a gesture so reminiscent of Jesse that I recoiled.

'You're really pretty, but . . . I mean, I don't actually have a boyfriend, but . . .' I shook my head, too confused to get the words out.

'What?' she questioned, backing up. 'You're straight? Seriously?'

I shook my head vehemently, staggering slightly.

'No,' I giggled. 'My first love was a woman. God, she's *stunning*. She's my best friend now. I still love her, but not in *that* way.'

The woman raised her eyebrows for a moment.

'Okaaay, no, that sounds . . . simple.'

'No, really,' I persuaded, 'it is. She loves a man, a cowboy, actually. And so do I. Not the same one, though.'

'You love a . . . cowboy?' she questioned. 'Here? In London?'

I giggled again, but it turned into a groan as a wave of nausea threatened to make this a violently embarrassing end to the evening.

'No! In *Wyoming*. I don't *just* love him, though, it's more than that. It's not about his dick, though. Although it's a very, very nice one.' I made the chef's kiss sign, watching as she fully backed away, eyebrows raised.

'Well, I'm happy for you. But maybe, if it doesn't work out . . . look me up.'

I nodded, suddenly remembering, with searing clarity, the reason I'd got myself into this state in the first place. That Jesse very likely wanted nothing else to do with me again, after Cal's stunt.

I'd messaged, tried to explain, but nothing. No response.

Which is why, after managing to crawl into bed, I didn't leave my hotel room for the next forty-eight hours. The realization that Jesse would not only be in pain but might actually hate me was more than I could bear.

After a long, fitful sleep, I lay awake for hours on end, curled in on myself, my brain slowly ticking over the worst moments of my life to date. The image in my mind of Jesse's face on the screen, thinking he'd realized what was going on, then hanging up seconds later . . . that had wormed its way right into the top spot.

My phone had been ringing on and off for the past two hours, on silent, but the screen lighting up the ceiling in the otherwise dark room. Eventually, irritation seeping through my comatose state, I dragged it onto the bed.

Lottie.

I tapped it to pick up.

'Hestia?' she said, her tone breathless. 'Oh thank fuck, are you there?'

'Yeah,' I croaked, brain firing as the anxiety in her voice filtered through the haze.

'Oh Hes, what happened with Jesse?'

I pushed myself up, pushing my tangled mass of hair back off my face.

'I don't know where to start . . .' I groaned, my head throbbing. 'I was speaking to him and . . . Cal, he acted like we were together – came walking into my room naked, pretending like I'd left underwear in his room, kissed me in front of Jesse . . .'

Her breath retracted, a horrified pause between us.

'Oh, fuck. Yeah, okay, that'd do it . . . oh shit, Hes. Listen, please don't hate me for asking, but you and Cal aren't really . . .'

'Jesus Christ, no,' I moaned, wincing as pain lanced behind my eyes. 'Why would you assume that? I've tried to message Jesse to explain. He's not responding.'

I swore, grabbing the stagnant glass of water from the nightstand and knocking it back as Lottie scrambled.

'I'm not assuming,' she said eventually, her voice firm. 'But I wanted to double check before I start trying to get Jesse back here. Come on, you know how you and Cal have a . . . different relationship. One minute you're fighting and the next you're fucking – I'm not blaming or judging you. I just wanted to get it straight for myself, okay?'

I rubbed my forehead, hating that I knew she was right, but focusing on what she'd said before.

'What did you mean, get him back here? What's going on?'

She stopped. I could hear Cole's voice in the background, his words just out of reach.

'Are you sure?' she asked him, letting out a volley of curses when he apparently confirmed that he was. 'He's going to fucking hurt himself, Cole. I don't like this.'

'Lottie, please – tell me what's going on?' I asked, finally getting up and turning on the room light, grimacing at the brightness. A fluttering sensation had begun in my gut, a sense that something was off as the pitch of her voice changed. 'You're scaring me . . . Lottie?'

'He's . . . oh fuck. Cole says he's getting ready to go up to the Livingston Peak rodeo a day early to practise. He's going with a bunch of the other guys and their crew . . . but it's the way he's acting . . . like he doesn't care. It's really fucking reckless, bad enough with his wrist as it is anyway, but . . .'

My heart was beginning to hammer.

'Put Cole on, Lottie. I want to speak to him, please,' I begged, gripping the phone as if it was my only lifeline.

'Hey, Hestia,' he said. Even in those two words, I heard it – an undercurrent of mistrust, of the same tenor as Lottie's question.

'Can you tell him not to go?' I asked, remembering our last conversation about this on horseback, what felt like a million years ago.

'I've tried,' he replied, his own anxiety now audible. 'I've never seen him like this, he's not listening to reason. I don't know what else to do, other than hold him down on the fucking ground. I don't know, maybe the other guys will help, maybe a bit of time and space on the drive up will clear his head . . .'

'But he can't do it,' I pleaded. 'What if he does something really stupid? What if he's not fucking focusing? Oh shit, Cole,' I begged, my voice giving way as I pictured what could happen, what'd happened to one of the riders at the first rodeo I'd seen, dragged out of the arena, limp and broken. 'Go down there, please, I'm begging you. I'll try and call, but he didn't answer my messages before . . . what if he doesn't pick up?'

I could feel the hysteria building. I was thousands of miles away and almost entirely helpless. If I was the reason something happened to Jesse . . .

'Okay . . . maybe that'll work. I'll see what I can do to make him pick up,' he reassured me. 'But Hestia . . .' He paused, clearly trying to arrange his words carefully. 'He's fucking devastated right now. Now, I like you a lot, but he's my brother. I can't let him get hurt all over again, you know?'

'I know,' I whispered, the familiar surge of self-hate washing through me. I fought it for a moment. 'But Cole, I didn't do anything with Cal. He was trying to fuck me over and make Jesse jealous. I fucking swear it on Lottie's life.' His breath caught for a moment, hesitating. 'You *know* how much I love that woman,' I added, shaking my head. 'I wouldn't lie about this, Cole. There's no other way I can prove it, but nothing happened with Cal other than me ending everything between us. We've always played this game . . . it's fucked up and sad and awful.' I stopped, drawing a ragged breath, desperate to keep it together. 'But I would never hurt Jesse like that. I haven't said it in as many words to him yet, but I love him, Cole, like you love Lottie. I love him *so fucking much* – I just don't feel like I deserve him.'

'Oh, sweetheart,' Lottie replied, her voice startling me as I felt tears building. 'Cole put you on speaker. Don't worry, it's just us.'

'I'm going down there now,' Cole said. I could hear movement in the background. 'Give me five minutes, Hestia, then try his phone, okay?'

I nodded to myself, more aware than ever of being alone.

'I fucking knew it,' Lottie croaked after a few more seconds, sniffing at her end of the line. 'I knew you loved him.'

'Smartass,' I murmured, trying to smile. She almost laughed, but it turned quickly into a sigh.

'It's not going well, then, being home?' she asked, keeping her voice low.

'No,' I said simply, getting up and walking into the bathroom, putting her on speaker as I attempted to sort my face out. Mascara smudged everywhere, hair sticking up at odd angles.

I briefly described the scene I'd walked into on day one, and then the state of the studio. Lottie listened in silence, with an occasional intake of breath at the particularly fucked-up moments.

'Oh, Hes,' she said after I'd finished. 'That's . . . a lot.'

'Yeah. And now I've got to somehow extract Cal from the studio and get that going again. The years of building up our client base, the work to get it where it is – well, was.'

'I know, I know. Look, are you sure –' She broke off as I paused with the face wipes.

'What?' I asked, the same feeling of panic resurfacing.

'He left,' Cole growled, cursing with frustration in his voice as clear as if he was standing next to me. 'I tried to talk to him but he wouldn't have a bar of it. Said he was going into town to pick someone up, give them a ride up to Montana.'

There was a heavy silence on their side, a silent communication I wasn't party to.

'I'll try him in his truck,' I said, suddenly determined, knowing it was the only way to service the panic. 'I'll just keep fucking ringing until he picks up.'

'Okay,' Lottie agreed, an uneasy undertone to her answer. 'Message me if and when you get through? You can call me any time, you know that?'

'I know,' I whispered. 'Thanks.'

We hung up and I gritted my teeth, tapping on Jesse's name despite the butterflies that launched as I did so.

Continuing to tidy myself up, I waited as it rang and rang, my eyes darting down as it went through to the answerphone.

Narrowing my eyes, I tapped call again.

'*Pick up, pick up,*' I hissed, almost growling as it cut off again.

One of three things was true. He was unable to pick up, or he hadn't seen it, *or* he was ignoring it. I knew his phone connected automatically to the Bluetooth in his truck, I'd seen it enough times. There's no way he wouldn't see it – mounted right on the dash in front of him.

'Stubborn motherfucker,' I breathed, now stabbing his name to redial. 'You can fucking hate me if you want, but I *will* talk to you,' I hissed, now brushing through my hair with unnecessary force.

For the next five minutes, I kept going. Cutting off time after time, until, after the fourteenth attempt, I came back into the bedroom and yanked open the curtains, the midday sun half blinding me.

Perching on the edge of the bed, instead I typed a message.

> I know you're ignoring me. I need to speak to you, Jesse. Please. If there's only more thing you do for me, please just pick up.

I waited for it to go through, watching as the message delivered, then the read ticks appeared.

> Please. For what we had.

I took a breath, waiting for that to go through too, blinking back the emotion it brought with it.

Waiting another minute, I pulled up his name again, my finger hovering over the button. But before I could tap it, he called me.

Heart in my mouth, I picked up. As the screen changed, I realized it was FaceTime again, not just a call.

Utterly bare-faced, the weight of the past three days under my eyes, I'd never felt more exposed.

'I haven't got time for this,' he said, barely looking at the screen as he stared straight ahead. In his truck, clearly parked up, he sighed. 'What is it?'

Momentarily stunned by his coldness, I could only gape for a moment, rearranging my thoughts into something that made sense.

'Please don't go,' I said, the words coming out with far less force than I'd intended.

He glanced at me then, his eyes guarded, so filled with pain and confusion that I almost choked.

'Don't go to the rodeo,' I blurted. 'Please don't ride feeling like this—'

'You can't just . . .' he started, real anger blazing in his eyes. 'You don't get to ask shit of me like that. What I am supposed to do, Hestia? You don't want me, you don't want us. You've made that real fucking clear. You've got right back to your old life, so I'm doing the same. Isn't that what you wanted?'

His words were like a slap, my eyes stinging as I struggled for breath.

'That's not . . . no, I mean . . .' My throat closed as my eyes did, my hand over my mouth as my head swam. I realized it, in the darkness: this was rock bottom. I'd been descending for so long that I barely noticed the feeling as I bumped down onto the lowest point.

'I've got to go,' he said, his tone softened. 'It's a long drive.'

'Why are you doing this?' I blurted, nothing left to lose, no further to go. 'How can you do this? Even if you don't give a fuck about me, what about your mum? Your sisters? Lottie, Cole, Bailey, Lil?'

My voice was rising, trying to fill the depths of the pit I lay in, as though all sound was pulled into a vacuum.

'Do what? Ride?' he asked, his tone responding in turn. 'What does it matter? It's just what we do—'

'*Not like this*,' I shouted, opening my eyes, almost shaking the phone in frustration. 'Not when you don't give a fuck what happens. Don't you fucking DARE ride in that state. I can't just stand by and let it happen!'

His eyes flicked up from the screen, following something outside of the truck.

'You've got no right to be angry with me,' he snarled, every angle of his face taut. 'Don't act like you care now—'

'*I do care*,' I yelled, standing up, almost punching the wall in frustration. 'It's *all* I fucking feel, Jesse! Why do you think I walked away and came home? Have you thought about that at all? That maybe I was trying to fucking spare you all of this?' I started to sob, my whole chest feeling as though it would disintegrate. '*Nothing happened* with Cal – he was deliberately trying to sabotage this, he set the whole thing up. I know I'm fucked up, I know I don't fucking deserve you. But *I love you*, Jesse. I'm selfish and I can't fucking help it. I love you so much that I can't feel anything else.'

There was a moment of silence, his face aghast, nothing but shock registering as I heard the passenger door of his truck open with a clunk.

A soft female voice began talking. The words were unimportant; his reaction said everything.

'I've got to go,' he repeated, his own voice empty. 'Take care of yourself.'

I stared, stunned, as the phone moved for a moment before disconnecting – a flash of long, blonde hair and the side profile of a pretty face.

In the silence that followed, still staring at the black screen, I knew.

Chrissy. His ex.

The next couple of hours became a blur. I moved from anger to indifference, from bone-shaking grief to a terrifying stillness that blocked everything out, that told me to get back into bed and never move again.

Buried deep in my gut was the urge to get back on a plane, to follow Jesse to Livingston Peak – five hours north of Jackson, in Montana, as a Google Maps search revealed – and put myself right between him and the fucking bull. *Under* the fucking bull, if it stopped him.

He could be with Chrissy if he wanted, if the idea of us was dead to him. But he couldn't get on that damn bull in a state that might fucking kill him.

This was my mess. My fault.

I ordered takeaway to my room. With my brain picking up speed as my first meal in two days hit, I grabbed my phone and started searching for flights.

Objection after objection, problem after problem bombarded my mind, ways this could all fuck up. But this was something I needed to be there for, in person.

After twenty minutes of working my way through flights to Denver, Salt Lake City and even Chicago, other than prohibitively expensive first-class seats, I couldn't find any that would get me there for Sunday evening. It needed to be a flight tonight, or at the latest, tomorrow morning.

There was nothing.

I couldn't do it. I couldn't get there in time.

Numb, about to put my phone down, I jolted as it buzzed.

It was the cleaning company, letting me know they'd finished up at the studio. I blew out a breath, willing myself into sense, knowing that staying in this room wasn't a plan.

I would shower, dress and walk over. Nothing more, nothing less.

If Jesse and I were ... done, then the studio was what I had left. That was the thing I could rebuild.

So I did, for once talking to myself as gently as I would a child, feeling myself come back to life gradually with clean hair, painting a semblance of myself onto my face with make-up. Occasionally I failed, caught off guard with a thought of Jesse, knowing he was in his truck right now with her – moving on, just like he thought I had.

That's when I had to stop, to lean over the bathroom countertop and hold myself in. The visceral effects of this fuck-up, I realized as I finally left the hotel some time later, were more than I'd ever known before. The scale of loss was like nothing I'd felt before.

The tainted city air was a welcome change, waking me up as I strode through the streets towards the studio, one foot in front of the other until –

Cal was leaning against the wall near the studio door, barely recognizable in clothes.

I came to an abrupt stop, eyeing him carefully.

'I'm not here to cause problems,' he said, holding up a hand. 'I swear. I just – I didn't want to leave things like that between us.'

'Give me fucking strength,' I hissed under my breath, walking round him as I got to the door, opening it with my key. 'How did you know I would be here?'

He shrugged.

'The cleaner replied to the studio email address. I figured you'd be here to check on it. You always did look for the details.'

I glared back at him for a moment, waiting for him to look away first before stepping inside.

The chaos was gone. There was no hint of the cesspit Cal and his dickhead, waster friends had created. But as I walked through the space, vast patches on the walls now scrubbed almost down to the plaster to remove the graffiti, it felt different. As though something of our history had been cleansed along with the mess.

My cherry blossom mural had almost gone, dozens of happy hours at the beginning of this adventure with Cal now erased.

'Hestia, I'm sorry,' Cal said, stepping into the room behind me, careful to keep his distance.

'I don't have the strength for this,' I admitted, turning to him.

'I did fake it,' he blurted, grimacing as I frowned. 'I didn't end up in hospital because I overdosed. I mean, I did get fucked up and go there for a few hours, but it was only long enough for Mum to visit before they made me leave.'

I stared at him, trying, failing to make sense of it.

'It was the only way I could think of to get you home,' he said, running his hands through his hair. 'Becca was . . . she was just a distraction, nothing important,' he dismissed. 'The timing of you coming back was fucked up, though. I never would've—'

'Stop, Cal,' I murmured, shaking my head. 'Just stop. Why did you think it would change anything? We ended months ago.'

'I know, I just thought . . . you were so fucking good to me when I was in hospital before, for real. Those weeks afterwards were some of the best of the past couple of years between us, weren't they? I guess I wanted to try . . .' He sighed. 'But, yeah. I don't know. I hadn't counted on you having changed so much since you'd been gone.'

I stopped, the build-up of disbelief and anger dissolving.

'Changed? What do you mean?'

He gestured at me, shrugging.

'You're . . . different. Something's changed in here,' he said, motioning to his temple. 'Whatever you think about me, Hes, I do know you. *Did* know you.'

We held each other's gaze then, registering an acute sadness at the distinction.

'And while I'm putting the truth out there,' he added, looking away for a moment, glancing at the scrubbed mural, 'it wasn't just a bender we were on in here. This was anger . . . revenge, I guess.'

Wide-eyed, I shook my head.

'Because I went on holiday?' I asked, not quite believing it, not even of him.

'No,' he replied, exhaling. 'Not because of you. Because the fucking landlord is selling this place. He used the break clause in our lease and gave us notice a couple of weeks ago. This place is being knocked down in a couple of months to make way for luxury flats.'

My jaw dropped open.

'We're out? Just like that?'

He nodded.

'Three or four weeks left on the lease. Years of work, establishing this place and . . . gone. Almost overnight. Story of this whole area, though, right? It was bound to happen sooner or later.'

And as I looked around the room – the memories faded to nothing, just the scrubbed, sterile remains left behind – the one connection holding me to London, to Cal and our old life, simply . . . disintegrated.

Gone.

'We need to sell the flat, Cal,' I said, a strange sense of calm pervading. 'We're both going to need the money to start again.'

He nodded.

'You're not staying here, though, are you?' he asked, scuffing at the floor with his shoes.

I shook my head gently, taking one last look around the space where I'd spent most of my adult life.

'No, I don't think I am.'

Chapter 22
Hestia

As I entered the restaurant that evening for Lil's leaving drinks, what sense of calm I'd had earlier in the day was rapidly evaporating.

In a little over twenty-four hours, Jesse was going to ride a bull with a broken wrist and barely a fuck left to give. And maybe, if he didn't get fucking trampled to death or break his neck, Chrissy would be all too happy to celebrate with him.

Despite the after-effects of my last hangover, I ordered a double whiskey, dead-eyeing the barman as he asked what mixer I wanted with it. Looking round the room, a smart, post-work banker bar in the City, I had a sudden pang for the bars in Jackson. The lack of pretentious voices and conversation; the easy-going, emotive country music that gave a depth and a vibe difficult to describe but impossible to forget.

I knocked back the drink in one as the barman handed it over, tapping my card on the payment machine as I finished, the heat of the whiskey searing my mouth and throat.

'Another?' he asked, his eyebrows raised, eyes flicking over my tattoos. The contrast between me and the usual customers was pretty stark.

'No, thanks,' I replied. 'Here for my friend's drinks party, actually. American, blonde, hot, Sabrina Carpenter vibes – seen her?'

He smiled, tilting his head as he took my empty glass back.

'Yeah, hard to miss,' he said, gesturing towards the very back. 'Bit like you,' he added, a suggestive curve to his mouth.

'Not tonight, hotshot,' I replied, giving him a half-smile in return as I began walking away, weaving through the sea of City boys with their slicked-back hair and signet rings.

'Hestia, hey!' Lil called from the centre of a small group of people at the back. I smiled, feeling yet another pang as I eyed her denim skirt and cowboy boots – just a cowboy hat away from her Jackson roots.

'Hey,' I replied, leaning into her huge hug, noting the way the group of others looked on with curiosity, Jamie raising his hand and grinning.

'I'm so glad you could make it,' she said, leaning back and smiling. 'I can't believe how quick this week has gone . . . I'll almost be home this time tomorrow.' She shook her head, leading me over to the others. 'How's it going with the studio and settling back in?'

'It's, uh . . . it's been difficult,' I began. Lil turned back to me, frowning as the other people began to introduce themselves – all friends of Jamie's.

'So what do you do, Hestia? Jamie says you live around here?'

He'd introduced himself as Dillon, one of Jamie's uni friends. He had a cocky edge to his voice and a swagger that suggested he was rarely refused anything.

'Yeah, I did,' I answered, catching Lil's eye for a moment. Her frown deepened. 'I'm a tattoo artist, although I'm considering different things right now.'

As he opened his mouth, eyes narrowed in on my neck, Lil interjected.

'Dillon, honey, would you do us the biggest favour?' she asked, laying her hand on his shoulder, waiting for him to turn to her. 'Hestia and I are just about gasping for another drink. Mine's a dirty martini, and I'd bet my life Hestia drinks those too?'

I hid a smile as I nodded, glancing down at my own cowboy boots, inconspicuous under my black, wide-leg jeans.

'Of course,' he simpered, another friend joining him to top up the whole group.

As he left, she grasped me gently by the arm, leading us away to a nearby standing table.

'You *did* live here? Considering new things?' she began, eyebrows in her hairline. 'What the hell happened in the past few days?'

I stared at her, hesitating, not quite knowing how to voice the thoughts that'd started developing this afternoon after I'd left the studio.

'The studio is . . . gone,' I admitted. I told her about the events of the afternoon, then rewound back to the painful moments with Jesse on the phone. My voice cracked a little as I finally admitted my simmering panic about his mental state, and about seeing Chrissy in his truck – and the lack of immediate flights to attempt to sort it out.

Lil's face, so like Lottie's, blurred at the edges as I blinked away the hurt and frustration. And, just as Lottie's would, her expression hardened, a steely core flashing through her wide blue eyes.

'C'mon, we're going outside for a moment,' she said, taking my hand and walking us through the building crowd and out into the cooling air, the relative quiet settling across us. 'This is bullshit. That man is a stubborn ass sometimes,' she added, pulling out her phone. 'But he'll listen to his boss. He'll have to.'

I held my breath as she called him, fighting back feelings of helplessness, grateful for her help but equally unsure how to accept it.

'Jesse, honey, how are ya?' she began, the friendly tone casing the hard edge of the expression. Her eyes narrowed as she took in his response. 'All of you, out on the town? That a good idea right before the competition?'

I balled my hands into fists, nails digging into my palms as she waited for his response.

'Oh, I'm coming home soon,' she suddenly replied, all trace of joviality gone. 'But changing the subject isn't gonna get you off the hook, Jesse.'

Shaking her head, she brought the phone down and tapped it onto speaker, holding it between us.

'. . . I get it, Lil,' he sighed, his voice only just audible over the babble of talking and music around him. 'I'll be fine . . . I just – these winnings could really change things, you know? Not just for Mom, but me too. Did Lottie call you? She and Cole have been bugging me all the way up here.'

'No, actually. I've been speaking to the one person you should be listening to. Hestia's worried sick, honey.'

Silence followed. My jaw clamped shut as I heard a now familiar female voice in the background – the sound that had reverberated around my head all day.

'Jesse?' Lil prompted, reaching out to squeeze my arm, her eyes too taut to be reassuring.

'Yeah, I'm here,' he mumbled.

'Listen, while you're out there drinking with God knows who—' she began, cut off by his angry sigh.

'Lil, I'm not doing this,' he growled. 'I don't know what to think about Hestia.'

I held my breath, trying to keep the hurt down.

'Honey, she cares what happens to you. She told you, didn't she?' Lil swallowed, as though this conversation was unlocking her own memories from a different time. I took her hand from my arm and held it instead, touched that she'd make herself vulnerable for my sake.

'She was just scared,' he replied, his voice suddenly becoming unbearably soft. 'Saying things to try and keep me safe, that's all.'

I opened my mouth, half gasping, half trying to respond, his words like a sharp stab to my gut.

'I don't think—' Lil cut in, but before she could finish, the sound of female giggling cut through; Chrissy was whispering his name.

'I've gotta go,' he said, his tone still despondent. 'Have a safe flight home, Lil. See you at the rodeo, if you make it.'

The phone cut off, the screen fading to black between us.

'Stubborn ass,' she hissed, opening it back up, ready to press call again.

But I stopped her, my eyes widening as an idea bloomed, like ink dropped into water.

'Your flight,' I murmured, not quite knowing if it was possible, or even if she'd consider it. 'When does it get into Jackson?'

Her eyes searched mine for a moment, widening.

'Tomorrow evening,' she breathed, taking back her hand and flicking away from the call screen and straight into another app. 'Are we thinking the same thing here?'

'I'm not sure I can pull off being you,' I stumbled, 'but if you can swap the name on the flight and don't mind waiting a couple of days to leave . . .'

She fell into concentration, pulling up her flight details and navigating around until –

'There,' she said, her tone triumphant as she turned the screen towards me. 'There's a fee to change the name on my ticket, but yeah, if you want to . . . I'll give you my seat home, sweetheart. You go rip that stubborn bastard a fresh one for me.'

With a noise somewhere between a sob and a laugh, I grabbed her into a hug.

She chuckled, surprise turning to a tight squeeze in return.

'Are you sure?' I asked, sudden guilt taking over. 'It's not too much? I mean, we can book you another flight right now, but...'

'Honey,' she replied, shaking her head. 'Listen, from what I know about you, from everything Lottie's said and what's going on with you and Jesse, I'm guessing you've been looking after yourself forever, right? Sweetheart, I say this from a place of knowing that feeling too damn well – you need to let people in, let them help you in the way you do for everyone else, okay?' She lifted her hand over her chest, staring at me square on. 'I am more than happy to give up my seat for you *and* I am more than happy to organize you a visa to stay on at the ranch, if that's what you want. I love Jamie's idea of running artist and writer retreats. We've been testing the waters these last few days with a bunch of people he knows, and we've got people signing up on a waiting list already. The ranch is gonna get real busy, real quick, so the work is there.'

I just stared at her, silenced by the size of her gesture, her willingness to share. Just as Jesse had shown me, from day one.

'I don't know what to say,' I admitted, allowing myself to smile as she did.

'Well, book me onto another flight for a start, then we need to go get our martinis. You need to go pack, and I need to tell Jamie he's got a few more days to put up with me.'

'Yes, ma'am,' I replied, grinning as she put her arm around my shoulder.

I left after transferring Lil the money for a new flight, getting her into Jackson in three days' time. Butterflies swarming in my gut, I knew that even though I didn't need to be at Heathrow until 4 a.m. for a flight just after 6 a.m., there was no way I would sleep in between.

So, with equal amounts of trepidation and excitement, I packed up my room at the hotel, trying not to focus on the hellish feelings that'd filled that space since I'd been there. Eventually, after triple-checking plug sockets and under the bed, I was checking out and climbing into an Uber.

We wound through streets I knew and gradually, through the evening traffic, pub- and party-goers on every pavement, we drove out into parts of the city I didn't wholly recognize, interspersed with memories of moments here and there over the years. I drank in every sight. London had been the first place to truly feel like home after the misery of my childhood and teenage years. It was vast and anonymous in so many ways but had accepted me for what I was, given me a place to start. But Jackson . . . that felt different.

Finally, almost approaching midnight, the airport loomed ahead.

Just six hours until I could leave.

Just twenty-four hours until I might see Jesse again.

More butterflies erupting in my chest, I set about the process of waiting, trying desperately to focus on one thing then another, careful not to let my mind wander too far. By the time we were finally boarding, then up in the air, I was ready to let the low drone of the engines pull me down into sleep.

Lottie's messages were waiting for me when I arrived into Denver, telling me that she and Cole had been trying to get hold of Jesse; that she was willing to drive on up to Livingston Peak once she'd picked Lil up from the airport if I wanted her to.

I smiled to myself, glad that Lil and I had agreed to say nothing about our swap – just let my arrival be a surprise.

But once I'd answered Lottie, my body and brain now fully awake after a solid seven hours' sleep, I could no longer ignore the thoughts that surrounded me; the ones that asked how the hell this would all work if Jesse and Chrissy were now back together. How would I cope seeing them together at the ranch? And would I be able to tattoo professionally on a work visa tied to the ranch?

At the back of my mind I was still turning over whether this would be a temporary trip or whether now, free of Cal and the studio, I could set myself up afresh in London. It was an option, I knew, but one that felt . . . empty.

Getting on the smaller plane to Jackson a couple of hours later, I noticed a couple of other passengers in cowboy hats, and reality began to hit. Gently, reverently, I took mine out of my case, running over the details with my fingers and remembering the day Dee had given it to me at the Collective.

That's where I could picture myself tattooing again – fresh designs, inspired by the endless landscape all around. And as we flew into the Grand Teton National Park, descending among the jagged tips below, my old signature cherry blossom design began to morph into the small, amethyst-coloured wildflowers all around the ranch. I could picture exactly the shading technique I'd use, the precise colour combinations. Pulling out the notepad and pen I always carried, I spent the rest of the flight sketching and was surprised when we suddenly bumped down onto the runway, the mountain peaks now soaring above the plane.

I spotted Lottie in the terminal before she saw me. She was still discernibly the Lottie I'd always known, more likely to choose pastel shades and simplicity over detail, but the western accents brought her to life – made sense of the untamed curls kept in check by her camel-coloured hat, city heels swapped for the stylish tan leather boots.

She just belonged here.

I wondered if – and hoped – I might be able to pull off my own version.

Approaching her from the side, knowing she was fixed on locating her cousin, I made an attempt at Lil's lilting drawl.

'Howdy, cowgirl.'

Head whipping towards me, confusion widening her eyes, she froze for a moment before squealing, running to catch me in a hug that almost send us both flying.

'What the fuck? Oh my God! Is this really happening?' she cried, laughing as our hats landed on the floor beside us. 'Where's Lil? Did she come too?'

I shook my head, still holding onto her. I'd never been more grateful to see someone I loved.

'She gave me her flight – there was nothing else for another couple of days. Besides, I made myself pretty popular with her new man; he gets a couple more days of her.'

'I can't believe you're here,' she breathed, picking up my smaller bag as I grabbed my big roll-on case. 'Does . . . anyone else know?'

I shook my head, updating her on the last conversation between Lil and Jesse as we walked out to Cole's truck. Lottie's brow pinched as I repeated his words, that he didn't know what to think about me.

'And don't even get me fucking started on Chrissy,' I spat as we climbed in.

'Yeah, I've had the lowdown on her from Bailey,' she replied, giving me a grim smile, holding up a finger as I was about to ask for all of it. 'Listen, before we get going – we can either drive up to Livingston Peak tonight, but we won't get there until late, especially as I'll need to grab a few things to stay over. Or, we can leave first thing, get there early and maybe stay over after the rodeo?'

Her hopeful smile was more than I could let myself join in with; she was clearly imagining an outcome I hadn't dared to hope for.

'Let's go first thing,' I replied. 'I don't want you driving tired and I'm sure Cole doesn't either.'

She nodded.

'Although . . . have you moved back to your room since I left?' I asked as we set off.

'Actually, no,' she said, the smile suddenly becoming a grin again. 'I meant to tell you when we spoke last, but everything was a bit . . . you know.' She paused, grimacing as I nodded my agreement. 'I, um . . . well, I've moved into the cabin . . . with Cole.'

I squealed, grabbing her for a half hug and trying not to land us in a ditch as she laughed, just about keeping control of the truck.

We chatted happily for the rest of the way back. As we finally turned off the highway and up onto the Diamond Back road, driving under the ranch sign and winding up the steep track, I was overwhelmed by the feelings it brought back.

It had only been three weeks since I left, but so much had passed since then that it felt like a year. Except this time, I realized as we pulled in by the house next to Bailey's truck – Jesse's truck conspicuous by its absence – it was very different.

'I'll give you a minute to unpack stuff – then come see the cabin?' Lottie clapped her hands, hugging me again. 'I thought it would be ages, months and months, before I could show you that!'

I laughed as we hauled the big case up the front steps together.

'Oh, and there's someone else who'll be glad to see you – other than Bailey and Cole, of course.'

I frowned, knowing she wouldn't sound so light-hearted if Jesse was back here, by some miracle.

'What? Who?' I asked, suddenly wondering if by some chance Dee could be here.

'Well, it was supposed to be a surprise for whenever you did visit next . . . and a way of holding onto you for a little longer, I suspect,' she began as we made our way to my old room – her old room. 'But Luci never did make it over to Rosie's sanctuary. Jesse called her up the day after you left, told her he was taking on Luci's training instead.'

I stared at her for a moment, not quite able to take it in.

'He worked on her every day, breaking her in for you, right up until he headed off for the rodeo yesterday. Even with his wrist. Wanted you to have your own horse here, to keep a place for you, if you ever decided to come home – back.'

I perched on the side of the bed. Somehow, I was back in exactly the same place, and yet . . . not. I couldn't help the tears that began to gather, and I gently shushed her concern as she took her place at my side.

'I don't know what I did to deserve it,' I murmured, shaking my head at her small smile. 'To deserve him.'

She kissed the side of my head.

'It's not about deserving him, or him you,' she said, her clear eyes calm as they rested on mine. 'That's the thing about love, right? Real love, I mean. It's not conditional. It just . . . is. I know our relationship didn't turn out as you wanted, way back in the beginning.' She smiled as I blinked back tears. 'But you know how much I love you, right? No conditions attached, not because you "deserve" it or either of us owes the other anything.'

I nodded, her words confirming the feelings that had dawned since I'd been away.

'You're way too pretty for a Yoda type,' I whispered back, bumping her knee with mine. 'And I know because I feel the same.' I paused, smiling as her wild curls cascaded over my shoulder as she leant on me. 'You're the reason I even know how that feels at all, Lots.'

It was her turn to well up, dabbing at the corners of her eyes.

'Okay, okay, enough of the heavy shit,' she said, exhaling. 'Meet me at the barn in ten? We'll say hi to Luci and then surprise Cole and Bailey.'

I nodded, closing my eyes briefly to the quiet as she left. There were so many memories in this room, in this bed, the bathroom . . . they were good memories, the best, only tinged with a little pain – right now. But after tomorrow, would I be able to bear being here?

Unpacking a little, I emerged into the corridor, reassured by the peaceful calm of the house. On impulse, rather than walking over to the front door to head to the barn, I carried on down the corridor and then headed up the stairs, hesitating as I reached the first room on the right.

I pushed the door open, immediately enveloped by everything Jesse. We hadn't spent much time together in here, with my room offering a little more privacy, further away from the others, but this room was a small piece of him – his wonderful smell, details that could only be his.

Not wanting to violate his privacy, I just stood in the doorway, fighting tears, until I noticed a shirt hanging from the handle on his closet door. Stepping across the floor, I picked it up and, unable to help myself, held it to my face and breathed it in for a moment.

My feelings were like a sledgehammer in response. The chest-crushing emotions of leaving him at the rodeo, begging me not to go. The sheer scale of the love I'd begun to feel and that had grown since, blanketing my insides like the wildflowers in the valley meadows.

I'd spent my life alone, relying on no one else, not even Lottie – definitely not Cal. I'd allowed myself to see glimpses of love, lust, and whatever else had passed through me over the years. But nothing that had consumed me like this, that I had no control over.

Jesse and me . . . if we got it right, I could finally see how we could be so much better together than apart. That to want and need another person didn't make you weak or vulnerable. There was so much strength in a relationship grounded in this kind of love – in holding each other's vulnerability and keeping it safe.

Replacing the shirt reluctantly, I made my way out of the house, knowing there was only one thing left to do. Work visas and everything else aside, Jesse had to know how I felt, how I *really* felt – all of it. I would have to bare my soul to him and be ready to have it ripped apart if he didn't feel the same; ultimately, it was up to him whether or not he could trust me again, love me again.

Chapter 23
Hestia

Lottie's cabin was beautiful.

Like a snapshot of her relationship with Cole, it was clearly built with so much care and love that the whole place sang with it, from the kitchen, paint matched to Lottie's favourite shade of pale, powder blue-grey, to the wraparound deck complete with a hand-made rocking chair – yet another gift from Cole.

'Hestia,' Bailey called, walking over as Cole lifted Lottie's case into the back of his truck, scooping her up into a kiss before she could climb in. 'I forgot to say. One of the guys at the Livingston Peak rodeo, Bill, he's an old friend of mine. If you need extra help getting round the back near the chutes, or if Jesse doesn't pick up, try him.'

I nodded, exhaling.

'You all right, cowpoke?' she asked, checking under the brim of my hat.

'Yeah, I guess. I just want to get there, you know?'

The truth was that nerves had churned up my guts since I'd woken up at 5 a.m. with jet lag kicking in, my body clock rejecting the time difference. The only thing that had calmed it was heading down to the barn, a walk so ingrained in my subconscious that I knew each step before I'd made it, heading straight for Luci's stall. Her greeting had been as sweet and heart-healing as ever; she had searched my pockets for treats and been rewarded with an apple I'd brought from the kitchen. I'd brushed her down, a fine haze of her fire-red hairs drifting across the shafts of sunlight that glanced across the wall, her head resting against my back.

'Know what I do before a competition, when all the stress kicks in and I'm wondering if I've got the stomach for it?' Bailey said, smiling as I looked up at her in hope. 'Either distract myself by talking about shit that has nothing to do with rodeo, something totally different. Or, maybe when you get closer, just focus on visualizing the thing you want. For me, that's racing over the line, everything feeling just right, hearing my time and knowing I've made it into first. For you . . . well. Whatever you want that to be.'

But as Lottie and I waved goodbye to them both and got onto the highway heading north, I just couldn't picture it. I couldn't see how I would get Jesse to trust me again, especially in terms of what he thought Cal and I had done. Hadn't I told him often enough how fucked up I was, told him I'd moved away to protect him from it?

'You want to listen to some music?' Lottie asked. Her voice was light, but I could hear the concern leaking through from underneath.

'Sure,' I said, shifting into a more comfortable position. 'But distract me, please, before my brain takes me over the fucking edge.'

She paused for a moment, selecting a radio station and keeping it on low.

'Cal's not all bad, is he?' she said, smiling as I turned to her, incredulous.

'What? Where did *that* come from?' I asked, trying to make sense of how she'd landed there.

'You said distract you, and I am,' she continued, a familiar glint in her eye as she turned back to the road. 'But he's not actually a bad guy, is he?'

I blinked, simultaneously wondering what she was up to, but suddenly plunged back into the complexity of his chaos, our chaos.

'No,' I said slowly, thinking of how we'd left things – the lack of animosity, in the end, despite everything. 'He's not. It's us, as a couple. Together we're toxic. We always were, I think.'

Lottie shot me a sympathetic look.

'I don't know, the early days were pretty good, right?' she replied. 'The ones at uni, anyway. He was always a bit of a loose cannon, but you guys had fun together, I remember it.'

I nodded, suddenly smiling as I remembered one particular night out where Cal had commandeered a battle of the bands night at the student union bar, belting out Linkin Park bangers and dragging me up on stage with him. Together we'd screamed at the crowd and they'd joined in, eventually blowing one of the speakers.

'Yeah, we had some good times,' I admitted. 'Although I guess ... with context, and what I know now ... what they should look like, what love actually feels like ... It just wasn't healthy.'

I stopped, my mind drifting back to Jesse again.

Lottie bit her lip, glancing at me briefly.

'What?' I said, curiosity thoroughly awoken. 'What's happened?'

She shook her head to dismiss it, but as she smiled, I knew she wasn't going to tell me. Yet.

'Nothing,' she said. 'I was just thinking about that time both of our parents came to visit in second year – remember? How we decided exactly what we *didn't* want from a relationship after that.'

I almost winced, remembering all too well. My stepfather's barely withheld disdain as he met Cal; the disappointment in my mum's face as she took in my building tattoo sleeve; the way Cal had looped his arm around my shoulders at dinner.

'Did I tell you what my mum said to me after that visit?' I asked quietly, suspecting I'd hidden it away at the time – ashamed to admit just how broken my family was, not thinking anyone would understand.

'I don't think so,' she replied, real concern winding through her expression now.

It replayed in my mind, the inflections in her voice still as clear now as they had been then.

'She told me never to rely on a man, on anyone but myself. That she was trapped by my stepfather, forced to stay with him for our sakes, for me and Theo. She said –' I paused, wanting to say the words aloud, wondering if it might release them. 'Relationships, marriage . . . is all a trap. People only ever use each other for their own gain.'

Lottie said nothing, just reached out to me with her right hand. I gripped it, swallowing down the emotion the words had brought up.

'I know how wrong she was now,' I whispered. 'I'm done living by that.'

Lottie nodded, turning off the highway towards Jackson, heading west for signs to Montana instead.

'No one's family is perfect,' Lottie said after a few minutes, the soft country tunes in the background filling the silence. 'I mean, look at me and Lil. Christ, the shit Lil's been through.'

I thought back to my conversations with Lil in London.

'Did Lil have a big relationship before?' I asked, watching as Lottie frowned. 'When we were talking about me staying in London initially, she came out with all this stuff about not giving up on a connection like the one I'd found with Jesse. It came from her own experiences, I think.'

She tapped the steering wheel, clearly raking over her memory.

'I don't think so,' she said slowly. 'But then, there was a whole chunk of time I missed out on right after her parents divorced and everything got serious with my exams. I think it had been eight years since I'd visited before this year.'

I mulled it over as we continued north, stopping briefly for lunch and snacks. By the time we crossed the Montana state line and drove into Livingston Peak, there were already queues of traffic building for the rodeo.

'Holy shit, this is huge,' I exclaimed, leaning forward for a better look ahead. The vast stadium-like walls were visible even with a couple of miles to go, and a colossal American flag rippling in the wind.

'Yeah, Cole said this is one of the biggest,' Lottie admitted, also staring out towards it. 'I just hope Jesse picks up if we call, because finding him in there is going to be a challenge.'

I gritted my teeth against a violent surge of anxiety as we edged closer, eventually crawling into the car park and coming to a stop.

Lottie killed the engine, turning to me.

'Are you ready for this?' she asked, a small smile appearing as she studied me.

'Fuck, no,' I murmured, unsure why she seemed so unperturbed. 'I can't believe I'm saying this, given I've travelled, like, what – the best part of five thousand miles to be here. But is this a good idea? Am I just going to put him off even more if we do manage to find him?'

Lottie rearranged her hat slightly, pulling it down a little at the back.

'Yeah, I did think about that last night,' she admitted. 'I asked Cole, given he's the only one who's actually done something similar with broncs.' She hesitated, her eyes flashing to mine for a moment. 'But he thinks Jesse will be okay. If you guys can talk even for a few minutes, it might set his mind at ease. There are always distractions, other shit going on in life when you're riding, whether it's bulls or not. Cole says it's when you move into the no-fucks-to-give category that things can go really wrong.'

She was holding something back, I knew. But before I could press her for more, she opened her door and slid out into the noise and streams of people heading past the truck and into the side entrance.

'I had a look online,' I said as we bought our tickets and squeezed through some time later, the sheer volume of people holding back progress through the entrance. 'The bull riding's one of the last events, I think.'

'Want to work around to the side, see if we can get in the back?' she shouted above the announcements and crowd noise.

I nodded, knowing I wouldn't have the strength to shout back. A growing feeling of nausea was cascading over me, threatening to become real. Knowing Jesse was right here in the same place, but not knowing if he cared or wanted to see me again . . . and not knowing Chrissy's role in all of it.

Slowly but surely we approached the competitors' entrance area, where the crowd thinned enough to let us see beyond the gates to a sea of cowboys beyond. My stomach lurched again.

'Howdy, ladies.'

An official stood by the gate, a walkie-talkie attached to his belt.

'Oh, hey,' Lottie said brightly. I almost chuckled at the shift in her expression, the way she looked up at him from under her eyelashes. 'A friend of ours is back there. My friend here has flown all the way from London to see him – is there any way at all we could sneak back there and say hello? We'll be out again within the hour, I swear it.'

He considered her, a smile growing.

'I wish I could, ma'am, but I'm afraid this is for competitors and their teams only – you'll need a badge to get in.'

They went back and forth for another minute before Lottie

took my hand, thanking him and walking us in the opposite direction.

'Okay, plan B,' she said, pulling out her phone and tapping on Jesse's name. 'Don't know how likely he is to answer now, not with everything going on back there.'

I already knew it wouldn't work, could feel my desperation growing as though my body sensed how close we were. Her phone rang and rang, and eventually, as it went through to the answerphone, I'd decided.

'Hang up,' I said, looking back towards the gate, watching as a competitor approached and exchanged a few words. The official simply slid back a latch on the gate to let them through. It wasn't locked.

'What?' she asked, puzzled, but doing it anyway. 'Why?'

'Because if you can distract him, I can probably get through unnoticed.'

She eyed me, deliberating.

'Okay,' she replied, clearly turning over the options. 'What kind of distraction?'

'Pass out,' I blurted, taking inspiration from the way I was feeling, my heart already hammering. 'I'll go over there.' I pointed towards the bathrooms in the corner, parallel with the gate. 'Then if you call out to him, maybe say you don't feel great and then fall down, preferably when no one else is nearby and he can't really refuse, I'll run out behind and slip through.'

The side of the chutes jutted out behind the gate. Once through, I'd be able to dive round the side and out of sight.

'Fuck, okay,' Lottie breathed, nodding. 'Well . . . guess I'll see you in the medical area, huh?'

I smiled, giving her arm a quick squeeze. Then I headed for the bathrooms and waited just inside the first door, out of the official's line of sight.

Within a minute or two, after waiting for a few groups of

spectators to pass by, Lottie edged a little closer to the official, looking down at her phone. Then, just as he reached down to his belt for the walkie-talkie, eyes on an area to her right, she called out, waiting for his attention to turn before her knees buckled. She landed side on in the dirt, her hat rolling off, hair splayed out.

He swore, opening the latch on the gate in seconds, leaving it open as he ran to her, pulling out the walkie-talkie in the same moment and speaking into it.

I bolted, holding onto my hat as I charged towards the gate, keeping my eyes on him as I ran right through, praying he would stay focused on Lottie until I was round the corner. Another second and I was out of sight, the edge of the chutes blocking me from view as I came to a standstill, breathing heavily, one hand on my chest.

Suddenly faced with far worse, I steeled myself as I looked into the organized chaos backstage. There were so many people – competitors with their numbers displayed on their fronts and backs, a maelstrom of hats, chaps and horses.

Staying clear of anyone official-looking, and very aware of my bright hair beneath the black hat, I stayed on the periphery, following the backs of the chutes all the way round, eyes searching for him. The noise was intense: the roar of the crowd from the other side of the stands, the occasional crash of hooves against steel making me jump.

'You okay there, ma'am?'

I flinched as an official approached from the side, eyes scouting for whatever ID was needed around here.

'Actually, no,' I said, letting my anxiety flood my voice. 'My friend just passed out round there, I'm trying to look for her boyfriend, he's a bull rider.'

Surprised, he grabbed his walkie-talkie.

'She with anyone?' he said, turning the dial on the top.

'Yeah, I think one person, I just know she'd want to see him, but I don't know—'

'It's okay – bull riders are mostly in that far back corner just around the side there, y'see?' He pointed, curving his hand around to indicate the other side of the biggest group of competitors in front of us. 'I'm gonna head over and see if she needs more help. Don't worry, we'll look after her.' He nodded and tipped his hat as he took off, talking into his radio.

Picking up my pace, I skirted what appeared to be the roping teams, keeping my head down. Rounding the corner, I slowed, looking down towards where the loudest animal noises were coming from. The volume of competitors thinned out there compared to everywhere else.

Then, just as I was about to turn back, unable to make anyone out, I heard a horribly familiar laugh that set my teeth on edge.

Chrissy and a small group of women, not twenty feet away, laughing together over drinks. And behind them, at the very far end of the chutes, three competitors leaning up against the chute.

The one in the middle looked up for a moment, his eyes scanning the crowd out in the arena, his face unmistakable in the golden-hour glow.

'Oh shit,' I choked, putting my hand to my mouth, my feet frozen to the ground. The need to go over there, to touch him, talk to him, was utterly eclipsed by my fear. The thought of his rejection playing out in front of everyone – especially her – was too awful to contemplate.

But before I had the chance to act or move away, I felt multiple eyes on me and heard someone curse.

'What the hell . . .' Chrissy said, marching over, half spilling her drink into the dirt. I backed up, my eyes still on Jesse; I was unable to take them away from every angle of his face.

'What do you think you're doing here? Hey! I'm talkin' to you!'

Jesse was too far back to hear her, the swell of the crowd cancelling all else out as the bronc riding was announced. Huge screens in the arena showed the first rider, his arms up to the crowd.

'Back off,' I said, watching as one of her friends came jogging over, her face just as thunderous as Chrissy's. 'This has nothing to do with you.'

Head tilted, hands on her hips, she took another step forward. She was pushing me towards the exit leading out to the stands, where small groups of spectators stood beyond the gates.

'The hell it doesn't,' she hissed, tossing her hair over one shoulder. 'You can't just show up and expect to walk back into his life after what you did.' Behind her, her friend was nodding.

'Listen, I've got no problem with you . . .' I said slowly, my anxiety giving way to building anger. 'But if you don't leave me the fuck alone, that's going to change.'

She shook her head slowly.

'Who the hell do you think you are, waltzing in here and assuming you can help yourself to him again? Huh? He's moving on, okay? With me.'

I stopped, fixed on her face, looking for the lie – hoping to find it beneath the self-righteous anger. But I couldn't.

'You're . . . together?' I breathed, a horrific wrenching sensation in my chest as she nodded, a cat-like smile rising on her lips.

'Oh, honey, you have no idea,' she replied, taking a sip of her beer, glancing at her friend. 'We were together for over a year before, in case he didn't tell you,' she added, her expression brightening as the pain inside made it through to my face. 'We've picked up right where we left off.'

I just stared at her. My pathetic, breaking heart wouldn't quite let me walk away.

'Fine,' I choked. 'But I still need to talk to him, just to clear some things up between us. It won't take more than a few minutes.'

I tried to move forward, but she reached out, pushing me back hard.

'No, he doesn't need this right now,' she said, shaking her head, her glossy blonde hair falling down her back. 'He doesn't want to see you ever again. He told me.'

I glanced down for a moment. Part of me, the larger, broken part, was ready to back off. But the other part raged at being pushed – at being told what I could and couldn't do – and decided to push back.

'I don't care,' I snapped, looking up at where Jesse still sat with the two other cowboys, oblivious to the gathering shitstorm. 'It's up to him, not you.'

She cried out as I shoved past her, dodging the rest of her drink as it fell from her hand.

'How dare you!' she cried, her friend joining in. 'Fucking bitch, get back here!'

I ignored her, now wholly focused on Jesse, on reaching him.

A vice grip on my arm yanked me back around as she used all of her weight, what little there was, to pull me back. I vaguely heard someone calling her name, calling mine from the staircase area, but as I tried to shake her off, her grip slipped and she reached out towards the front of my shirt instead. With another almighty yank, she ripped the front of it, tearing through the fabric and taking off the whole row of buttons in one go.

Feeling eyes on us, more heads turning from close by, I decided that if this was it – if Jesse was lost, and this bitch was the reason why – then *I* had nothing left to lose.

'That's your doing, not mine,' she snarled. Her friend backed away as I approached. Chrissy's eyes widened as I stopped, gently took off my hat and tossed it into the dirt nearby. I stared her down, watching her begin to squirm as I shrugged off what remained of my shirt, letting it fall to the ground at my feet.

'You owe me a fucking shirt,' I hissed, watching as her eyes travelled across my tats, over my bra: my favourite shade of purple, the colour of a bruised sky.

'Chrissy! What the fuck!' a female voice called from behind us – one I vaguely recognized.

'I don't owe you shit,' she said as I drew close, my fingers itching to slap the self-satisfied expression off her face.

'You know what?' I purred, taking a last step right into her space, feeling no small satisfaction in the way her expression faltered. 'It doesn't matter. Clothes never stayed on very long when I fucked Jesse. He'll like it better this way.'

With a scream she launched herself at me, nails gouging into my arm as she swung with her other arm. I dodged out of her way, grabbing her shirt by the collar in my fist, twisting it as I pushed her back, all but cutting off her air supply.

'Get off her!' screamed her friend, stumbling backwards in her eagerness to get away as I turned to her for a moment.

Chrissy struggled against me, panic rising in her eyes.

'Touch me again,' I whispered, suddenly pulling her close, 'and it'll be me tearing shit up next time. *You fucked with the wrong bitch.*'

She gasped as I released her, pushing her backwards with both hands instead and watching as she stumbled, landing ass-first in the dirt.

'Okay, okay, ladies. What's going on here?'

Two officials arrived, looking between us, their eyes lingering on my body, eyebrows raised as they took me in.

'She's fucking insane,' Chrissy yelled, her friend helping her up as she winced, trying to put weight on her ankle and failing. 'She attacked me, pushed me down.'

'Bollocks,' I spat, aware of someone approaching from the side.

'Look, we can't have brawling here,' the official said, scooping up my hat and shirt and handing them to me. 'And ma'am, you need to get dressed. This is a family show.'

They stared at me, eyes so diverted by my tattoos that it was suddenly very obvious. Living in London had afforded me a barrier from people like this – quick to judge anyone who looked different. But not here.

'Oh, fuck you,' I hissed, 'you fucking judgemental prick. She attacked me, ripped my shirt in the process. But just because she looks like fucking Rodeo Barbie, I'm the one at fault?'

'Ow, my ankle,' Chrissy moaned, her face creased in pain. 'I think she's broken it.'

The official gestured towards the gate by the stairs.

'I think you need to leave,' he said, just as someone brushed my arm. Startled, I turned to see Clara, Jesse's sister.

'I saw the whole thing,' she said, her voice hard as she stared Chrissy down, then looked at the official. 'Hestia was defending herself. *She* started it.'

'Don't worry, Clara,' I muttered, refusing to put my shirt back on as I began to walk away towards the gate, rolling my eyes as Chrissy pretended to cower away from me as I passed her. 'There's no point to me being here anyway.'

I kept walking despite the chatter behind me, despite Clara calling my name again. Still clutching my torn shirt as I let myself through the gate, I glanced back. The officials were still watching, one of them using his radio as they helped support Chrissy to a seat.

Lip curling, I balled up the shirt and threw it back over the gate with all the force I could gather. A dust cloud flared as it landed.

Only just resisting the urge to flip them off, and ignoring a series of catcalls from a group of men further up the stairs, I moved to leave, pulling my phone from my back pocket.

'What's going on?'

Jesse's voice was faint at this distance, but enough to send shivers cascading down my arms as I looked up, our eyes meeting for the first time.

As we stared, his eyes wide, mouth dropping open, Chrissy got up from her makeshift seat and limped over as she called to him. He mouthed my name, ignoring her until she yanked on his arm.

My broken heart leaping into my mouth, I put my hands on the gate, knowing that if I went back over, the officials would likely stop me.

Jesse moved towards me, trying to pry Chrissy's hands away, his eyes desperate as he looked back. He suddenly took in my lack of clothing. I saw Clara tell him something, looking between us as he then spoke to Chrissy.

Instincts kicking in, I backed up from the gate.

'Don't go,' he shouted, his gaze fierce as it held mine – but before he could move, the officials had walked over, blocking his path. The two cowboys he'd been standing with before joined the group, both staring in surprise.

Jesse moved his head to look around the official, and with one more glance, I gave a small shake of my head.

And left.

Chapter 24
Hestia

Lottie pulled a T-shirt from my case in silence, holding it up before handing it to me.

'This one okay?' she asked, her voice wavering as I looked back at her, knowing my eyes were as blank as I felt.

I took it from her outstretched hand, forcing it over my head. She helped me pull my hair free, smoothing it down without a word as I shifted to watching the one big screen visible from the truck, on the edge of the arena. It was still the bronc riders competing, being tossed around like rag dolls, the roar of the crowd rumbling through the frame of the truck.

'Now tell me exactly what he said,' Lottie said, clearing her throat a little and pushing her own hair back.

I turned to her, my mind still working in slow motion. A smudge of dirt on her cheek remained from when she'd fallen in the dirt for me, for no fucking reason at all.

'Not a lot,' I answered quietly, reaching out to wipe it away with my thumb. She eyed me, watching carefully. 'That poisonous little bitch was doing her best to distract him.' Remembering, I felt the first threads of emotion since I'd walked out of the stadium half an hour earlier. 'He just said, "Don't go," but . . .' I stopped, hardening myself to everything in my gut that threatened to spill up and over. 'The officials were talking to him. Half the people in the area were watching. I didn't want to make it worse, so . . . I left.'

Lottie bit her lip, looking up at the screen.

'There's no way we're going to get back by the chutes again,' she murmured, a calculating expression in her eyes. 'But there's something you need to know. Please don't be angry,' she began, wincing as I stared. Forcing myself to soften my gaze, I shook my head.

'Don't be a dick, Lottie. I can't ever be angry with you, not really.'

She ventured a small smile.

'I, um . . . I called Cal last night,' she started, taking in my surprise. 'We spoke for a while. Mainly it was him apologizing, regretting everything that happened in the past few weeks. But I also asked him to do something for me. For you, I mean.'

I opened my mouth to speak, but no words came out.

'I asked him to call Jesse, to leave a voicemail and explain, in his words, what he did at your flat. When he pretended you guys were back in a relationship.'

'Oh, holy fuck,' I breathed, the potential for Cal making everything so much worse amplified.

Lottie shook her head, grabbing my hands with hers as she smiled.

'No, Hes. It worked. Cal called me back when it was done, said he'd rambled until the voicemail had cut him off but he'd made sure it was clear nothing was happening between you two. That you deserved a real love, someone who could really return it.'

I swallowed. I couldn't quite bring myself to believe Cal would do something like that.

'Oh . . .' was all I could manage, not able to compute the dawning happiness in her eyes.

'But it was the call I got from Jesse early this morning that meant I knew everything would be okay,' she reassured, as my hands tightened around hers, eyes darting across her face, desperate to read her expression. 'He said he understood what'd happened, to pass my thanks on to Cal, and . . . tell you that he'd call straight after the rodeo. That he was booking tickets to fly to London, leaving tomorrow. That he can't live without you. I didn't want to say anything before, because I thought he'd get a chance to tell you himself, in person. But . . . well, obviously it didn't quite turn out like that.'

I choked then, the sobs rising up more quickly than I could push them back.

'It's going to be okay,' she said, holding tight as I struggled to gather myself. 'What just happened, whatever's going on with Chrissy . . . he wants you, Hes. He's in love with you – he has been for ages. That doesn't just go away, no matter what she says or wants.'

I let myself cry then, the relief reducing my body to jelly, leaning against Lottie as she held me.

It took some time to gather myself, to work up to sorting out my face and getting back out.

'Are you sure you want to watch?' she asked as we walked slowly back over to the entrance. It was now completely clear, everyone already inside. 'We could just wait round the back, for when he's done?'

I swallowed, trying a weak smile.

'If I'm going to be with a bull rider, I've got to get used to this, right?' I said, brushing off her excitement. I couldn't quite picture it all yet, despite what she'd told me.

We re-entered, this time picking up a couple of beers as we made our way to the stands. It was clear that finding a seat would be impossible now.

'You okay to just lean here?' I said, and she nodded. We had a clear view of both the area itself and one of the screens.

We watched the end of the bronc riding. My pulse was thundering as they finally announced the bull riding, listing out some of the competitors.

'. . . And from Jackson Hole, Wyoming's golden boy, right back on the circuit after a year off – it's Jesse Bennington!'

The camera panned to the chutes. Jesse pinched the brim of his hat as he sat astride one of the gates, the cast on his wrist visible below the cuff of his shirt. His face was set firm, every inch the Old Hollywood star, as the crowd roared – a very noticeable female contingent screaming from the stand we were in.

Lottie smiled at me, her mouth twitching as I rolled my eyes.

'His ego is going to be insufferable,' I said, sipping on my beer but unable to hide my own smile.

'I don't think he'll give a fuck now you're home,' she replied over the noise of the next announcement. The first rider was climbing into the bull pen, already struggling as the animal did its level best to smash him against the steel bars.

I shivered, folding my arm round myself, wishing I could go back there again and force Jesse to leave – just pull him right out of there and never look back.

Trying to distract myself, I focused on Lottie's words: the way she'd said *home*, even though this was neither hers nor mine. But then, neither was London, technically. And it sure as fuck wasn't that miserable hole in the Surrey suburbs where I'd grown up with my stepfather.

But this place – Jackson – had begun to feel something like home, even though I was barely more than a tourist. Turning it over and over, it wasn't until I glanced back up at the big screen as the announcer talked through the upcoming riders in more detail, the camera settling on Jesse one more time, that I suddenly got it.

With a jolt that felt almost physical, I realized it was the people, the connections I'd made, that gave me a sense of being at home here. That home could simply be people – a person – not necessarily a place, felt like a revelation so huge that when Jesse glanced up into the stands, his eyes tracking across the seats, it took everything I had not to run up to the ledge and jump up and down like a fucking lunatic until he saw me.

I knew then, reaching over to give Lottie a brief but hard hug and kiss her temple, why it felt like more than love for Jesse.

He felt like home.

'What was that for?' Lottie smiled, a quizzical expression blooming as the first rider was released out of the gate.

We both winced as he hung on for dear life – but with a particularly evil buck he was unseated, tumbling down into the dirt. The crowd groaned and began to clap as he walked away unscathed, the wranglers in the arena forcing the bull away into its pen.

'For never giving up on me,' I replied, all but shouting into her ear over the noise.

'I've always got you,' she shouted back, her eyes fierce. 'You're never alone, Hes. Especially not now.' She gestured towards Jesse, now visible as he sat on top of the gate.

I fought back more tears as I nodded, focusing on breathing steadily as I realized he was up next.

'What's the prize money for this, then? If he does win?' I asked, my thoughts drifting to his mum and what a difference this could make to her alone.

'It's a big one,' she said, also transfixed by the sight of Jesse in the pen, adjusting his left-handed grip, raising his right hand slowly. 'If he wins outright, it's a hundred and fifty thousand dollars. And I wouldn't be surprised if the sponsors come rolling back in. Cole told me Ariat and Wrangler have come knocking in previous years, and that's big money.'

'Shit,' I murmured, feeling a mix of pride in Jesse's obvious skill and utter terror as the announcer proclaimed his bull to be something of a Livingston Peak legend, known for his vicious temper.

'Hold my hand,' Lottie instructed, waiting for me to grip it tightly. 'It's just eight seconds, then it's over.'

We waited, everything else forgotten as the screens zoomed in, the bull fighters in the arena assuming their positions. Then, with a crack, the gate swung open, the crowd roaring in response.

Everything stopped. My body became stone, only my eyes able to move as I watched Jesse – the person I'd crossed half the world for, the man I loved, *my home* – on the back of something that could kill him.

The bull leapt clear of the ground, the huge digital timer above the arena counting up towards eight. Each second felt like a lifetime. But Jesse held on, his bound right arm raised just high enough despite the injury, utterly in line with each twist and turn of the bull. The crowd was screaming, the announcer proclaiming an incredible ride, when the buzzer sounded – and in one smooth motion, Jesse leapt off and landed with perfect ease in the dirt.

I let go of my breath as everyone around us shot to their feet, Lottie yelling with them. But in the next second, as Jesse turned to grin at the crowd, the bull – still spinning and bucking – turned too. And as Jesse pivoted to get out of the way, the bull put its head down and slammed him, side on, into the steel barrier.

He crumpled to the ground. A collective gasp made its way round the stadium as Lottie screamed his name, looking back at me as my legs began to give way.

'Oh my God,' I choked, leaning on her, my hands grasping at the wall beside us as the bull fighters rushed over to him. Seconds later, the bull was secured and paramedics ran out into the arena. 'Oh fuck, Lottie, no, no, no . . .'

'It's okay. It'll be okay,' she cried, but the uncertainty in her voice made what little strength remained in my body give way.

'Is she all right, ma'am?'

I heard voices coming closer, felt Lottie shaking as she held onto me, refusing to let go.

'C'mon now, honey, stay with us,' a new voice said. 'She ever pass out before like this?'

My head whirled, my pulse pounding as cool hands touched my forehead for a moment, fingers pressed to my wrist.

'Jesse – the bull rider just out there – she's his . . . girlfriend.'

'Oh, damn. Okay. C'mon, sweetheart,' the voice said. 'Let's get you some air. Jesse's gonna be just fine. Looks like he's conscious, okay? He's doing better than you right now.'

Seconds later, I was blinking up into the face of a stranger, a woman with a kind expression. She was holding out a bottle of water. I took it, my hand trembling. The arena was still spinning.

She talked to Lottie for a minute, discussing what to do with me as I turned my head, craning my neck for a look at the big screen. Only a corner was visible from this angle, but I could see Jesse being led out – walking, but heavily supported on one side.

'A terrifying end to one of the best rides we've seen in the past year! The score to beat!' the announcer roared. The crowd was clapping as Jesse left.

'I want to see him,' I murmured to Lottie, feeling her hesitate for a moment. 'Please – I'll be fine, I just need to see him.'

I gritted my teeth as she pulled me up, assisted by two others, and thanked them as we slowly walked out.

'You scared the shit out of me,' she said, letting out a shaky breath.

'Sorry,' I replied, attempting a small smile as my balance slowly returned. 'I seriously need to toughen up to all this, don't I?'

She exhaled, raising her eyebrows. 'That, or a bottle of whiskey beforehand,' she muttered, shaking her head. 'Fucking insane sport.'

I murmured my agreement as we made our way steadily

around the outside, the cooling evening air helping to dissolve the tension through my body, until . . .

'Is that –' I started, seeing an ambulance move in closer to the back of the building, picking up my pace as Lottie did the same.

A group of men emerged from the stadium, and there, between them, was Jesse. Still in full rodeo gear, covered in dirt.

'Jesse!' I yelled, not knowing if he would hear from this distance. I broke into a wobbly run as the ambulance doors opened. 'Wait – Jesse, please!'

The men around him stopped, parting as he turned towards me.

I continued at full pace, Lottie dropping back as we neared.

'Oh, thank fuck,' I cried, my heart rending as he tried to smile. It turned into a grimace of pure pain as I reached him.

'Ma'am, we need to get him to hospital,' one of the paramedics said, trying to step in my way.

'No, I can – let her through,' Jesse said, wincing as he stepped towards me.

We were suddenly face to face, all of the distance, the words and the pain of the past few weeks evaporating.

'Can you give us a minute?' Jesse asked the group, frowning as he struggled against the pain. He released his hold on the man to his right and grasped the ambulance door instead. 'Please.'

As they dispersed, I turned, hearing shouting behind us. Chrissy – her path blocked by Lottie, face red with rage.

'Lottie's got it,' Jesse whispered, his fingers tracing my jaw, gently turning my face back towards him.

And suddenly I couldn't speak; my eyes were filling, as his did.

'You came back,' he murmured, taking in my face.

'I never really left,' I finally admitted. The tears were falling freely now, too many to wipe away. Reaching up as he leant down, I closed my eyes as his lips met mine – the feeling I'd thought I would never have again. I almost gasped at the strength of it.

'I love you, Jesse,' I whispered, our mouths still touching. 'I meant it before, even though I screamed it at you.'

He choked a laugh, wincing at the movement.

'I know,' he replied, stroking my cheek, kissing me again. 'I felt it. I'm so sorry that I hung up . . . I'm so sorry about Chrissy. We didn't . . . I mean, she wanted to, but . . .'

I shook my head, not wanting her name between us.

'It's okay, I don't care. I just – I want to be with you, Jesse. I need to be where you are. Even if it's here, watching you get fucked up by a goddamn bull.'

He tried to smile, gritting his teeth instead as he held his right arm.

'Sir, we really need to get you to the hospital. That arm needs to be set.'

The paramedic stepped towards us and I nodded, not wanting to prolong Jesse's pain.

'I love you too,' Jesse said, his gaze on mine, watching as I absorbed the words. 'I can't wait to make up for the weeks we missed.'

I smiled, understanding everything included within that.

'I'll be there, at the hospital,' I replied, glancing at the paramedic as I stepped back. He took over as Jesse tried to smile back at me, others moving in to help him into the ambulance. I turned and headed back towards Lottie.

'Where's Chrissy?' I asked, glancing around before noticing the sly smile on Lottie's lips.

She shrugged.

'No idea. She took one look at you guys kissing and stalked off. I mean, I did say that if she didn't take the hint and fuck off, you would likely go full psycho, and ripped shirts would be the least of her problems.'

I laughed, the sound of it surprising us both after everything that had passed today.

'You're so sexy when you fuck with people,' I said, looping my arm through hers. We turned back to the ambulance, watching them close the back doors.

'They'll be going up to the Peak Memorial hospital,' she said, glancing at her phone. 'I messaged Cole. He's been there himself before. Says the food's pretty good.'

I shook my head. 'Fucking cowboys.'

———

And so the waiting began. An hour or so into it, surrounded by coffee and snacks, I looked up as someone approached.

'I knew you'd come back.'

Clara held her arms out as I got up, giving her a long squeeze.

'Your brother is a pain in my ass,' I sighed, smiling as she chuckled.

'Tell me about it,' she agreed, turning to shake Lottie's hand as I introduced them. 'And I want you to know that I filled him in on Chrissy's little game earlier.' She shook her head in disgust. 'That girl always did have a snaky side. Been that way since high school. She's been waiting for a chance to get back with Jesse ever since he dumped her the first time.'

'Thanks,' I said, glancing over to the doorway as a doctor emerged, heading for us as he recognized Clara.

'Are you Jesse Bennington's family?' he asked, looking between us as Clara nodded. 'Well, he's doing all right considering, but he's going to need surgery on his right arm. Maybe even a plate in his shoulder. It's pretty routine, nothing to worry about – but I'm going to need you to fill in some forms for us, for the insurance. If he has it?'

Lottie stepped forward then, nodding, offering her help as the one that dealt with payroll and benefits at the ranch.

'I totally forgot that you have to pay for everything here,' I said to Clara, rapidly realizing the financial implications of an injury like this.

She nodded grimly, frowning.

'Yeah, it's tough,' she said, watching as Lottie went over to the administration area. 'Even when you win. He did, by the way – I don't know if you checked.'

'Oh shit, he did?' I gasped, wondering why she wasn't mirroring the surge of relief in her expression. 'Isn't that good? Doesn't it help to pay for everything?'

She pursed her lips, considering it.

'I mean, I don't know the full extent yet, but I'd be surprised if this whole thing doesn't cost the best part of twenty thousand dollars, maybe thirty. Depends how long he stays, how complex the surgery is. Then there's physio afterwards . . . I doubt his insurance will cover all of it. It's gonna eat right into that money.'

My mouth popped open in disbelief. 'That's – holy shit. It's so much,' I replied, shaking my head.

'Yeah,' she agreed, sinking into the seat behind her. I followed suit, my mind whirring with the injustice of it. 'His insurance might cover some of it, but the rest will have to come from the winnings. It's a good job it was a decent payout this time. That's why you end up with so many people having to use things like crowdfunding to try and prevent getting into debt. The amount of times I've donated for different people is crazy. Our system is so fucked.'

I nodded, turning over the implications.

'Do you know what he was planning to do with the money?' I asked tentatively, not wanting to pry, but trying to gauge how big of a disaster this was.

She nodded, biting her lip as she looked at me.

'Some of it was for Mom, as you know. About forty thousand is what she needs to pay for an ongoing supply of her new meds for the next few years. But the rest was . . . well, I don't want to spoil anything. I think he wants to tell you himself.' She smiled, but it was tinged with sadness. 'But maybe . . . now, I don't know. Maybe it won't work out yet. I guess we need to focus on getting him better, right?'

I didn't press her for more, just listened as Lottie came back over, repeating what the doctor had said.

Clara got up, heading out to call her mum and Belle, while Lottie sat next to me.

'What I wouldn't give for the NHS right now,' she sighed, shaking her head. 'I know it's not perfect, but at least people don't go fucking bankrupt because they get injured.'

I told her what Clara had told me about crowdfunding, suddenly wishing there was a way I could help, maybe find a way to try to replace the money Jesse would lose. But without a visa to work, there was no way I could charge people for tattoos, even if I could do enough to amount to twenty or thirty thousand.

Lottie side-eyed me as I became quiet.

'What are you think—' she began, stopping as I gasped, an idea hitting me squarely between the eyes.

'I can't work yet here in the US,' I explained, trying to stay calm as more and more ideas poured into my thoughts. 'But I can give away tattoos, right? For charity?'

She frowned, not following.

'I mean, I'd have to check, but yeah, I imagine so? But why?'

'What if we did something for Jesse? A way of raising the money to pay for his hospital bill?' I said, watching as her face changed, the idea dawning on her too. 'If we all offer something up that people could bid on, like a charity auction, back in Jackson – locals and tourists. I could offer up tattoos. Maybe, if you and Lil don't mind, we could offer a weekend stay at the ranch? Bailey might be able to give riding lessons . . .'

'I fucking love it,' Lottie breathed, nodding. 'Who wouldn't want to help Jesse? Especially with what he had planned . . .'

She tailed off, her cheeks colouring a little as she glanced at me.

'What?' I said, frowning. 'What now?'

'Nothing,' she said, dismissing it with a wave. 'It's not for me to say. Let him tell you once he's out of surgery, okay? Seriously, Hes,' she added as I gave her shit-eye. 'I don't want to ruin it for him, okay? It's nothing bad.'

'Fine,' I grumbled, pulling out my phone. 'But we need to gather up as many prizes as possible – and see if we can find somewhere to host this, make a party out of it. C'mon now,' I added, trying my best Wyoming drawl. 'Y'all the best marketer in the state, or what?'

She snorted, already halfway to making a call.

'Hope your powers of persuasion are better than your accents,' she joked, dodging me when I tried to swipe her as she got up.

'Rude,' I murmured, smiling as she winked back at me.

Opening my phone, I pulled up the first person I could think of, tapping the call button.

'Howdy, stranger! Hang on – are you calling from the UK? The dial tone sounded different?'

'Um, not quite,' I began. 'Listen – I'll explain everything, but Dee, I have a favour to ask.'

Chapter 25
Jesse

I had to admit it: despite the surgery and the shitshow that was my shoulder and arm, the rest of me felt . . . good. Out of hospital and staying in a hotel nearby, I could finally get some sleep away from the constant noise of machines and other people. I still had to go back in for a few hours a day for check-ups and physio, but I would be ready to go home in a couple more days. It was one of the few downsides of living somewhere remote like Jackson – the hospital facilities just weren't set up for major trauma.

It was late, but I hovered over the last messages from Hestia earlier today, rereading and smiling, hearing her voice through the fragments of our written conversation. The sheer fucking relief of being on the other side of losing her, of knowing she was waiting for me, right now, back in Jackson.

Goddamn, I wanted to call her, talk to her, touch her . . .

But she'd be tired. Lottie had hinted before they left that she'd be busy filling in at the ranch, and that I needed to focus on getting better – and back to the Diamond Back as soon as possible.

Desperate for a distraction, I opened my phone up to voicemail, still fascinated by the message from her ex, Cal. I'd listened to it a couple of times, the first with wary disbelief, the second with a sense of hope and relief so great that I'd hardly taken it in. A third time – for, what, confirmation maybe? – I tapped the play button.

'Hey . . . uh, so Jesse, right?' His voice was deep, a different accent entirely to Lottie's or Hestia's. Possibly London, but undeniably British. 'It's Cal. Hestia's . . . ex. Look, man, I know I don't know you and there's no reason why you'd believe me, but . . .' He stopped, sighing, cursing under his breath. 'Me and Hestia . . . we're not a thing, not together. The whole situation on your call with her the other day was all me, okay? We're not fucking, I swear it – I mean, we're not even *speaking*, for fuck's sake. Especially not after *that*.'

He paused again, taking a breath to steady himself.

'But . . . I do love her though, you know? I know we're over and just not right for each other – I mean, she seems to know that on a way deeper level than me now, and I guess that's because of you. And look, I don't blame you if you think this is all bullshit, but I just wanted you to know, for what it's worth, that I just want her to be happy. Like, *really happy*, with someone that can help her get through all the shit she's been through. She's . . . well, I'm sure you've seen the fire under the surface and *fuck me*, she's got a bastard of a right hook . . . but the way we are together brings it out – and not in a good way. And that's what we've done to each other, for years. Under all that, she's one of the best people I've ever known.'

I swallowed a surge of emotion as his voice caught: a recognition that he was on the other side of what I'd felt, knowing she was gone.

'Don't judge her on what I've done, okay? She deserves better than that. Way more than that.'

The message ended, the voicemail cutting him off.

I almost felt sorry for the guy, despite what he'd done since Hestia had been away – all the shit since she'd returned to London, all explained in a long call a few nights ago. It was easy to take the wrong path, for shit to get messed up. I'd always known that, but seeing it first hand, living it through someone I loved . . . it hit different.

Shifting on the bed, I felt the familiar ache in my shoulder restart as I moved, cutting through the painkillers. Clenching my teeth to it, I started unbuttoning my shirt, frustratingly slow with just one hand. But given I couldn't do T-shirts yet with the sling, I would just have to get really good at it.

My phone rang, startling in the silence as I finished the last button. My heart leapt at the screen, a wave of feeling crashing into me.

'Jessica,' I said, opening FaceTime and catching the way her lips curved in response.

'Hey, you,' she breathed, her face unbearably beautiful in my palm. She'd taken off any trace of make-up, had her hair up in a high ponytail, just her tats and a small smile. My heart squeezed at her willingness to do this now – to be entirely herself with me. I felt so fucking honoured that she trusted me in that way.

'I miss you,' I murmured, lost somewhere between those incredible ocean eyes, down to the definition of her delicate collarbones, where the flames sprang from the forest canopy of the Sleepy Hollow scene. '*Fuck*, I want to touch you.'

Her smile broadened for a moment as she glanced down, then back up, a mischievous thread winding through her expression.

'Where?' she asked, biting her lip as I groaned, feeling the inevitable sensation of my dick responding to her voice.

'I'd take a fucking handshake right now,' I admitted, setting the phone on the nightstand while I finished shrugging off the shirt.

'Oh . . . are you . . .? Okaaay,' she said, putting a hand to her neck as I sat back down, her eyes tracing my abs.

'You all right there, honey?' I chuckled, secretly pleased that my lack of shirt had an effect on her. Somehow it evened up the balance between us, of the constant undercurrent of attraction charging my body day and night.

'Fuck, yeah,' she sighed, leaning on her side, hand propping up her head. 'I want you too. There's only so much I can do by myself.'

We stared at each other through the screen, knowing exactly where this would be going if we were together. The thought of it, the memories of all the times before, the last time, over a month ago . . .

'Will you show me?' I asked before I could stop myself – but instantly regretted it, knowing how tired she likely was, how hard she was working. I didn't want to take more than she had to give.

But . . . this was Hestia.

'Depends,' she replied, her eyebrow raising as her smile deepened with mine. 'You going to give me some inspiration to get going?'

'Holy fucking hell,' I hissed, my dick now so hard it almost hurt.

Godfuckingdamn, I loved this woman.

She just laughed, propping her phone up against the footboard of her bed, crossing her arms in front of herself and peeling off her T-shirt in one smooth motion.

There was nothing underneath, just her bare breasts, nipples hardening even as I stared.

She was going to be the end of me, the absolute fucking undoing – and I wanted it, wanted her, more than I wanted anything else this world had to offer.

'So why were you taking your shirt off before?' she breathed, fingers inching into the top of her pyjama shorts.

'I was gonna take a shower,' I admitted, my words stilted as my focus faltered, unable to process anything other than her breasts, the slow descent of her hand inside the waistband.

'Well . . .' she began, breath hitching a little as her hand sank low enough, clearly touching herself, her mouth parting slightly as she let out a breath. 'Why don't we combine the two? You take your phone into the bathroom and . . . I'll watch you if you watch me.'

'*Jessica*,' I groaned, picking up the phone and moving to the bathroom, shrugging off my shorts and underwear in seconds, thanking the fucking hotel design gods that they'd thought to include a built-in alcove in the shower wall.

'Don't get the phone wet,' she purred, eyes all over me, hand beginning to move again as I propped the phone up against my shampoo bottle. I turned on the shower and aimed it down, away from my arm. 'Doesn't look like the bull fucked up any . . . more important parts of you,' she added, her voice strained.

I stood in the water for a moment, letting it run down the length of my body, fisting my cock in my left hand.

'He had the good manners to fuck up the hand I don't need anyway,' I replied, watching as she closed her eyes for a moment, her head tilted back and throat exposed.

'*Fuck, Jesse*,' she breathed, so reminiscent of our moment outside the line dance that suddenly I was back there, right on the edge of coming inside her, gripping her beautiful, full ass in both hands.

I moaned with her as I rested my forehead against the tiles, the warm water cascading over my shoulder and down my back.

'Take off the shorts – I want to see exactly what I'm missing,' I said, my voice rough now, knowing I'd have to take it easy or –

She pulled them down without question, eyes holding mine, only dipping briefly to watch how I moved my cock. I only just held it together. Weeks apart, the past week or so with nothing to take the edge off in hospital, and now . . . Hestia laid bare right in front of me, her legs apart, fingers drifting in lazy circles.

I stopped for a moment, transfixed as slowly, without breaking our stare, she pushed her fingers into herself, moaning as she did so and finally closing her eyes.

Jaw clenched hard enough to crack teeth, I just about held on long enough to see the image in front of me for what it was.

A woman more beautiful, more incredible than I ever knew existed, who I loved with my whole fucking heart. Somehow, I'd been lucky enough to meet her and, even more incredibly, she loved me back, trusted me enough to be vulnerable and her whole self, from crying and shaking through an anxiety attack to *this*.

She really was every single fucking inch a goddess, just like her name.

'I miss you,' she whispered, and I shuddered as I resumed the movement, sliding my cock gently, then with harder, rougher movements as she withdrew her fingers, then pushed them back in again. 'I want you in me. I want you to fuck me so hard and so deep that we don't know where you end and I begin.'

I groaned, knowing it had been too long, my stamina reduced to dust as I imagined it, knowing exactly how good she felt around me.

'I swear to you, Jessica,' I murmured, only just able to form the words, knowing I was so close. 'As soon as I see you again, I will be fucking you wherever you want me to within the goddamn hour . . . and I won't stop. I want to be inside you for days.'

She gasped, letting out a long, low moan, just as the familiar tingling sensation began as I started to come.

'Jesse,' she called, her voice raspy and desperate, the sound of my name on her tongue more than I could process as I moaned with her, the orgasm taking over. 'I love you . . . I need you.'

I couldn't reply. My breathing stalled as I gripped my cock and held my gaze between her legs, up to her breasts, her face as she came too. Her look of pained pleasure, the sounds coming from her parted lips . . .

'Oh, honey, you have no idea how much I need you,' I panted, leaning my head back against the wall for support, trying to plant my legs down to keep myself steady as the orgasm faded. I felt a physical ache, right next to the one in my injured shoulder, at not being able to be with her. 'I've never missed anyone like this. It fucking hurts not to be with you.'

It took her a few moments to find me again. Her eyes were glazed and a dusky glow was forming across her cheekbones.

'Then let's agree,' she murmured between breaths. 'We'll never do this long apart ever again. Two days, max. Or maybe one. Just one, absolute max.'

I smiled, imagining how it would feel to brush the hair from her face right now, to kiss her forehead gently and tuck her in against my body.

'Deal. I'll be wherever you are, Jessica.'

Chapter 26
Hestia

A few more days of brutal graft later, Jesse was due home from the hospital in less than forty-eight hours. Lil, now back and firmly roped into our plans, had come down to help us prep everything for the auction at Shelby's bar.

'Okay, what's with all the looks?' I said, nudging Lottie as she glanced at Cole yet again. 'I mean, I get it, Cole's hot, but c'mon – you see the guy every day.'

Lottie actually giggled. Even Bailey paused as she laid out the printed auction catalogues on each table. 'Spit it out, girl,' she urged, winking at me from under her hat. 'It stays between us.'

'Oh, nothing, it's just . . . this is where I first met Cole,' Lottie shrugged, the tops of her cheeks turning pink.

'You did?' I questioned, confused. 'I thought – didn't you tell me he was chopping wood or some shit, woke you up?'

'That a euphemism?' Bailey asked as I cackled. Lottie was blushing fully.

'Oh, fuck off,' she replied, grinning. 'I mean, that was *officially* when it happened, when I found out who he actually was.'

'Sooo, what happened here, then?' I asked, following her gaze over to the door that led out to the corridor, the bathrooms beyond that. 'Hang on – wait – oh God, Lottie! You horny motherfucker – did you guys get busy in the bathrooms?'

It was Bailey's turn to laugh, almost dropping the box of catalogues.

'No, not quite,' Lottie said, unable to help herself giggling again as Bailey's eyes lit up, waiting for her response. 'Almost. It was in the corridor – we didn't make it to the bathrooms.'

'That's my girl,' I laughed, shaking my head at her. 'That's one way to deal with jet lag.'

'Want some of this?' Lil said as she sidled over, carrying a small tower of glasses and a massive jug filled with something iced and bright orange. 'It's some kinda cocktail – enough alcohol in there to get all of us ready for this whole thing, I think.' She looked up, noticing the amusement all round. 'Hold up, what did I miss?'

'Oh, only that Lottie defiled the corridor out there with Cole on her first night in Jackson,' I chuckled, enjoying Lottie's resignation, knowing there was no way out of the merciless teasing now.

'Ahh, that where it happened, huh?' Lil replied, raising an eyebrow as she poured from the jug into the glasses, passing them round.

'You knew?' Bailey questioned, looking between Lil and Lottie as they shared a look.

'Oh, I knew, honey,' Lil confirmed, knocking her glass back and pouring another. 'There's not much that happens in this town without me hearing about it. I knew right then that either my cousin was staying, or my ranch manager was leaving.'

I knocked back my own glass, taken aback.

'Jesus,' I rasped, 'the fuck is this?'

'The ticket to survival,' she answered, refilling it. 'Now, I've heard about you and Jesse,' she said, the faintest hint of a smile on her lips. 'And from what I hear, you guys make Lottie and Cole sound like Joseph and the blessed Virgin Mary.'

It was Lottie's turn to laugh, half choking on her own drink.

I shrugged, grinning.

'Y'all okay here, ladies? It's getting mighty rowdy this early,' Cole interrupted, sidling round to Lottie and enveloping her with his vast frame.

Bailey snorted.

'I'm just doing my job,' she said, holding up a catalogue and carrying on round the tables.

'I was just getting the lowdown on Hestia's adventures,' Lil chuckled. 'Sounds like I missed a hell of a summer.'

Cole caught my eye for a moment, a glint in his eye.

'I tried to keep them busy,' he replied, 'but you know Jesse. When he's decided on something, there ain't a damn thing anyone can do to change his mind.'

Lil nodded, smiling as she looked back to me. 'And he has no idea about this, right? All a total surprise?'

I nodded, thinking back to the range of calls we'd had on the phone this week: from short and sweet when his meds had kicked in, to the one call that would be branded in my head for ever. The surgery had gone well – even if he was pissed at the thought of a huge hospital bill, he was still somewhat consoled at likely having enough to help his mum. But, frustratingly, he wouldn't tell me what the other plans were, and no amount of trying to pry it out of the others was working either.

'Clara's bringing him home tomorrow,' I said, not quite able to hide my smile.

'You know how he's gonna have to be real careful with that arm for a while,' Cole added, tilting his head as he looked down towards Lottie.

'Don't worry, it's not his arm I've been missing,' I replied, taking another drink and watching Lil and Lottie dissolve.

Cole laughed with them and shook his head.

'Cocktails, huh? You building up the courage, Lil?'

She grimaced between laughs.

'Something like that,' she said, glancing back to me. 'You know I'm not technically single any more?'

'People are bidding for a *date* with you, Lil, not a wedding,' I shrugged. 'Besides, Jamie understands. You said he thought it was a great idea, right? It'll be a couple of hours, a bit of conversation, a nice meal, maybe even . . . dessert – fuck it, breakfast, if things go really well?'

Even she cracked at that, looking over to the door, noticing the guy walking through it. 'That's John, the auctioneer guy. I'll go get him set up, distract myself.'

I looked around the quiet bar, hoping . . . no, knowing that in a couple of hours it would be rammed with people here to support Jesse.

Every one of my requests for help to the Jackson community, although I'd been hesitant and apologetic at first, had been met with a yes. From displaying flyers and posters in local hotels and bars, to announcements at the Jackson rodeo. Prize donations from local stores and venues had all but flooded in, leading us to need professional help to conduct the auction, given its growing size. Shelby's had offered to host it, even at this short notice, totally free of charge. Even the Cowboy Bar had lent their mechanical bull, which I'd been eyeing with a mix of suspicion and curiosity ever since.

'You want a go?' Lottie said, walking over as Cole disappeared to help get the small stage for the auction ready. She'd followed my gaze, nudging me with her elbow.

'After those cocktails?' I replied, only to be met with narrowed eyes.

'Chickenshit,' she hissed, walking over there, glancing back at me over her shoulder, waiting for me to follow.

Within another minute Lottie was on board, right arm up just like the real thing. I could see Cole from the corner of my eye, trying desperately to stay focused on building the stage, and failing miserably.

Rolling my eyes at her request to time her, she was eventually unseated twenty-eight seconds later as it changed direction erratically. Sliding off with a squeal into the mats below, she stayed down as she laughed, Cole chuckling to himself in the background.

'Your turn,' she said, breathing heavily. 'Left hand to hold on, right arm up. Lean back and hold on tight.'

'The fuck am I doing?' I murmured, wondering how it was that lying down to get ink injected into my skin for hours on end was utterly fine, but twenty seconds on a plastic bull seemed unreasonable.

Bailey wolf-whistled as I climbed on board, chucking my hat over to Lottie as she pressed the button. Thankfully I'd gone with my corset top, and while it definitely emphasized my sizeable rack, it held them in tight too.

'C'mon, Hes, just twenty-nine seconds to beat me,' she called, holding up the timer on her phone.

'What's the forfeit?' I yelled, hyper-aware that everyone in the bar was now watching.

'You don't want to know,' she laughed, spinning out of focus as the bull twisted round.

I gripped on, leaning back like Lottie had said, imagining, for half a second, that this might be a fraction of what Jesse would feel.

People had started cheering as seconds ticked by, my knuckles on the rope going white with the effort of staying on, my head and body whipped around in every direction.

Eventually, barely able to make Lottie out any more, but catching her looking back towards the entrance, I fell to the side, managing to roll off and spring back up with ease.

'Did I win?' I said, shaking my hair back as I finally looked up. 'What was my time?'

Only then did I realize that the rowdy cheering had stopped, and a different kind of sound – full of exclamation and surprise – had taken over. Right there, walking into the bar, was Jesse, staring straight ahead at me as Clara grinned.

'Sorry, honey,' she shouted over to me. 'Your girl Lottie made me promise not to say a word.'

I just gaped for a moment as he took his hat off, looking me up and down from my now wild and tangled hair to the corset – the same one he'd instructed me to leave on in the truck all that time ago. His eyes lingered there before coming up to meet mine.

Running over the mats, I vaulted over the low fence in front without a thought and launched myself in his direction, only slowing very slightly as I reached him. I buried myself into his body on the left side, careful to avoid his right arm; the cast was visible under his jacket. He closed himself around me.

'Jessica,' he murmured, breathing in my hair, kissing my head. I lifted my face to him.

'Bull riding's a piece of fucking cake,' I murmured, watching his slow smile break out, feeling my whole heart lift at the sight of it. 'No idea how you fucked it up. I'll do it next time, okay?'

'*Never again*,' he whispered. And right in front of the whole bar, he kissed me, hard.

It was like the time at the rodeo, when I'd left – a thousand thoughts and words all channelled into one feeling – but this time, unlike the last, I knew that he loved me as much as I did him.

He slowed as a chorus of cheers and whistles broke out, chuckling as I tried to carry on, not giving a flying fuck who saw.

'Hold that thought, sweetheart,' he murmured, his lips moving up to my forehead and kissing me there before he looked over towards Lottie. Grinning, barely able to contain her glee, she walked over and dropped a set of keys into his hand.

'See you in a few hours,' she said, giving me a little wave as Jesse turned us around. 'We'll take care of everything here.'

'But – what – ?' I exclaimed as Jesse led me out to Cole's truck.

He just smirked, opening the door for me, waiting as I lifted myself in.

'Seriously, Jesse, what the –' I began as he jumped into his side and shut the door, leaning over and taking my chin in his hand.

He kissed me again, this time with a force that took my breath away, the implication clearer than any words.

'I said,' he breathed, pulling back and starting the engine, seemingly utterly unimpeded by his right arm, 'hold that thought.'

Stunned, I just sat back, unable to do anything other than glance at him as he drove us a few minutes out of town. He turned off the highway to what looked to be a very expensive, very beautiful hotel, only speaking to confirm our names at reception.

Only when he'd closed the door to the room behind us, a vast suite laid out in front, did he begin again.

'Are you still holding that thought?' he whispered, drawing me to him, his fingertips working across my shoulders, following the outlines of my tattoos.

I nodded. All other thoughts of the auction, of keeping it as a surprise for him, vanished as his eyes took me in.

He moved us to the bed, the hunger in his expression so fierce that I could already imagine the feeling of him on my skin.

'*Now* you can take it off,' he murmured, gesturing to my corset as I sat on the edge of the bed. My eyes widened as he knelt between my legs.

I unhooked the catches at the front, feeling his low moan rumble through me as he brushed my hands aside once I was halfway down, my breasts all but exposed.

'I can't tell you how many times I've thought of this,' he whispered, putting his lips against mine, his tongue tracing them. 'You are so fucking precious to me.' He kissed me so softly, with such care, that it reminded me of our goodbye.

'As you are to me,' I answered, my breath hitching as he

continued to unhook the remaining catches, finally taking it off. 'I'm yours, as long as you want me.'

He moved his mouth down, his tongue circling my nipple as he started to undo my jeans, then pulled off my boots.

'What about your clothes?' I complained, barely able to concentrate enough to form the words as my waistband was tugged down, revealing the black lace underwear beneath.

'Oh, no, no,' he groaned into my skin as he gently pushed me back onto the bed, his mouth reluctantly leaving my breasts and working down to my hips. 'This is all about you, *for you*. I know what you've been up to, running yourself into the ground to organize this auction all week.'

'What? You know?' I gasped as his fingers slipped into the lace, stroking low between my legs.

'Oh, I know,' he confirmed. 'And I have never felt so fucking loved in my life.'

I raised myself up onto my elbows, hearing the change in his tone. I watched as he kissed the side of my thighs, stopping as he saw me, gradually kissing his way back up to my face.

'I knew how you felt about me before you even left,' he said, looking into my eyes, his hand brushing stray hairs back from my face. 'Maybe before you did. But *my fucking God*, Hestia, I want you to know, *to feel*, how much I love you right back.'

My breath caught on the intensity of his words, but now my gut instinct was to draw closer, to show him what I knew inside. Any desire to run, to avoid it – gone.

'I didn't know how to tell you – what it meant,' I whispered back as his lips covered mine again, his hand now wandering down towards my hips.

'I know, honey,' he agreed, 'but you showed me. You always have done. This week is no fucking different, which is why Lottie called me. You deserve the fucking world too. So I'm going to give it to you, starting right now.'

As he laid me back down, his fingers slipping into my underwear, into me, I wondered how this could be real – how it was possible to feel this way about someone, physically and emotionally.

And as he pulled the rest of my clothes away, his kisses lingering longer, circling me, teasing me, I stopped being able to think at all.

———

The daylight was dimming behind the craggy peaks outside the window before we resurfaced. I stared out at it, still naked, transfixed by the colours across the snow-tipped peaks, the way the setting sun leached coral light over the slopes, setting them ablaze.

Jesse emerged from the bathroom, stopping as he saw me.

'What does the viper mean?' he asked softly, eyes drifting from my ass and down my left leg to where the snake wrapped around my skin. He skirted the edge of the bed, his cast and sling somehow still neatly in place despite the physicality of the past couple of hours.

I smiled as he reached me, kissing my shoulder as he pulled my body into his.

'Transformation, rebirth, renewal,' I said, tilting my head back to rest on his shoulder. 'Why?'

'What would you choose if you wanted to signify "forever"?' he whispered, brushing my ear with his mouth.

I turned around fully, goosebumps forming across my arms as he gazed at me, his eyes shifting down to my lips as I spoke.

'The ouroboros,' I replied with a smile, using my nail on his collarbone to make a circle, then a figure of eight motion. 'It's a snake eating its own tail,' I explained, his fascination clear as he stared. 'It means infinity, the eternal cycle.'

He nodded, swallowing, hesitating for a moment as he looked down.

I used my fingers to tilt his head to meet my eyes, just as he always did to me.

'Yes, I'll tattoo it for you,' I said, smiling again as I watched his dawning realization, that I knew what he was thinking, what he wanted to ask. 'And I'll do the same design for myself too,' I added, feeling him become very still.

'Where?' he whispered, taking my hand, his eyes beginning to glaze a little.

I knew what he was asking, knew he was too afraid to say it.

'I'm not scared,' I reassured him, knowing, at every single level, how much I meant it. 'I'm never leaving you again,' I added, reaching up to touch his mouth with mine for a moment. 'Where would you like us to have it?'

He closed his eyes briefly. Then, lifting my left hand to his lips, he held my gaze as he kissed the lower half of my fourth finger.

We said nothing for a moment, not needing words for what this was, what it meant.

But as I nodded my answer, he used his left arm to reach down and scoop me up, choking a laugh, his face alight with something between complete happiness and disbelief. I placed my hands either side of his mouth as we kissed.

We gave everything we had to each other, every last barrier removed.

So, with everything spoken and unspoken, we eventually arrived back at Shelby's. The auction was well under way, the bar packed tight as we approached the doors.

Jesse stopped me for a moment, raising my left hand to his lips again.

'I can't believe you organized all this for me, for my mom,' he said, pulling me into him, the feel of his body against mine after the past couple of hours setting it alight all over again.

'Team effort,' I breathed. 'Finally figured out that most things in life are better with others, shit that I could never do by myself.'

He smiled, his eyes holding mine.

'Guess I need to figure out whether this whole bull riding thing is worth getting back into again,' he said slowly. 'I don't want to be stressing you out every weekend.'

I shook my head.

'It's your decision,' I replied, adamant that I wouldn't be the reason he gave up on anything. 'And I'm going to need your help here, because, fuck . . . this will be my first healthy relationship,' I admitted, butterflies releasing as his gaze softened with such obvious adoration that it almost stopped me. 'But if it's something you love, that you're passionate about, I'll be right with you. I might need a whiskey or three just before you ride, but I'll toughen up.'

He chuckled, shaking his head.

'First of all,' he started, releasing my hand to brush his thumb over my lips, 'I don't ever want you toughening up. The way you care, how much you feel everything – it's one of the things I love most about you.' He leant in, his lips touching mine for a moment, not quite letting us take it further before pausing. 'And second of all, it is my decision, but we'll make it together, as partners. Because whatever I love about bull riding doesn't come close to loving you, to what I know we're gonna have together.'

I grabbed him then, pushing us gently against the doors as I opened my mouth to him, heard him groan as my tongue teased his lips.

'Hey! Didn't you book a damn hotel room for that? C'mon, Lil's up next!' Lottie poked her head round the door, winking as I pulled back reluctantly.

'Cock-blocker,' I muttered as she disappeared back inside.

Jesse laughed.

'You know I booked two nights there for us,' he whispered, leaning down to brush the edge of my ear. 'A whole weekend alone, away from the ranch, to show me what you can do with that tongue.'

I arched my eyebrow as we followed Lottie inside, hands clasped firmly together.

'I'm going to need longer than that,' I replied, feeling my whole heart melt under his gaze, the way he stroked my ring finger.

'We can take as much time as you need,' he said, his tone changing, expression turning serious.

I smiled, knowing exactly what he meant and feeling nothing but excitement and happiness welling up at the thought of him, of us.

'Thank you,' I whispered, squeezing his hand as we walked into the main area, where the auctioneer was currently selling off a weekend stay at the Four Seasons penthouse downtown.

I clutched at Jesse as eventually, after working its way round the room, it was sold to someone in a group of tourists near the back. They whooped and hollered when he shouted, 'Sold!'

'Holy shit,' I exclaimed, catching Lottie and Cole's eyes across the floor. Both were grinning – partly at the eight thousand dollars the lot had raised but partly because, as Cole lifted his hand in greeting, Jesse had put his left arm round my shoulder and pulled me close, kissing my hair.

'Next lot for sale is . . . well, ladies and gents, a real Jackson exclusive!'

There were a few laughs from the crowd and a long, loud wolf whistle from Bailey.

'That's right, this lot is a date night with none other than Jackson's very own Elizabeth Dean, Jackson High's most beautiful Prom Queen and fifth generation Jackson Hole rancher!'

There was a chorus of encouraging whoops, shouts and yells as Lottie brought Lil up to the stage area.

'Now, sadly, her equally beautiful cousin isn't part of the deal,' the auctioneer went on, prompting a hard glare from Cole, 'but we're only accepting top quality bids here for the chance to take Miss Dean out for dinner. Let's start the bidding at four hundred dollars. Do I have four hundred dollars?'

Jesse chuckled as Lil exclaimed, turning to face the auctioneer with a bemused expression, clearly unable to believe anyone would bid that much. But, in the same moment, one, then two, then three people raised their hands. As the price went up, Lottie barely covered her laugh as she watched her cousin's expression.

'*Man*, there's some money in this town,' I said, Jesse humming in agreement. 'I mean, Lil's gorgeous and fucking hilarious, but fuck – fifteen hundred dollars for a date?'

The bidding paused as things slowed, until –

'Five thousand dollars,' a voice called out from the back, hidden from view by the crowd.

'Well!' the auctioneer called, above a burst of cheering and clapping. 'Now, Miss Dean is a mighty fine date, but that is quite the generous bid! Do we have any further advance on—'

'Eight thousand!' another voice called from the opposite side of the room – a similar tone to the previous bid. It was almost as if the same person had shouted twice. Lil's face, already incredulous, drained of all colour as a figure began striding forward through the crowd.

'Who the hell . . .?' I asked, turning to Jesse, but he shook his head in confusion, frowning as he noted Lil's reaction too.

'Ten thousand,' the first voice said, the accent now clear. It had a Wyoming edge, but the rest was all British. This bidder too appeared to be making his way through the crowd towards the front of the room.

As he stepped into view, I felt Jesse go rigid. Lil's mouth fell open.

'Ten thousand dollars,' the man repeated as everyone stared at him. He was tall, dressed in an expensive suit, with short, dark hair and a tanned, chiselled face. He nodded a greeting to Lil, his expression firm, then glancing in the direction of the other high bidder as if challenging them to continue.

There was a silence, broken only by whispers throughout the crowd. After a pause, the auctioneer carried on, clearly as stunned as everyone else.

But no one was more astonished than Lil. As the auctioneer declared the date sold, the room erupted. The man in the suit glanced at her, gave one more nod in her direction and then turned away, stepping back into the crowd.

'What the fuck just happened?' I breathed, turning back to Jesse, following his stare to Cole. Then both of them looked up at Lil.

Lottie was with her, concern in her eyes, talking rapidly as she supported her cousin.

'That right there was Ryder Sinclair,' Jesse said, frowning, his gaze still on Lil. 'Son of Zach Sinclair, the owner-in-waiting of the Diamond Back's biggest rival, Elk Creek. And . . .' He winced, shifting his gaze back to me. '. . . Lil's onetime fiancé.'

Chapter 27
Hestia

It wasn't until the first flurries of snow had fallen, coating the fir trees around the ranch house, that I realized how quickly time was passing.

Pressed against the biggest window in the kitchen, I all but forgot everyone's drinks order as I gazed out at the view beyond. The valley floor had partly disappeared under a fine crystalline blanket. It was almost too beautiful to take in.

I heard footsteps approaching.

'Happy first Thanksgiving,' Jesse whispered, appearing behind me, his lips automatically grazing over my neck as I closed my eyes, leaning back into him.

'Does it normally snow this early?' I breathed, trying to control the impulses his mouth usually inspired. Even now – two months since the auction, living and working alongside each other – every time we touched, it still felt the same. Somewhere between relief, like taking a deep, calming breath, and lighting a taper. It burnt low and slow with a desperate urge to be alone together, whether it was physical or not, hours spent getting to know each other in every possible way.

'Sometimes earlier,' he murmured. 'Means we'll need to stay extra warm, honey.'

His hands circled me; his right arm was moving more freely by the day. Both hands slipped under my sweater, one heading north and the other south, my breath catching as his fingers slipped into my jeans.

'I need to get drinks,' I whispered, barely able to stifle a moan as he started to work his hands in the way he knew I liked.

'It's not my fault my girlfriend's a goddess,' he rasped, his own breathing becoming erratic as I felt him becoming hard, pressing into my back. 'Or maybe it's just remembering our first time in this kitchen.'

Slowly approaching the point of no return, I turned around to face him, his hands reluctantly withdrawing.

'Later this evening, when everyone else has gone home, I'm going to fuck you until it feels like summer again,' I promised, digging my nails into his ass as I squeezed it. 'But it's about Lottie tonight, right?'

He smiled down at me, leaning in for a long, heart-stopping kiss.

'Always thinking about other people,' he said eventually, biting his lip as I reached up to run my fingers through his hair.

I shook my head.

'Mainly you,' I admitted, rewarded as his smile grew. 'But right now, Cole.'

His outraged expression was worth it, making me laugh as I kissed his cheek and moved over to the fridge, desperately trying to unscramble my thoughts and pick up the right drinks as well as the magnum of champagne.

'So what exactly is your role in this?' he asked, eyebrows raised as I turned back to him.

'See,' I smirked, reaching over to grab a tray from one of the drawers. 'This is what it's like to tease someone with a secret and keep it to yourself.'

He grinned, looking down as he scuffed his boot against the wooden floor.

'All right, that's fair enough, I guess,' he began. Then, looking back up, he added, 'But I was planning to tell you later – show you, actually.'

I studied him for a moment as I gathered flutes and glasses together, placing them next to the bottles on the tray. Two months he'd kept this a secret – his plans for the rest of the rodeo prize money.

The auction had been a huge success. So much so that not only could Jesse buy his mum all of the medication she would need for many years to come, but he could donate significant sums to both the Livingston and Jackson hospitals, where his physio treatment was rebuilding his strength at pace.

But the rest of the money – that was still a mystery. And there was one other part of the auction that had remained a secret, barely mentioned since.

As far as we knew, Lil's ten-thousand-dollar date hadn't yet happened. Avoiding all conversation around it, she wouldn't even open up about it to Lottie, let alone actually go through with it.

'You're gonna show me, huh?' I asked, secretly proud of my increasingly convincing Wyoming accent.

He chuckled.

'C'mon, better do this for Cole before the poor fucker combusts.'

I nodded, imagining how strung out Cole must feel, and picked up the tray, carefully balancing everything as Jesse held the door open.

A blazing fire in the gargantuan fireplace had warmed every part of the living room, throwing a honey-coloured glow across everyone in it. Everyone from the ranch was there, as well as Dee and her new guy, Austin; her cousin Rosie and little Addie, now curled up on the sofa, fast asleep; Jesse's mom, who couldn't stop smiling at Jesse and me together; and his sisters, Clara and Belle, with their husbands.

The vast space was finally full, Lottie at the centre of it. Her cheeks rosy, her dark, wild curls pinned half up, she looked completely and utterly beautiful in the pale pink dress I'd suggested. Thankfully she hadn't questioned it, my ulterior motive nicely covered by my genuine admiration.

I set down the drinks, asking Jesse to take over with serving them. Looking up, Cole gave me a small nod before heading out of the room.

'Hey, girl,' I said, sidling up to her, hand on my phone. 'So, this is pretty fucking nice? That Thanksgiving dinner was unreal. You've set a bit of a high bar though.'

She shrugged, her expression so happy and contented that I almost welled up on the spot at the thought of what was coming.

'It's just a big Sunday roast, really, isn't it?' she admitted, smiling as I laughed. 'But I know this time of year is a bit rough for Cole. And Lil . . .' She trailed off with a glance at her cousin, now talking animatedly with Clara. 'So, yeah, I just wanted to make it special for them. And you.'

She took one of my hands.

'This is more than I ever thought could happen,' she said, holding my gaze fiercely. 'This is the family I choose. I can't believe I got this fucking lucky, to have you here too. It wouldn't be right if you weren't.'

I drew her into a tight hug, tears already starting.

'First off,' I said, pulling back, my hands on her shoulders. 'You're a bitch for trying to ruin my make-up.' She chuckled, reaching out to gently wipe under my eye. 'And secondly, if we weren't in love with cowboys, I would be happy to just be here, with you. I know you never got your gay awakening,' I added, both of us smiling at the other. 'But you'll always be my first love, in every sense.'

'Same,' she whispered, holding me tight again. 'Thank fuck Lil swung the work visa situation.'

I nodded, a shiver of excitement at the thought of all the plans for the creative retreat slowly coming to life, combined with my growing tattoo waitlist here in Jackson. With my London flat sold and the studio wrapped up, there was nothing left but good things on the horizon.

'Although there *are* other means to getting more permanent visas and green cards,' I murmured, waiting for her to let go, her eyes suddenly wide.

'What?' she began, sudden, fierce excitement brewing.

I shook my head, grinning, holding up a hand.

'All in good time,' I promised, my own excitement deep down, knowing what I had planned for Jesse tonight. 'But first, I've got something to show you. C'mon.'

She trailed behind me as I headed out, giving Jesse a wink and mouthing, 'Two minutes.'

In the hallway, I gently urged Lottie ahead of me towards the back door and the porch beyond. It was golden hour, the waning sun tinting the valley a molten bronze, the snow glistening on the trees and rocks.

'What . . .?' she began, but I shooed her to the door, prepping my phone.

'It's outside. Brace yourself,' I said, her puzzled smile so fucking precious that I almost reached out and squeezed her again.

Opening the door, letting the cold wash over me, I held up my screen to capture every second.

'Seriously, what's . . .' she began; then, as what Cole had set up became obvious, her hand went to her mouth, covering it.

The huge fir tree ahead, snow weighing down the branches nearest the house, was strung with fairy lights. A small path, lined with pillar candles and storm lanterns, led to the base of the trunk.

Cole stood there, utterly fixed on her, his expression as it often was – in perpetual disbelief at his luck that Lottie was his, that she loved him back just as much.

He gestured to her to walk over, and I captured the glow of the lights reflected in the fabric of her dress as she passed under the canopy.

Before she reached him, Cole went down on one knee. I moved around to the side, my own heart in my mouth; I didn't want to intrude on the words, but I captured her expression as Cole asked her, his voice low and rough, to be his wife.

Tears beginning, hands still over her mouth, Lottie nodded and knelt down right in front of him, taking his face and kissing him, the tears brimming as he returned the kiss.

I could barely see the phone screen, now just hoping they were in shot as Cole pulled out the ring box and opened it. Lottie's eyes grew wide as she saw it. He took it out, taking her left hand and gently slid the ring onto her finger.

My hand, now unsteady from my own emotion, held still just long enough to hear her say yes and to see Cole's raw joy, the way his smile lit his whole face.

'You fucking knew, the whole time,' she cried as she hugged me a minute later, staring at her finger in disbelief while Cole grinned at us both.

'You're not the only sneaky motherfucker, you know,' I chided her, drawing her back onto the porch and handing her over to Cole. 'Now, go tell everyone. I need to wrestle with a huge bottle of champagne.'

Barely an hour later, celebrations well under way, Jesse took my hand.

'This way,' he said, smirking as he took us out, grabbing both of our jackets and hats off the rack. 'You're gonna need these.'

Frowning, wondering if we were going down to the barn, I came to a stop as he opened his truck passenger door.

'C'mon, Jessica,' he urged, squeezing my ass as I climbed up.

'Is this finally the big secret, huh?' I asked as we set off. We got straight onto the highway, heading away from Jackson.

He said nothing, just smiled, reaching out with his hand to hold mine.

I went with it. I'd long since learnt that all things came to those that waited with Jesse, and that it was always worth it.

So when we took a right off the highway, heading down a wide dirt road, I didn't question it. Up ahead, nestled into a group of fir and birch trees, was a small, one-story ranch house: a miniature version of the Diamond Back.

'That looks just like . . .'

'The Diamond Back?' he finished, grinning as he turned up the short drive, coming to a stop before the closed wooden gate. 'Yeah, it was built by Lottie and Lil's grandfather as a spot to come fishing and hunting here down in the valley. He loved the main ranch so much, he built a smaller version right here.'

I could see the river snaking through more trees; beyond it, the Tetons puncturing the fading sky.

We climbed out, Jesse taking my hand and leading me to the gate. It was beautiful, so peaceful and private. Just the sound of the river and the birds in the trees around us.

'Do you like it?' he asked, his voice soft, hesitant.

I exhaled.

'It's fucking gorgeous,' I exclaimed, unable to take my eyes from any of it. It felt as though we'd landed in our own personal paradise.

'Hestia,' he said, taking both my hands and leaning on the gate, 'I didn't want to tell you about the rest of the money, in case it didn't pull off. But . . . it did. Thanks to you, for what you did for me . . . and Mom.'

I searched his face, not following.

'I already had some money put aside from my last bull riding season, when shit went really well, before Mom got sick. But this win . . . this pushed me over the line. Hestia, honey, this place – I've bought it from Lil's mom.'

My mouth opened, unable to process it.

'What? But – all of this?'

He nodded, smiling.

'This house and a hundred acres, stretching down to the river,' he said, reaching out to brush my cheek. 'It's ours, sweetheart. If you want to share it with me – hell, there's plenty of room for Luci too. I don't want anything else in this world. Just you and our own space, together.'

Tears rose up again as I blinked at him, almost unable to comprehend the size of the gesture he was offering. Generosity was like breathing to Jesse – I'd told him as much weeks ago as I'd thanked him for keeping Luci at the Diamond Back, for breaking her in for me.

'In fact, Cole and I, we kinda agreed we'd both do something today,' he added, holding my gaze with such an intensity that I felt my insides begin to melt. 'I wanted to ask you, again, maybe in a more traditional way than I did in the hotel room.' He released one of my hands and, as my brain moved into slow motion, he dropped down onto one knee.

I could barely breathe, but it was happiness – of a kind I'd only just come to recognize – that filled me up instead.

'Hestia, whether it's on an official piece of paper or not, I don't fucking care. I just want you to be my everything, for ever, even if it's just us that know. I love you more than I ever thought was possible, honey. Will you be my friend, my partner, the love of my life?'

I knew I was crying, but I couldn't feel anything, see anything but him. Our future.

'Yes,' I whispered as he stood, pressing his lips into mine for a moment. Neither of us could speak, only hold onto each other. His thumb brushed away my tears before he bent down to kiss them away. 'But – I think . . .' I began, my throat thick with feeling, 'if you want to, I – I want to marry you.' I saw his eyes widen. 'In a way that's just about us – right here, if we can,' I decided, looking up into the trees. The first stars were appearing above the eastern peaks in the distance. 'Just us, and the same people up at the ranch right now.'

'You want . . . to be my wife?' he murmured, his voice cracking a little.

I nodded, holding his gaze as he stared, his disbelief turning to something else, tears forming in his eyes.

'I know where all of the negative feelings have come from, about marriage. They have nothing to do with us, with what you are to me. I . . . I want everyone to know what we are to each other.'

There was a silence as he gathered himself, just the rush of a breeze through the trees.

'You have no idea what that means to me,' he murmured finally, searching my face.

'I love you, Jesse. I think I always have,' I whispered, smiling as I remembered. 'I think I felt it, back there in the kitchen, the first time. The start of it all.'

He smiled back, his hand lacing through my hair, making my scalp tingle.

'I remember,' he replied. 'But I . . . I didn't get you a ring yet, I didn't want to assume—'

I shook my head, my smile broadening.

'Don't need one. We agreed, remember?'

And so, back in my room at the ranch, we decided to keep our news quiet, wanting Lottie and Cole to have their own moment. Instead, we snuck into my room and I set up my kit at the small table as he watched.

I took the fourth finger of his left hand first, smiling as he suggested he might need distraction again. Within twenty minutes, using just a simple outline, his ouroboros was complete. Lacing round the base of his finger, it made the perfect match to the one I then added to the same finger on my own left hand.

As I finished, taking off my glove, we compared them, my hand in his.

'When do you want to do it?' he asked as he kissed me again, twining his fingers into mine.

I almost laughed as a sudden thought popped into my head.

'Do you remember when we got completely wasted that night, on fireballs?' I said, watching as the thought registered on his face, a small smile blooming.

'Yeah, course I do,' he grinned. 'Well, I think I remember the bit you're meaning, anyway.'

'I didn't cancel it, the booking,' I admitted, watching as he absorbed the words. 'I couldn't bring myself to . . . not when it felt like I was cancelling out the evening. But – we don't need it if we're going to do it at your – our place.'

He considered me for a moment, bringing my fingers to his lips and kissing them.

'You thinking what I'm thinking, Jessica?'

I arched my eyebrow.

'Other than how much longer you're going to keep me waiting before I finally get laid tonight?' I started, my heart so fucking full as he laughed. 'Yeah, I'm thinking the same. See if they want to take the booking instead. Lottie would love a spring wedding – especially at that place – I know it. I think . . . maybe I'd prefer summer. Maybe the same day we met this year.'

He considered it, nodding, then broadened his smile.

'We better go offer it to them, then,' he said, getting up from the chair, stopping as I did the same.

I shook my head.

'Not a fucking chance, cowboy. Clothes off, now. You've been dressed for way too long today.'

Almost growling as he grabbed me by the waist, he lifted me up and carried me over to the bed.

'I can't wait to fuck you in our kitchen,' he whispered as he laid me down, bracing himself over me as I unbuttoned his shirt.

I could picture it so clearly, the feelings I had for him ingrained in every cell.

'Neither can I.'

Acknowledgements

Once again, the biggest thanks are reserved for my absolute diamond of an agent, Judith Murray. It's your belief in me – your genuine, heartfelt support and warmth as a person, not just as a professional, that's led to all of this. I can't quite believe where this journey has taken us so far, Judith, but GOOD GOD it's been amazing! You and the whole Greene & Heaton team – Kate Rizzo, Imogen Morrell and Mia Dakin most notably – are an author's dream. On that note, huge thanks also to Sanjana Seelam at WME; I'm so lucky to have you on my side on the other side of the pond! Here's to more cowboys . . . in this world and others . . . !

Kinza Azira, you absolute rock-star editor. This last year has been so brilliant, and I can't thank you enough for your faith in me at all stages. Can't wait for everything to come – it's already everything I could've imagined and more. To the wider Pan team – Katie Loughnane, Daisy Dickeson, Charlotte Dixon, Rosie Friis, Anna Shora, Mairead Loftus, Lloyd Jones and Siân Chilvers – you've absolutely smashed it and I'm so grateful for your hard work and expertise.

To my international publishers – it makes me so happy to see my characters in other languages and knowing just a little piece of my Wyoming is making it around the world. Thank you.

To my family and friends – your support with *Untamed Heart* and this book have meant the world, thank you to all of you. It's been wonderful to know so many of you have read and had fun at the Diamond Back; sharing it with you has been surreal and lovely in equal measure.

Emma Lucy – thank you so much for our first cowboy crawl last year. It's been lovely to get to know you a little and tear up the south of England with you . . .! Looking forward to more in the future, and so pleased for your own well-deserved success.

Erin – little did I know that I would actually run into the actual physical Hestia inspo when my local Waterstones opened . . .! You are beautiful – inside and out – thank you so much for your support and friendship, and long live book club!

Elle – we did it again, girl! Somehow you managed to beta read this on the fly (as always) while setting up an incredible business with Kate (see, Kate? Didn't forget you this time!). I loved getting to write more about Lottie and Hestia's friendship, esp as it's based on threads of our friendship, as you know. You mean the world to me, I hope you know that – and I can't wait to be there at Cora's first book signing. (Finn and Tom – I can't not mention you too now, right? Thanks for letting Elle be on call for reading support!).

Hannah – you are the wisest and loveliest of all sages in this world, and such a smart and generous reader and friend. I'm so happy we got a chance to trauma bond at work (jokes . . . kinda) for all those years . . . and then continue afterwards with a lot more laughing involved!

Rich – there's never a succinct way to sum up how much I appreciate you, especially given my crash writing schedules and erratic brain. Just as Hestia finds in this book, home isn't necessarily a place, it can also be a person. You and the boys are my home, and always will be.

Finally, to the readers, reviewers and booksellers that took a chance on reading *Untamed Heart* and now *Reckless Vow*. You'll never know how some days you were the difference between giving up and keeping going. That meeting some of you, as I've been lucky enough to do, has reaffirmed a belief in people that'd waned over the years. I appreciate you all SO MUCH, and know that I'll be writing my little heart out for you in time to come – so leave a little more room on your bookshelves for me, okay? There's plenty more on the way . . .

If you enjoyed *Reckless Vow*, discover Gemma Morr's steamy debut cowboy romance . . .

Welcome to The Diamond Back ranch: where the cowboys are hot, the drama is real and city girls like Lottie Wright are in way over their heads.

Lottie has spent her whole life chasing success – or at least what it's supposed to look like. The perfect job, the perfect boyfriend, the perfect London life. But when she's suddenly fired and catches her boyfriend cheating, she does what any totally rational person would do . . . and gets on a plane to her family's ranch in Wyoming.

Cole Miller is a rugged ex-rodeo star and absolutely not interested in a city girl playing cowgirl on the Diamond Back ranch – even if they did end up in a steamy tangle on her arrival in Jackson Hole. But as Lottie trades designer suits for cowboy boots, she starts to realize she might be a little more country than she thought . . .